Praise for *Pergam*…

Meticulous in her research as t… ronment of the day, Dow's nov… and now *Pergamum: Satan's Throne*, accurately reflect the times of the mid to late first century. In addition and most importantly, Sharon Dow has communicated a vital spiritual lesson of faithfulness—a gracious God to His people, and His sold-out people to Him at whatever the cost. I encourage you to read with both pleasure and an open heart. You will be blessed!

Reverend Lance Johnson, past director, FEB Central; associate pastor, Emmanuel Baptist Church, Barrie, Ontario, Canada; author, *Pastor Search 411*

Reading Sharon Dow's first novel, *Antipas: Martyr*, I felt the gritty sand between my toes, heard the sharp crack of the whip, and smelled the searing flesh roasting over the fire. Best of all, it reaffirmed that the love and power of God is much stronger than the forces of the evil one! Sharon Dow's second book, *Pergamum: Satan's Throne* proves to be another eye-opening novel, dramatically portraying the power of God and the life-changing relationship one can experience with Jesus Christ.

Jean Morby, host, Young at Heart Show on Faith FM 94.3 Kitchener, Ontario, Canada; author, *Rainy Day Activities* and *Hands of Gold*

Do you want a journey? Well, travel with Sharon Dow as she continues the spiritual adventure story of Antipas's family and their search for real truth in the midst of false religion. A story like this applies to our world of today, more so now than ever. This sequel, *Pergamum: Satan's Throne*, is a must-read. Sharon's writing style will not only invite you, but it will draw you into this journey. So let's go and find the truth!

Reverend Mark Cudney, chaplain, Riverside Glen Retirement Centre, Guelph, Ontario, Canada

Pergamum:
SATAN'S THRONE

To Darlene,
So happy for you in
your new apartment! May
it be a place of peace and
joy and God's blessing on
your life. Enjoy Paulus' story!
Blessings!
Sharon
2013

SHARON DOW

Deep River
BOOKS

Pergamum: Satan's Throne

Published by
Deep River Books
Sisters, Oregon
www.deepriverbooks.com

ISBN-13: 9781937756734
ISBN-10: 1937756734

Library of Congress: 2012953978

Printed in the USA

Cover design by Robin Black, www.blackbirdcreative.biz

Dedication

To my three sons: Andrew, Greg, and Glen. You bring me joy every day. I am so proud of each of you and what you have accomplished and are continuing to accomplish in your lives. Your support and encouragement has assisted me on my journey to become an author. I love you, my three sons.

In the previous book *Antipas: Martyr . . .*

"I know where you live—where Satan has his throne. Yet you remain true to my name. You did not renounce your faith in me, even in the days of Antipas, my faithful witness, who was put to death in your city—where Satan lives" (Rev. 2:13 NIV).

Antipas, a young boy, lives with his family in Pergamum. His family is steeped in the worship of Zeus and the emperor, except for his grandfather, who spends time telling Antipas about earlier times before the Romans came. He believes life offers more than Zeus or emperor worship and encourages Antipas to seek the truth.

Throughout Antipas's growing-up years, his grandfather's words return to him again and again until he is invited to Rome to continue his studies. He knows he cannot go to Rome and talks with his father, telling him of his struggle with both Zeus worship and emperor worship. His enraged father disowns Antipas, telling him he will no longer have any contact with the family. He has no son named Antipas.

Frightened and alone, Antipas ultimately joins a caravan and leaves the city. On his travels, he becomes acquainted with Epaphras, who leads him to Christ. Antipas soon experiences God's call to preach the good news of Christ. The apostle Paul becomes his mentor, and eventually he is led back to Pergamum to lead the fledgling church in that city where Satan reigns. His life is in danger from his father and brothers as well as from the city leaders and priests of Zeus.

His love for the Lord increases, and he fearlessly preaches the gospel on the steps of the altar to Zeus. Eventually he is arrested and sentenced to death. The book ends when he is sacrificed on the altar to Zeus and meets his Lord.

Prologue

Earlier in the Day

Justus Anthony gave the order, and Antipas was lifted from the step and carried to the edge of the smoking altar.

Time stood still. The arms lifting him were surprisingly gentle, wrapping themselves around him. The heat was intense as they approached the altar. The smoke bent down and circled him, enclosing him in its fragrance. His vision was limited, but he could see the dancing light from the flames; ever rising, ever retreating. The smoke curled away and back again at the whim of the wind.

"The time has come for the god Zeus to be avenged," Justus Anthony shouted. "Commit him to the flames!"

And with that, Antipas was thrown on the altar. As the arms encircling his body fell away, he floated through space. Now the only sound was the hissing of the flame. It called to him, luring him on.

Then his body made contact with the altar. Searing pain shuddered through him, sharp and consuming. The flames welcomed and embraced him. He could make no sound. The only sound was the roaring of the flames. The cloth melted at the touch of the feverish blaze. Mercifully he could no longer feel. The flames licked the fabric away then devoured his garments. With great finality, they attacked his body.

Chapter One

Then the tears came. Silent and leaden, they slipped unbidden from his eyes. Paulus stood tall, eyes riveted on the altar, and watched the long tongues of flame consume his brother Antipas. A shudder passed through his body, and sweat beaded on his forehead, but he made no effort to wipe it away. He focused on his brother's body.

I can't believe how brave he was when he faced the flames. He was confident that this was God's will for his life. And I agree. It hurts, but I agree.

He focused on the altar until movement from the side caught his attention. Marcus moved in beside the governor, Justus Anthony.

Marcus: I ache for you, my older brother; ache for the hate and evil that seem to consume you; ache for the divide in our family.

The contrast struck him: Antipas, filled with the light of God; Marcus, filled with the darkness of evil.

He noticed that the governor seemed frozen in place, head bowed in a stance of utter defeat until Marcus leaned in and whispered in his ear. His head came up, and at that moment a piercing scream split the air. Paulus knew without looking that the sound had come from Father—filled with evil like his firstborn son, responsible for the sacrifice of Antipas, his second son. Yet his heart went out to him, saddened that evil consumed him, saddened for the loss of a father's love.

Two priests grabbed his father, Julian, and dragged his limp form into the temple.

Paulus turned his attention back to Justus Anthony, who seemed to become aware of the people waiting at the foot of the steps.

"Guards, remove the body to the burial chamber in the prison. And get these people out of here," Justus Anthony said, flailing his arms in front of him. He turned on his heel, marched up the steps, swept past the startled priests, and disappeared into the temple.

Turning his head, Paulus watched the silent Christ-followers begin to stir and move slowly away from the altar. Eunice clung to his arm on one side, wiping her eyes with her other hand. Her soft weeping touched his heart, and he pulled her closer.

What must she be feeling after watching her husband committed to the flames?

His mother was beyond her, surrounded by friends who supported her while they walked toward the street. He gave Eunice a hug before she joined the others, leaving him standing alone at the foot of the stairs.

What does the future hold for me? Will I ever be the man Antipas was? Lord, Your Spirit is moving through me. Your strength and love fill me.

He raised his hand in salute to his brother. He whispered the words to the gathering wind. "Your sacrifice will not be in vain."

Once inside the semidarkness of the temple, Justus Anthony fled through the halls to a door recessed in the back wall. A servant opened the door when he approached, and the governor moved through and into a waiting chariot. They sped through the streets, arriving at his quarters, where he leapt from the conveyance, up the steps to the house, along the dark passageway, and into his own chambers.

"Lock the door and allow no one to disturb me until further notice." He ground out the words to the guards. Stumbling into his room, he fell onto the couch near the window. The heat of the afternoon penetrated his room, nearly suffocating him. He had never felt so drained in all his years of being governor.

Jairus, his personal physician, slipped into his room, stopping just inside the door. "I know you asked not to be disturbed, but I felt you needed my ministrations. I take full responsibility for forcing my way in." He moved farther into the room, keeping an eye on Justus Anthony.

"You're right, I do need you. I can't shake this melancholy feeling. Do what you must to give me some peace." He waved his arm at the physician and closed his eyes, laying back his head.

"I've brought powders with me that will help you sleep. When you awake, the melancholy should be a distant memory. So you have wine in your cabinet?" He lifted the small packets while pointing at the cabinet.

"Yes, yes, there's plenty. You know where it is. Just be quick about it." Justus Anthony rubbed his hand over his chin.

"I'll need to heat the wine to release the healing powers of the potion. It'll only take a minute." The doctor was already gathering the supplies he needed from the cabinet. He worked quickly with practiced hands, handling utensils deftly. He soon had the drink ready and brought it to Justus Anthony.

"I will stay with you while you sleep. That way, I can make sure no one else is able to convince the useless guards that they need to see you. Sleep now, and may your rest be peaceful." He touched Justus Anthony's forehead lightly.

Justus Anthony was already drifting into slumber when Jairus reclined on another couch from where he could watch him. He had feared for the governor's mind recently. Since the prisoner had first been arrested, Justus Anthony had not been of the same sound mind as before. Something about the prisoner had had a profound effect on him. He would make sure he watched him closely in the future.

Jairus unrolled the scroll he had brought with him. He prepared a pen and began to make copious notes while the governor slept. He glanced at him from time to time, studying each feature in repose. He then made more notations in the neat columns. He wanted to remain loyal to Justus Anthony, but he felt it was wise to be prepared with documented notes if the need to change loyalties ever arrived. Of late, he wondered.

Ekrem, the high priest, led a company of priests down to the altar and watched while they circled it. The guards had removed the body after Justus Anthony disappeared into the temple. Smoke still curled from the altar, making Ekrem's eyes sting.

The priests had come to cleanse the altar, which was defiled from the pagan sacrifice. Ekrem, clothed in a white tunic trimmed with gold thread and embroidered with vines, raised his arms and, with closed eyes, swayed back and forth.

"All hail to Zeus." Ekrem's voice carried to the others, who took up the response to the chant, the gold threads in their tunics shining in the sunlight.

"The god of Pergamum."

"You have been avenged."

"Supreme god of Pergamum."

"Cleanse your altar."

"Great god of Pergamum."

"Cleanse your altar with a purifying fire."

"The one god of Pergamum."

The rhythm of the priests' chant rose and fell. Ekrem moved to the altar, opening a leather pouch tied at his waist. Extracting a portion of the contents, he threw it on the altar. The flames leaped again toward the sky, obscuring his vision momentarily. He turned toward the priests and raised his arms; they began circling the altar. White robes swirled around their legs. Hands were lifted high, exposing bony arms. Round and round they went, chanting continuously. As the flames became weaker, the chanting of the priests increased in intensity.

Marcus swung his horse around, scanning the crowd, looking for one particular person. There, he saw him. He worked his mount through the fleeing crowd until he was face-to-face with Paulus, who paused and looked at him with raised brows.

"So, you join the infidels, brother." Marcus glared down at him, his lips curled in a sneer. His horse sidestepped nervously while he tightly held the reins.

"Yes, I am happy to say that I have. I can only hope that one day you, too, will join with me." Paulus shaded his eyes and looked up at his brother.

"Now that has a touch of humor to it." Marcus threw his head back and laughed. "You are now the enemy, my brother, and as such, you should stay out of my line of vision, or you may find yourself on the altar joining our brother, Antipas."

"I would consider it a great privilege to join him." Paulus looked steadily into his brother's eyes. His face was peaceful as he stood quietly before Marcus.

"That was an unwise thing to say to a temple guard. I could have you arrested on the spot. Do you know that?" Marcus stiffened his back and leaned over, snapping his fingers in his brother's face.

"Yes, I'm well aware of it, but I don't think you'll do that today. The day may well come, and when it does, I hope to be as courageous as our brother. I will be praying for you, my brother." Paulus turned and walked away from Marcus. He never looked back.

Marcus let the shock show in his eyes. Where had Paulus gotten this boldness? He had always done his bidding and the bidding of their father. Maybe there was something to this "Christian" thing. He shook his head in bewilderment.

"But it's not for me." He lifted his head high as he turned his horse and rode off to join the other guards. He would have ample time to replay the scene over and over again in his mind and decide what to do about Paulus, but for now he had work to do.

Chapter Two

The people needed to be together. Some returned to their own homes, but most went to homes open to welcome them, where they could talk over the events of the day.

When David, one of the prominent church leaders of Pergamum, entered his home, a large group had already assembled. Quiet talk was coming from the atrium. He entered and surveyed the crowd. They hushed when they became aware of his presence.

"I'm glad you've come, friends," he said. "This is no time for any of us to be alone. We need to mourn the loss of our brother, Antipas, and then we need to move forward for the cause of Christ. That's the way we can best honor Antipas." He moved farther into the room, taking up the space in front of the believers.

"What an example to all of us." Emin stood as he spoke, a look of sadness and loss troubling his face. He breathed deeply and managed a slight smile. "Did you see the light around him as he stood there with Justus Anthony?"

"Yes, yes," a murmur of voices responded.

"I thought Justus Anthony might release him," Mattias said. "I've never seen him so upset, so disturbed." He shuddered and wiped his forehead with the edge of his robe.

"I think he would have had it not been for the priests," Voss said with an emphatic nod of his head. "They were out for blood, that's for sure. The priests will exact revenge on any of us they can arrest on their trumped-up charges."

David faced the group, eyes flashing. He lifted his shoulders as he faced them. "Friends, the time for hiding is over." He spoke with deliberation. "Antipas has left us a legacy we can't reject. We must move forth boldly. We took a stand today, and we can't back down now. Are you with me?"

David nodded with the group, all in agreement. Today had been remarkable. They had lost their leader but in a glorious display of solidarity in Christ. There was now no doubt in his mind and in the minds of the people of Pergamum that the Christians had come to stay. He rejoiced that the priests were blocked in their desire to clear the city of all believers. Oh yes, they would try again, but he knew the power of the Holy Spirit would keep them, would keep alive the flame of their love for Christ. Christianity was moving forward.

Mattias responded by standing to his feet. He was a big, strong man, but at this moment his eyes were moist with tears. "Fellow believers, I'm moved as I've never been moved before. I loved Antipas like a son. His wife and son are part of my family, so the tears you see are partly for them, partly for me, but most of all they are for our Savior who filled us today. I don't think I'll ever be the same. I felt His power like never before." He lifted his right arm high in the air before he sat again.

David agreed that what they had witnessed today, what they had experienced, was life-changing.

The talk continued while servants, led by the lady of the house, Miriam, circulated among the guests, serving cooling drinks and a light meal. The believers began to relax, and the talk became more general.

Eunice was in one of the bedrooms of the house, holding Simon close to her. Larium, her dear friend, was with her as they poured out their hearts in prayer.

"Larium, I don't know how I'll ever be able to carry on without him," Eunice sobbed as she rested her head on Larium's shoulder. Larium rubbed her back gently while she cried. "But I know God has given me peace that He'll be everything I need. Antipas and I talked about this many times as he was certain he would be killed."

She lifted her head to look into her friend's eyes. "I'm just so thankful I had him for the short time we had together, and Simon, our baby, is worth everything. Every time I look at him, I see Antipas in him." She wiped her eyes with a cloth Larium handed to her.

"He'll certainly be a comfort to you. He's such a wonderful baby. I'm so glad, too, that you have him." Larium too wiped her eyes. "Mattias and I want you to know that our home is your home for as long as you want to stay. Grandmother Lois says the same thing. I think you and Simon have brought new life to her." She brushed hair back from Eunice's face, where it had fallen.

"Thank you, Larium. I'll be happy to stay for the present. I don't yet know what God wants me to do about the future, but that's not a decision for today." She sniffed, lifted her head, and closed her eyes. "I think I'd like to join the others now. I think they need to see that I'm going to carry on with the work, even through grief. I also want to thank them for how they've stood with Antipas through all of this."

"Are you sure you feel up to this?" Larium frowned as she looked at Eunice.

"Yes, please, let's join them."

Larium held Simon while Eunice wiped her face and tidied her clothes. Together the two women moved out of the bedroom and along the hall to the atrium. When they appeared in the doorway, two of the ladies ran to them and hugged Eunice. Soon several had gathered around her, many with tears spilling from red eyes.

Eunice was overwhelmed as prayer broke out from the lips of many present. They fell to their knees in prayer for her and Simon, for the church, for reaching the lost of Pergamum, for Justus Anthony, for Julian and Marcus, for the temple priests and guards, for peace, and for strength to carry on the work. Tears slid down Eunice's face as the prayers ended. She felt the presence of God in a new and vital way.

"God has not forgotten us." David leaped up from his knees, punching the air with his fist. "He's here with us. I can sense His presence."

Led by David, the group surrounded Eunice with cries of victory, which made their way into her heart, warming it and giving her courage.

By early evening the converts, much encouraged, started out for their homes. Mattias was the last to gather his group together. He was reluctant to take Eunice from this place of encouragement. Would she still feel strong once they got home?

He rose reluctantly but of necessity. They must make it across the city before nightfall. It would not be safe to be out after dark tonight. Who knew what the temple guards would do, what the priests had instructed them to do?

"Come, Larium, we must leave. Eunice, are you and Simon ready?" Mattias put his hand on Larium's shoulder and looked at Eunice.

"Yes, Mattias. I feel it's time to get Simon home to his own bed," Eunice said. "It's been a tiring day for him." She hugged Simon to her and wrapped his blanket closer around him. She placed a kiss on his forehead.

David and Miriam embraced them and promised to do whatever they could to help Eunice in the days ahead. Paulus was ready to leave as well.

"May I walk part way with you?" Paulus walked over and joined Mattias and the women.

"We'll certainly be glad of your company," Mattias said. "Don't put yourself in any danger though." He gripped Paulus's shoulder in response. They left by the front door and began walking down the path to the street.

"I'm not afraid. I think it will be quiet tonight," Paulus said. "The priests will need to assess the situation and make plans. That will take some time." He nodded to Mattias. "They won't want a public demonstration such as they saw today. They've got a different view of the Christians. We're not the cowards they thought we were." He smiled at Mattias triumphantly.

"What about your brother? Will he not want to harm you?" Mattias drew his brows together and pursed his lips.

"I can deal with Marcus. He sought me out in the crowd today. When I stood up to him, he backed down. He has a lot to think about." Paulus adjusted his cloak, pulling it tighter around him since the evening air was cooling.

"Your father seemed in bad shape." Mattias frowned.

"Yes, I plan to visit my parents' home tonight to see if there's anything I can do to help him."

"I really think he is beyond help at this point." Mattias shook his head sadly.

"You're probably right, but I need to at least try. My mother may need help as well. I'm hoping I can get her to leave their house and live with me for a while." He ran his fingers along the edge of his turban. "Her life is in danger since she appeared at the altar today. But Marcus may have figured that she was just there because Antipas is her son. What a mixed-up family we are." Paulus shook his head, lines gathering between his eyebrows.

"But look what God has already done for your family. First, he brought much good out of the evil done to Antipas, saving him and then calling him to be an evangelist. Then your mother saw the truth and also came to Christ, and now you. I would say that God has His hand on your family in a very real way." Mattias put his arm around Paulus's shoulder, gripping it tightly.

Paulus opened his arms to Simon, and Eunice gratefully handed him to his uncle. "You're right. I need to be encouraged and start praying for Marcus and my father. That seems so strange when neither would appreciate it." He settled the baby comfortably in his arms. "They wouldn't want to know Christ. They're so hard."

The women walked ahead with Mattias and Paulus following closely. Mattias carried a lantern they could use if needed.

"But you don't know what effect this sacrifice of Antipas will have on them," Mattias said. "It may well be too late for your father. I think his mind is destroyed. But Marcus saw everything. God may well be working in his heart."

Simon shifted in his arms, and Paulus hugged the little boy closer to him. Simon snuggled his head on his Uncle Paulus's shoulder and drifted off to sleep.

"I want to be a big part of this little fellow's life." Paulus patted his back and placed a kiss on his head.

"Know that you are welcome in my home whenever you want to come. Be there often for Simon but also for Eunice. You're really all the family she has here in Pergamum." He reached up and put his hand on Paulus's shoulder. "But also come for you. It will do you good to be a part of a Christian family."

"Thank you, Mattias. You'll never know how much that invitation means to me. Our family has been troubled since the day my father banished Antipas. My life has been a lonely one. Your offer is happily accepted." And then he grinned. "You may get tired of me before long. I may show up every day."

Mattias laughed with Paulus. It felt so good to laugh after all the tensions of the day.

"You already remind me of Antipas, and he was just like one of the family. I expect you will soon be in the same position with my womenfolk. They like to have someone to fuss over. You'll do nicely." They smiled again, then lapsed into a comfortable silence.

Larium and Eunice talked over the events of the day as they walked in front of the two men.

"I will grieve deeply for Antipas, but I don't want to and don't plan to do it sitting by the fire or resting in my room. I want to get out and resume the visits to the families that I had started while Antipas was in prison." Eunice nodded and clasped her hands together.

"I think that's a very wise idea. It would be so easy to just slip down into your grief. I think God will reward you for that kind of attitude." Larium shifted the basket she carried over her arm. Her eyes were red from crying, but she curved her lips into a smile.

"Do you think Tabitha will look after Simon for me sometimes? There are times when I might want to make a visit where it wouldn't be appropriate to take him." Eunice put her hand on Larium's arm.

Larium chuckled. "Try to stop her. Sometimes I think she pretends he's *her* baby."

Eunice could see the house up ahead. One part of her wanted to get there quickly. Another part held back, not sure how she would feel doing the ordinary things without Antipas.

Grandmother Lois had a hot meal waiting for them. They persuaded Paulus to stay and sup with them. His presence helped all of them tremendously. Eunice listened as they recounted the events of the day, hugging each word close to her heart.

Paulus rose from the low couch where he had been reclining. "I must leave, but I thank you for including me. It has been a blessing to me." He spoke to each of them with his thanks. When he reached Eunice, she stood.

"I would like to accompany you to the door," she said.

"Thank you. I would like that."

She followed him down the narrow stairs into the shop below.

"Paulus, I can't tell you how much it means to me to have you in my life and in Simon's. I look forward to getting to know you better. I know Mattias has invited you to come often, and I wanted to add my voice to that. I would love you to be the father figure in Simon's life. He already loves you." She glanced shyly at him, folding her arms around her waist.

"Nothing would give me greater pleasure, Eunice. Believe me, you'll be helping me more than I could ever help you." He leaned over and gave her a brief hug. "I want to try to make it possible for you to spend some time with my mother as well. I think it would be good for both of you."

"Oh, thank you. I would love to get to know her, and for her to get to know Simon. I think Antipas would be pleased with all our plans." A little smile curved her lips upward.

"I think so, too. I'll probably come by tomorrow night if that is all right with you." He raised his eyebrows in a question to her.

"I'll look forward to greeting you." She took his hand in hers and gently squeezed it. He patted her hand before he turned to leave.

Paulus left through the shop door and disappeared into the night. He knew his life was held in balance tonight, as were the lives of Eunice and all the believers. The priests and civic leaders would seek revenge for the open display of solidarity today. Of that he was certain.

Chapter Three

Paulus walked quickly, lost in a haze of memories of the day. He prayed as he walked, thanking God for the great display of courage the Christians showed at the altar to Zeus. Antipas had been beyond belief.

He stopped briefly at his home to collect his horse and chariot. The horse was frisky, covering the distance at a good pace. Paulus gazed into the night sky as he sped through the city.

God, I don't yet know You the way Antipas did, but my desire is to have that same peace and boldness he had. I want to do Your will, but I'm not yet sure what it is. Show me the way, Lord.

Night noises surrounded him as he clopped his way through the streets. Late birds flapped frantically, hurrying home to snug nests, calling to each other in their flight. Gentle moonlight etched the trees, casting a soft glow over his way.

Peace filled his heart as he neared his parents' house. He slowed the horse and approached quietly, wondering if Marcus was there. He really didn't want to encounter him tonight. That time would come, he knew, but he hoped not for some time.

Leaving the horse at the front of the house, he went to a side entrance he used to enter as a boy. He slipped into the area where the kitchen slaves worked. Beulah was still mixing some concoction that would need to sit overnight. Yeast: he would recognize that fragrance anywhere, a memory from childhood. Beulah's wooden spoon hit the sides of the clay bowl in a rhythmic beat. She was dressed simply but colorfully, favoring the rich blue so popular with the servant classes. Her hair was invisible beneath her head covering, and flour dusted her face and arms.

He cleared his throat so as not to startle her.

"Paulus! How nice to see you." She beamed at him, wiping the flour from her face with her arm.

He knew he had always been her favorite, being the youngest of the three boys. He had also been a great lover of her pastries.

"But why are you coming in this way? Surely you should be coming in by the front entrance." She put the bowl down on the worktable and planted her hands on her hips.

"Actually, I had hoped to see you first and get some information." He winked at her and eased farther into the room.

"What do you want to know? You know I'll tell you anything, my boy." She drew her hand across her forehead, adding more flour to her face.

"Thanks, Beulah. Is Marcus or my father here?" He eased out of his cloak and folded it over his arm.

"No, Marcus isn't here. Your poor father. He may never be the same again. He's been taken to the physician's house. That's all I know about it." Tears hung in her eyes.

"Is my mother still up?"

"She went to her room only minutes ago. Her maid is with her. She'll want to see you, so go on up." She pointed the way with her wooden spoon.

"Once more, thanks." He gave her a hug.

He left the kitchen area and proceeded through the empty rooms, his footsteps echoing on the marble floors until he reached the curved staircase. The house was beautiful but cold, oh so cold. His mother was the only one who ever showed love in his family. He planned to change that. She deserved his love and support.

What a brave and gentle lady she is, he thought.

As he approached her room, he paused to compose himself. Breathing deeply, he knocked softly on her bedroom door. He lightly tapped his foot while he awaited a response.

The door slowly opened the merest space, only enough for her maid to peer out at him. Her eyes grew wide at the sight of Paulus's face outside the room. Paulus had never seen her before and assumed she must be a recent addition to the household.

"I'm Paulina's son, Paulus. Would you ask my mother if I may come in?" He forced a smile to reassure her.

His mother appeared in the doorway. "Johanna, you may take a break until I call you."

The maid bowed respectfully to her and Paulus, then walked off toward the kitchen.

Paulina turned to her son with tears in her eyes. "Oh Paulus . . ."

He wrapped his arms around her and just held her as she wept. After a time she stepped back and wiped her eyes.

"I'm so glad you've come," she said. "Please come into my room. I didn't know how I was going to make it through the night. I know God will see me through, but I'm so new at faith that I sometimes wonder if God will really do all the others say He will." She twisted a tiny cloth round and round in her hand. It was damp from her tears.

"Mother, I'm here to help you now. I know I'm even newer in the faith than you, but I'm more than convinced that Christ is everything and much more than we've even dared to hope. I'll be right by your side, and we'll go through this together." He put his hand against her cheek. She covered it with her own.

"And to think I thought you were as hardened as Marcus and your father." Paulina wrapped her arms around her son again and clung to him.

He rubbed her back as they stood in a silent circle of grief mingled with hope.

"I was certainly under their power," he said. "I was afraid to break from them. I really had nothing to turn to. And then Antipas came back. That made all the difference for me." He paused to swallow and sigh. "I couldn't believe the stories I was hearing about him. Marcus and my father were incensed by his boldness. I was intrigued. He was doing what I had always wanted to do: stand up to Father."

"Oh my son, life hasn't been easy for you," Paulina murmured into his shoulder, still softly weeping.

Paulus continued. "Then when Antipas wanted to meet with me, I knew I had to go. When I saw him, I wept. I wept for all the lost time from our boyhood, for the threats to his person, for our family, which was falling apart, and for my lost self. When he told me his story, I wanted so much to believe, but I was afraid, afraid of Marcus and afraid of Father."

He stepped away from her and walked to the window. It was open, inviting into the room the warm air redolent with the hint of fresh blossoms. Stars were flung with abandon across the black expanse of sky. He clasped his hands behind his back, still staring sightlessly at the night.

"Then when Eunice wanted me to go to prison to visit him, I was shocked, but again I wanted to go so badly." He turned to face his mother, who now sat on a carved wooden chair. "I wanted to see him again and talk to him. You understand how I felt?"

"Yes, my son, continue your story." Paulina had stopped crying and was watching her son intently.

"When we talked in the starkness of his cell, I knew beyond everything that this was holy ground. God was there in that cell. I could feel His presence, and

He was calling me. I can't explain it, but I felt compelled to bow before Him." Paulus began pacing as he became more passionate about his beliefs. He crossed his arms and faced her. "Mother, He's real. He's more real than anything that happens on this earth. I will serve Him until the day I die, gladly serve Him. We'll make it, Mother, you and I."

Paulina watched her son, eyes shining with tears. She wiped them away with the back of her hand, then looked into Paulus's eyes, smiling tentatively.

"Paulus, you amaze and excite me. You sound just like Antipas. I think you'll follow him as a leader right here in Pergamum. I'm so proud of you, Son."

Paulus leaned forward and lovingly placed his hands on his mother's shoulders. He looked deeply into her eyes.

"Mother, I want you to come and stay with me until things settle down. You can bring your maid and anyone and anything you want, but I want you out of this house. You're not safe here."

One lone tear escaped from her eyes and slid down her face to her chin.

"Oh, Paulus, you have no idea how much this means to me. I wondered how I would cope here, especially if they let your father come home. I will happily come with you." She stood and once again circled him with a hug. He held her tightly, savoring the warmth of mother love he had so long neglected.

"Just bring what you need for tonight, then the servants can get the rest tomorrow."

She was ready quickly and appeared with her cheeks glowing rosy from excitement. It was her one moment of happiness in a day filled with grief and fear. She didn't know what the future held for her, but for now she felt safe leaving with Paulus. God was good to her. She had lost one son but gained another all in one day. How strange life was. Her husband could no longer hurt her, at least for the moment. She did not fear Marcus. He might be as tough as his father, but she didn't think he would hurt her. She might even be able to protect Paulus from the grasp of his brother.

The horse and chariot were waiting at the door when she stepped out into the night. She never looked back at the house where she had lived so many years but known so little happiness. She was content to leave it all behind her and just trust God to lead her into the future He had prepared for her.

Her maid, Johanna, came quickly behind her, carrying a bird cage and the last of the luggage. She hurried into the chariot and had just seated herself when the horse leaped into motion. Paulina knew she would never return, knew she never wanted to return. She knew the future would hold pain and heartache, but she would have to face those when they came.

Chapter Four

As they fled through the night, Justus Anthony stirred in his quarters. Jairus became alert immediately, watching his patient regain consciousness. He noted how his eyes moved constantly. As his eyes gradually opened, Justus Anthony looked around with a vacant stare, almost as though he didn't know where he was. His eyes finally made their way to the couch, where Jairus sat looking at him closely.

Justus Anthony gave a start of recognition. "What are you doing here?"

"I've been here the entire time you've been sleeping." The calm voice and hooded eyes gave away nothing.

"How long have I been sleeping?"

"It's now almost night, so you've been asleep for several hours. You'll be in need of food. I'll call one of the servants." He rose from the couch to give the order to the servants waiting outside the door.

"No, I need to talk to you first." He gingerly sat up, rubbing his hand across his eyes and forehead.

Jairus sat down again and looked expectantly at Justus Anthony. "So speak."

"I need to know that whatever is said in this room will remain between you and me." Justus Anthony narrowed his eyes as he stared at Jairus.

"I never disclose patient information." He lifted his chin slightly and pursed his lips.

"This is more than that. I need your promise before I speak." He folded his arms over his chest and waited.

Jairus gave a wave of his hand. "You have my promise. Now begin."

"I'm disturbed by a communication I received from Rome. It came by courier late last night. The soldier who brought it was exhausted from the journey since he had been instructed to bring it with all haste." Justus Anthony shifted on the cot. "It seems the emperor has received word of what is happening here in Pergamum regarding the Christian sect and the unrest among the priests of Zeus. He, in his great wisdom, wants action, and of course he wants it yesterday."

"What kind of action does he have in mind?" Jairus narrowed his eyes and ran a finger over his lips.

"My theory, for what it's worth, is that he sees this as a way to not only get rid of the Christians but to seriously damage the worship of Zeus. That way he would benefit from more worship himself. Replace Zeus worship with emperor worship." He shrugged his shoulders and gestured with his hands.

Jairus jumped up from his seat. "Mind-boggling." He stood staring down at Justus Anthony. "Is he crazy?"

"I think that's highly possible. I've felt for some time that he is getting dangerously close to insanity." He shook his head slowly.

"Those are traitorous words, my friend." Jairus raised his eyebrows.

"I'm well aware of that. That's why I needed your promise that our conversation would never be repeated."

"What does he want you to do?" Jairus now returned to the couch and sat, chin in hand.

"He wants me to pursue the Christians, step up the persecution to wipe them out, and then expose the priests for what they are—'cheats and liars,' according to the emperor. He doesn't have any suggestions as to how all of this should be accomplished, just for me to do it." He spread his hands wide in front of him.

"That's typical of the emperor." Jairus shook his head back and forth.

"As my physician, I say to you, all this is unbearably stressful. I don't know if I have the heart or the stomach for it." He massaged his forehead, brushing stay hairs back from his eyes.

Jairus took his time answering. "Let me ask you a few questions. Are you looking for help in doing this? Like a magic potion that will give you the courage and stamina? Or are you seeking a way out?"

Justus Anthony rose to his feet, balancing himself carefully. He still felt weak from the sedative the doctor had given him. He walked over to the window, looking out on the street. His mind played tricks on him, and the scene from earlier in the day tried to play itself out in his mind. He shook his head and turned to face Jairus.

"I don't really know. If I decide to do his bidding, what can you do to help?"

"There are potions out there, which are available to me. I could get you something that would strengthen you." He spoke the words slowly and deliberately.

"At least that is good news." Justus Anthony grimaced, sitting on his cot once again.

"They do, however, come with a price." Jairus eyed him intently.

"Yes, I know I would have to pay—"

"Not that kind of a price . . ." His voice trailed off after the soft words were spoken.

"What are you saying?" Justus Anthony stared at him. He sat up straight, focusing his attention, awaiting the answer.

"Oh, political clout, servitude . . ." He used his hands to emphasize each point.

"To whom?" His voice rose in intensity.

"To whatever power grants you the stamina and the possibilities . . ."

"Are you talking about demon involvement?" Justus Anthony cried, a hot flush burning his face.

"I wouldn't be as blatant as that." Jairus sat back and crossed his ankles.

"You are, I can tell by your face. There will be no demons driving the course of my life. Have you not seen enough in what happened today?" He clamped his teeth until they hurt.

"But sir, if that is where the power is . . ."

Justus Anthony bolted from his seat, his face hot, his body shaking. Lifting his right arm, he pointed his finger at Jairus. "Leave my presence. Leave at once and don't come back."

Jairus started to protest, but Justus Anthony waved his hand at him. "You have overstepped your position. Leave and leave quickly."

Jairus stood, and as he neared the door, he turned to face Justus Anthony. "I'm leaving now, but there will come a day when you will remember this hour, this minute, and rue the day you were ever born."

He swept from the room, closing the door with finality.

Justus Anthony sank to his knees, trembling wildly. "What have I done?" he whispered. "What is happening to me?"

He eased himself down on the floor and allowed the entire day to play out before his eyes. As the scenes flooded over him, he gasped for breath. He was in deep trouble on many levels and he knew it. What would happen next, only God could determine.

Now that is an interesting assessment, he thought. *This is getting to be all about God, isn't it?*

He didn't know how long he lay there on the floor. His mind slipped around all the events, all the thoughts of the day. What should he do next? He knew he was not the man he had been before Antipas was arrested. Everything had changed at that point in his life. He felt the hardness he had worn with pride sliding away from him. He didn't seem to have the stomach for Caesar's demands anymore.

Then there were the priests. They weren't going to let this go either. They had watched him with critical eyes and had formed their opinions. They were in all likelihood plotting his downfall even now. That's what they did best, plotting and scheming.

And now the doctor, one of his few friends, but he couldn't trust him either. He was a friend only when it was to his advantage. That little scroll of his, with the multitude of words, undoubtedly contained enough information to destroy many people in high places, including him.

Who would get to his servants first? Would they bring poison in a cup or something mixed in with his food? Or would a paid assassin burst through his door, blade zinging through the air?

And now what about Caesar? And Marcus? And the temple guards? His life was over and he knew it. The only people not angry with him or out to get him were those who had the most right to do so, the Christians. He felt only compassion from them.

Should he approach them? He had long thought about that, then discarded the idea. How could they trust him when he wasn't even sure he could trust himself? And his presence with them would only increase their risk of intensified persecution. If he left his office to join them, Caesar would handpick the man replacing him to destroy him and the Christians, probably the priests as well. He couldn't be responsible for all the repercussions from a choice like that.

He finally rose from the floor. He had a plan and he knew he must follow it. He must be ahead of his enemies. He must be gone when they decided to strike.

Chapter Five

He made his way over to his cabinet. The door opened readily, exposing a myriad of potions in covered cups. He read labels and chose five from the group, moving slowly and methodically. Choosing a half skin of strong wine from one of the provinces, he nodded. It would do quite nicely.

He was surprised that his hands weren't trembling now that he had reached his decision, the only decision that made any sense. He carefully measured out portions from each container, mixing them meticulously in his drinking cup. When he was satisfied with the amount and combination, he poured the wine and mixed it with the medicines.

Leaving the brew sitting on his desk, he opened drawers and closets, choosing his finest robe and all the trappings of his office. Next he washed carefully at the basin and then arrayed himself in his finest clothes. He sat at his desk for a few minutes, pondering his future. At last he bowed his head low on his desk.

God of the Christians, if You're out there, I need to talk to You. I don't know how to do that, so I'll just talk. You know how impressed I was with Antipas and now with all the Christians who so bravely stood before the steps of the altar. I've done some terrible things in my life, and I'm really sorry for them. I know I don't deserve anything from You, but if You'll have me, I'm Yours.

His tears stained the leather covering of his desk, but that didn't matter anymore. Nothing did. He lifted the drink and slowly swallowed the contents, including the last few bitter drops. When he finished, he took the cup to the basin and washed it thoroughly. He dried it, then placed it back in the cabinet. He wandered to the window and watched the scene below until a tiredness began to seep into his body. It was time to lie down and face his future, the one he had planned for himself.

Sleep overcame him quickly, and in the early hours of the evening, before the servants brought him his evening meal, he faded from the earth, which had become unbearable to him, and entered eternity.

Larium found Eunice weeping uncontrollably in her room one afternoon a few weeks after Antipas's death. She was surprised since Eunice had seemed so strong, so positive, so trusting in God. She had even been a support to Antipas's mother, brother, and the other converts. What could have happened to send her into this sobbing bordering on hysteria?

Larium approached the bed and bent over her. "Eunice, what's wrong?"

Eunice lifted her distraught face and flung herself into Larium's arms.

"Oh my dear, whatever has happened to put you into this state?" Larium wrapped her arms around her.

"I can't bear it." Eunice beat her fists against Larium's shoulder.

"You mean losing Antipas?" She brushed hair back from her face.

"No, no, I have come to terms with that." Eunice gulped and eased her weeping.

"Then what is it? Maybe I can help." Larium looked into her eyes, her forehead wrinkling.

"Oh, Larium, I think I'm expecting another baby." The sobs wracked her body again.

"Are you sure, Eunice?" Larium gripped her shoulders.

"Yes, I'm sure. How can I bear to have another child without a father? This child will never know its father. Antipas will never hold it or see its face. Oh, it's too much." She flung her head back on Larium's shoulder.

Larium sat on the edge of the bed and just held her. She rubbed her back and let her sob until gradually the weeping subsided to a few sniffs. Eunice sat up and rubbed her eyes.

"I'm so sorry, Larium, to involve you in my problems."

"My dear, that's what I'm here for. I want to help you. I know you're feeling a great sadness and an overwhelming fear right now, but let's try to see the positives in this situation. And there *are* positives, Eunice." Larium offered a bright smile.

"Please remind me of them. Right now I can't even think." She dropped her face into her hands, shaking her head.

"Well, first off, you'll have another beautiful baby, another blessing from your life with Antipas, a little brother or sister for Simon. He'd really like that." She lifted Eunice's chin so they were eye to eye. "And two, I feel sure Antipas will somehow know about this." She counted them off on her fingers. "Three, if God can provide for you and Simon, I'm sure He can handle a little one like this baby.

And four, remember that God has promised to never leave you nor forsake you. You've held onto this thought all through the time of his death and the weeks following. God hasn't given up working just because there's another baby." Her hand massaged Eunice's shoulder.

"You're right. I couldn't see past the thought of having a baby without Antipas by my side." She smiled shyly at Larium. "This will make more work for you, too."

"Another baby? I can't think of anything more welcome right now. We'll all make it our baby, and we'll raise it together." Larium wiped the tears from Eunice's face.

"I think I'm all right now. I think I can face it. Maybe it'll be a little girl." She actually giggled.

"Why don't you wash your face and take a walk in the garden before mealtime? I'll be happy to look after Simon for a while. Tabitha is home as well, and she's really good with him."

Eunice gave her a tight hug and agreed.

The air was fresh with a light breeze rustling the leaves and fanning her face as she walked. She prayed earnestly as she wandered through the flower beds and trees at the back of the property.

Presently she heard footsteps behind her and turned. Her brother-in-law, Paulus, walked toward her. When he caught up with her, he greeted her and took her arm. The two continued walking and talking quietly.

"Eunice, I hope you don't mind, but Larium told me your news." He smiled at her, eyebrows raised in question.

"I don't mind, Paulus. In fact, I'm glad you know." She smiled back.

"I don't know how to say this, but I would really like to be the father figure in this little one's life. I love Simon already and really want to be a big part of his life and of the baby's, if you'll let me." He glanced at her hesitatingly, awaiting her answer.

"Paulus, that would please me very much. Simon loves his Uncle Paulus, and I know this new little one will as well. Thank you for offering." Her lips curved upward.

"I have something else I'd like to discuss with you." He paused and cleared his throat before continuing.

She looked up at him, eyebrows raised in question.

"I'm not sure how to say it or how you'll respond." He stopped walking and looked at her.

"Why don't you just ask me?" She laughed as she turned to face him.

"All right. Mother and I have been talking. You know she lives with me now." Eunice nodded. "We would really like you to move in with us. I have a big house, my mother would love to have you near her, and we're your close relatives and would like to look after you." He dropped his hands to his sides, a serious look on his face.

"Paulus, that's a wonderful offer. But I'll want to talk it over with Larium and Mattias; they've done so much for me. I wouldn't want them to feel I was ungrateful."

"Of course. I would expect you to do that. Take your time and think it through. I know you'll want to pray about it, too."

She took his arm again. "Thank you, Paulus, you're so understanding. And thank you for your offer. I'll make the decision quickly after I've talked to my friends."

They kept walking in silent companionship until they heard Larium calling to them for the meal.

Eunice already felt like she was a part of the family. She marveled at how they had accepted her and Simon, and now Paulus was becoming very dear to them as well. After a joyful time eating together, Eunice and Larium cleared the table and began washing dishes.

"I can't believe how much Paulus reminds me of Antipas," Larium said as she dipped a dish in the hot water. "There are differences, of course, but the resemblance is remarkable."

"I've noticed, too," Eunice agreed. She smiled inside, not wanting to admit that she was drawn to him. "I never was close to my own brothers since they were older, but also because they were against my belief in Jesus." She closed her eyes, remembering their surly comments when their father wasn't around to defend her.

"It must have been hard for you when you became a believer." Larium swished around another dish in the clay bowl.

"Only at times. My father was a Christ-follower, too, so when he was there, they didn't dare say anything to me."

“It amazes me to see how Paulus has grown in his faith. Sometimes he simply glows from his walk with the Father,” Larium said.

“I’ve noticed that, too. His faith seems deeper every day.” Eunice carefully dried the wooden knives and spoons they had used during the meal, placing them in the basket Larium had put on the table.

“His care for you and his concern for you and Simon are touching.”

“I know, and especially now that there is another baby.” Eunice’s mind drifted off to his offer. She decided she would talk to Larium and Mattias once the children were in bed.

Chapter Six

Larium sank down on a low couch beside Eunice once the children had retired for the night. She sighed once, putting her head back against the cushions.

"I'd like to talk to both you and Mattias," Eunice said, twisting the embroidery on her sleeve nervously.

"Mattias, will you join us?" Larium looked to where he was sitting at the table, going over figures on the scroll open in front of him. He looked up at both of them.

"Please, Mattias. Eunice wants to talk to both of us."

He placed the quill pen beside the scroll and stood from his place. With a big grin he headed for the couches. "In that case, of course I'll come," he said as he lowered himself among the cushions.

Still twisting her sleeve, Eunice looked from one to the other. "Paulus has made an offer to me. He'd like me to move in with him and his mother. I've been praying about it and want your opinion."

"What are your thoughts since you prayed?" Mattias leaned toward her, his hands in his lap.

"I've felt peace about it. Somehow it seems the right thing to do."

Larium's arm came around her shoulder, and she hugged her. "I know Paulus has a large house, and it would be a great place for the children."

"Yes, and don't forget that Paulina will be delighted to have both you and Simon there. She's had a hard life. Not much joy in it." Mattias stroked his beard and nodded. "But you do know you're welcome to stay here. Everyone in the household will miss you." He cleared his throat.

"I do know that and am very grateful. You two are family to me. I just sense that God is in this offer and I think I need to get to know my family. It will be good for Simon to know Antipas's family, and I want to get closer to Paulina." She hugged both of them.

"We do understand, Eunice. We'll really miss you, but I too feel God is leading in this." Larium returned the hug, holding her tightly.

"You have our blessing on your decision, Eunice," Mattias said.

"Thank you, my friends. We'll probably see Paulus here tomorrow, and I'll give him my answer. I've kept you up long enough now."

When Eunice was escorted to her new quarters, she couldn't believe her eyes. She had never lived in such opulence, such magnificence. Her quarters were on the ground floor at the back of the house. Long, narrow windows opened into a spectacular garden with paths through the flower beds, ending at a small bower with blooming bushes and comfortable benches.

She gazed at the scene, longing to walk the paths and drink in the heady perfumes of the flowers in bloom.

"Would you care to walk in the garden with me?" Paulus stood beside her.

"Oh, please, nothing would give me greater pleasure." She turned from the window and looked into his eyes, which reflected the smile on his lips.

He offered her his arm, and they strolled along the walkways, enjoying the freshness of the day. Simon ran ahead of them, exclaiming over every new thing he encountered.

"Can you be happy here, Eunice?" He leaned toward her, eyebrows raised.

"How could I not be? This is wonderful. I only have to look out my window if I'm feeling down, and all this beauty awaits me." She swept her arm in a circle to encompass the flowers and trees.

"I've assigned one of our young girls, Marina, to be your servant. She'll help you look after Simon and do anything else you ask her to do. Please use her services, or she will feel she has not pleased you." He drew her closer to his side.

"I will certainly have to get used to this lifestyle. I've never had a servant." She grinned at him. "But I promise to make friends with her. I would rather have her do things for me because she wants to than because I order her to do so." They continued their stroll.

"You are an amazing lady, Eunice. Antipas was very fortunate to have your love."

"Thank you." She lowered her eyes as a blush burned her cheeks.

They soon returned to the house, and Paulus brought his mother to greet her. Paulina made her feel so welcome. She hugged Eunice warmly.

"I have longed for this for many days," Paulina said. "I want to get to know you better and to be a big part in my only grandson's life. It will go a long way to making up for what I lost of Antipas's youth. You have made an old lady very happy." She wiped tears from her eyes.

"I, too, am looking forward to getting to know you," Eunice said. "Antipas always spoke of you so lovingly and warmly. I know he missed you terribly when he had to leave home." She swallowed with difficulty, forcing the tears back. "Simon and I will be pleased to try to make up a small portion of what you've lost."

Paulina slipped her arms around Eunice. "I've been storing up love for years, and I hope you'll let me pour it out on you and Simon, and you too, Paulus," she said as she turned to him. "I've never been happier in my life." A single tear slipped from where it had been hanging on her eyelashes.

Eunice hugged her tightly. "We'll treasure your love and return it." The tears she had tried to contain now flowed.

Later, while Paulina rested in her room, her mind replayed the reunion with Eunice and Simon.

How I shall enjoy getting to know both of them. I'm afraid I've lost any love I may have had for Julian. His cruelty squeezed it out of me. I will never live at his house again. It seems strange to me that I've never considered it my house; I was merely another of his material possessions. Never a wife, never a partner.

Eunice sat in the garden, watching Simon play. She loved these times, watching the delight on her son's face while he ran along the paths, sniffed the flowers, and picked up pebbles and tiny insects. The tread of sandals caught her attention, and she turned to see Paulus approaching.

"Paulus, I didn't expect to see you this early." She watched his mouth widen in a smile.

"May I join you on the bench?"

"Of course," she said and moved over to make room.

"I hope you're enjoying the garden, Eunice, and I can see that Simon loves to play here. Look at him watching the birds."

"Simon begs to come out here each morning. I know he misses Larium and Tabitha, but this is his place of joy."

"Have you seen Larium lately? I know you must miss her, too." Paulus lifted his eyebrows and looked directly into her eyes.

"I try to visit once a week, and sometimes I leave Simon with Tabitha for an hour or so to visit some of the families in need that I used to visit before Antipas died."

"I'm happy you continue to see friends, especially the ones who look for your help and encouragement. You have a wonderful gift of encouragement." Paulus squeezed her hand, then stood. "I'm going to spend a few minutes with Simon and see if I can help catch those birds or at least a bug or two." His face creased in a grin.

"Simon will love it." She watched as the two of them walked together and stopped to look at things. She smiled to herself.

How special it is to live here. I will always miss Antipas, but this has been a place of healing.

She studied Paulus as he bent down to Simon's level.

Paulus has done so much for me, but I think he enjoys having us here, as well.

"Mama, Mama, come see what we found!"

The voice of her son delighted her, and she rose to join them. "I'm coming, Simon." When she reached the two, she pushed other thoughts from her mind and focused on Simon and Paulus.

Amid the peace of the garden, it was easy to forget the persecution, the unrest following her husband's death. But she knew in her heart that Pergamum was quiet—too quiet. The church leaders were expecting another outbreak of persecution. The news of Justus Anthony's suicide had stunned the converts. What would it mean for them and for the young church of Pergamum?

Chapter Seven

The evening meal was over. Marina took Simon to his bed, and Paulina went to her room. Eunice and Paulus reclined and talked quietly.

"I stopped in to talk to the doctor today," Paulus said, "and the news of Father isn't good. In fact, it's grim. He has yet to regain his sanity, if he ever will."

"Oh Paulus, it must be so hard for you." Eunice put her hand over his.

"It wrenches my heart each time I get a report, but I believe God wants me to keep in touch and help however I can. The doctor said Father spends his days pacing the room, ranting and raving about Antipas, Justus Anthony, and the priests."

"Isn't it interesting that Antipas is still on his mind?"

"I think, at least I hope, that he feels guilty for his treatment of Antipas. He's apparently developed a persecution complex and invents sinister plots of people determined to kill him."

Eunice squeezed his hand. "He needs the Lord, Paulus. All his terrors and fears would leave him."

"I know, and that's why we need to keep praying for him. I'm so thankful the church is praying for him, too. The last time I saw him, he screamed at me to leave. He apparently thinks I'm part of one of the plots to kill him."

"Oh Paulus, how terrible." Eunice wiped the tears from her face with the edge of her scarf. "Have you been able to talk to Marcus about him?"

"No, I tried to talk to him one day, but he's closed himself from the family. He's angry that I have Mother here. There may not be much hope for Julian, but there's still hope for Marcus, so we'll pray."

Eunice awoke one morning in great pain. She gasped when she tried to sit up in bed. Pains gripped her abdomen and circled around to her back. Taking a deep breath, she sent Simon to look for his grandmother and bring her to their room. Although he was still very young, he knew the way to her room, and soon Paulina entered, carrying him.

Her eyes widened, and she drew her lips together tightly. Eunice reached out a trembling hand to her.

"Eunice, I'll take Simon to the nursery and have Marina look after him. I'll send Paulus for the doctor. Then I'll be right back."

Eunice only moaned in reply, so Paulina hurried away with Simon. When she returned to Eunice, she bent over her, smoothing her hair back from her face.

"Eunice, I'm going to bathe you with cool water. I think you're running a fever." She placed a cool hand on her forehead, then found a clean cloth, dipped it in water from the pitcher on the table, wrung it out, and began to wipe her face.

"Thank you, Paulina. That feels so good," Eunice whispered, then fainted.

Paulina gripped her hands together as fear tightened around her heart. She kept dipping the cloth in the cool water and bathing her face. Once Eunice stirred but then slipped into stillness again.

It seemed forever before she heard Paulus and the doctor arrive. Paulus brought him to Eunice's room and slipped in with him. Paulina took one look at her son and knew he was terrified. His eyes widened, and a muscle twitched in his cheek. She decided there would be no help from him.

"How long has she been like this?" The doctor's words intruded into her anxiety.

"Just a short while. It started with pain and then she fainted. I've been bathing her with cool water."

He opened his pouch and extracted vials, some containing herbs and others a dark liquid. He mixed their contents together in a clay bowl.

He glanced toward Paulina. "Please, hold her head."

She knelt beside the doctor and lifted Eunice's head slightly while the doctor spread the mixture on her lips, forcing some between her teeth.

Eunice moaned and opened her eyes. Paulina was distressed to see how pale her skin had become. With an intake of breath, she closed her eyes tightly, drawing her knees up and rocking back and forth on the bed.

"It'll take a few minutes for the medication to take hold and ease her pain." The doctor stood from the side of the bed. "Paulus, I have some things I need. Would you be able to get them for me?"

"Yes, of course. Tell me what you want." He left the room once the doctor gave him the list.

Paulina watched him return with towels and other items, while she listened to the doctor. Paulus joined them.

"She has gone into premature labor," the doctor said. "It's far too soon for the baby to be born. I can't hear a heartbeat. My opinion is that the baby is already dead." He shook his head.

The words hit Paulus hard. Why did this have to happen to Eunice? Hadn't she had enough trouble already?

He handed the towels to the doctor and left the house. His feet turned to the garden, where he had walked with Eunice and Simon on many occasions. She loved the peace and beauty of the flowers and shrubs.

As he walked, he prayed.

Lord, I know I have to trust You with her life and the baby's. Please spare her, Lord. Give her peace if she loses this baby. Ease her pain. I know You have her in Your tender care and that You have a plan for her life. Lord, I need peace, too.

As he walked and talked, he felt renewed. He reentered the house and returned to Eunice's room, where all was quiet. The doctor held a tiny bundle. Eunice appeared to be sleeping quietly.

Paulus glanced at his mother, his eyebrows raised in a question.

"It's a little girl. She's so tiny that we don't know if she'll live or not. Come see her, she's so beautiful." She beckoned him closer.

The doctor passed the bundle to Paulus. He hesitated to take it, but the doctor insisted. As she was passed to him, he looked at her small face and marveled at the perfect little features. She opened her doll-like eyes, and Paulus fell in love with her. He couldn't explain the feeling as he held her. He kissed her head, where dark curly hair rimmed her forehead.

"Oh, Lord, protect this little life." He closed his eyes, holding her gently.

Eunice awoke and watched Paulus holding her baby. The tender look in his eyes moved her. She spoke his name, and he moved over to the side of her bed and laid the baby in her arms. Though she was weak, she managed a beautiful smile.

The doctor gathered his things and told Paulina he would return in the evening to check on the baby's progress. "She seems healthy even though she is so small. She may yet live. Keep her wrapped warmly and send for me if there's any change." He nodded to Paulus and left the room. Paulina left the room with him.

Paulus smiled at Eunice. She returned the smile. He knelt by her bed, and she reached out and touched his face.

"Thank you for everything, Paulus. I don't know how I would have managed the last few months without you."

He looked deeply into her eyes. "Eunice, you must know that I have come to care for you very much."

"Yes, I know you do, and I appreciate your care." She put her hand on his arm.

"It's more than that. I love you, Eunice. I know it's too soon to talk about it, but I wanted you to know." He touched her face gently with his fingers.

"Oh, Paulus, that is beautiful. I didn't think I could ever love again as I loved Antipas, but God has shown me that I can. I have felt love for you, too, but didn't think you could ever care for me in that way." She looked into his eyes and tipped her lips in a smile.

He smoothed the hair back from her forehead. "You need to rest now, but you've made me a very happy man. We'll talk again when you're stronger. Just know I'll be here for you and Simon and now for this beautiful baby girl. Rest now, I'll see you a little later."

She closed her eyes after he left her. God was so good. First the baby was born alive against all odds, and now Paulus had declared his love for her. She hugged the knowledge to her heart, wishing against all hope that the future would be bright.

But she had the feeling that the fires of persecution were moving ever closer, dimming the hope she held.

Chapter Eight

Eunice lifted her baby from the basket beside the bed, holding her close to her heart. "Helena, my baby girl." She kissed the top of her curly head. "I think your daddy would have been pleased with your name, my sweet baby. I promise you, Helena, that you will know your father through my eyes. I'll tell you and your big brother stories about him, how brave he was and how much he loved God." She kissed her again, marveling at her soft skin. "You have an incredible heritage, little one."

A sound in the doorway made Eunice look up. "Paulina, come in. Helena and I have been having a little talk." Laughter tinkled from her lips as she held the baby out to Paulina. "Would you like to hold your granddaughter?"

Once she was safely in her grandmother's arms, Paulina kissed her cheek. "I can't believe how much she's grown in her three short months."

"That's because everyone in this house takes special care of her." The laughter bubbled up again. "How could she not thrive?"

As if on cue, Helena giggled and gave them one of her lopsided smiles, while little gurgling sounds escaped her tiny lips.

Eunice watched her mother-in-law kiss Helena. "I'm so thrilled to have you a part of Simon's and Helena's lives. Not only is it good for the children, but it's been good for me, too. I feel so close to you and enjoy our sweet fellowship."

Paulina put Helena on her shoulder and patted her back. "It's been a blessing for me. I had long ago ceased to expect this joy. But now to have these two children, and also our special times of praying together and sharing; my heart overflows. Thank you, Eunice."

Eunice stood and approached Paulina, leaning over and wrapping her arms around the older woman. "No, Paulina, the thanks goes to you." They shared a hug around the baby, who peacefully sucked her thumb, making little cooing noises.

"Are you visiting any families today, Eunice?"

"Yes, I hope to spend some time with Sophia today. Her life has not been easy since she lost her husband in the farming accident. Marina is so good with the children that I feel comfortable taking up these duties again."

"I'll look in on the children while you're gone to see if they need anything. I'm glad you're able to do this. I know you're a blessing to Sophia and to the others you visit."

Paulus had been away on business and returned while Eunice was visiting Sophia. After greeting his mother and finding that Eunice was out, he decided to look for Marina so he could visit with Simon and Helena. Simon's face lit up when he saw his uncle enter the room.

"Up, up," he shouted happily, lifting his hands over his head. Paulus bent down and lifted the little boy up in his arms. It felt so good to just hug the child. He was humbled to accept such trust. Together they leaned over Helena's little bed and watched the sleeping baby. To Paulus she was a miracle.

He felt such a great responsibility for these two and a love he hadn't even known existed until a few months ago. He hoped to one day adopt them as his own, whenever Eunice was ready for such a step.

The evening meal was a festive occasion. Paulina had planned a special meal for her son's homecoming. Simon was allowed to stay up as well, adding to the excitement. Eunice was reminded of the warm, loving meals taken at Larium and Mattias's table. The conversation was pleasant and included talk about the Pergamum church and the studies they were involved in.

"I never imagined peace like this was possible." Paulus took in all of them around the table with his glance. "Just knowing Christ has made a tremendous difference in my outlook on life, even in the way I do business. I owe so much to my Savior, and so much to you, Eunice, and to Antipas."

"I agree." Paulina nodded in reply. "It's interesting to compare our situation with Joseph's in Egypt—how his brothers meant it for evil, but God meant it for good. It's hard to think of the time your father sent Antipas away; he certainly meant it for evil, but just look at the good God brought out of it."

"As painful as it is to think about"—Eunice leaned forward to join the conversation— "even Antipas's sacrifice has made a huge difference in the Pergamum church. People have never been so bold for Christ. I miss him so much, but I have to accept God's plan for his life and mine."

"You are one of the bravest people I know." Paulus looked at Eunice with a smile. "The love of God just shines through you."

"You're embarrassing me, Paulus." Her cheeks warmed under his gaze.

The talk shifted to Eunice's visit to Sophia that day and her plan to visit David tonight. "Sophia needs help with the farm, and I'm hoping David will know someone looking for farm work."

"I'll go with you," Paulus said. "I've been planning to visit him as well."

"Thank you, Paulus. I was going to have the gardener take me, but I'd rather go with you." She clasped her hands before her.

"We'll leave as soon as you're ready after the meal." He nodded to her across the table.

Simon was nearly asleep, so Eunice carried him to her room, where Marina was sitting with Helena. "Marina, I'll be out for a few hours. Please put both children to bed for me. Simon is ready now, and Helena looks like she is almost ready as well."

She lifted her daughter in her arms, never tiring of just looking at her and feeling her warmth. She was truly a miracle. How she wished Antipas could see her. But she must not become melancholy now; she needed to talk to David. She handed Helena back and grabbed a warm cloak, leaving the room and seeking Paulus.

The two left the house together, entering the dusk of the evening. Stars were just beginning to appear in the eastern sky. Streaks of sunset still showed low in the west. Paulus offered her his arm to lean on while they walked the short distance to David's house. She was thrilled to walk arm in arm with him, content not to talk as they moved through the streets. Deepening shadows crowded the alleyways, turning the city from day to night.

Lights shone from David's home when they knocked on the entrance door. One of the servants greeted them, then went to inform David of their arrival.

"Greetings, friends. What brings you out this fine night?" David greeted them heartily and led them to an inner room.

"We have different reasons for seeking you tonight," Paulus said. "I am hoping for time to ask some questions, and Eunice has a request." He shook out of his cloak and laid it on a low couch.

"Well, sit down, friends, and we'll see if I can help. Eunice, why don't you tell me your request?" David motioned toward low seats near the fire.

Eunice sank down on the comfortable couch, tired after their walk in the evening air. Taking a deep breath, she began by giving him some background on Sophia. Her hands were graceful in motion while she spoke. When she mentioned Sophia's need for someone to help her, David gave her a gentle smile.

"God is so good, isn't He?" He rubbed his hands together and nodded. "Just this week a family arrived from the country to stay with us."

David rose from his seat, his form tall and slim, and leaned on a low divider. Dark hair was pulled back from his face, and his beard was trimmed. Everything about him was neat and orderly. He eyed his visitors. "The husband is very young with a younger wife and a wee babe. His father died, leaving the farming business to his older brother with the idea that he would be kept on to help work the farm. The older brother made it very clear after the funeral that he was no longer welcome on the farm. Desperate, James decided to come to Pergamum to seek work. He is unskilled so has not yet found a position. I think he'll jump at the chance to work on a farm. Do you think there would be enough room for his wife and baby?" David lifted his brows as he posed the question.

"I'm sure Sophia would make room," Eunice said. "She'll be so thrilled. It's all too much for her. God really does answer our prayers before we even pray them, doesn't He?" She folded her hands and rested her chin on them, meeting David's eyes.

"Then let's meet James and make some arrangements." David called his servant and asked him to bring James to him. A few minutes later a stocky young man with sandy hair entered the room, eyes lowered and hands at his sides.

"James, this is Paulus and Eunice," David said. "Eunice has come to me with a request that I think you will find interesting. Eunice, please tell him what you told me."

Eunice told the story again. James was beaming by the time she was finished.

"Please," James said, "if you think I would be acceptable to your friend, I could start tomorrow." His voice had a plaintive tone.

"I'm sure it's acceptable," Eunice said. "I'll be happy to walk to the farm with you and introduce you to Sophia."

James agreed, so they arranged a time for them to meet. He hurried off to tell his wife the good news.

Eunice clapped her hands together. "I'm excited about how fast God answered my prayer." She turned in a circle and grinned at the two men. "God is so good. Sophia's greatest difficulties have been solved."

"God does things like that," David said. "I'm so pleased that things have worked out for James and also for your friend Sophia." David gave her a warm hug and shook Paulus's hand.

"Would I be able to speak with you privately?" Paulus asked David.

"Certainly, I'd be happy to talk with you. Eunice, why don't you visit with Miriam while we talk? She's in the garden with the children."

"I know the way and would love to spend some time with Miriam." Eunice turned toward the garden while David led Paulus to an inner room.

When they were seated comfortably, Paulus told David the purpose of his visit.

"A few months ago, you mentioned to me that you thought I could one day become the leader of the Pergamum church." Paulus looked to David, taking a breath and holding it.

"Yes, and I still think that." David put a hand on his shoulder, giving him a light shake. They grinned at each other.

Paulus became serious again. "At the time, I didn't really believe I would ever be ready for such an assignment. But God has been working on my heart, nudging me in that direction. I wanted to talk to you and see if you think I'm ready to assume such a responsible position. I feel inadequate, but God won't take it off my mind."

David put his hand on Paulus's shoulder again. This time a thoughtful look crossed his face. "Paulus, I have prayed for this moment for many months. No one has the leadership ability you have; no one since Antipas was martyred. I have watched you grow spiritually day by day. You have a depth to your character that is beyond compare." He gave his shoulder a shake. "You are certainly ready and the church is ready for strong leadership again. The leaders are growing weary of trying to carry the burden thrust on them with Antipas's death. They're doing their best, but clearly it's a temporary solution."

David shifted in his seat to face Paulus.

Paulus bowed his head as David spoke.

"Are you willing to meet with the leaders this week and put some plans in place?" He gave his shoulder another shake.

Paulus raised his eyes to look directly at David. "I'm humbled by your words, but yes, I'm ready. I must follow the Lord's leading. He's done so much for me. I can only be obedient."

“Have you considered that you will now be the center of the persecution? The priests will want to get their hands on you.” David pointed a finger at him, his mouth set in a straight line.

“Yes, I’ve gone over all that, and I have a great example in my brother. I know that he willingly went to the altar. My heart was torn in two as I stood and watched him face the flames. God gave him the courage to bear all the hardships.” He paused and pursed his lips. “I know his fate may be my fate; the danger is out there. My brother and the priests will make certain we don’t forget.”

Chapter Nine

Early the next morning Paulus sought out Eunice. He found her in the garden, playing with Simon. Marina was close by, holding Helena. As Paulus approached, Eunice looked up and smiled. His heart leaped when he saw her; her smile always seemed to make his knees feel weak.

"Good morning, Paulus," she said. "We don't usually see you in the garden this early in the day."

"I was hoping I could talk with you for a few minutes." Palms moist, he wiped his hands on his robe. *I'm acting like a young boy,* he thought. Simon saw him and hurled his little body at his uncle. Paulus leaned over and picked up the squirming boy.

"How's my boy today?" Paulus asked with a grin.

"I'm good, Uncle Paulus." A big hug followed his answer.

"I'm glad to hear you're good. Then you won't mind going back to the house with Marina so I can talk with your mother." Paulus softened his request by returning the smile and the hug.

Simon pouted for a moment, then agreed to go with Marina.

Once the children had disappeared into the house, Eunice looked questioningly at him.

"Let's walk." Paulus offered her his arm with a slight bow.

She slid her hand in the crook of his arm and they sauntered down the path toward the trees. A companionable silence followed while they strolled along between the rows of flowers and small shrubs. A heady mixture of fragrances greeted them with each step. Vibrant colors welcomed the sunlight. A small bird flitted from branch to branch with dried grass clenched firmly in its yellow beak.

When they reached the back of the garden, Paulus suggested they sit on the rustic bench overlooking the stream. Sunlight danced off the water, adding more sparkle to the day. Paulus turned toward her.

"Eunice, I have so much I want to say to you. First, I want to tell you about my decision and a meeting I'm having tonight."

He told her the story of his struggle over the past few months, about God's gentle nudging. "I finally submitted to God, and that's why I talked to David last night." His shoulders relaxed, and peace settled in his heart. "I'm going to meet with some of the other church leaders tonight."

"Oh Paulus, I'm so happy. I've been praying about this, sensing that God was leading you." She folded her hands in her lap and looked out over the water before facing him. "I am so proud of you." He could see the tears shining in her eyes.

"I have so many dreams and fears for the Pergamum church," he said. "But I know God is in control, and I don't need to be anxious."

She listened intently, watching the play of emotions on his face. How like Antipas he was—in many ways—yet how different. What she heard impressed her, and she silently thanked God for this man and the spiritual growth she had witnessed over the last few months.

"But I also want to talk to you about us." He took her hand in his, squeezing it gently.

Eunice sat very still. Her heart seemed to stop in anticipation of his words. She glanced at her hands, aware of warmth on her neck and cheeks. She was not afraid, at least not for herself, but it might be hard for him to step into his brother's shoes. He was already doing that for the church; maybe in his personal life it would be too much.

"Eunice, I haven't spoken to you about us since the day Helena was born. I wanted you to have all the time you needed to enjoy your baby and recover from a difficult birth. I also wanted you to have the time to adjust to thinking about another relationship so soon after Antipas." He reached for her other hand as well, entwining his fingers with hers.

A thrill ran through her at his touch. "Eunice, look at me." He cupped her chin with one hand, gently turning her face to his and looking deeply into her eyes. "It's been three months now, and I want you to know that my feelings for you have intensified over that time."

Her lips trembled as she gazed at him. Was this really happening? Her heart began to sing.

"You are a beautiful person, inside and out. I would love to have you for my wife, if you could even consider marrying again." He sat quietly, holding her gaze with his own.

Her mouth opened, but no words came. Joy bubbled up inside her until her lips curved; she was overwhelmed with emotion. With a tiny gasp she whispered, "Yes. Oh yes, I don't deserve to be this happy, but I am. I will be happy to become your wife."

Paulus gathered her in his arms, whispering promises to her. He ran his fingers through her hair, then lowered his face to hers and kissed her. Her heart raced, and she returned his kiss. The garden faded until only she and Paulus were there. Her gaze was riveted to his until she was almost breathless.

He leaned back a bit, still holding her gaze. "You'll probably want to wait longer before we're wed, and I understand . . ."

She pushed away from him and looked deeply into his eyes. "No, Paulus. There's no need to wait. Antipas and I talked about just such a possibility. He wanted me to find someone to love, someone who would be a father to Simon. I see no reason not to be married as soon as possible." A rush of warmth to her face stopped her. She was sounding too eager.

"Then let's set a date." He sat back, lips curving upward to meet the gleam in his eyes.

"Oh yes, I agree." A giggle escaped her lips.

"How about a month from now? That should give Mother and our friends time to adjust to the idea." He ran his hand over her hair again. "Will that give you time to prepare?"

"Plenty of time."

"I think we need to tell Mother our news. I know she'll be thrilled." Hand in hand, they walked back up the path to the house.

"I can't wait to see her face when we tell her."

When they entered Paulina's room, a smile broke out on her lovely face.

"I think you have good news for me," she said. "Your faces are shining with a special glow."

"Yes, Mother, you're right. Eunice has just agreed to become my wife." He squeezed Eunice's hand and grinned at her.

Paulina gasped, hands pressed to her heart. "My prayers have been answered." She rose from her resting place and approached them with open arms, gathering them both in her embrace. "I wish you much happiness."

She reached out and took Paulus's hand in hers. "I know Antipas would be pleased that Eunice has chosen you and that Simon and Helena will be raised by a good man." She paused to wipe a tear from her eye. "May God richly bless you. May your faces always radiate the love I see on them today. May you have many years together in blissful harmony. God bless you, my children."

As Paulina was blessing them, Eunice felt the tears start. When she glanced at Paulus, he, too, had tears in his eyes.

"Thank you, Mother. Whatever time God has given us, we want to use it for His glory." He then told her about the meeting this evening. While he spoke, the smile lines deepened on her face.

When he was finished, she clapped her hands. "I'm so thrilled, both for you and for the church." She looked from him to Eunice, lifting her chin. She nodded. "I can't think of a better leader. Antipas would be so proud of you. Now if only Marcus would find our Lord. How wonderful our family would be—and of course Julian, too. But the news isn't good there."

Paulus knew he needed to visit his father, but it was with reluctant steps that he turned into the street where his father was kept. Breathing deeply, he knocked on the door and followed the servant down the hall. He was left alone, standing before the door to his father's room.

To enter or leave; I'm never sure which I should do.

Thrusting his shoulders back and lifting his head, he slowly pushed the door open. Julian stood in the center of the room, pulling on his hair and emitting a low growl.

"Father, I'm here to visit you." Paulus took a step into the room.

Julian swung around, grinding his teeth and snarling. "You, you." His shrieks pierced Paulus's heart. Julian grabbed a book from the night table and threw it at him. "Deserter, deserter! That's who you are. No son of mine. No, no son. No son."

Paulus was alarmed not only by his words but by his appearance. He was dirty, and his clothes were ripped in several places. Almost to prove a point, it seemed, he grabbed his tunic and tore it from his shoulders, standing before Paulus bare chested.

"I can help you, Father, if you'll let me." Paulus swallowed, almost choking on his grief. "Please let me help you."

A piercing scream poured from Julian's open mouth, followed by obscenities. He ran around the room in dizzying circles. "No, no, no . . . Get out."

Paulus left. Back on the street, he walked a league before he realized where he was.

Why do I go?

He stopped on the edge of the street.

I know I go because he's still my father, and I'll go again.

He pushed thoughts of Julian aside and returned home for the evening meal, where he enjoyed time with the family. Once they were finished, Paulus kissed his mother and Eunice good-bye and left for his meeting with David and the other church leaders.

As he strode through the descending dusk, he wondered what assuming leadership of the Pergamum church would mean for him and his family. He knew the news would not go unnoticed by the antagonistic leaders of the city. Rumors abounded of more persecution to come, and his stomach tightened at the thought of facing execution like his brother.

Will I be next?

Chapter Ten

Lights gleamed from the open doors and windows of David's house. As Paulus approached, a mixture of emotions roiled inside him. He couldn't help feeling incredibly excited with anticipation, but a sense of fear also hovered over his heart. Would the leaders accept him? Would they feel he was only trying to replace Antipas? Could he do the job? Of himself, he couldn't, but with God he could do anything. The feeling was very strong that God was leading him in this direction. He couldn't say no to God.

When he entered, several leaders were already gathered. Emin stepped away from the group and approached Paulus. He reached out his hand, lips stretched wide.

"Friend," he said. He gripped his shoulders and kissed him on both checks. "You are most welcome. I can't help but be thrilled with your willingness to come forward. I, for one, embrace you in your decision to offer yourself to the Pergamum church."

"You make me humble, Emin. Thank you, thank you for your support." Paulus squeezed his arm and turned toward David, who also greeted him and led him to the front of the gathered group.

"Let's all find a place to sit and we'll get started." David stood, arms at his sides, while the others moved around the comfortable room, finding soft couches to recline.

David moved closer to the group, making eye contact with each man. "It is with great joy that we meet tonight." He paused a moment to look down, clasping his hands together. "We have mourned our brother, Antipas, for many months now. He would not want to see us continue and hinder the work to which he so willingly gave his life." His gaze roved over the expectant faces.

Murmurs of "yes, yes" resounded throughout the room.

He drew Paulus closer to him, placing a hand on his shoulder. "My heart is full as we meet tonight to discuss our next leader. We've watched Paulus grow from a spiritual baby into a strong leader. We know him, we know his heart."

He glanced at Paulus, who stood with his head bowed, wondering if the others would accept him or if he was even capable of leading them. His heart raced until it was pounding in his ear.

Lord, I need You if I'm to lead these people.

David scanned the men once again. Tense silence filled the room. Paulus lifted his eyes, afraid there would be opposition to his leadership. Attentive faces watched him.

"Paulus came to see me last night," David said. "After many weeks of praying and struggling, God prompted him to offer himself as leader of the church of Pergamum."

More sounds of "yes, yes" filled the room, along with a whispering among some men at the back.

"Our purpose tonight is to decide if we will accept him as our leader," David said. "If we decide yes, we have plans to make. We must organize ourselves again to be effective in reaching our great but evil city."

The whispering at the back continued. David glanced toward the back but made no comment to address it. "We want to make the process as smooth as possible. We'll start with giving you time to question Paulus, to assure yourselves of his suitability to be our leader. So feel free to ask your questions."

David stood back and motioned for Paulus to stand before the men. Paulus faced the men. His stomach clenched with fear or excitement; he wasn't sure which.

Mattias rose first. "Antipas and I prayed for you for a long time before you surrendered your life to Christ." He faced him with his back straight and shoulders back. "Paulus, please tell us how and why you came to believe in Christ. I know your story, but not everyone here does. I think it will give a good picture of your heart." He gave Paulus a nod before he sat down.

Paulus's stomach tightened. He bowed his head and prayed for the right words to say. Then he studied each man's face before he briefly but emotionally told his story. He told how, under the influence of his father and brother, Marcus, he had been opposed to the believers. But Antipas had reached out to him, and he had ultimately surrendered to Christ.

"That was the best day of my life. I gained so much. Christ revealed Himself to me through the words of my brother. It became evident to me that Jesus is the Christ and that the only way to eternal life is through Him. I want nothing more from life than to be able to serve Him."

Silence lingered for a few moments. Each man seemed to be absorbing his answer. Many had heard his story before, of course, but hearing him deliver it in person gave a new perspective to his commitment to Christ.

Peter rose from his seat. “What are your plans concerning your father and your older brother, Marcus? You will become the enemy in their eyes.”

Paulus hesitated. Just thinking about his father and brother brought a whole gamut of emotions rushing through his body. “I want to be very open and honest with you regarding my family. We have never been a close family, other than in our attempt to wipe out the Christians. Now, however, the threat is greatly reduced. Antipas was the first of our family to come to know Christ. My mother was next. Then I, too, met Christ.”

Paulus shifted his feet nervously. He bowed his head and breathed deeply. “My father has not regained his sanity since Antipas was sacrificed. The doctors feel he may never do so.” He shook his head sadly. “He is no longer a threat to the believers. I pray each day that he will regain enough reason for me to present the gospel to him again. As for Marcus, he has not troubled me since the day Antipas died. We had an encounter that day, and he gave me the distinct impression that he was greatly moved by the courageous way our brother faced his death.”

Some of the men gave nods of encouragement. Mattias waved a hand at him. Paulus drew comfort in the fact that he was among friends. “I firmly believe it is only a matter of time before Marcus believes. It will be very hard for him because he is a proud man, deeply involved in temple worship. I’m not afraid of Marcus or what he can do.”

Voices burst forth in hearty support.

“Well spoken.”

“We’re with you.”

“Yes, brother.”

Their encouraging words washed over him, bringing comfort and strength. A number of other questions came next before the group again fell silent. Then from the back of the room came a shuffling sound. Antonius, a new believer and a powerful merchant, rose to his feet. He towered over the others, and well developed muscles rippled under his tunic; he was a very imposing presence.

“I must speak,” he said. “It would be foolishness for us to submit ourselves to Paulus’s leadership.”

A gasp sounded from the front of the room. Mattias jumped to his feet, but Peter pulled him down, leaning close to whisper in his ear.

Antonius glanced over the others, cleared his throat, and continued. “It is well known in the inner circles of Pergamum business that he is a marked man. It’s only a matter of time before the priests and civic leaders destroy him.”

He clamped his lips together and glared at the group again. He folded his powerful arms over his chest. "Excuse me for being so blunt, but all our lives are at stake as well as our businesses." He lifted his right arm and clenched his fist. "I say no to Paulus." He swept the crowd with his gaze and sat down.

David moved to stand beside Paulus, resting one hand on his shoulder. "Brother, I understand your concern, but don't you see that we serve a higher power than the priests and leaders? Yes, they have control of many things, but Christ has control of our hearts."

Many yeas filled the small room. Men looked around uncomfortably.

Antonius rose again, face flushed. "If you're bent on putting our lives on the line and our livelihood, I for one won't be a part of it. Is anyone with me?" He gazed at the group, arms folded across his barrel-shaped chest.

No one moved. No one said a word.

"Then you will see me no more," he said, "but be assured, I will do everything in my power to protect my business, even if it means compromising yours."

While everyone watched with open mouths, he grabbed his cloak and swept out of the room.

"What will we do?" asked one of the men, the one with deep lines lodged between his eyebrows. "He's very influential."

Murmurs followed.

David raised his hand, quieting the men. "Do? We won't do anything. He may be influential, but in God's scheme of things his influence is insignificant. What we will do is pray—for him, for us, for our families, but most of all, for God's will in our lives and in our church."

Heads nodded in agreement.

"If there are no more questions," David said, "it's time for us to make a decision, either for or against Paulus as our leader. I want us to be very open and honest about our choice. If you feel Paulus isn't the right person or isn't ready for the job, you need to say so. We only want the will of the Father in this decision."

He ran a hand over his beard. "I will ask each of you individually for your answer. Both Paulus and I are prepared if you have a negative reply. Again, we both want to be in the Lord's will."

David stood still before the group. When all the shuffling stopped, he asked each one in turn.

Paulus stood with bowed head, asking his heavenly Father for His will in the decision. His body had begun to relax when Antonius left. To him it seemed the opposition had left with him; there was now a sweet spirit of unity in the room. He glanced up to watch each man answer the question.

"Mattias?"

"Yes, absolutely!"

"Emin?"

"Yes from me as well. I think Paulus is exactly who the Lord has chosen to lead us."

"Hera?"

"There is no hesitation on my part. Yes, yes."

"Peter?"

"I have no reservations, so my vote is 'yes.'"

There were no negative replies. Paulus was very humbled by their support of him.

A beaming David turned and hugged Paulus. A wild cheer broke out from the men. The room rang with their laughing and backslapping as they congratulated Paulus and each other. They celebrated for a few minutes, then David brought them back to order.

He swung his arms out to include the whole group. "We now have work to do. There is a big city just waiting for someone to tell the people about Christ. We need plans."

The group was ready.

Paulus assumed control, suggesting they first commit their way to the Lord in a time of prayer. While he prayed silently, his thoughts turned to Antipas.

Oh my brother, your mantle has fallen on me. May I wear it with the grace and courage you showed. Lord, only You can give that to me. May I be faithful to You.

"I believe we need to resume preaching on the temple steps," Paulus said after the prayer. "If David agrees, he and I will begin at once, and then the rest of you can take turns with me."

David stepped up beside Paulus. "I count it an honor to stand with you."

One by one the others came and stood beside Paulus until a circle had formed around him.

"I think we're all in agreement," Mattias said. "It's frightening to think about standing on those steps again after watching Antipas die there, but I feel God is prompting us to be there." He gripped Paulus's shoulder on one side and David's on the other.

"I agree," Peter said, "but I admit I'm afraid of what Marcus will do, and now we have Antonius as a new burden."

"Brothers, we're going to pray that my brother will not only see and hear us, but that our message will touch his heart." Paulus looked at each one of these dear brothers, and his heart swelled with love for them.

The meeting ended with a great feeling of hope and excitement. The church of Pergamum would once again be visible and vocal within the city. What that would mean for the church and individual members would unfold in its time. They knew that darkness was gathering in the city.

Chapter Eleven

When Paulus stood on the temple steps, he surveyed the area surrounding him. This was the view Antipas had seen just before he was committed to the flames. This realization should have made him sad, but instead he felt a great longing to minister to the citizens going about their daily routines. He wanted to reach them for Christ.

He looked at David who stood beside him, then squared his shoulders and faced the people. In a loud, commanding voice he said, "People of Pergamum. People of Pergamum."

Many questioning faces turned to him. He recognized some of them.

"People of Pergamum." He turned his head from side to side, making eye contact with as many people as possible. "I'm here to tell you about the one and only God who came to earth in the form of a baby, who lived His life as a man, and who died to bring us into a relationship with Himself. His name is Jesus."

The crowd responded with whispering voices.

"Isn't this what Antipas was talking about?" someone asked.

Another voice: "How dare he stand there talking about this cult. Doesn't he know his life's in danger?"

But Paulus talked on. David stood beside him, eyes fixed on the gathering crowd. The people were restless and surly.

It wasn't safe to be here, Paulus knew, but he talked on. At length he drew his message to a close. "If any would like to talk to us about what you have heard, we'll be happy to meet with you."

No one came forward, but neither did they hurl insults.

"I think I'm pleased with how things went today," Paulus said to David after the crowd dispersed. "I was able to say the things I wanted to say, and people listened."

"I wasn't sure if we'd be successful, but I didn't look at it that way. I'm impressed by your optimism."

"It's only that I follow the leading of Christ. If I do what He asks me to do, then I am content."

They descended the temple stairs. When they reached the bottom, a man stepped out from the side of the building. "Excuse me, sirs, but I would like to talk to you," the man said. He quickly added, "But not here."

"Where would be a good place for us to meet you?" Paulus leaned closer to catch the man's soft voice.

"Do you know the stall in the market where they sell leather goods from Sardis?"

"Yes, I'm familiar with that one," Paulus said.

"Meet me in the lane behind it." With that the man disappeared down an alley between buildings.

David rubbed his beard. "Now that was a strange encounter."

"There must be a reason he doesn't want to be seen talking to us. Let's work our way over to the market and see if he's there."

David looked intently at Paulus. "It may be a trap."

Paulus gripped David's shoulder. "I promised myself that I wouldn't let my fear dictate how I go about the Lord's work. If someone wants to talk about Christ, then it's worth any risk."

"You're right, Paulus. Sometimes I still worry about the persecution, but I want to be bold. Let's go."

The two friends directed their feet toward the meeting place, while David's eyes roved from side to side. Paulus anticipated sharing Christ with this stranger.

Finding the stall was easy. It was located on the far side of the market with only a lane running behind it. Several carts were lined up, and several horses were tethered to posts. Refuse from the day's buying and selling was scattered along the lane. Paulus and David paused behind the leather stall and looked around for the man who had spoken to them.

Paulus saw him first. The man pulled his turban down low over his brow and clutched a homespun cloak around his thin body. His gaze darted from side to side as if to assure himself no one was watching him. He approached the two men with hesitant steps.

"Greetings, friend." Paulus lifted his hand in greeting. "You wished to speak with us?"

"Yes, yes." With downcast eyes, the stranger scuffed one sandal in the dirt.

"Did you have questions about our message today?' Paulus moved closer and had to lean closer to hear the muffled reply.

"Yes, yes, I do."

David also leaned in. "Aren't you Decimus, the owner of the stall yonder?"

"Yes, yes. I'm he." Decimus's hand shook as he tugged on his turban. He turned his head toward the stall, then looked Paulus in the eye.

"Do you want to know more about Jesus?" Paulus touched his arm.

Decimus looked up into Paulus's face and spat out the words. "I keep hearing His name. Everywhere I hear His name; even my wife talks about her friend who knows His name." He released his hold on the robe and gestured wildly with both hands. "The crowd chanted His name when that innocent man was sacrificed. And now you say His name again. What's with this Jesus? What power does He hold over people?" He raised his hands in the air.

"You ask really deep questions, friend." Paulus stepped back from him, making eye contact.

"I'm getting on in years. Life has been hard, sometimes hopeless. I need to know about this Jesus." He bowed his head and scuffed his sandal again.

"Would you be willing to come to a meeting tonight? It's at David's house." Paulus gestured to David.

"It's my wife. She won't take kindly to me being out after dark." He sighed heavily.

David entered the conversation and studied Decimus as he asked the probing question. "Is your wife Juliana, the woman who sells the woven goods and wooden household items in your stall?"

"Yes, master, that's her." Decimus shook his head slowly.

David said, "I've seen you sweeping the area in front of the stall, have I not?"

"Yes, master, that's me. It didn't used to be like that, but that's another tale, too deep to tell today." He gathered the robe around his frail frame again.

"Decimus, I fully believe God wants your heart," David said. "He wants you to take a stand with your wife and come to the meeting."

"Oh, sirs, I couldn't do that. She has me under her control." His hand shook again.

David stood straight as he made this declaration. "I think it's time you came out from under there. I challenge you to defy her and come. Mayhap she'll come too."

Decimus pulled himself up to his full height. He looked straight at David before he replied. "Can this Jesus give me the power to do that?"

"Decimus, you need to hear more about Jesus," Paulus said. "You need to break away from the bondage that is holding you down. Jesus has the power to change lives, both yours and Juliana's. Come tonight."

Decimus thrust his thin shoulders back and clamped his lips together. With a decisive nod he said, "I'll come. I need a change in my life. And I'll challenge my wife to come with me."

David gave him directions to his house, and with his shoulders back and a firm step, Decimus left them, moving past the stalls and out of the marketplace.

"Do you think he'll come?" David turned to Paulus, eyebrows drawn together in question.

"We're going to pray right now that God will empower him to stand up to his wife and come." Paulus bowed his head there in the laneway and petitioned His father to give Decimus the courage he needed.

Meanwhile, Decimus approached his home and decided to talk to his wife immediately before this newfound courage left him. He opened the door and entered swiftly. Juliana looked up from her work, eyebrows raised and head tipped to one side.

"Wife, I'm going to talk and you're going to listen." He gave his head a curt nod.

Juliana raised her eyebrows higher but didn't speak.

"I need to hear more about this Jesus you've heard about. Tonight I'm going to a man's house to listen to him tell about Jesus. I want you to come with me." He stared straight into her eyes.

Her eyes widened and her lips pulled together. She was silent for a moment, then her lips curled upward. "All right, I'll go with you." She set her work aside in a slow motion.

His knees turned weak, and shock ran through his body. He gathered his wits about him. "Then we'll leave as soon as the meal is over."

She nodded in agreement. As Decimus ate his meal in silence, he wondered what the evening would bring for them, wondered about their change in roles today. Would this Jesus make a difference in their lives?

Chapter Twelve

Evening was closing in as Decimus and Juliana left their humble dwelling. Few words had been exchanged between them since Decimus had made his declaration. He had no idea what was going through her mind as she hugged her cloak around her and bent into the wind, which had risen as the sun went down.

Though fear gripped Decimus's heart, he was exceedingly excited. Whatever the man who had been sacrificed had, he wanted it. The answer was all tied up in this Jesus. That name seemed to be the word on everyone's lips these days.

He followed David's directions easily, and soon they entered the street where he lived. As they neared his house, others approached it as well. Juliana neither slackened her pace nor looked sideways at her husband. She seemed wrapped up in her mind and intent on getting to David's.

David and Miriam stood at the door, welcoming their guests. When it was Decimus and Juliana's turn, David welcomed them warmly, inviting them to join the group already in the large area where the meeting would take place. They slipped into seats near the back of the room.

Juliana scanned the group but, seeing no one she recognized, sat quietly and waited for David to begin. When he began to speak, Juliana couldn't take her eyes off him. Decimus seemed transfixed as well.

At the close David asked if anyone would like to talk to him about what he or she had heard that evening; he and several other leaders would be available.

A sob escaped Juliana's lips, her mind a tangle of emotions—emotions she had carefully kept hidden for years. All the lost babies, all the hateful words spoken to her husband, all the blame for their lost relationship piled on him, all the bitterness she had built up in her life. Miriam slid in beside her and put her arms around her, letting her continue her wild weeping.

The others left quietly until only David, Miriam, Decimus, and Juliana were left. Gradually the weeping subsided, and through tear-filled eyes she looked at the three of them.

"I've lived a terrible and bitter life," she said. "I don't deserve this Jesus, but I want Him so badly."

She turned and looked into Decimus's eyes with her tear-filled ones. "I've taken happiness from you. I've treated you shamefully." She gulped and swallowed the lump in her throat. "Can you ever forgive me?"

By now, all four of them had tears on their faces. David and Miriam sat quietly, just letting the two talk to each other.

"Oh, Juliana, nothing would give me greater pleasure than to forgive you," Decimus said. "Consider it done." He smiled at her through his tears, then took her hand. She leaned toward him and hugged him tightly.

Decimus looked over her shoulder and spoke to David. "I think we're both ready to accept Jesus as our Savior. Tell us what to do."

David and Miriam had the great joy of leading them both to the Lord. When the last prayer trembled on their lips, the faces of Juliana and Decimus radiated a joy beautiful to behold.

"I can't believe how I feel." Juliana shivered and folded her hands in her lap. "I've been unhappy for so long that I hardly remember how to have joy, but now it's just overflowing in my heart."

Decimus just sat there and beamed.

They talked far into the night. Juliana had so many questions that she could hardly express herself. Decimus continued listening quietly, still shining with joy. At last they knew they had to leave; morning would still come at the same time, and the market awaited.

David and Miriam hugged them both warmly and promised many more sessions with them. The two, so long disconnected, went out into the night with hopes of a bright future, where their love would be rekindled and peace and joy would once more return to their household.

Chapter Thirteen

"Eunice, come walk with me in the garden."

Eunice rose to greet Paulus. "Yes, I'll gladly come. Marina is playing with the children, so I have some free time."

They left the house together and strolled down the path leading to the stream at the back. It was quickly becoming their favorite place to be. Paulus placed his arm around her waist as they walked in unison.

It feels so right to be here with Paulus like this, Eunice mused.

"We need to make plans to announce our coming marriage." Paulus drew her closer in his embrace.

"I've been thinking the same thing. It's been nice to hold the secret in our hearts, but people need to know." Eunice laid her head on his shoulder.

"I think we should visit David tonight and talk to him and Miriam. I feel like they are our best friends. Then we can decide how to announce the news." He turned to face her, looking deeply into her eyes.

"That's a great idea. Miriam has become a true friend to me. They are both dear people." She smiled up at him.

"Can you arrange for Marina to put the children to bed after the evening meal so we can leave right away?"

"That'll be easy. The children love her and will be happy to have her put them to bed."

"I want them to be a big part of our lives," Paulus said. "Let's sit here on the bench for a while. I find it so peaceful watching the stream."

"It's my favorite place to sit in the garden." She snuggled close to him on the bench.

"I've been thinking about those two large rooms next to my room. What would you think if I have them prepared for Simon and Helena?" His arm rested along the back of the bench, caressing her shoulder as they talked.

"Oh Paulus, that would be wonderful. They do still need me in the night, and Marina could be close to them, too." She breathed in the fragrant air and felt her body relax as they discussed plans.

"I love when we agree on so many things." He twisted his fingers through her hair and laughed.

They returned to the house in time for the meal. Paulina encouraged them to go quickly to David and Miriam's since there was so little time before the wedding. As they walked through the streets in the early evening, inner peace and a great excitement filled Eunice. God seemed to be in their plans.

David was surprised to see them at his door. Paulus hadn't said anything about coming tonight when he stopped by earlier in the day.

"Come in, Eunice and Paulus. You're always welcome." He led them into the garden at the back of the house. "We love sitting in the garden this time of evening. There's a refreshing cool breeze tonight." He pulled a chair out for Eunice and placed it where she would be able to see the rose bushes.

"Would we be able to talk to both you and Miriam?" said Paulus.

David noticed the red creeping up Paulus's face and smiled to himself. "Of course, I'll get her." He left them, guessing in his mind the reason for their visit.

Miriam came back with David and greeted them with a kiss. "It's always such a pleasure to visit with both of you." Her white gown reflected the colors of the setting sun.

After a few minutes of talk, Paulus wrapped his hand around one of Eunice's. "We have news we'd like to share with you."

His face glowed, but David didn't think it was coming from the sunset. "Please tell us." He sat back and watched both of their faces, keeping in the smile that threatened to spill onto his face.

Paulus cleared his throat and glanced first at David and then at Miriam. "Eunice has agreed to become my wife."

"I'm so happy for you." Miriam jumped up and rushed to Eunice, wrapping her in a tight embrace. "I can't think of news I'd rather hear. God is certainly in this. You both deserve to be happy after all the heartache you've suffered. We all know there'll be difficult days ahead, but you'll have each other."

David, too, rose and clapped his hand on Paulus's back. "Good news. You are certainly a special couple, and I believe God will use you together to further

His will. Congratulations to both of you." He leaned over Eunice and planted a kiss on each cheek.

"We'll need to let the church families know. How should we do this?" Paulus looked to David.

"Why don't I make an announcement on Sunday morning after the morning teaching session," David said.

"That's a great idea," Miriam agreed.

"I'd like to visit Emin and tell him the news myself, so I'll go there before Sunday," Paulus said, then turned to Eunice. "And I think you'd like to tell Sophia, Eunice."

"Yes, of course. I'll walk out to visit her tomorrow. I know she'll be thrilled." A dimple showed in Eunice's cheek, which was tinged with pink.

With hugs all around, Paulus and Eunice left David's house to return home.

Sunday was overcast, with fog strung out along the fields, obscuring the grass, as well as low-lying clouds that threatened rain later in the day. Eunice wrapped the children warmly in their little cloaks as Paulus brought the chariot to the front. Paulina helped Eunice carry the children out to meet him.

Although the weather was depressing, Eunice couldn't suppress the great excitement welling inside. Today was the day the church would hear of her approaching wedding, and she hugged the delicious thought to herself.

"I don't think David will need to make an announcement," Paulina said as she settled in her seat in the chariot. "Everyone will know if they take just one look at you two." She, too, smiled with joy.

Eunice blushed and smiled back at her mother-in-law.

"I only wish Marcus would join us," Paulina said. "I think it's too late for Julian, but Marcus is young and bright. I don't know why his eyes are so blinded." She lowered her head, lips pressed tightly together.

"Just have patience, Mother, and faith in our great Father," Paulus said. "I believe Marcus will come to the Way. We've all been praying for him. I hope to see him soon. Eunice and I have discussed the possibility of approaching him." Paulus glanced at his mother, then encouraged the chariot horses to begin.

"Is it safe to do that?" Paulina looked up at him, forehead wrinkled, fear in her voice.

"I remember when Antipas and I felt compelled to pray for Paulus," Eunice said. "There was fear in many of the believers' hearts, but we felt strongly that God was prompting us, and look how that turned out." Eunice beamed at Paulus and squeezed her mother-in-law's hand.

"It has turned out rather well, hasn't it?" Paulus grinned back at her. He turned serious. "If God is in it, Mother, we don't need to be afraid." He kept his eyes on the horses as they left their area of the city.

"Yes, I know that's true." Paulina's shoulders slumped and she sighed. "I guess I'm just so happy to have you two after all the barren years, that I don't want anything to take it away. But you're right; Marcus *does* need Christ, and who better to approach him than his own family? I promise not to worry anymore. Just pray." She held tightly to Eunice's hand.

"Thanks, Mother, that's what we need." He flashed her a special smile.

As they finished the conversation, David's house swung into view. Many people were hurrying along the street toward his house. Thankfully his house was large and could accommodate many people. The family moved along with the others. David and Miriam greeted them.

Miriam shot a gleeful glance at Eunice before reaching out and taking Helena in her arms. "I can't believe how much she's grown. She was so tiny, and now she's healthy and beautiful. Henna has volunteered to look after the children today, so let's take them to her."

Eunice followed Miriam into the quiet courtyard, where three other children were already playing. Simon ran ahead and greeted his friends. Helena was sleeping and would probably nap for most of the morning. The women sauntered back to the meeting area, chatting as they went. Friends greeted them as they moved through the rooms.

An older lady stopped to speak to her, gripping her hand in a warm clasp. "Eunice, you are looking especially lovely today."

"Thank you. You are very kind." Eunice smiled shyly.

"I haven't seen you looking this happy for a long time." The woman cocked her head to one side as though trying to find out the reason.

"I do feel happy today. Thank you." Eunice's face began to burn, so she kept walking to avoid spoiling the coming announcement.

Once everyone had gathered in the largest room, which the household had made ready by filling the room with benches, David opened with a moving prayer, asking that each person present would feel the power of the Holy Spirit on this day. Then Paulus rose to address the group.

"Friends, today Jesus wants to come near you. He wants to guide you on this earthly journey. He wants to walk each step of the way with you. He hasn't promised to take away all earthly pain, but He promised to walk through it with you, to be your comfort, your guide."

Paulus continued teaching the people about the great love Jesus had for them. Eunice watched him as he spoke, impressed with his speaking. He seemed filled with enthusiasm and fervor. She marveled at the change Christ had wrought in this man. He looked especially good today. When he was immersed in teaching about Christ, an inner glow seemed to flow from him. He was indeed a mighty power for Christ here in dark Pergamum. How she loved this man. She knew Antipas would be pleased that she had found the love of a man so near and dear to his heart.

When Paulus finished speaking, David rose and stood beside him.

"Friends, I have two things I want to say to you today," David said. "First, if you don't know the Christ Paulus has been talking about, we would love to tell you more about Him and how you can enter into a personal relationship with him. Just talk to us when we dismiss."

He cleared his throat, covering his mouth with one hand. "The other thing I have to say is a personal announcement, one that will bring great joy to your hearts as it has to mine." He paused to put his hand on Paulus's shoulder. "Our dear brother, Paulus, and our sweet sister, Eunice, want you to know that they have decided to marry."

David could go no further with his announcement because a great cheer rose from the group. The men were on their feet clapping, and many of the women wiped tears of joy from their faces. David waited until the room quieted, then continued with the details.

"Our dear friends in the Lord have decided to be married at Paulus's home, in their beautiful garden, a fortnight from now. And the really good news is that all of you are invited."

Another cheer greeted this announcement.

"Come after the midday meal, enjoy the beauty of the garden, and support this couple as they seek to follow God's leading in their lives. This will be our first Christian wedding!"

Eunice began to think her face would stay permanently in a smile as well-wishers swamped them with their blessings and many promises to help with the setup and the food to be served. She gratefully accepted their offers, knowing they were given in love and with a desire to be part of this very special time.

In another part of the city, Marcus sat brooding in his chair, revenge in his heart. Evening shadows deepened but still he sat.

I'm the only one left.

He cupped his chin in his hands and stared unseeing from his window.

My father is a lunatic, Paulus has joined the other side, Antipas is dead, and my mother has never been useful.

He rose from his chair and circled the room, slamming a fist into his hand.

What happened to our plan? Our plan to destroy this cult, this Jesus-man they all seem to worship?

He paused in his pacing and thrust his shoulders back.

I'll do it myself. I don't need them. A plague on them. He shouted to the walls, shaking a fist in the air.

He vigorously rubbed his hands together.

When I get finished with them, they'll wish they'd never been born. I won't rest until every last one is dead . . . dead . . . And I'll start with Paulus, weak Paulus, deceived brother.

He laughed uproariously and threw himself on his bed.

Chapter Fourteen

Who would ever have believed that a fortnight could go so quickly or so slowly? Eunice couldn't decide which it was. She had so many little details to attend to that she didn't seem to have enough time to do them all. On the other hand, she thought her wedding day would never arrive.

Paulina worked with her on the details. "Eunice, I'm so happy for both you and Paulus, but I'm happy for me, too." She was cutting ribbons to tie around flowers for the wedding.

"I'm excited but also a little apprehensive. This is a big step for me and the children." She swept her hair back from her face, which had fallen as she leaned over the table where they were working. "I want to make Paulus happy." Her sleeve brushed the table, knocking the ribbons onto the floor. She bent down and gathered them in her arms.

"By the look on his face, I don't think that'll be a problem." Paulina's lips curved up. "My son is very much in love, I'd say."

One afternoon, as she sat in the garden alone, she felt compelled to talk to her heavenly Father. "Lord, I only want to do what's right, so please stop me if I'm taking a wrong step."

She sat in silence for a few minutes, just letting her thoughts dwell on her Lord. As she sat, waiting, a quiet voice spoke in her heart.

Fear not, my child, I am in this. I go before you, making the path smooth.

"Lord, was that You?" She raised her eyes to the heavens, watching the puffy clouds drift across the sun.

My child, I am always with you, always seeking your best. Never fear.

"Then, Lord, I know this is the right thing to do. Thank You, thank You. I love Paulus so much, but I would give him up if I thought it was not in Your will." She folded her hands in her lap as she quietly waited.

Fear not, my child.

Eunice sat for several minutes, just enjoying the peace that had come to her heart. She basked in the presence of the Lord. Footsteps pounded on the path. She raised her head.

Paulus approached the bench where she sat. "My love, you look serious." He leaned over her, looking closely at her face.

"Sit with me, Paulus. I want to tell you about my talk with the Lord." She patted the seat beside her.

He consented and listened closely as she spoke. As she finished, a smile crossed her face, and she gazed tenderly into his attentive eyes.

"Now I know beyond a shadow of a doubt that we're taking the right step. Oh, Paulus, I'm so happy."

They stayed in the garden while the sun beamed down on them, showering them with warmth in the late afternoon. When they rose to leave, one of the servants hurried down the path to meet them.

"Master, you have a visitor," he said, gasping out the words as if in a hurry.

"Who is it, Saul?" Paulus drew his brows together in a frown.

"I don't know, master, but he wears the insignia of the temple guards." Saul visibly trembled.

Paulus glanced at Eunice with a frown, excused himself, and strode into the house. As he approached the room where the visitor waited, his stomach clenched. He entered the room and greeted an officer unknown to him. The officer was standing at attention, shoulders back and arms at his sides. With his chin jutting out, he faced Paulus.

"Greetings, Paulus." The officer bowed low to him. "I have a message for you. You are to appear in the temple tonight after sundown. It is in your best interests to arrive. And now I bid you good day." He turned on his heel to leave the room.

"Wait," Paulus called and followed him out.

"I wait for no man." The officer glanced back over his shoulder once with a stern look, and then he was gone.

Paulus watched the man climb into his waiting chariot and disappear down the road.

"What could this mean?" His thoughts ran wild through his head. "Should I go? Am I in any danger?" He paced the length of the room, hands behind his back, face muscles tight.

By this time Eunice had entered the house. He led her into a small, private room where they could talk without interruption and without being heard. As he told her his story, fear crossed her face.

"Paulus, I don't like the sound of this. Who wants to see you and why?" She wrung her hands. "Do you have to go?"

"I may be in more danger if I don't. I feel I should go." He rubbed his chin and nodded.

"I feel you should, too. I'll pray the whole time you're gone; you can be sure of that." She held his hands in hers and searched his eyes.

It seemed as though darkness delayed its arrival in the city tonight. Sunlight still sparkled as they finished their evening meal. A beautiful but unappreciated sunset spread its vibrant colors over the western sky. On any other night, Eunice would have exclaimed with delight, but not tonight. She paced back and forth in the still-warm evening air of the garden.

Right after the meal Paulus had gone to his rooms to spend time alone in prayer. She knew he had peace as she did, but the unexpectedness and uncertainty of what lay head disturbed her. She, too, prayed.

At long last the hues became muted, and lamps in the house and garden were lit. It was time for Paulus to leave. Eunice decided to stay in the open air longer. She couldn't bear to see him leave the house.

Paulus donned his cloak and entered the waiting chariot. His driver had been given directions earlier, so no words were spoken between them. When they reached their destination, Paulus slipped out and stood facing the temple.

It looked sinister tonight, not at all like it did in the daytime hours when he so boldly spoke the truth of Christ on its steps.

He remembered David words.

Greater is He that is in you than He that is in the world.

With those words of confidence playing in his mind, he placed his foot on the first step.

Chapter Fifteen

An eerie silence filled the temple. The massive statue of Zeus filled the open space in the center; tonight it stood like a dark, foreboding shadow. Paulus stopped just inside the main entrance to let his eyes adjust to the darkness.

He looked around stealthily and began to pick out shapes. His visitor hadn't told him where in the temple to go or who had ordered him to come.

He walked slowly toward the statue, his fear welling up and threatening to overwhelm him. He circled the statue, but no one appeared on the other side.

Is this a trap? he wondered.

Suddenly, a light sprang up in front of him, the flame momentarily blinding him.

"You came," a voice whispered from behind the light. "I wasn't sure you would."

"Who are you?" Paulus said, also in a whisper.

"Don't you recognize your own brother, or have you disowned me by now?" The voice seemed to hang motionlessly in the stale air.

The voice didn't seem familiar. "Marcus?"

"Who else?"

Paulus relaxed. He knew the sarcasm in that voice too well.

The lamp was placed on a table, and Marcus materialized out of the shadows. He beckoned to Paulus with his hand. "Do come nearer, brother. I wish to speak with you privately."

Paulus approached the table. Two chairs had been placed beside it.

"Sit, Paulus."

Paulus consented. Marcus took the other chair.

"I have an offer for you," Marcus said.

No preamble, no warning. *Typical Marcus style*, Paulus thought.

He leaned his head closer to his brother, trying to look into Marcus's eyes. "An offer?"

"Yes. I know you have been persuaded by our dead brother and all his cohorts into believing a lie. You are a condemned man unless you accept my offer." He leaned back in his seat, jaw tightly clenched.

Paulus didn't respond. Where was Marcus going with this?

"Would you like to hear my offer?" Marcus appeared to be studying his fingernails in the faint light, keeping his gaze away from Paulus.

"Of course. It would be rude of me not to listen, brother." Paulus kept his eyes riveted on Marcus.

"You're getting just like Antipas. You always have an answer, don't you?" He looked up this time, and the angry twist in his brother's face shocked Paulus.

"Marcus, I don't wish to upset you or argue with you. You sent me a command to come, and I've come. Please tell me what you want of me." He lifted his hand to his brother.

"I want the old Paulus back. Haven't you had enough of this nonsense yet?" His chin jutted out as he flexed his shoulders.

"What do you mean by 'nonsense'?" Paulus tried to read his eyes.

Marcus responded sharply, jerking forward on his seat. "You know what Antipas believed wasn't true. He was a disillusioned fool. Even you must recognize that."

"Marcus, believe me, every word Antipas believed was and is true. It has been proven to me over and over again that Christ *is* the Son of God. I know in my heart that He has saved me. His power far exceeds any earthly power." He nodded. "I pray daily that you will come to see the truth as well."

Marcus didn't move. Paulus wondered what he was thinking. He seemed to gather himself together.

A plaintive note crept into his voice. "It's all nonsense," Marcus said. "I thought you would be able to see through it. That's why you haven't been bothered by the guards. That's been on my order." He finally looked directly at Paulus.

"Thank you for that, Marcus." Paulus reached out his hand to touch his brother's arm.

Marcus yanked it away from him. "Don't thank me. I thought you would have come to your senses by now. There is work to be done, and I need you by my side, not standing against me." He sat up straight in his chair, chin in the air.

"What work is that?"

"You know as well as I do that the emperor has insisted that we rid our city of this blight." He was working himself into another rage. Saliva ran from the corner of his mouth. He quickly swept it away.

"Blight?"

"Your cultish ideas." Marcus sneered. "You've caused me a lot of trouble, Paulus, and I won't stand for it any longer. The priests are agitated, and there's a new governor coming who is the emperor's own man. Things are heating up. I should have been chief guard by now, but your desertion has hampered my career."

Marcus was on his feet now, shouting at Paulus. He was shaking, and the spit flew from his mouth.

Paulus wondered if Marcus was going to have a seizure. He jumped to his feet and tried to push him back onto his seat. "Get yourself under control, Marcus. You'll harm yourself."

The words seemed to make an impression on him and he sat. He was silent for a few moments. Then he began to speak in a more normal voice.

"Back to my offer to you, Paulus," he managed to say. He gestured with his hands and shook a finger at Paulus. "Leave this cult, denounce this leader you think is a god, join me in cleansing our city, and I will make sure no one harms you. I also have the power to see that you rise in power. When you join me, I'll be made chief guard. That will open doors for both of us to become important men in this city." He emphasized his point with a determined nod of his chin.

"And if I don't agree?" Paulus raised his eyebrows in question.

Marcus stood up. He rushed at Paulus and grabbed him by the throat, hauling him to his feet.

He's going to kill me. Lord, help me to be as courageous as Antipas. I can't breathe.

"Then I'll no longer be responsible for what happens to you." Marcus spat out each word. "What's your answer, Paulus?"

He shook him vigorously until Paulus pushed away from him. The brothers faced each other.

Breathing heavily, Paulus looked into his eyes. "There's only one answer I can give, brother," Paulus said. "I will never deny Christ, and I will pray for you daily that you will come to see the truth."

With both hands Marcus grabbed him around the throat again and squeezed while he shouted at him. Paulus thought his life was over.

"Then go!" Marcus shouted. "I can only hope you will soon join Antipas. You two deserve each other!"

He threw him to the floor, and Paulus landed painfully on his side. He scrambled to his feet just as Marcus took one last disdainful look at him and stormed out of the temple.

Paulus lay there for a moment, just trying to catch his breath. He started to rise to his feet when someone close by whispered his name. He didn't recognize the voice.

"Paulus, I've come to help you. Lean on me. I'll take you back to your home." Gentle hands gripped his arms.

"Who are you?" Paulus squinted to see in the darkness.

"I'm one of the priests' helpers. I couldn't help but overhear your confrontation with your brother. I didn't dare interfere since he would have me skinned alive at the blink of an eye. I waited until I knew he was gone." The gentle hands helped him to his feet.

Paulus was grateful for the small shoulder to lean on. "You're a boy, aren't you?"

"Yes, but I'm strong for my age. I can help you."

"Why were you here in the temple in the darkness?"

"It's my job to check the main room after everyone has gone. I had just come in when I heard voices. I didn't light my lamp. I hid behind the statues in the corner."

"I don't want to put you in any danger. Just help me to the steps, and I can go on alone from there."

"I've heard you talk on the steps many times. I . . . I like what I've heard," he said in a hesitating voice. "In fact, I'd like to hear more."

This admission thrilled Paulus. He turned over different ideas as to how he could help this young boy. The priests would certainly kill the boy if they knew he was inquiring into Paulus's faith.

"Would you be willing to come to my house with me?" Paulus asked. "It would mean you couldn't come back here, but I will do all I can to protect you."

The boy's voice broke. "You would do that for me?" He sighed. "My life is miserable. When I hear your stories about Jesus, I feel like crying. I would be happy, happy, happy to come to your house."

Paulus leaned on his shoulder, and the two began their walk to the entrance. When they stepped onto the top stair, no one was in sight. The street was deserted. Marcus was gone.

Torches circling the altar where Antipas had been sacrificed illumined the steps. The scene looked peaceful tonight, almost serene. The flickering torches cast dancing shadows on them as they slowly descended.

Once they reached the main street, Paulus turned to the left, and they proceeded through the city by an alternate route. He wanted to keep the boy from exposure to the temple guards if any should be patrolling the main thoroughfare.

As they neared the house, the boy gasped.

"This is where you live?" His mouth fell open.

"Yes, this is the house. You'll be very welcome here." He stopped before the entrance and faced the boy. "I don't even know your name." He gripped the small shoulder.

"It's Leonius, master." The boy lowered his eyes. Dark, curly hair covered his head and spilled over his forehead, making him look very young and delicate. Thin hands and feet dangled from his robe, affirming his youth.

"Do you have family who will be looking for you?"

"Oh no. My mother took sick last year and brought me to the temple. The priests didn't want me, but she persuaded them that I could be a servant to them. They told me she died." His brows nearly touched each other, and his lips stretched in a thin line.

"Then please consider my family your family now. Let's go in and meet everyone." Paulus led him with gentle pressure on his shoulder.

Everyone welcomed Leonius. Paulus had a room made ready for him, and for the first time in his life, he slept in a comfortable bed in a room he had all to himself.

Eunice was filled with questions—Paulus could see it in her eyes. But she made no comment about his meeting until Leonius was looked after and they were once again alone.

"Let's walk in the garden," Paulus said. "The evening air is refreshing, and the moon is full tonight." Paulus slipped an arm around her, smiling.

"Let me get a shawl. It sounds like a wonderful idea. If we don't soon talk, I think I'll burst." She soon returned, wrapped in a warm shawl, and they left the house arm in arm.

When they reached their favorite bench, they sat in silence for a time. Then Paulus told her everything that had happened since he left the house.

"What do you think Marcus will do now?" She frowned, turning toward him on the bench.

"Really, I'm not afraid of Marcus. Underneath it all, I think he's seeking something deeper in his life. I think part of this meeting was to see how strong I would be in my faith. My guess is he would have been very disappointed if I had agreed to his offer." Paulus shook his head.

"I hadn't thought about it like that," Eunice said with wonder in her voice.

"Well, he could easily have killed me tonight. He had his hands on my throat, and it wouldn't have taken much to finish the job. I don't think he wanted to do that. I'm convinced he was testing me. I can only hope that I've passed the test." He shifted on the bench, drawing her closer to him.

"Paulus, we really need to pray for him with increased fervor." She laid her head on his shoulder.

"You're absolutely right. We'll pray with Mother. I won't tell her all the details of what happened tonight, only that I met with Marcus. She would be needlessly upset if she knew all the things he said and did. Tomorrow I'll talk to the other church leaders, and we'll have a special time of prayer just for him. They also need to know that the persecution could start up again."

They fell silent for a time, and Paulus thought about Marcus and his need for the Lord.

He changed the subject to get her mind on more pleasant thoughts. "How are the plans coming for our wedding? Did you meet with some of the ladies today?"

"Yes, we met this afternoon." Eunice grinned at him. "Our quiet wedding is about to become a big event. I know we just wanted something small and simple, but I've come to see that it's not just about us at all. I think the believers want this to be very special. I think they need this in the midst of the uncertainty here in Pergamum."

"I think you're right. I guess we can handle that. What do you think?" He leaned back lazily in his seat.

"Oh yes, the women were so excited as they discussed plans. It'll be very special."

"I can't wait. We're not going to let thoughts of what Marcus might do spoil our day."

Chapter Sixteen

Eunice stepped into the garden to watch the morning break on her wedding day. Rose streaks marked the horizon, crossing the rising sun, while long shadows lingered beneath trees and bushes lining the paths that had been swept clean in preparation for today. She breathed the cool air, rejoicing in the beauty around her and letting her mind wander to the ceremony to take place here in her favorite place.

"Eunice." A voice behind her startled her. Turning, she saw Paulina coming toward her.

"Good morning, Eunice. What a pretty day for your wedding." Paulina hugged her. "I can hardly wait for the ceremony. I love the time you chose—just as the sun reaches its highest elevation."

"Paulus and I both want this to be honoring to God and wanted God's beautiful creation to be shining down on our union." She linked her arm with Paulina's, and they strolled along the paths, entertained by birdsong.

"This wedding will be so different than when Antipas and I were married. For one thing, it was a Jewish celebration, and my whole village celebrated with us. Now it will be a Christian wedding with the whole church with us."

Paulina squeezed her arm and drew her closer. "I'm so happy I can be at this one. It almost broke my heart to know Antipas was being married and I couldn't be there. It was a hard time for me because I couldn't even let on I knew about it. Julian was such a hard man." Her voice drifted off, apparently lost in memories.

"David and Paulus have spent hours planning the ceremony. This is the first Christian wedding in Pergamum. It'll set a tone for future weddings." Eunice let her eyes wander over the garden, a riot of color, just perfect for today.

"Mama." A little voice called them back from their walk. "We're hungry."

"I guess we'd better get back and feed the little ones." Eunice let a smile curve her lips, and she moved toward the house.

My precious children.

"It's time, Eunice." Miriam entered the bedroom and raised her eyebrows. Her lips formed a perfect circle. "You look stunning."

"Thank you, Miriam. I feel like a young girl again. Are the children ready?" Eunice blushed and touched her cheek.

"Oh yes, and Simon is so excited he can't sit still. I hope he's still clean by the time the ceremony starts." She laughed and adjusted the shoulder of Eunice's robe.

Eunice laughed. Today felt so right.

"I'm ready. Shall I start out now?" Her hands trembled with excitement.

"Yes, everyone is in their places, just waiting." Miriam stepped aside and beckoned Eunice to lead the way.

As Eunice stepped out into the garden, she couldn't believe the number of people there. They lined all the paths leading to the back of the garden, where the ceremony would take place, at her favorite spot. As she appeared, a great cheer arose. A gasp caught in her throat and she forced back tears. Her love for these people welled up in her heart.

She drifted down the path, and the children handed her flowers. Miriam came behind her with Simon and Helena. The sun, warm on her face, touched the faces of the others lining her way. At last she could see Paulus. He stepped out onto the path to meet her. He smiled his gentle smile and took her hand. They walked the rest of the way together.

Eunice had chosen to wear the ornamental dress she wore at her wedding to Antipas. Its brilliant whiteness and elaborate embroidery shimmered in the sunshine. She was unveiled today.

Paulus wore a white robe. Embroidered gold threads etched the outlines of the garment and the tasseled belt. They made a dazzling sight for those watching their every move.

David and Emin waited for them by the stream. Paulus and Eunice faced them. As planned, David lifted his hands to the sky and asked God's blessing on this day and on this marriage.

"Today we gather to celebrate the marriage of Paulus and Eunice," he said, "two people strong of faith in God, followers of His Son, Jesus Christ, and leaders in the church of Pergamum. It is my great honor to join these two together.

"Paulus, will you accept Eunice as your wife . . . ?"

Paulus turned to face Eunice and took her hands in his. A thrill ran through her as she looked into the eyes of the man she loved; the man she was entrusting with her heart and life.

With a tender, loving look he promised to love her for always. "Yes, I accept Eunice as my wife."

She, in turn, pledged her love to him.

David stepped closer to them and covered their joined hands with his. "In the presence of these Christ-followers, and with God's blessing on your lives, I declare you, Paulus and Eunice, husband and wife."

David placed a hand on each of their shoulders and turned them to face the group. Cheers and clapping greeted the couple. Eunice thought her heart would burst with love, not only for Paulus, but for each person present. Her eyes were dry as friends gathered around them, exchanging embraces and words of love and encouragement.

When Emin reached them, he touched each of them on the arm. "God has been glorified today. You are indeed a unique couple. May God shine His blessings on you."

Eunice closed her eyes as he spoke. A cool breeze shivered across her arms, and she thought about Marcus and the persecution they might have to face. *But we'll face it together, and with God's help, we'll overcome.*

"Eunice, what are you thinking? You look like you are far away from me." Paulus circled her shoulders with his arm and gazed at her.

"I'm just a little overwhelmed, but oh so happy." She touched his face with her fingers.

"Come, little one. The ladies have been busy, and I'm getting hungry."

Her laughter bubbled up as she looked at his face. "Me, too. I don't think I ate much at breakfast. I was too excited."

"Then let's head over to where the tables are set up. I think they have a special one for us."

Hand in hand they moved through the well-wishers until they were seated at a small garden table, decorated with flowers cut fresh from their garden.

Miriam set plates of food before them, kissing Eunice on the forehead. "I'm so happy for you," she whispered in her ear.

Eunice watched the children at play, Simon and Helena with them. How wonderful to see her children enjoying this special day. Everywhere she looked, people were eating, strolling the paths, or sitting in the sun and talking together.

"Paulus, what an incredible day."

He lifted her hand to his lips. "And you are the most incredible part of it."

"Oh Paulus, I don't deserve you."

"Hmm. Let's hope you never change your mind," he said in a teasing voice.

"Look at your mother, Paulus. She's everywhere—talking to people, serving food, playing with the children . . . I don't think she's ever been happier."

"I was thinking the same thing," Paulus said. "I love seeing her like this. She's missed so many of life's pleasures."

As the celebration reached its height, Emin approached David and spoke quietly. "One of the servants came to me and reported that a temple guard on horseback has passed the house a number of times."

David looked at him in alarm. "Did anyone question him?"

"No. Everyone is afraid of the guards, but they did leave one young servant to watch the front of the house and bring them reports each time the guard passed."

"Do you suppose it could be Marcus?" The lines in David's forehead stood out.

"That was my thought. Should we check for ourselves?" He turned and looked toward the entrance to the garden.

"Agreed." David was already moving, his stomach muscles tightening. *Who could it be except Marcus?*

The two men slipped into the house and stationed themselves close to the front door. They could see the street well from their position. It wasn't long before the clomp, clomp of shod hooves approached. The horse and rider slowed as they neared the house.

"Let's go." Emin gave David a little push.

They stepped out from the doorway so the rider could see them. He glanced their way with a frown, pulled on the reins, and, with a command to his horse, galloped off down the street.

"I've only seen Marcus a few times, but I'm sure that was him." David rubbed his head as he followed the rider's progress down the road away from the house.

Emin, too, stared in the distance, his eyes shaded against the sun. "That's my assumption as well. What do we do now? Was he here for harm or out of curiosity?"

"I don't want to disturb Paulus on his wedding day, but we need to take this seriously. Why don't we ask two of our brothers to take turns watching the house tonight? Paulus doesn't need to know about this until after today." David turned to Emin and gripped his arm.

Emin nodded and pursed his lips. "I think that's the best plan. Marcus is a brutal guard who has threatened all believers. He bears watching."

They set the plans in place and returned to the garden. The young servant boy would watch for now.

As evening approached, families gathered their things together. Paulus and Eunice bid each one a good night and thanked them for sharing their day. When they were finally alone, Paulus took her hand, and they entered the house.

"Come with me to say good night to the children," Eunice said.

"Of course. They must be tired. It was a big day for them, too."

They heard their giggles before they opened the door to their room. Marina was just finishing their bedtime routine.

"They're all ready for bed and hoping you'd come for good night hugs and kisses," Marina said.

As Paulus leaned over the bed, Simon jumped into his arms. Eunice picked up a sleepy Helena and hugged her closely. "Good night, my darling girl." Eunice loved the smell of her daughter after her bath—lavender, a lovely fragrance.

"Simon, you know Marina will be in my room if you need her in the night."

He nodded and reached out his arms for her hug.

Paulus and Eunice left the children and met Paulina in the hall.

"What a wonderful day," she said, enclosing them both in an embrace. "I'm tired, but so happy." She left them for her room.

At last, Paulus led Eunice to the rooms that now belonged to both of them.

The moon rose over the garden, bathing the scene with its gentle light. Birds had long since said their farewells to the day, and flowers had closed up for the night. Inside, the night was quiet. Outside, the self-appointed guards kept watch, wondering if Marcus would return.

Chapter Seventeen

Marcus paced the hall nervously. With his hands clasped behind his back, he took long strides in the small space. *Why is he keeping me waiting? Doesn't he know I'm the chief of the temple guards?*

A guard, clad in a short, dark tunic, complete with a leather belt, stepped into the hall where Marcus paced. "Governor Magnus will see you now."

With a short nod to the guard, Marcus swept past him and into the ornate chamber, where Magnus sat on an elevated chair. Dark straight hair, cropped short, Roman style, fell over a deep forehead, which shaded a prominent nose. A strong chin jutted out, and piercing eyes watched Marcus enter.

"Marcus, I have many questions for you."

The tone seemed curt, but Marcus bowed his head to acknowledge him. He had heard rumors that Magnus was a hard taskmaster.

Magnus leaned forward on his seat and fixed his eye on Marcus. "I've been told you're the new chief temple guard. Tell me this isn't true."

"Your Honor, it is true." Marcus's hands were beginning to sweat, but he resisted the urge to wipe them on his tunic.

Magnus eye's narrowed, and lines appeared between his eyes. "But how can that be? I believe you're connected with that new cult."

"That's not true." He straightened his shoulders and faced the piercing stare.

The governor leaned back in his seat, his lips slightly lifted. "How can that be? Isn't the cult leader your brother?"

"Yes, your Honor, but we do not agree."

His hand stroked his chin, and he appeared to be assessing Marcus. "Then I can count on your help to rid the city of this cult?"

Marcus felt his muscles relax. Maybe this wouldn't be so bad after all. "There is nothing I would like better than to see this cult eradicated and the leaders punished." He knew the words were brave.

"We shall see. I will have tasks for you, but for now, you are dismissed."

Marcus turned to leave.

"One more thing." The voice carried a challenge that was not lost on Marcus. "You can tell the priests that I see them as part of the problem, and I'm expecting them to bring the city back to Zeus and emperor worship." He paused. "It will be in their best interests. Now go."

Once Marcus had relayed the governor's message to the chief priest, he called a meeting of the priests and several of the guards. Magnus had not been included. As Marcus hurried into the temple, the meeting was already in progress.

Old Ekrem was on his feet when Marcus slipped into the room.

"These are tough times we live in, fellow priests," Ekrem said. "I have lived a long time, and never have I witnessed such a turning away from the old ways. These followers of the Jesus cult are strong. We must convince them to return to the ways of our fathers." His thin, upraised arms poked out of his tunic sleeves. Bent back and sloped shoulders were outlined under the worn fabric.

"And just how do you suggest we go about that?" Rifat, one of the younger priests, asked in a scornful tone. He towered over Ekrem, arms folded over his ample chest. "Haven't we done everything we can?"

"Oh, we've given them a little taste of our displeasure," Ekrem said, "but that will seem as nothing compared to what I have in mind." Ekrem's body was twisted with the ravages of age. His humped back seemed to draw his shoulders forward, but his sharp mind gleamed out of his beady eyes.

Several voices could be heard around the room. "Tell us, tell us."

Ekrem drew himself up to his full height, as far as his back would allow, which still left him far short of average. His face was stony as he looked each priest in the eye. His gaze scanned the rest of the room, coming to rest on Marcus.

"Ah, Marcus. Just the person I wanted most to see. You will be a major player in the scene I have played in my head. Listen carefully everyone." His faded eyes peered out at each of them; one bony finger poked the air before his face. "We must infiltrate this group."

A gasp escaped a priest's lips.

"We need to know everything about them," Ekrem went on, "what they believe, what they think, what they plan to do next, what they say, whom they say it to. In fact, everything about them."

The room was still as he shook the bony finger once more. "Who better to infiltrate them than the brother of the leader?" He rapped his walking stick on the floor to emphasize each point.

Loud cheers greeted these remarks.

"Brilliant, Ekrem." Musa jumped to his feet. "That's the best plan I've heard yet."

Meanwhile Marcus sweated beneath his tunic. He let nothing show on his face, but his heart almost stopped. Fighting Antipas was one thing, but Paulus? He couldn't do it.

All eyes turned to him as Ekrem outlined the plan.

Marcus was to contact Paulus and show interest in his message. Paulus would, of course, be delighted and never suspect Marcus was anything but serious. It was a fail-proof plan. Everyone began to say so.

Ekrem said, "I want to meet with you tomorrow night, Marcus, here in the temple. We'll talk about all the details then." Both hands were tucked inside the arms of his robe. "That will give you a few hours to come up with some ideas of your own. This must seem as natural as possible."

Ekrem pointed one of the bony fingers at Marcus once more before turning his gaze on the group. "Each of you, pray and sacrifice to Zeus for success in our endeavors. We can't fail. There is no room for error." Once again his walking stick emphasized each word. "I don't need to remind you that secrecy is utmost. Good day to you now."

He turned slowly and stiffly, using his stick to walk to the door with dignity, the brown tunic trailing on the floor behind him.

Marcus left the meeting, feeling like he was suffocating. His breath came in quick gasps as he considered the plan.

I hadn't expected it to come to this. I thought the worst was over, and now this.

He wiped away the sweat seeping beneath his turban.

What can I do? Paulus would say to pray. Pray to who or what? Zeus has never done anything for me, and the emperor is far away and inaccessible. Paulus says pray to God. Okay. God, if You're up there, I need help.

He glanced at the sky, almost expecting a sign.

Nothing. What did I expect anyway?

He threw his arms up in the air.

He roamed the streets in central Pergamum. Eventually he found himself in the market area, glancing at the stalls he passed. He had been here many times on horseback, quelling potential riots and generally stirring up trouble if there wasn't any.

As he walked, deep in thought, he bumped into an old man who was sweeping the path before one of the stalls. The old man toppled to the ground.

"Get out of my way, old man!" Marcus shouted, then immediately felt ashamed. "Are you hurt?" He bent over the man, checking him for obvious injuries.

"I think I'll live. Help me up, won't you?" The man lifted his hands to Marcus.

Marcus assisted the old man to his feet.

"Say, aren't you Marcus, the temple guard?" Bright eyes under bushy brows looked him over.

"Yes, I'm Marcus. Who are you?" He looked closer at the man, noting his worn tunic.

"I'm Decimus. I own this stall along with my wife, Juliana." He pointed back to the stall. The woman was waiting on a customer, and bargaining was in full swing.

"Aren't you also Paulus's brother?" Decimus squinted at him, lips pursed.

"Why do you ask?" He folded his arms over his chest, his mind wondering how this man knew him.

"I know Paulus. He's a fine man. He's brought happiness to me and my household. I never thought it was possible, but the name of Jesus changes people." Decimus stood tall with his shoulders back.

"You're a bold one to speak that name in the open market and to a temple guard at that. I could have you arrested, you know." Marcus spat on the ground beside him.

Decimus nodded. "Yes, I'm aware of that, but speaking the name of Jesus is more important than being arrested."

Marcus couldn't believe his ears. This humble, lower-class man had more boldness than he did. What was it about these Christians? Marcus bade the old man good day and strode out of the market, shaking his head. The name of this infidel kept coming up, hounding him.

Maybe I should meet with Paulus. But I can't until I settle in my mind what I'm going to do.

A troubled Marcus went home to brood long into the night.

Chapter Eighteen

Decimus picked up his broom and shuffled up the path to where Juliana was arranging fruit in their booth. She turned when he drew near.

"Hello, my husband. Is the sweeping finished?" She put the last fresh date on the pile and wiped her hands on the cloth she held.

"Yes, for now. The path gets a mess with all the footsteps going back and forth. Not that I'm complaining because more footsteps mean more business." He leaned on his broom.

"How right you are, my husband."

Decimus tried not to laugh. He was still getting used to this "new" Juliana. *What a change in a woman,* he thought.

"Did you see me talking to that gentleman?" He pointed the way Marcus had left.

"Yes, it looked like one of the temple guards, but I figured it couldn't be that. They wouldn't talk to the likes of us." She shook her head and tilted it to one side as she studied the fruit.

"Well, there you are mistaken. Not only was it a temple guard, it was Marcus, the chief guard." He stood straighter and faced her.

"You don't say! Was it really him?" Her head swung up, eyes wide with disbelief.

"Him in the flesh. He was walking along, lost in thought, and bumped into me and knocked me over. When I saw who it was, I expected a good kick and tongue lashing. Instead he apologized and helped me up." He scratched his head under his dark turban.

Her eyebrows almost disappeared in her hairline. "You don't say. That's unheard of."

"Not only that, but I was able to speak the name of Jesus to him and not get arrested." He grinned, lifting the broom from the ground.

Fear flashed across Juliana's face, then she regained her composure. "Tell me more." She leaned against the side of the stall and watched her husband.

He quickly nodded. "I also asked him if he was Paulus's brother."

"Never. You didn't say that!"

"Yes, I did, and he didn't deny it." Decimus loved her attention.

"What else did you say?" She plunked her hands on her hips.

"I told him I knew Paulus and that he was a fine man and that he had brought happiness to us through the name of Jesus." He leaned on the broom again.

"Oh!" she gasped. "I can't believe how brave you've become."

"The name of Jesus has changed our lives, you and me." He smiled at her.

"That it has, my husband." She wiped her forehead with the back of her hand.

"But I'm troubled about Marcus. He seemed to be far away in thought, like he had some big problem on his mind. I think I'll go talk to Paulus and tell him about seeing Marcus. It might be something important. I just feel the urge to go." He nodded a few times.

"Then go, my husband. I'll pray for you while you're gone. Paulus needs to hear anything that might help bring his brother to The Way." She waved her hand at him and turned as a customer approached.

At Paulus's home, Decimus knocked on the door of the servant's entrance.

The door opened. A jolly face peered around the door frame.

"Decimus, it's not you, is it?" asked the lively voice.

"Of course it's me." Decimus laughed. "Martha, you've got to be the happiest person I know." Decimus, smiling from ear to ear, greeted her.

"And why wouldn't I be happy? What's there to be sad about? Come in, come in before you let all the flies in." She held the door wide for him to enter. "You've no doubt come for a reason, and it's probably not to see me." She laughed and wiped her floured hands on a towel.

"I really need to see Paulus. Is he here?" Decimus glanced around the busy workspace where a meal was being prepared.

"Indeed he is. Bella, go tell the master that he has a visitor." Martha poked a young girl, prodding her to move.

Paulus greeted Decimus as an equal, a fact he knew still made Decimus feel uncomfortable. Once they were seated in Paulus's rooms, he asked Decimus what had brought him here today. Decimus related his encounter with Marcus.

"I wasn't sure what to do but felt you needed to know. Something's not right with Marcus today." He shook his head, shifting in his seat.

"Thank you for telling me, Decimus. You did the right thing. I'll need to pray about it and decide what I should do, or maybe not do."

After Decimus left, Paulus paced the room, hands behind his back, head bowed.

What a strange encounter. It was out of character for Marcus to show compassion. Maybe it meant nothing, but then again, it might be a sign.

Was Marcus softening, or was he becoming even more dangerous?

Chapter Nineteen

While Paulus mused on what Decimus had told him, in another part of the city his brother fretted over the meeting he had attended and the mission assigned to him. He had a full day before his meeting with Ekrem. He had decisions to make.

He threw himself down on his bed and stared at the walls. No answer there. Up again and another turn around the room. The room was filled with treasures Marcus had collected from many sources over the years, but they meant nothing to him tonight.

He finally decided.

I'll do it, he said to himself. *Paulus is the traitor, not me. I need to stay focused on my goal to rid the city of this cult.* He was snarling to himself by now. *Antipas and Paulus both discarded the traditions of our family. I won't. If Paulus gets hurt, so be it.* He flung his clothes on the floor and stumbled into bed. Sleep was almost instantaneous.

"Marcus."

Marcus didn't move.

"Marcus," the disembodied voice whispered in the darkness.

Marcus threw off the covers and sat up. He rubbed his head, then lay back down.

"I've got to talk to you. Paulus is right." It was Julian's voice.

Marcus slept on.

"I've been greatly troubled by visitations. Horrible, ugly creatures appear in my room. Oh, take them away . . ." The sobbing voice faded from the room.

When Marcus awoke, an oppression lingered in his head. Fragments of a dream hung in his mind, but he was unable to capture the scenes. He shook his head to dispel the thoughts and rose to begin his day.

This morning he was more resolved than ever to go through with Ekrem's plan. "This could be good," he spoke aloud to the silent room. "Paulus will be very surprised. It'll serve him right for deserting father and me."

Marcus hurriedly prepared for the day. Thoughts about his plan put glee in his step. He rubbed his hands together in anticipation and caught a glimpse of himself in the shiny bronze shield hanging on the great room's wall. His disheveled appearance startled him, but he didn't take the time to groom himself further.

He moved through his home, muttering to himself. "Ekrem is clever—no question about that. I wouldn't have thought of this myself; I'd have proceeded with the plan to destroy them from without. Destroying them from within will be much more effective." He chuckled to himself.

His first stop of the morning was the temple. Ekrem had suggested that they offer a sacrifice to Zeus in preparation for their mission. He stopped along the street at the side of the temple steps, where vendors sold birds and animals for sacrifices.

Many customers milled around the stalls, making their selections. Marcus joined a ragged line, approaching the goat pens. Loud laughing and talking swirled all around him, but he heard little. Children played in any open space they could find, shouting their joy in their games.

The closer he got to the pens, the stronger the smell of goats and sweaty bodies. He held the edge of his robe under his nose, trying to lessen the nasal assault. A scuffle broke out in front of him; one customer elbowed another, who was pushing ahead of him in line. The word battle continued even after the pushing stopped.

At last it was Marcus's turn. He quickly chose the goat he wanted and produced his bulging purse. The vendor's face twisted in a grimace as if realizing he could have held out for a greater price. But a bargain was a bargain, and the goat was soon placed, frantically struggling, in his arms.

"Be quiet, goat." Marcus hissed at the animal, still gripping it tenaciously. The goat suddenly stilled, a look of panic gleaming in its slanted eyes.

Marcus ignored the eyes and moved to the side of the lane. He reached under his robe and extracted the short knife he always carried. He lifted the head high and deftly slit the throat. Warm blood washed over his hands. The goat gave one last heave, then went limp. He prepared the animal for sacrifice, then washed his hands in the stone basin next to the temple wall.

He lifted the carcass onto his shoulders, worked his way through the crowd, and ascended the altar steps. He stood to the side as an old man presented his offering to one of the priests officiating at the altar. When it was Marcus's turn, he handed the goat to the priest, whose robe was stiff and discolored after the number of sacrifices he had committed to the altar this morning.

Marcus wasn't prepared for the wash of feelings that came over him as he glanced at the altar. *My mind is playing tricks on me; the goat has the shape and form of Antipas.*

He shook his head to clear his thoughts and motioned to the priest, who had paused to look at him, to continue.

I need to get control of myself if I'm going to succeed at this assignment, he scolded himself. He backed away from the flames and stench.

The chanting over his sacrifice began as the priests circled the altar. Marcus turned his attention back to the ritual, imploring Zeus to give him success in his venture. That completed, he strode down the steps and elbowed his way through the crowd to the building where the guard was housed. His office was empty, allowing him to complete the tasks requiring his attention.

When his day's work was completed, he approached the temple once again for his appointment with Ekrem. As he mounted the stairs, his thoughts turned to Paulus and the chilling surprise he would soon deliver to him.

Chapter Twenty

Marcus's dress sandals made no sound as he paced across the marble floor of the temple foyer. He pushed aside the curtain of the anteroom, where the meeting would take place. Ekrem looked up, eyebrows raised.

"What? Did I startle you?" Marcus asked with disdain in his voice. He wrinkled his forehead.

"On the contrary, I've been expecting you," Ekrem said in his strident voice. He shuffled some scrolls lying on the table before him.

"Then get to the point. I have other uses for my time." Marcus towered over the seated priest.

"My, my, we're thorny tonight. Cold feet Marcus?" The smooth tones of the priest grated on his nerves.

"Listen to me, Ekrem. I want to rid our city of this cult as much as you do. Let's get this meeting under way so we can accomplish that." Marcus shook his fist in Ekrem's face. He'd never had respect for this old priest. The priest had once chastised him in front of his friends, and Marcus had never forgotten.

"Sit down, Marcus. We have much to discuss. Have you made plans for approaching Paulus?" Ekrem motioned to the only other chair in the room.

"I have a few things in mind, but I'd prefer not to share them since a secret shared soon becomes the nation's gossip." Marcus sat heavily in the chair. He swept his gaze over Ekrem and focused on the wall behind his head.

"You hover on the line of disrespect," Ekrem said. "Perhaps the new captain of the guard is not the right person for this scheme of mine." He shrugged.

Marcus stared at him. "I can accomplish what no other can. Tell me your plans."

They soon agreed to meet secretly once each week to share information. Marcus would continue with his duties as chief guard, keeping his new role under cover. It would be a dangerous game, a fact that made it more appealing to Marcus. All thoughts of softness toward Paulus had vanished. In their place smoldered intense hatred and hardness.

As he left the temple, the night air was cool. A few people milled around the streets, but most had turned into their homes for the night. As a cool breeze from the north gusted down a side street into his path, Marcus pulled his robe tighter around him. He swore softly under his breath and pushed against the breeze.

He marched with purpose toward the doctor's house where Julian was still housed. The facade could soon be discerned in the distance. Larger than other houses on the street, it bore the sign of the physician on the front. The double doors were closed, but a light shone from inside.

Marcus approached the door and rapped heavily on the wooden panel. When the door remained closed, he raised his fist to knock again, only to meet air. A young servant girl had opened the door; she looked frightened as she looked him over. She was tiny with a fringe of tight curly hair escaping her servant's hat.

"Well, are you going to invite me in or stare at me all night?" He flicked his fingers in her face.

Fear flashed across her face. She bowed before him and bade him enter in a high, frightened voice.

"Take me to my father."

She bowed again and made no sound, then turned and led the way down a wide hallway. Dark tapestries hung from the walls, interspersed with shelves holding small bronze lanterns, which were lit. They cast a smoky light along their passage. She stopped before a partly open door and stood aside to let him enter. He brushed past her roughly, causing her to quickly step back. He firmly closed the door in her face.

Julian sat on a low stool beside the window, his back to his son. He gave no indication that he knew Marcus was there. His shoulders were thin under his tunic. Matted hair hung limply from under his turban. He lifted a claw-like hand to brush hair from his eyes.

"Father, sit up," Marcus said. "It's me. I've come to discuss a matter with you that will greatly interest you." His attempt at pleasantry fell short. Julian didn't move.

He walked over to the stool and grasped his father's shoulder, shaking it. "Father, I said it's me. Attend to what I have to say."

Slowly Julian's head swung around, and two pale, vacant eyes stared at him. For a moment recognition seemed to pass across his face, but that was quickly dispelled by a blank look.

Marcus tried again. "I know you can hear me."

This time he got a response. Julian tried to rise from his seat. Drool dripping from his lips, he hissed at Marcus.

"What you want." His labored breathing made his words sound harsh and slurred. "Get out. I don't need you . . ." Arms flailing, he lost his balance and fell back on the stool. He stayed quiet while Marcus watched him.

"I don't believe you're as bad as you let on." Marcus crossed his arms and lifted his nose in a sneer.

This sent Julian into a spasm that twisted his face, turning it a dark shade of red. He gasped for breath in his attempt to speak.

"There's no point in me staying longer," Marcus said. "You're obviously crazy."

Marcus took one last look at his father, who now writhed on his stool and screamed obscenities at his son. Marcus nodded to the aide, who waited to minister to Julian's needs. This time he closed the door softly. Without a backward glance, he left the building and entered the darkness of night.

From now on, he would be alone in his fight against Paulus, yet something had changed. A strange power stirred within, a power opposed to the power Paulus claimed to possess.

"Let the battle begin," he yelled into the night air, his clenched fist held high.

Chapter Twenty-One

Marcus stood at the back of the crowd gathered around the temple steps, where Paulus held forth in preaching. He watched his brother closely, observing his every move, observing the look of joy on his face, the purposeful gestures while he listed his points, observing the patient way he responded to questions.

He will be a worthy opponent, Marcus mused. *We may be on different sides of this issue, but we are alike in many ways.*

When Paulus finished speaking, Marcus turned quickly and disappeared into the crowd. He wasn't ready to meet him yet. He needed more time to polish his approach.

Paulus must believe me right from the beginning. There's no room for error. The guise must be complete.

He chuckled to himself just thinking about it.

Paulus shared his concerns about Marcus with Eunice. They discussed what Decimus had said but couldn't decide what it meant.

"It seems best to leave it alone and see what happens," Paulus finally concluded.

"I agree, husband. We already know Marcus is dangerous and that our lives are held in his hand, except that really they are held in God's hand." Eunice gave him a soft smile.

"Then we do nothing until we have reason to do otherwise."

A week later Marcus rode his horse along a country lane one morning. He hadn't seen Paulus in the intervening time, having avoided the temple area when he knew his brother would be there. This morning he felt ready.

He wound his way around the low hills, slowing among the rocky outcrops. He relaxed, knowing it was only a matter of time before he encountered Paulus.

He deliberately steered the horse toward the city gate, mingling with the carts and donkeys entering the city. Today he would search for his brother.

"I can't wait to see his face," he said aloud, a wide grin spread over his face. "It'll be the revenge of the millennia."

Many turbans bobbed in front of him. The air was warm and moist, intensifying the already odious smell of beasts and men. He pulled his scarf closer around his nose, hoping to mask the stench. He was finally through the gate and able to detach himself from the lot. Glad to be rid of them, he turned his horse's head toward the market. He decided to leave the horse tethered with the blacksmith and proceed on foot.

He would have to be careful. The encounter must look natural to Paulus and any onlookers.

"There he is," Marcus said in shock. He stopped where he was, chin in hand as he studied his brother.

Paulus was finishing his teaching on the temple steps. The last of the listeners were moving off in several directions. Marcus approached.

He spoke with what he hoped was the right degree of humility. "Paulus, I need to speak with you. In private." He watched his brother's eyes and thought he saw a flicker of surprise, but Paulus reached out his hand to touch Marcus's arm.

"Good day, brother. Of course we can meet and talk. Where would you suggest?" Paulus looked into his eyes with a smile on his face.

"I'd like it to be someplace private; there are eyes everywhere." Marcus scanned the crowd to see if anyone was watching him.

"Would you care to come to my home tonight?" Paulus asked.

"No, no. I can't put you in danger." Marcus shook his head from side to side.

"Then what do you suggest, brother?" Paulus raised his eyebrows.

"How about our father's house? There are only servants there, and they won't be alarmed if we both happen to arrive on the same night." Marcus spoke quickly, fidgeting with the edge of his cloak.

Paulus watched his brother's hands fingering his cloak.

Something's wrong. The thought flashed across Paulus's mind. *I know him so well; he's nervous. Why does he want to meet?* He swallowed his uneasiness.

"Our old home is fine with me. Shall we meet as darkness falls?" Paulus tilted his head.

Marcus's gaze darted back and forth. "Agreed."

He wasted no time turning his back on Paulus. Pulling his military cloak tightly around him and jerking his turban lower on his forehead, he disappeared into the crowd. Paulus stood watching him with a puzzled look on his face.

That was strange out-of-character behavior for Marcus. Now I'm doubly concerned after what I heard from Decimus. Is it possible that our message is getting through to him, or is this another ruse to destroy me and other believers?

Paulus entered the market area, puzzling over his encounter with Marcus. The dazzling array of fresh fruits and vegetables was lost on him today. Even the fragrance of expensive perfume, coming from one of the more prosperous stalls, failed to elicit any response from him. He hurried on, wanting to meet with David, share about the unusual meeting, and elicit his prayers for tonight.

Finding his father's house lit up when he neared the front entrance surprised Paulus.

Marcus must already be here.

He knocked on the door.

An unfamiliar servant opened the door promptly, ushering him in without questioning his identity. The servant took his outer robe and led him to a small enclosure at the back of the house; it had once been his mother's workroom. Marcus sat on a low cushion but jumped up when Paulus was shown into the room.

He looked at Paulus intently. "Please be seated, Paulus. I have something to discuss with you."

"Marcus, is something wrong that you've brought me here tonight?" Paulus hesitated before he sat where Marcus indicated.

"No, no, nothing is wrong." Marcus shifted his feet and clasped his hands into fists.

"Then what is it?" Paulus leaned forward on his seat.

Marcus took a deep breath and lifted his face to his brother, an inscrutable expression in his eyes. "Paulus, I want to know more about your religion."

"Do you mean my relationship with my Savior?"

"Yes, yes, whatever you call it." He gestured with one hand.

Paulus gathered his thoughts for a moment before answering. Was this a trap, or was Marcus really interested?

"Why do you want to know?" Paulus sat back and watched his brother.

Marcus cleared his throat, wiped his hands on his robe, and without looking up said, "I want to join your group."

Something stabbed Paulus's heart. How should he reply? "Marcus, do you realize what you're asking?"

"What do you mean? Of course, I know what this means. I could lose my job and my head." He had snapped out the words.

Paulus was at a loss as to how to proceed. He stared at the floor and gathered his thoughts. "Marcus, do you believe that Jesus is the Christ, the Son of God?" Paulus kept his face still as he questioned him.

"If you say that's true, then I'll believe it." Another wave of the hand accompanied his answer.

Something was wrong. Paulus was perplexed yet excited. They had been praying for Marcus, and now this was the answer. "Do you understand that you have sinned and that Jesus wants to forgive you?" He touched his brother's arm.

"I guess we all sin. What do I have to do?" He didn't throw off Paulus's hand, so that was encouraging. His answer, however, seemed unsatisfactory. Paulus had no choice but to take his brother at his word and proceed. He explained the way of salvation to a now-silent Marcus and asked him if he would like to pray and ask Jesus into his heart.

"Just tell me what to say." Marcus had lowered his eyes.

Paulus led him in prayer. Even though all did not seem right, he had to let God work in Marcus's life. Not everyone reacted to the gospel message the same way. A long road lay ahead for Marcus to travel.

"Thank you, Paulus," Marcus said stiffly. "What do I do next?" He finally made eye contact.

"We need to meet with some of the elders. You need to tell them about your conversion."

"My what? Conversion?" He raised his brows and opened his mouth.

"Your change of heart, brother. Your desire to follow Christ." Paulus looked closely at Marcus.

"Yes, yes, of course. Let's do it." He opened his arms in a wide gesture.

"I'll need to set up a time for us to meet with them."

"Can't we do it tonight?" Marcus was talking fast.

"I really need to talk to them and find a time that's suitable."

Marcus almost barked out the words. "Then do whatever you have to do. Meet me back here tomorrow night with the information."

"I'll be here. Brother, I'm glad you're joining us." He put his hand on Marcus's shoulder again.

"Yes, yes. Just get the meeting set up." He rose without another word, grabbed his fine cloak, wrapped it around him hurriedly, and left the house without a backward glance.

Paulus rose slowly, a puzzled expression on his face.

"Was that real, or is there something else going on?" he mumbled to himself. "But why would Marcus even approach me if he wasn't sincere? He's putting his own life on the line."

Paulus decided his only choice was to accept what Marcus had said and move on from there.

As the brothers went their separate ways home, Marcus walked with his head bent, long strides flapping the material of his cloak.

"I need to be more careful. I can't raise any suspicion in Paulus or the others."

He lifted his head high and whispered into the darkness. "I'll do this. By Zeus, I'll make this work. Beware, Paulus. I'll win this battle."

Chapter Twenty-Two

Paulus paced his room, hands clasped behind his back, head lowered. Everything in him wanted to believe Marcus was truly a believer, but a lingering doubt played around the edges of his mind.

No, he thought, *I'm going to accept what he says as the truth. I really have no reason to doubt him.* And with that, the decision was made. Now to talk to the others.

David was home and welcomed Paulus warmly, stepping aside to let him enter. "Come in, brother Paulus. It's always such a joy to see you."

Paulus stepped into the house, no smile of welcome on his face.

"I detect something is troubling you," David said. "Come sit with me and we'll discuss it." He stared at Paulus, then guided him into another room.

"Thank you, David. I do need to talk to you. I'm not really troubled, but I do have a weighty matter to discuss." He followed David and removed his cloak as he walked.

The two sank into soft cushions on the low couch. Miriam had decorated the room with earth tones to please the eye, and many intricate silver vases and bowls were scattered on low tables, adding a feeling of comfort and beauty for her guests. Paulus let his gaze roam the room while he gathered his thoughts.

"Take your time, Paulus. I'm in no rush." David sat back and watched him.

Paulus leaned forward as he spoke. "I've met with Marcus." Bold statement. It hung in the air between them.

"Is this good news or bad?"

"It's good news. He wants to join our group. I told him he would need to meet with the elders." Paulus took a deep breath and firmly pressed his lips together.

"Now, wait a minute. That doesn't sound like good news to me. The man is dangerous. I can't believe he really wants to have anything to do with us." David's eyes flew wide open. He held up a hand.

"He says he does. I accept his word."

"What are you thinking, Paulus? He's trouble. He must have some ulterior motive. I can't believe this." David frowned and watched Paulus. "Why don't you tell me the whole story right from the beginning?"

"Yes, that's what I should have done first," Paulus said, a relieved sigh in his voice.

He recounted the story from the moment Marcus approached him until he'd decided to accept his word. When he finished his story, he sat back and looked at David.

David had his head down and was seemingly staring at his feet. His shoulders were slumped, a furrow between his brows. He appeared to be deep in thought. Paulus sat quietly, waiting for him to speak.

"I'm sorry, Paulus. This doesn't sound real. I don't think we should meet with him." He shook his head slowly.

"But David, I explained the way of salvation to him, and he said he wanted it. He even prayed with me." His hands were restless on his lap.

"Marcus is like a fox. I wouldn't trust him. I know you want this for him, Paulus, but I can't see that's its true."

Paulus hung his head. David was a man he trusted, depended on, needed. "Brother, I know it sounds suspect, but what if it's real?" He raised his eyes to look at David. "Shouldn't we give him the chance to prove to us that he has accepted Christ? I have to take him at his word. Why would he humble himself like this if it wasn't true?"

David was silent for a long moment. Then he lifted his head, the worried frown still between his eyes, and looked Paulus in the eye.

"If you are so determined that we meet, I'll agree. For *your* sake, Paulus, you understand that? I'm not worried for myself; he already knows who I am, so it's no threat to me personally."

"Thank you, David. This means so much to me. I'll bring him by tonight. Will you speak to Emin and ask him to come as well?" Paulus rose from his seat.

"Yes, certainly. I'll explain the situation to him. I think you can count on him coming."

After Paulus left, David paced the room for many minutes, praying aloud. Heaven seemed far away this night, and no revelation came as an answer to his prayer. Fear gathered around the corners of his heart, and he contemplated the step they were taking.

Marcus can't be trusted. That's a fact. I'm afraid he's up to something. Something I won't like. The die is cast. I can't turn back now.

Chapter Twenty-Three

A cold wind swirled the dust along the deserted street. Lights flickered in the houses set back from the road. Clouds obscured the moon's light as the two brothers walked along side by side in silence. Paulus tightened the belt on his robe and pulled his cloak tighter to keep out the dust. A shiver ran across his shoulders as a strong gust played with a loose piece of his turban, hitting his neck in a rhythmic beat.

He glanced at Marcus, who had not spoken since they'd greeted each other at his father's house and begun the journey through the city. He wished he could read his brother's expression, but that was impossible in the dim light.

"How many people will be there tonight?" Marcus's voice lacked his usual arrogant swagger.

"Just two, David and Emin."

"And they're prepared to accept me?"

"Just tell them your story, and we'll let them decide for themselves." Paulus glanced sideways at his brother. "Are you nervous, Marcus?"

"Nervous?" Marcus snorted. "Why should I be nervous? I could have them both thrown in jail tonight." He jerked his head upward.

Paulus hoped Marcus couldn't see the shocked look on his face. "I don't think I'd mention that. They certainly won't believe you're serious if you start to threaten them."

"No, you're right. I have so much to learn." He said this in a subdued tone, shoulders slumping.

"That's David's house up ahead." Paulus was glad to change the topic.

Marcus stopped abruptly and turned to face Paulus. He laid his hand on his arm. "You believe me. Don't you, Paulus?"

"Yes, Marcus, I believe you, and I'll do everything in my power to convince the others that you've really given your heart to the Lord." He held Marcus' gaze.

Marcus didn't reply.

Paulus ended the silence. "Let's go. The others will be waiting."

Paulus couldn't believe what he was hearing. Marcus had done his homework somewhere. He answered every question Emin and David put to him.

He's even answering graciously, Paulus mused.

Marcus answered one of David's questions in a soft voice. "I know I have much to learn."

David looked at Emin, then at Paulus. "I think we can accept Marcus into our group."

"Thank you, David." Marcus sat back as though relieved.

Emin stood and took a turn around the room. When he returned, he stopped in front of Marcus. "You have to understand that this will be hard for our people to grasp. They have only known you as a feared temple guard. We'll have to go slow until they learn to trust you."

"Yes, I understand, Emin." Marcus looked him right in the eye.

"I suggest we start with some studies, just the four of us, before we introduce you to any of the other converts," Emin said. "Then when you do meet them, you'll have some grounding in the teachings of Jesus."

"When would you like me to meet with you again?" Marcus glanced from one to the other.

"Why not tomorrow night?" David met his gaze.

"Can we make that the next night? I have an appointment tomorrow night."

"Agreed. We'll meet here if that is acceptable to Paulus and Emin."

Later, in the privacy of his own home, Marcus contemplated his evening. Anger rose in his chest as he recalled their words.

"Ha, they'll accept me, they say. What drivel. I should send in the guards tonight. I've never been so humiliated in my life. Study with them? I'd rather run a nice sharp sword through them."

He strutted around his room, getting more agitated with each sweep of the area.

"I don't have to put up with this." He punched his fist into the wall. He punched it again and again until the wall began to crumble at that spot and blood poured from his fist.

He stalked some more, pausing to kick at a pile of scrolls on a low stool. With one swipe of his foot, they came tumbling down at his feet. He glanced at the fallen scrolls and became more incensed, to the point of violence. Punching and kicking at anything in his path, he systematically destroyed his room. When his anger was spent, he called to a servant.

"Yes, master?" The servant appeared quickly as if he had not been far off. He stepped into the room with a blank expression on his face.

"Clean this up." Marcus pushed past the servant and marched down the hall and out of the house.

He stormed his way through the streets and up the temple steps.

I'll find Ekrem, tell him I quit, then send the guards in. The Christians are history!

Chapter Twenty-Four

"Calm down, Marcus." Ekrem raised one hand, shaking a finger at him. "Sending in the guards won't accomplish our purpose as effectively as having you in the midst of them. We would only take out a few of them, and the rest would go into hiding, gaining strength as they go. Look what happened when we sacrificed Antipas."

Ekrem folded his hands in front of him and kept an eye on Marcus.

I will not let him see how much he irritates me.

"This is different. I can't do this. I don't want to do this. I feel like a fool doing this." Marcus half-lifted himself from his seat, his face twisted in a grimace.

"Oh, too hard for you, is it?" Ekrem said. "I should have known you wouldn't have the backbone to carry it through." He stood and started to gather his things while Marcus sat with his head in his hands.

"I'll be going now," Ekrem said. "I expect there'll be some discipline since you have defied a direct order."

Marcus sprang to his feet and angrily ground out the words. "Just a minute now. I haven't said I won't do it."

"Really? It certainly sounded like that to me." Ekrem continued to pick up his scrolls.

"Sit down, Ekrem. You annoy me." Marcus flicked his hand in Ekrem's face.

"I annoy you? That's rich. You annoy half the people in this city, and that appears to be acceptable to you. Why should I sit down?" He crossed his arms and drew his brows up.

Marcus flung his hands in the air. "We need to make more plans."

Ekrem leaned over Marcus's seat until he stared directly in his eyes. "Let's get one thing straight, Marcus. You may be the chief temple guard, but I'm the temple itself." His chest puffed up as he took a deep breath. "What I say goes in this city. This new governor thinks he has the power, but he has a few things to learn." He snapped his fingers. "I know he plans to wipe out the Christians and the priests of Zeus as well. If he is successful, where will that leave you?"

Marcus glared at him, lips tight in a straight line.

"Yes, I see you get the point. Without priests, there won't be a temple. Without a temple, there won't be temple guards, not even a chief temple guard." Ekrem stood back, adjusting the belt around his robe.

"Get to your point, Ekrem."

"My point, Marcus? My point is that you have no choice but to do my bidding. Unless we wipe out this sect, you stand to lose as much as the rest of us. Now stop your foolish ranting about not being able to do this and get out there and get it done."

Ekrem straightened, took one last look at Marcus, turned his back, and walked away. At the door he turned and looked back into the room. "Meet me here in two nights with your report, your success report." Then he disappeared into the darkness of the temple foyer.

The next five days were feast days in worship of Zeus, and controlling the crowds in the city kept Marcus busy. Pilgrims flocked from many distant places to pay homage at the great altar. As foreigners poured into Pergamum, Marcus kept a guard posted on each gate. Magnus, the new governor, was a hard taskmaster who demanded that Marcus control the crowds. Riots in the streets were not allowed. The governor had made his wishes very clear, with veiled threats of consequences if anything disturbed the fragile peace.

Not only that, but today he needed to meet with Magnus, who had refused to disclose the matter for discussion.

"What terrible timing," Marcus said to himself. "I have Ekrem down my back, the church leaders questioning my honesty, crowds swarming the streets, and now Magnus."

He circled the city on his regal, dusky black horse, checking each contingent of guards to ensure they were following his orders exactly. Everything appeared quiet, so he directed his horse's steps to the governor's office.

As he neared the city's core, the press of people increased. The noise grated on his ears as hawkers shouted their wares, animals bleated in frustration, children shrieked in glee, and men and women yelled at each other in offensive language. Their guttural sounds were irritating to him. He was assaulted with the smells of vendors cooking over open grates, ill-kept animal pens, and unwashed human bodies. The display before him disgusted him.

By the time he reached Magnus's door, he was exasperated and angry. He entered the outer foyer and approached the guard at the door.

"I have an appointment with Magnus." He barely glanced at the guard, keeping his nose aloft.

"Yes, you are expected." The guard opened the door and ushered him in.

He hadn't seen Magnus in some time and was unprepared for the changes that had taken place since his last visit. The room was drenched with color and light to such a degree that it offended the eye. The opulence astounded him. Marble pillars circled the room, with carved sculptures and bronze trophies gracing their tops. Ivory images complemented gold dishes displayed on ornamental tables. Heavy draperies hung from the walls and windows. The intricately carved chair holding Magnus was wrought in marble. Women draped in costly materials lounged around the room, chatting lightly and eating cakes with honey. Over all hung a heavy scent unfamiliar to Marcus. He absorbed all this in seconds, then let his eyes rest on Magnus.

"Welcome, Marcus. I'm glad to see you arrived promptly. I like punctuality." Magnus nodded, his chin jutting out.

Marcus bowed low, gritting his teeth and planting a false smile on his face. He rose and looked Magnus in the eye.

"What do you think of my audience room?" Magnus asked. "Quite an improvement over the last occupant, wouldn't you say?" He swept his arms around, drawing the eye around the room.

"You have certainly made changes, my lord." Marcus bent his head.

"But do you like the changes, Marcus?" Magnus leaned forward, a gleam in his eye.

"It is not for me to like or not like, Your Honor." Marcus bowed low again.

Magnus snapped to a sitting position. "You'll like what I say you'll like!" he roared.

"Yes, my lord, certainly, whatever you say." Marcus bowed again.

"That's not why you're here." Magnus changed the subject. "I've heard rumors."

Marcus waited, unsure where the conversation was headed.

"I said, I've heard rumors. Have you nothing to say?" He frowned at Marcus.

"There is often little truth to rumors." Marcus waited uncomfortably.

"Do you not wish to know what rumors I've heard?" He sat back in his chair, crossing his legs. His Roman toga was a brilliant white. It seemed to shine in the light of the room.

"I know you will tell me when you're ready, my lord." Marcus remained still and gave a slight dip of his chin.

"You're coy, Marcus. You wear your cleverness like a badge, and yes, you're right. I will tell you when I'm ready, which is right now." The legs uncrossed, and the chin jutted out again. "You've been seen consorting with the enemy." Magnus let this drop between them and then waited, watching Marcus with keen eyes.

"What enemy is that, my lord?" Marcus's stomach muscles clenched. He tried to show nothing on his face.

"You know very well of whom I speak. Your detestable brother." He said this in a low voice while banging his fist on the arm of his chair. "What do you have to say to this charge?"

"Family business, my lord." Marcus bowed again, his mind working in circles. If he admitted to infiltrating the group, he would have to implicate the priest. That would not be a good option. He was already on shaky ground with Ekrem. Magnus would be infuriated with both him and the priest for going beyond his authority. This was indeed a difficult scenario.

"Family business," Magnus said with a faint smile. He continued to bore his gaze into Marcus. "I don't believe you!" He sprang from his chair.

The women in the room gasped and fanned themselves rapidly as they turned their eyes to the two men.

"You've become one of them," Magnus said. "That's the charge. I charge you with treason." He shouted toward the door, "Guards?"

Marcus sank to his knees before Magnus. "I assure you, my lord, that it is not true. I would never turn my back on you and the emperor." He was begging, something that went against everything he believed about himself.

A sly smile worked its way across Magnus's face. He sat back in his chair and contemplated the kneeling Marcus. "What will you do to prove to me that you aren't one of them?"

"I'll do whatever you command," Marcus whispered.

Magnus rose to his full height, thrust back his shoulders, and folded his arms. He stared at Marcus for a fraction of a second. Finally, he spoke.

"Then bring me your brother's head."

Chapter Twenty-Five

Marcus sat by the open window of his bedroom. The full moon was rising, casting a golden glow over the garden. Light breezes rustled among the bushes, bringing puffs of air laden with the heavy scent of flowers and damp earth. A night of beauty.

But it was all lost on Marcus.

How did I ever get myself into such a complicated and dangerous situation? he asked himself once again. He had been asking himself that question since Magnus shattered his mind with his declaration.

Ideas flashed through his mind one after the other, only to be quickly discarded.

It's an impossible situation.

He sat, head in hands, thinking far into the night. Toward morning he stood up, stretching to release cramped muscles, and leaned on the window frame. The cool air revived him as he gazed out without seeing.

"I'll do it." He slammed his fist on the window frame. "I'll prove I'm more cunning than all of them."

"Cato." He strode to his door, flinging it open and calling to his servant. "I'll break my fast early."

While his meal was being prepared, he retrieved his favorite quill and a small scroll. Using a small knife he always kept close by, he trimmed the quill and quickly wrote several words. He first blew on the scroll to dry the ink, then shook it vigorously. His ring made a deep impression in the circle of wax he dripped on the rolled scroll.

He grabbed a clean robe from a hook, broke his fast, then left the house.

As he moved briskly through the streets, he kept his head low, making no eye contact with passersby. He strolled along the stalls in the marketplace, seemingly intent on the wares displayed, stopping a number of times to lift fabrics and pottery as though interested. Covert looks slanted his way, but he pretended not to see them.

Eventually he arrived at the stall where Decimus and Juliana bartered their goods. Bright piles of woven fabrics and wall hangings were interspersed with wooden bowls and utensils. He lifted a large cooking spoon and rubbed his thumb over the smooth wood.

He could see Juliana watching him with wide eyes and open mouth. She shuffled over to where Decimus had just finished with a customer and elbowed him, nodding her head in Marcus's direction. Decimus looked, shook his head slightly, then moved toward him.

"May I help you, my lord?" Decimus nodded in Marcus's direction.

"Are you the carver?" Marcus held out the spoon.

"Yes, my lord, I've carved all you see here in our stall." Decimus lowered his eyes.

"You have a talent." Marcus picked up a small bowl and rubbed his hands along the sides.

"Very little talent, I fear, but it's a living." Decimus kept his eyes on Marcus's hands.

"I believe you know my brother. I think we once established that." His voice was low and casual.

"Oh yes, I know Paulus. Very fine man, he is." Decimus smiled at the mention of Paulus.

"Yes, well, I need to get a message to him. Would you be able to do that for me?" He fixed his gaze on Decimus's face.

"Anything, my lord." He bowed his head again, keeping his hands clasped together.

"I'll first purchase these articles." He handed them to Decimus. "How much do I owe you?"

Decimus named the usual price. Instead of bargaining as was usual, Marcus withdrew double the amount from his money bag and handed it to Decimus.

"This is too much." Decimus backed away, hands raised.

"Consider it payment for delivering my message." Marcus actually smiled. He still held out the money, which Decimus took with a trembling hand.

Marcus reached inside his cloak, withdrew the small scroll, and handed it to Decimus. He bowed low, then turned and quickly walked away.

Paulus entered his room and noticed a small scroll on his desk. He lifted the scroll in his hands.

From Marcus? Maybe he can't meet tonight, but he seemed most anxious to do so.

He pursed his lips, released the seal, opened it, and began to read. His brows moved closer and closer together as he scanned the message.

I need fresh air, he thought.

The afternoon sun slanted through the trees, casting beams of filtered light across the garden paths. The gardener was working in a distant part of the garden, clipping wilted heads from flowers. Paulus could hear him whistling as he moved along the rows of plants. He barely noticed the warmth of the sun as questions swirled through his already-crowded mind.

Why the strange message from Marcus?

The words swirled around in his mind: "Meet me outside the north gate after sunset tonight."

Is this a trap?

He tried to think rationally, but more questions than answers arose.

I said I trust him. So why am I troubled by his message?

He reached the back of the garden and sat on the bench, which rested on the bank of the stream. The water languorously glided between the banks. This had always been one of his favorite places; it was his refuge when he felt threatened, his refreshment when he was tired, his solace when he was troubled. Today it would have to accommodate all three.

The sleepiness of the scene began to soothe him. He relaxed his shoulders and bent his head into his hands. Slowly he came to the realization that he already knew what he would do. Rising from the bench, he stared into the sluggish flow before him and made his decision. With more purpose in his step, he returned to the house.

He found Eunice; she was mending one of Simon's tunics. "Eunice, I need to talk to you."

She looked up from her work with a sweet smile. "It's always my pleasure to talk with you, my husband." She laid the fabric and needle on the low table beside the bench where she was seated. Paulus sat beside her and took her hand in his.

"Eunice, I've had a message from Marcus. You know I've been seeing him, but I've withheld some of the details so as not to involve you in any conflict that might arise from meeting with him." He paused and looked into her eyes.

"I trust you, my husband, to make the right choices for me. I know when the time is right you'll tell me everything. Until then, I am content with what you tell me." She tilted her head to one side as she watched him.

"You make things so easy for me, my love. Be assured, I only withhold information when I think it might harm you." He squeezed her hand and planted a kiss on her forehead.

"I know. Now tell me why you need to talk to me and what this message from Marcus is."

"He wants to meet with me." Paulus paused, not sure how to proceed.

"But surely that's not troublesome. You've been meeting with him recently. There must be more to this." She patted his hand.

"There is. He wants to meet me outside the north gate after sunset tonight." He gripped her hand tighter.

Eunice sat up straight, covering her mouth with one hand. "Paulus. Outside the gate? They close and lock the gates at sunset. How will you get back in?"

"That's the problem. I won't get back in until sunrise." He bowed his head, shaking it slowly.

"What does he want?" She leaned closer to him, looking up into his eyes.

"He didn't say." He watched her face carefully and saw the fear in her eyes.

"But you don't have to go. Send him a message that you can't come."

"I can't do that."

"But it's dangerous outside the gates."

"I know."

"And why *that* gate? That's where the thieves and robbers and all kinds of wicked people dwell at night." The tears now slid down her cheeks.

"I know."

"Oh, Paulus. Why there?" She pressed her hand to his face.

"I can't answer that. I only know I have to go. It must be something important if he needs to meet me outside the gates." He covered her hand with his.

"Then God go with you, Paulus. I'll try not to worry, and I'll be praying for your safety." She leaned her head on his shoulder.

"Thank you, Eunice. I knew I could count on you." He held her face in his hands and kissed her forehead. "I'll need to leave soon to get through the gates before they close."

He stood, drawing her up beside him. She clung to him briefly, then stepped back and let him go. He gave her one last wave before he left the room.

He gathered his cloak and turban and left the house without drawing attention to his departure. He wanted to be as unobtrusive as possible.

He passed through busy city streets. Children played in the laneways, chasing each other with shouts of laughter. Mothers called children in from play, and dogs barked, adding an air of the ordinary to the scene. It was an ordinary day in the city, but not in his heart.

What did Marcus want?

Chapter Twenty-Six

Once he passed through the center of the city, the homes became less prosperous. The flimsy dwellings of the poor of Pergamum clustered together as if to share their poverty and unfortunate circumstances. The smells hanging in the hot breeze were unappetizing. Voices rose in argument from the alleyways.

Paulus bent his head and hurried by. He felt a deep sympathy for these people but knew lingering in the quarter was unsafe. As he drew closer to the north gate, the structures became more and more decrepit until they resembled discarded tents. Men in rags sprawled in front of their shelters, while others cooked over an open fire. Debris from their communal living littered the ground around them.

As he passed by one group, an unkempt man rose before him.

"What brings you here?" His tone was sharp and belligerent. He reached out to stop Paulus.

Paulus paused and glanced at the stranger. "I have business beyond here."

"You have no business here." The man gave him a shove that almost knocked him off his feet. He jeered at Paulus. "Go back where you came from, rich boy."

"I must continue." Paulus steadied himself and pulled his cloak closer around him.

"Yeah." A short, dark man carrying a large stick stepped forward. "Take yourself out of here. We don't want no one like yourself around here."

Two others shuffled toward them. Paulus tried to remain in control but knew he was in imminent danger. He tried to walk away from them, but the first man tripped him. Paulus fell heavily to the packed earth, the wind knocked out of him. One of them fell on him and began pummeling him with his fists.

"Enough!" a new voice cried. A large, impressive-looking man entered the space around them, striking out with powerful arms. A blow to the head of the one pounding Paulus was enough to knock the man out, allowing Paulus to rise to his feet.

He dusted himself off, wiping his hands together to remove the dirt. The others faded into the background until Paulus was alone with the giant.

"Be on your way. You're not welcome here." The giant folded his brawny arms over a bulging chest. His authoritative tone left no room for negotiation.

Paulus didn't need a second command. He turned and moved out of their reach without looking back. His back and shoulders felt raw from the beating, but he didn't stop. Once the north gates were in sight, he sighed but knew this episode was only beginning.

Many people were moving through the gates and entering the city. Few were leaving. Shepherd boys herded flocks of sheep and goats with the inevitable dogs. The raucous bleating and shouting jarred his ears; the animals pushed and shoved, trying to enter the gate all at once. Their bodies tumbled over each other as the push continued. The sight resembled a fast-moving stream heading toward him. He stepped out of the way just in time as the mass of animals reached him. They rumbled by in a heap of smelly hides and discordant outbursts.

At last the press of people entering dwindled to a trickle, and Paulus was able to resume his passage. He glided out through the gates as the sun was setting, painting the sky in soft shades of pink. Once through, he paused to consider his route to the destination mentioned in the note. As he continued, the gates clanged shut behind him, and the guards shouted from the wall.

There was no turning back.

It was only a short distance to the grove of trees Marcus had indicated. As he approached, he could see Marcus sitting beneath a large, pale tree.

Marcus stood as Paulus approached. There was no welcoming smile. Marcus looked frightened.

Marcus spoke when Paulus was near. "Thanks for coming."

"I never considered anything else." He eyed his brother warily.

"You always did have a streak of loyalty, didn't you?" Marcus spat to the side and wiped his mouth with the back of his hand.

"Marcus, believe me, I only have your best interests at heart." Paulus stepped closer.

"Yes, I believe that's true."

After a pause, Paulus studied his brother. "Why did you want to meet with me, and why here? We could have met anywhere in the city."

"What I have to say needs to be said where there is no chance of being overheard. I could think of no other place and no other way to do this." Marcus pointed to the ground. "Let's sit down and I'll tell you my story."

The brothers sat side by side. Paulus remained silent, letting Marcus gather his thoughts.

"I'm in deep trouble," Marcus said.

"Trouble?" Paulus asked, alarm in his voice.

"Oh yes, trouble." Marcus rubbed his hand over his eyes.

Paulus glanced at him. He couldn't distinguish his features in the darkness, but the outline of his face looked tense.

"I'm listening, Marcus. I may not be able to help, but I can certainly listen."

"That's why I asked you to come. I need someone to listen."

Marcus stood, facing away from him. Paulus stayed sitting, watching him. He knew Marcus would begin when he was ready. He sent up a quick prayer for guidance.

Marcus swung around and sat down again. "I've discovered a plot to assassinate the new governor."

Paulus gasped. "Are you sure, Marcus?"

"I'm sure. Some of the guards assigned to him have banded together in a conspiracy. Apparently they've had enough of his arrogance. The rumors say he is cruel and that some heads are already in jeopardy. I know from personal experience that he is brutal." He shook his hair back from his face.

"But how are you in danger?" Paulus reached out a hand to place on his arm but withdrew it at the last minute.

"I was caught while listening in on their conversation. I, of course, threatened to go to the governor. They, in turn, threatened me. If I go to the governor, they will kill me." He put his head in his hands.

Paulus tried to hide the shock in his voice. "What are you going to do?"

"I don't know. It really doesn't matter. I'm a dead man." His shoulders slumped and he sighed.

"Why do you say that?" Paulus looked intently at him, trying to determine what Marcus was feeling. This time he laid his hand on his arm.

"If I tell, they'll have me killed. If I don't tell, they'll believe I did, and the result will be the same. I know too much." He cupped his chin in his hands.

"What can I do to help you, Marcus?"

"I'm not sure. For now, I just needed you to listen."

The two men fell silent. The night sounds swirled around them. An animal cry sounded off in the distance. The wind soughed through the big tree, sending shivers through Paulus's body.

He waited for Marcus to continue, but nothing more was said. The events of the day and night began to take their toll on Paulus. His mind continued turning over scenes until he started to drift off. Light dreams slithered across his brain as his body relaxed against the rough texture of the tree trunk.

As consciousness began to return, he sat up abruptly. Marcus was gone. He called softly to him, then searched the area, but he was gone. What did it mean?

In front of a gate on the far side of the city, Marcus paced, awaiting the dawn. *I think he bought my story. Now for the next part of my plan!*

Chapter Twenty-Seven

"I don't like this, Paulus." Emin rubbed his hand over his head. "There are too many questions."

"But his life's in danger. I can't stand by and do nothing." Paulus wrung his hands together.

"I know how you must feel," David said, "but I agree with Emin. Something's not right."

Emin walked over to Paulus and put his hand on his shoulder. He leaned over and made eye contact.

"Paulus, you're an incredible man. The hand of the Lord is on you—I don't doubt that for a moment. I've watched you grow from the time Antipas sent you to us. I'm proud to call you friend."

"Thank you, Emin. You too, David. I don't know what I would do without your guidance. I'm not thinking clearly. He's my brother, and I want to see him be a part of us, but you're right. There are many questions." He shook his head sadly.

"Let's start at the beginning. Why did he leave you in the middle of the night, and where did he go?" David ticked off the points on his fingers.

Paulus shrugged. "That's been bothering me. I stayed awake the rest of the night, but no one came near. I would have heard him come back. Once dawn broke, I went to the gate right away, but he wasn't there. When the gates opened, I came in with the others waiting there and came directly here. There was no sign of Marcus anywhere."

"And that's only the first question," Emin said.

"Another thing that's bothering me"—David ticked off another point—"is his story. It doesn't have the ring of truth. If he had discovered a plot, why wouldn't he go to the governor right away? He's the chief temple guard. It would be his duty to report it. His life wouldn't be in danger because Magnus would have dealt with the conspirators immediately, and that would have been the end of it."

"I did think of that, too." Paulus rested his head in his hands. He was so tired from having sat on the ground most of the night that he was having trouble ordering his thoughts.

"So, if we all agree that his story is suspect, what was his purpose in telling you this?" Emin looked up at the ceiling, lines creasing his forehead.

"That's it," David said. "That's the most important question. We all know Marcus is not only clever but cunning. He has a purpose in this." He began to pace. "I think he may want your sympathy to soften you toward him, so you'll believe whatever he says."

Paulus lifted his hands in the air and asked in a searching voice, "But what about his profession for Christ?"

"It's all very confusing, I'll admit," David said. "How we respond to this could be very important in the days ahead for not only you but for Marcus and for the other converts." He put his arm around Paulus's shoulders.

Paulus searched David's face with his troubled eyes. "I certainly don't want to do anything to endanger the other believers. That's why we've kept this quiet for now. But I need to approach him with your blessing and with a plan in place. He may be unwilling to accept it, but as his brother, I need to offer." He put his hands over his face.

There was no sound in the room. From another part of the house drifted murmuring voices, servants quietly going about their duties.

Emin stood in front of Paulus and David. "What if we offer him sanctuary in one of our safe houses in the country? Maybe Hera's. We've used his place before when we needed to hide people. It would accomplish more than one thing; if his story is true, it would certainly give him safety. Hera is a strong follower, so Marcus could learn much from him. If his story isn't true, Hera is astute and would likely see the falsehood." Emin looked at the other two, his brows furrowed in a frown.

David was the first to speak. "That's a great idea, Emin. What do you think, Paulus?"

Paulus closed his eyes, deep in thought. He wanted this to work so badly. The ring of children's laughter filled the courtyard as he pondered the problem. They reminded him of less stressful days before Marcus had intruded into his life. Although he was happy his brother was interested in the Way, he had certainly complicated everything.

The other two were looking at him closely, waiting for his answer. He rose and approached the window. It opened onto the garden, where David's wife was talking with the gardener. The day seemed so peaceful. The aroma of warm olives ripening on the trees in the distant vineyard drifted in through the window. Life outside this window gave the aura of peace. But within his heart, all was turmoil.

He turned and faced the other two. With a shrug he said, "I think it's the only answer. We can't house him here in the city. It would be too dangerous for him and for any of the brethren. David, will you send someone to Hera's to ask?"

"Even better." David smiled for the first time. "I'm headed there tomorrow on business. I'll discuss the whole thing with Hera."

Paulus trudged along the dusty street in front of the great altar. It was quiet today: no sacrifices were being offered or pilgrims approaching the altar on bended knees. As usual, thoughts of Antipas flooded his mind as he passed along the familiar street. So many memories. Unexpectedly, he was transported to the day Antipas had participated in the annual ritual to become a man. His family had still been intact then; the troubles had not begun.

What had changed things? He had always felt safe and secure in his home until the day Antipas disappeared. His mother had been distraught, bringing down the wrath of his father on her head. His father had been so adamant that Antipas was no longer a member of their family. Everything had changed that day. He almost thought he could trace Marcus's hardness to that time. He seemed to side with their father and distance himself from his mother.

Why am I going over all that now? he asked himself with the shake of his head. *That's forgotten history.*

He forced himself back to the present, trying to focus on his surroundings. He entered the street behind the temple, which was abuzz with activity. Soldiers drilled in a grassy area at one end, while others readied their horses for a foray. The ring of the iron-shod hoofs resounded on the Roman pavement prevalent in this area of town. The large barracks stretched along one side of the street. The colorful tunics cloaking the soldiers livened up its gray exterior.

Commands were shouted above the snorting of the horses, the barking of barrack dogs, and the shouting of children who played a game of chase in front of the living quarters. Paulus had secured the scarf from his turban around the lower part of his face. He wanted to see Marcus but didn't want to risk being recognized. The fact that so many people milled about could mean danger for Marcus.

I should have sent a servant, he realized. He turned back and traveled along the same route by which he had come.

I don't think anyone recognized me or even noticed me in the melee. Maybe Decimus will take a message for me.

He turned his steps toward the marketplace. Its sounds reached his ears before his eyes encountered the sights. Hawkers plugged their goods in shrill voices. Cattle, sheep, and goats bellowed in protest, contesting with the vendors for attention. Due to the richness of the din around him, focusing on his errand was hard.

The press of people in the laneways was not conducive to quick movement, so he slowed his pace and began to enjoy the bustle. Fresh vegetables sat side by side with leather goods, spices, perfumes, and all sorts of marvelous things, both local and from the caravan trade. When he approached their stall, Juliana was shouting in an exchange with a customer.

An old man with a bent form lifted his rusty voice while bargaining with her. As the exchange continued, he shook a bent finger in her face. His ancient turban had lost most of its color and showed signs of fraying around the edges. He stuffed a stray piece of edge behind his ear as Paulus watched the two. Juliana was fully engaged with the man and didn't seem to be aware that Paulus was watching them. He knew that, because of her changed heart, she would have willingly given the goods to the old man, but his pride would have been injured, so she kept bargaining.

They finally came to an agreement. A pleased smile crossed the old man's face, and Paulus knew Juliana had done a good thing. He guessed the old man would be on his way, feeling he could still provide for his family.

Juliana looked up as Paulus approached. "Paulus, how pleasant to see you. What brings you to our stall today?"

"Greetings, Juliana. I would speak with Decimus if he is here."

"He's helping a customer load his cart and should be returning shortly. Why don't you wait beside the stall? There's a bench there in the shade."

"I'll do that. Thanks Juliana." He waved and walked around to the side.

Another customer arrived, drawing her attention away. Paulus sat on the bench and looked around. The wooden goods displayed in front of the stall had the redolent flavor of cool woods. They reminded him of the wooded area near his home, where he and his brothers had so often played as children.

Funny, how so many childhood memories are crowding my mind today.

He gazed around the market. Decimus was working his way through the crowd.

What a change in a man.

He smiled as he observed Decimus walk with a swagger in his step, head held high.

Decimus caught sight of him. "Paulus!" he shouted. He waved his arm and moved in his direction.

Paulus stood as he approached, smiling a welcome.

"Welcome, my friend," Decimus said while greeting him enthusiastically.

"Thank you, friend." Paulus greeted him with the traditional kiss of welcome on each cheek. "I would speak with you privately if it's convenient for you."

"Of course. You look troubled. Let's move behind the stall. We can talk undisturbed there." Decimus led the way, and the two were soon ensconced on a low ledge facing away from the market lanes.

"What is it, my friend? What troubles you?" Decimus laid his hand on Paulus's arm, studying his face.

"I appreciate your concern, Decimus. I have need of your help, but it must be kept private between us. You must not even share this with Juliana. I know I can trust her, but it's for her own protection. The fewer people who know about this, the less potential for harm."

"Paulus, you have my pledge. Juliana understands there are things that she will not know. She won't even question me."

"Thanks, Decimus. That makes the telling easier for me. I guess the best thing is to begin at the beginning. So what I ask of you is fraught with danger; for you, for Marcus, and for all of us."

Chapter Twenty-Eight

The final clang of the north gate closing was followed by shouts from the guards on the wall.

"All is well to the north." The guard standing on the wall to the left of the gate raised his hand over his head in a salute.

"All is well to the east." Another hand raised in salute.

"All is well to the west."

Under cover of the noise, a lone figure glided along the side of the alleyway facing the gate. He didn't want to be recognized, so he moved along slowly with head bent and glanced surreptitiously from side to side. He turned into the side lane and proceeded along a rough path until he reached a temporary shelter. A big man was waiting for him in front.

"I hope this meeting is necessary." The large man stood stiff and tall with arms folded. His rough tunic clung to his legs in the breeze. A heavy, unkempt beard bushed out from his jutting chin.

"I wouldn't be here if it wasn't necessary," the figure said, spitting on the ground.

"None of your haughty talk here," the giant, Izak, said. "If you have work for me to do, tell me and it will be done. Otherwise, I'd prefer not to see your ugly face, almighty Marcus." A mock bow followed.

"Shh, not so loud. And I thought we agreed no names." Marcus put his finger to his lips, drawing his brows tightly together.

"Names, names. Who cares? No one here cares anything about you, who think you run the universe. All we care about is living. If you pay us enough, we'll do your bidding." He flung his arms about wildly.

"You'll be well paid. That I can guarantee." Marcus stepped closer until he was almost nose to chin with Izak. He was beginning to sweat even though the day cooled as the sun set. "Maybe it was a mistake to come here." He needed to get the upper hand of this beast.

"Don't be so hasty in your talk. We'll do your dirty job. Where else could you get that kind of service?" Izak bent down until his eyes were level with Marcus's. His lips were curled in a snarl.

"Then we understand each other." Marcus leered at him.

"Money first, then talk." Izak stood back, folding his arms again in his tight stance.

Marcus withdrew a leather pouch from under his nondescript cloak. He handed it to Izak, who weighed it in his hands, then opened the drawstring. He poured out the coins, counted them, then dumped them back in the pouch, which quickly disappeared beneath the folds of his cloak.

"Now tell me what you want this time." He beckoned him to come closer.

Decimus shuffled along the side street which housed the barracks. A wind had blown in from the east, causing debris to scatter over the street. Puffs of dust rose before him, compelling him to pull the top of his cloak over his nose. He pressed on, leaning into the wind, looking neither left nor right.

Night was settling on the city, forming shadows in every crevice. Voices drifted from the living quarters, where housewives prepared the evening meal for husbands and children.

Just beyond the main barracks, Decimus turned into a side alley. He moved along the path until he reached a small outbuilding. Through the open door, a tall man bent over a low table, working on a piece of wood with a small saw. Decimus knocked on the casing, and the man looked up from his work.

The man called a friendly greeting. "Come in, whoever you are."

Decimus entered, pulling back his cloak to expose his face.

"Decimus, is it you?" The occupant jumped back from his table and moved toward Decimus.

"Yes, Aulus, it is." Decimus stepped farther into the room.

"What brings you out after dark? The roads aren't safe." Aulus greeted him with their traditional greeting, kissing both cheeks.

"I needed to speak to you. The matter is urgent and not one I wish to publicize." Decimus spoke softly but earnestly.

"Speak, my friend. You know I'll help you in any way I can." Aulus stretched out his hand to his friend.

"I seek Marcus," Decimus whispered in a halting voice.

"Marcus? You surely don't mean Marcus, the captain of the guards." At the mention of the name, Aulus put his hand over his mouth, eyes widening.

"The very same." Decimus nodded.

"But you know he's not here." Aulus opened his hands, palms up.

"Not here?" Decimus raised his eyebrows.

Aulus moved closer, lowering his voice. "He hasn't been seen for a couple of days. No one knows where he is. Some think he's out on business, but I'm not so sure. I've heard a few rumors about him."

"Rumors?" Decimus asked.

"Something about him being in trouble with Magnus, the governor. It's dangerous to be on the wrong side of Magnus." A slight shudder passed across his shoulders.

"Why is Magnus upset with him?" Decimus peered intently at Aulus.

A shrug accompanied his words. "No one seems to know. At least no one's talking."

Decimus leaned toward Aulus. "When he arrives back, could you get a message to me?"

"Sure, friend, I can do that. Can I still find you at your market stall?"

"I'll be there."

"Now, Decimus, you need to head on home before the night gets any later." Aulus fluttered his hand toward the door.

"Thanks, Aulus. I'll hope to hear from you soon." He gave a wave and turned back to the entrance. Decimus slipped out and groped his way back down the alley. His mind was reeling.

Where is Marcus? Something about this is not right, and I fear it bodes ill for us all.

Chapter Twenty-Nine

Juliana hummed to herself as she packed up her wares at the end of a long but productive day. How different she felt at day's end now than she had months ago. Christ in her life had made a dramatic difference to everything about her. People told her she even looked younger. She pushed her hair back with a smile as she thought about that.

She struggled to lift the last basket onto the old cart and sighed with relief when it was in place beside the others. She turned to check the area once more.

Something was wrong. The sound of someone crying drew her attention, but no one was in sight. Her heart beat faster as she cautiously moved in the direction of the sound.

The other side of the stall. Who could be there?

Her hand flew toward her mouth and covered it.

She paused, listened again, then inched to the end of the stall. Leaning against the flimsy wall, she drew in a deep breath. Warily she edged her head around the wall.

A young woman crouched in the dirt, hands over her face. She wept mournfully.

Instantly compassion filled Juliana's heart. She crossed the distance between them and knelt beside the girl. "Is there any way I can help you?" She touched the girl's shoulder.

The young woman didn't answer but only kept weeping and buried her face deeper into her hands. Her shoulders now shook from the force of her sobbing. Juliana observed the slim shoulders and bright color of the robe before speaking again.

"Are you in some kind of trouble? I'd like to help." She leaned in closer, trying to see her better.

The crying stopped. The young woman raised her tear-streaked face to look at Juliana. "If only you could." She returned her face to her hands.

Juliana laid a hand on her arm. "I'm not sure what I can do for you, but I can listen, and maybe together we can find a solution to your problem."

"I can't talk about it," came the muffled reply.

Juliana shook her head in bewilderment.

What should I do next?

She sent up a quick prayer for guidance. She asked the girl, "Do you live near here?"

"Live?" She moaned. "I can't ever go home."

"Then you're coming home with me." Juliana sat back on her heels, surprising herself with her own boldness.

The girl was silent. Slowly she raised her face again, this time looking into Juliana's eyes. She wiped her tears with the back of her hand, pushing her hair behind her ears. The hood of her robe had fallen back, exposing her luxuriant dark hair. Deep, wounded eyes looked solemnly at her.

"Would you really do that for me?" she asked.

"Not only would I do it. I insist." Juliana held out her hand.

"Then I'll come." She nodded vigorously so her curls shook, shimmering dark and beautiful.

Juliana helped her rise to her feet. The girl was trembling.

"What is your name, dear?" She put her arm around her shoulder.

"Octavia." The girl clasped her hands in front of her tunic.

"And I'm Juliana. My cart is just behind the stall. Let's get you settled. My husband will be back soon, and we'll be on our way." She touched Octavia's shoulder, indicating the direction of the cart.

Octavia stopped abruptly. "Husband? Oh, I can't come then." Her face fell and she lowered her head.

Juliana experienced a moment of insight unusual for her. "You have no need to fear my husband. He is the most tender of men and would never betray a confidence. Come, we waste time."

Octavia nodded and moved forward again with Juliana. When they rounded the corner of the stall, Decimus was already at the cart. He looked startled at first but soon covered the expression in a smile of welcome.

"Who have we here, wife?" he asked in his gentle voice.

"This is Octavia, and she is coming home with us." She nodded, letting him know there was no discussion.

He bowed to Octavia. "It's a pleasure to meet you. In the cart, both of you, and we'll soon be off."

When they arrived at their humble dwelling, Octavia glanced around her. It was impossible for Juliana to tell what she was thinking. Octavia went in with them and was quickly made comfortable in a small but tidy room.

"I'll bring you some warm water and clean towels," Juliana said. "You can refresh yourself and rest a bit while I prepare the evening meal. We'll talk once you're rested and we've eaten." She bustled around the room, adjusting this and that, smoothing imaginary wrinkles from the blanket on the bed.

Octavia smiled for the first time since Juliana found her. "Thank you, Juliana. You'll never know how much this means to me." Her lips trembled as she watched Juliana.

"I'm just happy I found you." Juliana gave one last pull on the blanket and left the room.

Later, the meal over, Decimus excused himself to work in his shed, while Juliana made Octavia feel comfortable around their table. "Do you feel you can talk now?" she asked.

"Are you sure you want to hear all this?" Octavia's head was lowered, but she looked up with wide eyes.

"I'm very sure. Just tell me anything you want." Juliana settled back in her chair.

"It's a very long story, but I would be so happy to share it with someone. I've carried the burden too long myself." Her hands were restless in her lap, twisting around each other.

"I'll just be quiet and listen."

"When I was a little girl, I always wanted to come to the big city and be someone important, to live an exciting life. But we were poor country farmers, so the chances of that happening were almost nonexistent." She paused, looking to Juliana as though for support. Juliana just nodded at her. "As I grew, I realized this and became resigned to the fact that I would probably marry a local farmer and raise a number of children." She shook her head and adjusted her robe around her.

"But one day, all that changed. I was walking along the main road close to our property when I heard a horse approach. As the horse drew closer, I could tell it was going to stop by me. I looked up to see a magnificent man riding a regal horse. Not one of our poor farm horses. The man was dressed in a rich riding outfit that almost made my eyes pop out. I was a young, impressionable girl, and I had never seen anyone like this." She put her hands over her heart. "He smiled at me as he reigned in his horse."

Octavia's eyes had a faraway look, almost as if she'd been transported back to that country road. Her body gave a little shake before she continued.

"'Hello beautiful maiden,' fell softly from his lips.

"'Greetings, sir,' I replied.

"'I seem to be lost. I was on my way to Albina. Do you happen to know the way?'

"'I'm not sure, master, but my father would know.'" She looked at Juliana, who stared at her intently. Juliana smiled at her, fluttering her hand for her to continue.

She took a deep breath, her shoulders relaxing.

"'I'd rather talk to you.' He had such a smooth voice. I lowered my eyes from his intense stare. I'd never experienced this type of conversation before.

"'What is your name?' he asked me, still in his silky voice.

"'Octavia, master.' I didn't yet know that I shouldn't be talking to a strange man so freely.

"'Octavia,' he said, 'a beautiful name for a beautiful maiden.'"

She put her hands over her face. "I was embarrassed, yet pleased. No one had ever spoken to me that way before.

"He slid from his horse and came closer. I was fascinated and my feet wouldn't move away from him. I knew he was going to kiss me and I couldn't stop him. He leaned very close to me. I was captivated. His nearness was overwhelming. I was aware of his startling eyes, his manly perfume, his height towering over me, his warm breath on my face. He kept leaning closer but at the last moment straightened and rubbed his hand over his chin."

"'I think I would like to speak with your father after all,' he said.

"I could see my father in the distance along with two of my brothers. He looked up as he heard us approach. I could see the startled look in his eyes as he took in my companion.

"'Father, this man would speak with you,' I said. 'He's lost his way and needs direction.'

"'I would speak with you alone,' he said to my father.

"'Children, leave us,' my father said.

"My emotions were swirling inside me as I climbed the ladder to the loft where I slept. He didn't even say good-bye, was all I could think.

"I sat beneath the small window above my pallet. Shock registered slowly. The stranger and my father were walking back to the house together.

"They entered from the yard, and I could hear them talking to my mother.

"'I am the head of this house and what I say is what we abide by.' I had never heard my father speak to my mother that way before.

"Much to my surprise, I was shortly called to the main area of the house. When I arrived, the stranger had vanished, and I was facing a teary-eyed mother and a stern father.

"'Octavia, the nobleman you brought to see me requests your hand in marriage.'

"I couldn't have been more surprised if he had asked me to sacrifice myself in the flames. Something was not right. Why would a nobleman want me for his wife?

"'You will gather your things together as he wishes to leave within the hour.'

"At this, my mother completely broke down. She made such a fuss, my father ordered her from the room."

Octavia paused at this point. Juliana reached over and held her hand. "Take your time. I'm not in any hurry," she said in a soothing voice.

"Yes, I'll go on. That was the last time I ever saw my mother." She was finally able to gasp out the words.

Juliana made sympathetic sounds and patted her hand.

"My father's words were law to my brothers and me, so it never occurred to me to contest his decision. I climbed the ladder again and was ready to leave in a very short time. My father was waiting for me at the foot of the ladder and bade me farewell. Not so much as an embrace or a word of encouragement.

"I walked out into the sunshine, which now felt like dark clouds, and looked toward the incredible man before me. In the midst of my sorrow was a certain measure of excitement and anticipation. He was gorgeous.

"'I don't even know your name,' I said haltingly.

"'How negligent of me,' he replied with that smile of his. 'It's Marcus. I'm one of the temple guards.'"

Juliana gasped softly but made no comment.

"Marcus. I let the name roll around in my mind. Marcus. A nice enough name. I mounted the horse with hope in my heart. Were my childhood dreams about to come true?

"We rode hard until the gates of Pergamum came into view. As we entered the city, several men called to him, some laughing and pointing at me. It was very uncomfortable. After the first few stares, I kept my eyes lowered.

"We reached his lodgings and entered the spacious rooms. I had never seen so much splendor. He led me to a room that he said would be mine. I was dazzled by everything.

"He left me to refresh myself after our journey. Once I was ready, I wandered from my room along the hallway outside my door. I could hear voices coming from the last room on the right. I walked slowly toward the sounds, expecting to meet some of his family. Imagine my surprise when I encountered several girls around my age, all scantily clad and giggling in a silly manner.

"I felt shock rip through my body. Who were these girls? I entered the room and asked them outright. This only brought on more tittering, and strange looks passed between them. One of them stood before me, hands on hips, and demanded to know who I was.

"'I'm Octavia, and I will soon be Marcus's wife.' Now they laughed uproariously. Once they had spent their laughter, the leader, who had spoken to me first, laughed and asked me if that is what he told me.

"'Yes, of course it is,' I said. 'We're to be married.'

"'Sure you are, dear, and so are we all,' she replied to me. 'That's what he told each one of us. The sooner you realize he's a liar—albeit a good-looking and rich liar but still a liar—the happier you'll be.'

"I was so naïve. I asked them why we were all there if he didn't intend to marry at least one of us. They again shared that look of knowing, which I was to learn later that night exactly what it meant.

"I left them in a huff and strode back to my room. What did it all mean? Oh if only I could have gone on forever not knowing. But, later that night, when I had settled into the soft mattress and fallen asleep, Marcus arrived. I soon realized he had been drinking and was undoubtedly drunk. He staggered into my room, turning the air frigid with his curses. I don't want to recall the events of the next two hours. Suffice it to say, he is a cruel, vulgar, evil man."

"But you're here with me now. How did you get away?" Juliana was so absorbed in the story that she hadn't even heard her husband come in and go to his bed. It was very late, but it seemed important to let Octavia tell her the whole story, uninterrupted.

"Get away? I did the unthinkable in his eyes. I carry his child."

The room fell silent as this revelation fell between them.

"He wants me to visit the sorceress who lives beneath one of the gates," Octavia said. "I have refused, and he has threatened to drag me there personally or have me killed. I didn't know what to do, but then he left town for a few days and I ran. When I reached the marketplace, I was exhausted, both physically and emotionally. Once I arrived there, I didn't know what to do next, so I sank down beside your booth and cried. And now, here I am." She opened her arms and gestured toward herself.

The two women sat in silence. Juliana processed what she had just heard. Ideas flashed through her mind, to be discarded one after the other. Octavia had rested her head and arms on the low table, where they were sitting. Juliana rose from her seat and slid down beside Octavia. She opened her arms and engulfed her in a compassionate embrace.

"Octavia, look at me," she said and released her. The girl raised her head. "I would really like you to stay with me."

"Oh, but I couldn't impose on you like that. I'll think of something. It's been so good just to be able to share all this with someone."

"Octavia, I'm serious. You'd be doing me a favor." She brushed some damp hair from Octavia's face. "Someday I'd like to tell you my story. I have so longed for a child, but God has not granted one to me. If you would consider staying with me for now, you would bring great joy to my heart. Please say you will."

Octavia turned into her embrace and hugged her tightly. "Nothing would make me happier than to stay with you. I feel so comfortable and at home here. But what about your husband? He won't be pleased."

As they pulled apart, Juliana smiled at her. "You have no idea how happy he will be. If it makes me happy, it makes him happy. You'll see. He'll be as delighted as I am."

"But you could be in danger from Marcus."

"Aren't we always in danger from the captain of the guards? I'll not let him come between what I want and what makes me happy. Besides, he would never suspect you of being here. You'll be safe from him for a long time." Juliana nodded emphatically. "Let's get you settled for the night. I have sleepwear you can use, and tomorrow we'll see about getting you more to wear."

"Thank you, Juliana. This is the best thing that has ever happened to me. I can't go back home. My father can never know that I was not married to Marcus. It would bring shame on the family. I am so grateful for your goodness and kindness." She hugged her again.

Later, Juliana crept into bed beside her husband. He stirred.

"You're late tonight, my love," he whispered.

"Yes, Octavia had much to share." She slid down in the bed, getting comfortable.

"What's her story anyway?"

"I've invited her to stay with us as long as she wants. She's had a hard time."

"What kind of a hard time?" He sounded groggy.

"Well, I can't give you all the details tonight, but she's been living with Marcus and now is carrying his baby and—"

"Marcus?" Decimus sat straight up. "Get her out of the house. She can't stay here. All our lives are in danger!"

Chapter Thirty

Juliana sat staring at her husband, unable to find the words to reply.

"I can't tell you why, Juliana, but you must get her out of our home." Decimus gathered the blankets around him and stared at his wife.

"But Decimus, I can't. I've promised her." She sat beside him, wiping tears from her eyes.

He reached an arm around her, pulling her close. "Juliana, why don't you tell me more of her story? I can see you are bent on having her here. I hate to refuse you anything. Maybe we can come to some compromise."

"Then I'll tell you everything. You need to know why she's here. Then I think you'll see why she must stay." She blew her nose, swallowed, and took a deep breath.

When Juliana finished the tale, Decimus looked very serious and thoughtful. He got up from the bed and went to the small window. Moonlight illuminated his face as he gazed into the heavens. He turned and watched Juliana, still sitting in their bed.

"Juliana, I can see she needs us. If we keep her here, we will all be in great danger, but I can't see how we can turn her away. If you're willing to take the risk and if she's willing, then I'm willing to put our lives on the line to protect her. I can now see it's the right thing to do." He walked back to her, leaned over, and rubbed her back.

"Oh, thank you, Decimus. I know it's dangerous. But since we have Christ in our hearts, I long to make a difference for Him and in other people's lives. I believe God sent her to us, and He'll protect us as we conceal her." She looked up at him, smiling through her tears.

"Then we're agreed," Decimus said. "She'll need to stay close to home and not draw attention to herself. Even the neighbors could turn us in."

"I know, Decimus, but this is the right thing to do. I just know it is." She squeezed his arm.

"Then let's get some sleep before the night is totally gone."

"Where is Marcus?" Magnus bellowed.

"He hasn't been seen for a week, my lord." The soldier snapped to attention, keeping his back straight.

Magnus sat forward on his seat and fixed his sharp gaze on the soldier. The words came out like sharp knives hitting metal. "And why haven't I been notified sooner?"

The guard threw his shoulders back and lifted his chin. "We thought he would have returned by now." His lip curled slightly as Magnus looked away.

"We thought, we thought!" Magnus pounded the arm of the chair, where he'd been reclining but was now almost coming off the seat. "You are not paid to think." The words shattered like pottery before them.

"Yes, my lord. I agree." The soldier bowed his head slightly.

"Oh, you agree, do you? My, my, how that makes me feel better." He sat back in his seat while a red flush climbed his neck and face.

The guard remained silent and still.

"Speak, slave. And just how do you plan to find him?" He flapped his hand in the soldier's face.

"My lord, there is a contingent being formed to look for him even as we speak." The soldier looked up into the brutal face of Magnus. He had turned purple in his rage. Spit dripped from his twisted lips.

"Then you'd better go and join them if you value your worthless life," came the rejoinder.

The soldier wasted no time in leaving the presence of the governor. He rushed past the waiting servants in the hall outside the governor's anteroom, leaving them staring at his back. As he gained the pavement outside the building, he breathed deeply, mounted his horse, and rode off for the military stables attached to the barracks.

If we don't find Marcus, we'll all be rotting in prisons in Rome, he thought.

Decimus had reported to Paulus his unsuccessful attempt to find Marcus. No one had seen him for several days. Paulus began to believe that something must have happened to him. He sought David and Emin for advice.

David walked the length of the room, hands behind his back. "I think we need to be on the alert. He may be in hiding. If his conversion is real, he's in danger. If it isn't, then all of the converts are in peril. I don't think we can take a chance on this."

Emin lent his voice to the discussion. He was seated to one side of the room and watched David pace. "I agree."

Others had gathered with them on David's invitation, eight men gathered on couches at David's house. The room was tastefully and comfortably decorated. Miriam's touch was evident. It exuded a peaceful atmosphere, which had no effect on the guests today.

Mattias looked grave as he turned to Paulus. "Paulus, I trusted Antipas with all my heart, and when he died, I shifted the trust to you. I want to hear what you have to say. You know him better than all of us, even better than Antipas."

"Yes, yes," several of the others agreed. "Tell us what you think, Paulus."

Paulus lifted his body from the couch. It felt so heavy today, just like his heart. "Friends, I'll be as honest with you as I can possibly be. The church is at stake as well as some of our lives. I owe you my innermost thoughts on this."

He rubbed his hands together and tapped his chin. "Marcus has been trouble since we were children. One of his favorite pastimes was torturing small animals and insects. It used to make me sick to watch him, but once Antipas was out of our home, I had no one else." He smiled sadly. "He used to make me watch and even participate in his cruelty. Our father was always cruel, and Marcus wanted to be just like him."

The others riveted their gazes on Paulus as he spoke. Silence filled the room except for Paulus's words.

"As he grew older, his passion to hurt grew to include servants and what he considered lower-class people. It was not such a big leap to be part of the temple guard and to rise to the top. I saw him involved in terrible incidents where he displayed a total lack of feeling for another human being. There's no question of his lack of character and humanity." He walked to the window and looked out, unseeing. He turned back to the men.

"When he approached me, showing interest in becoming a Christian, I was overjoyed. I wanted it to be true more than anything. But subsequent events have caused me to gravely question his conversion. Paul has said we'll recognize other believers by their actions and by their love. I have seen nothing in Marcus to indicate a change of heart." He rested his hand over his own heart.

"It pains me to say this," he continued, "but I think we need to proceed on the assumption that he is not a believer and therefore a threat to each of us and our families." He clamped his lips tightly, pain filling his heart.

Emin spoke up. "Do you think he is working with anyone else?"

"Marcus is quite capable of working on his own, but I think we have to assume that he's involved in some sort of plot." Paulus turned to Emin and shook his head.

One of the others said, "So, Decimus is trying to locate him. Is that correct?"

"Yes," Paulus said. "He's been in contact with one of the metal workers at the barracks. Someone he knows and trusts. He'll get in touch with Decimus if Marcus appears."

A new convert rose to his feet to ask his question. "Can we trust Decimus?"

"I'd trust him with my life," David said. Emin and Paulus nodded in agreement.

"The reason we've called all of you together is to discuss this and to get your input on how we proceed from here." David included each man as his eyes scanned the room.

A lengthy discussion ensued. At the end, they all agreed they couldn't do much but watch and pray. The converts numbered too many to go into hiding, and home churches were too numerous to consider. God would have to protect them or not as He saw fit.

They decided that Paulus would keep them updated on any information that came into his hands. He still had some influence in the city and would make discreet inquiries, as well as keep in close contact with Decimus.

As they dispersed, Paulus spoke one last time. "Prayer is our only hope. We're in God's hands. Whether He wishes us to live or die, it's His choosing."

Chapter Thirty-One

Izak huddled under the edge of the wall beside the north gate, avoiding as much of the rain as possible. The rain had started several minutes ago and showed no signs of stopping. His thin cloak was soaked through, and his stringy hair was matted and soggy.

"Marcus will pay for this," he growled to himself. "I'd at least be out of the wet if it wasn't for him and his dirty work. Where are they?" He drew the cloak tighter around him, shivering as he did so.

Two forms materialized out of the mist to his left. He watched them furtively as they approached. As they neared him, they slowed their pace.

Without looking at him, the larger one muttered, "Zeus wants revenge."

Izak moved out from the wall and fell in beside them. They walked in silence until they neared the river. Slipping under the bridge, where many of the homeless had their dwellings, they moved on until they had passed the decrepit hovels and were on the bank of the darkly flowing river.

"It's about time you showed up." Izak shook his fist in their faces.

Jamus stepped back, lifting his hand before his face. "We had things to do to prepare for our meeting."

"When I send for you, nothing is more important." Izak leaned in closer until he was nose to nose with him. He drew his brows together and ground his teeth. "Do you understand?"

"Oh yes, lord and master, I should have been here on time." Jamus backed up and gave a stiff, exaggerated bow.

The caustic words bit deeply into Izak's brain, making him promise himself that Jamus would soon outlive his usefulness.

Izak swept the words away with his hand. "Enough of that. I have important things to discuss with you. It will be worth your while to listen, and listen carefully."

Jamus and Gallus drew closer to Izak. He beckoned them farther along the bank until they came to a shallow cave partly hidden by low bushes.

"We'll enter here to talk." Izak nodded to them to enter.

Once the three were inside, they huddled along the wet wall of the cave. It was barely large enough for one, so the three were toe to toe when they squatted down together in the damp dirt. It had been dark outside, but here the blackness could almost be felt. It was thick and potent, with the moldy smell of rotting roots and other things better left unthought.

Something rustled in the far corner, causing Gallus to jump.

"Perhaps this is too taxing an assignment for you." Izak smiled his evil smile, unseen in the blackness.

"I'm fine," Gallus said. "Just changing my position."

"No more now, only listening," Izak said in a rough, commanding voice. He shifted his position so he could feel their breath on his face.

"I've had a visitor this week that moves in high places." He paused to let that piece of information sink in. "He has a sordid task that needs our expertise. Yes, there is danger involved, but the rewards exceed anything you can imagine." He jabbed at them with his finger, causing Gallus to jump again.

"I like the sound of that. We're in." Jamus said.

"Not so fast, my mangy friend," Izak said. "You must first hear the task, and then I must decide if you're the ones for the job." He spat between them.

Gallus put his hand over his mouth. "I don't have to listen to this kind of talk." He rose to his feet or got as close to standing as he could in the cramped quarters.

"Sit down, fool." Jamus ordered him, pulling on his damp cloak. He turned him back in Izak's direction. "Tell us more. We're interested. If we can fit it in our schedule, we may consider it."

Izak really laughed this time. His eyes were adjusting to the darkness, and he could now see the whites of their eyes. He was sure he could see the greed shining in Jamus's gaze. He considered whether he really needed them but concluded it wasn't a one-man job. Characters like Jamus and Gallus were hard to find. He'd have to be content with their mental weaknesses.

"Let me outline the mission," Izak said in a superior tone. He would be the boss regardless of their attempts to be in charge.

Three heads remained together for many minutes. Sometimes hoots of laughter could be heard, other times cries of protest as the plan unfolded.

"Do you think you can complete this assignment?" Izak gave each one a push on the chest.

"We'll do it." Jamus pushed back.

Two forms slipped from the dank cave into the sodden night and disappeared along the river bank. Their departure was silent, with only a promise to meet again next week to compare progress.

Izak sat alone a long time. From the mouth of the cave he watched the rain hit the river, sending little splashes of water skyward. A ghastly night for a ghastly deed, he decided.

"I wouldn't want to be a member of that pagan cult for any mythical promise," he said to himself. "After tonight, the Christians will soon be history."

He eased his way out of the cave and stretched leisurely into the wet sky before turning his face toward his shelter. He gave one mighty cheer, breaking the night air with his triumphant cry.

Chapter Thirty-Two

As the days moved on, Paulus realized he must talk with Eunice about the events surrounding Marcus. He had been trying to spare her from the threatening details, but the city was rife with rumors, and it was only a matter of time before they reached her ears. His mother, too, needed to be aware of circumstances that could affect both of her remaining sons.

As he pondered how best to approach the subject with the ladies, the decision was rudely and abruptly taken out of his hands.

Evening was approaching as he neared the house. After several days of clouds and rain, the sun had broken through earlier, bathing the earth in a silvery glow. The trees shimmered in their wet attire, shaking their leaves to dislodge showers of crystal granules. Puddles along the roadside flashed back the brilliance of the sun, blinding the eye but warming the heart.

Paulus wished this feeling of content could remain with him forever, but he knew it was an illusion. This lull in the affair was only temporary. He knew it had to break soon. As his home came into view, the sense of peace continued until he entered the front gate.

The front door flew open, and one of the servants rushed out to meet him.

"Master, master, come quickly. Something terrible has happened." He turned and fled back into the house without another word to Paulus.

Paulus broke into a run and entered the house right behind him. Distant crying and wailing beckoned him. He hurried through the rooms to where he would find Eunice.

He arrived at the door and looked into the room. She lay prostrate on the floor, beating her fists on the carpet. Paulina knelt beside her, grief evident on her face.

"What's wrong?" Paulus shouted as he neared them. "What's happened?"

He leaned over and lifted Eunice to her feet. "You must tell me what has happened."

Eunice raised red, swollen eyes to his face. She appeared to be in shock and seemed hardly aware of his presence.

"Eunice, tell me."

"They've taken Helena," she whispered through her tears, then went limp in his arms.

Ekrem worked at the back of the temple. The light filtering in from the slightly parted curtain over the door was weak and uncertain. The small room held no window and depended on the little light that came from the larger room beyond or from lamps. Nevertheless, he studied a scroll and muttered to himself. As he continued to ponder the document, the curtain moved slightly, and a figure materialized in front of him, causing him to drop the scroll.

"Where have you come from?" He thrust his hands in front of him, his mouth falling open.

The figure put a finger to his lips and closed the curtain. Then he turned and scowled at the priest.

"Where I come and where I go is *my* business." A dark cloak was slung over his shoulders, and a darker turban covered his head. The scarf from the turban was wound around his neck.

"For someone with a price on his head, you are certainly arrogant." Ekrem sat back and studied his visitor.

"Oh, so now I have a price on my head, do I? I'm amazed at how important I've become." He pushed the scarf down from his chin.

"Marcus—"

"No names." Marcus thrust a finger to his lips again and drew his brows together.

"So, no names, is it? Well, you certainly are a bold one; I'll say that for you."

"I'd prefer it if you didn't say anything."

"Then you'll not find out what I know about the price on your head." Ekrem folded his arms across his chest, pushed his shoulders back in defiance, and glared at Marcus.

He had a point, Marcus conceded. He stared thoughtfully at the priest. Disdain showed on his face, which he quickly concealed. He needed the priest for the next part of his plan. It would never do to provoke him at this point.

He swallowed his irritation and actually managed a smile. "My apologies, Ekrem. I do want to hear what you have to say, and then I want to tell you where we are with the plan." Marcus shrugged out of the cloak and hung it over his arm.

Marcus's apology seemed to mollify Ekrem, and he appeared ready to talk. "Magnus has his spies out looking for you. I'm not sure how you managed to get here without attracting their attention." He leaned forward and searched Marcus's face.

A shrug of the shoulder accompanied the words. "I have my ways."

"Well, however you did it, I'm glad you're here. The city is rife with rumors. It's being said that you have been assassinated or are in prison or have escaped the country and are on the run from the governor. But I see all the rumors are false." Ekrem nodded with a small smile slanting his lips. "Where have you been?"

"Let's just say I never divulge my secrets. I may need to use the same ploys again. I'm here, and that's all that matters at the moment." Marcus folded his arms and lifted his chin. "I have much to report and then a request." He sat down across from Ekrem.

He proceeded to explain his meeting with Izak, who remained nameless, and the implications of their meeting. Ekrem shook his head in agreement throughout the narration, smiling at some of the points. Toward the end, he lifted his head and stared hard at Marcus, while his jaw dropped.

Silence replaced talk as the two pondered the ramifications of what had just been said. Ekrem rolled up the scroll and secured it almost as though he needed something to do with his hands. Sounds drifted in from the room beyond where they sat, bringing a sense of the normal back into the room. Marcus leaned forward, hands on his knees.

"Ekrem, I need you to hide me for a few days, then get me out of the city."

"But . . . that's not possible." His eyes grew large as he looked at Marcus. "I would be risking my life."

"And I'm not putting my life on the line? If I remember correctly, it was *your* idea that got us all into this in the first place." Marcus leaned over until his face was close to Ekrem's. "Has our plan changed? Do we now want these infidels to overrun our city?"

"No, no, of course not. It's just that I don't see how I can possibly do what you ask." Ekrem fluttered his hand in front of Marcus's face.

"You must." And Marcus said no more.

Ekrem sat with furrowed brow for several minutes. He removed a cloth from under his tunic and wiped his face repeatedly. He finally grimaced and looked up at Marcus, who remained perfectly still.

"I can see only one way to hide you," he whispered, "until I can work out a way to carry out the rest of your request. You will have to be housed with the dead."

"That's appropriate." Marcus chortled. "I'm numbered with them already."

Ekrem did not speak but rose from his chair. He slid his finger along the curtain edge, moving it enough to see the room beyond. He let the curtain slip back into place before facing Marcus again.

"Wait here until I'm sure there is no one along the route we must take. It's the hour for sacrifice, so most of the temple priests and visitors will be near the altar."

He vanished through the curtain, leaving Marcus to sit alone, frowning now that he no longer had an audience. He felt that his life was out of his control; it was a place where he didn't like it to be.

Once we've rid the city of the cult, I can resume my life again. Everything was going well until Antipas appeared on the scene. My father was right; he was nothing but trouble.

Ekrem glided into the room again, cutting short his reverie. "Come with me, but don't speak or make eye contact with anyone we should happen to meet."

Marcus rose and followed him through the curtain. The larger room was empty and quite dim. The afternoon had faded into dusk, which threw deep shadows among the statues of Zeus and the other gods. Only the golden face of the emperor still gleamed from a tiny ray of light shining full on it. Marcus observed all this as he padded softly after the priest.

They entered an unfamiliar back hallway. Marcus's temple dealings as a guard had mainly been limited to the outer areas, where the local people and visitors swelled the halls and rooms. This area was reserved for the priests alone.

He ducked under a low archway leading around a turn and away from the main corridor. Ekrem pushed back a creaky door to reveal a rough stairway descending into the depths of the earth.

As Marcus put his foot on the top step, a rancid odor assailed his nostrils. As they descended, the scent only intensified. He knew it was the smell of death.

What fate awaited him below the temple grounds?

Chapter Thirty-Three

Feet pounded the packed earth as Paulus's servants chased the man who had lifted Helena from her play in the garden. Fortunately, Marina had screamed frantically, bringing Saul and Leonius immediately. She pointed to where the intruder had escaped, carrying Helena.

Saul fell behind, but Leonius had youth on his side and was determined not to stop until he had Helena in his arms. Her shrieks pierced the air, spurring them on to the chase.

The kidnapper made his first mistake by taking a right turn at the end of the garden.

This led to a wide-open meadow, where they could easily see him. A turn to the left would have eventually led him into the forest, where they might never have caught him.

His second mistake came when he veered off the hard path and into the sandy soil along the side. He slipped and nearly fell, giving Leonius an advantage.

Leonius was on him almost immediately. He jumped on his back, but a twist of the powerful shoulders threw him off. Leonius jumped again but missed.

The scoundrel kept running but was definitely slowing.

Saul now caught up with Leonius, and the two jumped at him. This time they knocked him off balance, and Leonius was able to grab Helena, who was whimpering pitifully by now. He quickly handed her to Saul and continued his chase of the escaping abductor.

Without the encumbrance of Helena, he sped off on powerful legs and soon left Leonius panting behind him. After another feeble attempt, Leonius stopped the chase.

He bent over at the waist and held his aching sides. A muscle in his leg twitched and cramped.

I can't catch him. He's too fast for me. But at least we have Helena.

He turned back to rejoin Saul and Helena.

"You're safe now, darling," Saul said to her. "We're going to take you back home now."

"I'll carry her, Saul," Leonius said. "You must be spent by now." He reached for the little girl, who came willingly.

"I'm not as young as I used to be—that's for certain. But I'm grateful we could get her back. Let's go. Her mother will be beside herself with worry." Saul turned back toward the house.

Paulus paced the length of his room and back. This had to be the work of Marcus. But why take Helena? She was his niece.

He stopped in his tracks as thoughts rushed through his mind.

That's it! Helena belongs to both Antipas and me. He could get back at both of us at the same time. I'm sure he thinks we abandoned him, especially me.

He rubbed his hands through his hair.

I must talk to Mother and Eunice. They need to know the danger we face.

He broke the news to them as gently as possible, but there was no hiding the awful threat that hung over their heads.

"But where is Marcus?" Eunice's hand had covered her mouth through most of Paulus's talk.

"No one has seen him for several days," Paulus said. "I have Decimus looking for him, but rumor in the city claims that Magnus as well as others are also looking for him. He has completely disappeared." He put his head in his hands.

"Do you think he really gave his heart to the Lord?" Paulina said at last through a veil of tears.

Paulus leaned over her and gave her a warm embrace. "Oh Mother, how I would love to say yes, but I've come to believe like the other church leaders that it wasn't real. He's up to something."

"He's my firstborn son. I had such high hopes for him. But it wasn't long before I saw the cruel streak coming. I tried to quell it, but it was too strong, and it was encouraged by your father. It fell in with his plans for Marcus." Paulina sighed and shook her head, rubbing her hand over her face.

Paulus grabbed her hand. "Mother, it's not your fault. We can only pray that Marcus will come to know our Lord. It's not too late for him yet."

Eunice looked at Paulus, eyes wide with fear. "Do you think he had anything to do with Helena being taken?"

"Unfortunately, I believe he may have. We're in danger; don't ever forget that for a moment. I don't want to alarm either of you, but you must know the truth of our situation."

Both women nodded their agreement.

"Neither of the children is to be outside without at least one of the male servants nearby," he said. "Both of you must remain on the property for the present. If you must go out, I need to be with you." Paulus watched each of them carefully.

"But what about you?" Eunice asked. "Won't you still have to move around the city?"

He nodded. "Yes, of course."

"But won't you be in danger, too?" Eunice shifted in her seat to face him directly. She put her hand on his arm.

"Yes, but no more danger than Helena was right in our own back garden. We'll need to keep alert wherever we are." He rubbed the back of her hand.

Eunice sat up straighter. "Then I'm going to be brave. When Antipas was taken, at first I thought I couldn't handle it, but he showed me that *I* couldn't, but that God could. And He did. I'm going to trust Him the same way now as I did then." Eunice gave him a dazzling smile.

"Thank you, Eunice. You're making this whole situation much more bearable for all of us." He bent and placed a soft kiss on her forehead.

"Then, if Eunice is going to be brave, so am I," Paulina said. "You don't need your mother to deal with as well as your brother. I can only commit Marcus to the Lord, and I've already committed you and Eunice to Him. If this can be overcome, we'll do it." She nodded emphatically.

Paulus smiled at the two women in his life, so different—from different backgrounds—but so united in their love for him and his heavenly Father.

When they went to their rooms, Eunice wrapped her arms around him. "I'm so much happier and more at peace now that we've talked. We can face this together, Paulus."

But he hadn't told them about the latest rumor he'd heard, the one that left his flesh cold and his heart barely beating.

Chapter Thirty-Four

The stench became unbearable, the air thick with it. Marcus tried to swallow the lump in his throat. The stairs came to an abrupt end, with Marcus bumping into Ekrem at the bottom. They turned sharply right and moved along a narrow passageway. Torches smoldered in brackets along one side. The smoke had a greenish hue and hung low along the dirt-packed wall.

The passageway soon opened into a larger area lined with crude shelves. The remains of deceased priests lined the shelves in wooden receptacles. This truly was a place of the dead. A shudder passed over Marcus's frame, but he reminded himself that for him this entombment meant life.

Ekrem stopped in a shallow alcove just beyond the rotting shelves. A pallet lay on the earthen floor but little else.

"This is where you must stay until I can make arrangements. I'll bring food and water when the others have retired for the night. Enjoy your stay." Ekrem laughed and turned on his heel, whipped his robe in place, and walked away.

Smoky torches burned in this room as well—in respect for the dead, Marcus supposed. He dropped onto the pallet and leaned against the wall. It was damp and soon soaked through his coarse tunic. He fondly remembered his fine fabrics at home, where he could no longer go. The robe and tunic he wore now were "gifts" from a homeless man, who had happily traded them for coins.

This is only temporary, he reminded himself. *All for the cause, but what a mess. Magnus wants Paulus's head, Izak wants more money, and now Magnus wants my head, too. The plan to kill Paulus was going well with Izak until Magnus decided to charge me with treason.*

He shifted his position in an attempt to find a comfortable one, but to no avail.

Now I need to hide to save my own head.

He closed his eyes, but thoughts of the place where he sat opened them.

No, I'm not superstitious.

He closed his eyes again, only to open them wide when he heard a noise.

Now I'm hearing things. Get a grip on yourself, Marcus.

He decided to walk around and see if the underground rooms went any farther.

I'll count each turn and remember whether it was right or left. He didn't want to get lost in the warren of cubicles.

His exploration only confirmed his theory that all the place contained was corpses and more corpses.

"Depressing," he muttered.

He was ready to turn back when a new sound stopped him again. It seemed to be coming from a grate in the ceiling. He moved under the grate and looked up.

A face stared down at him.

He didn't pause to think. He just turned and ran as fast as he could back to where he'd started. Now he fell on the pallet, heart pounding, sweat pouring from his brow. His hands and knees trembled.

It must have been my imagination. What else could it have been?

He decided not to mention the incident to Ekrem when he returned.

Time seemed to stand still. Where *was* Ekrem? Why hadn't he returned with food and water by now?

Finally, Marcus relaxed, and sleep overtook him. Wild dreams filled his sleep until he woke with a start.

Ekrem bent over him. "Here's food and water for you. I even found a little wine. I may have a solution for you, but it can't be utilized until tomorrow night just after midnight."

Ekrem's voice was soft, but the words fell like shards of broken pottery in his mind.

"Tomorrow night?" Marcus whispered. "You expect me to stay here until tomorrow night?" He jerked away from Ekrem's leering face.

A hard light played around Ekrem's eyes. "You can always leave whenever you want. You know the way back to the great room of the temple. The choice is yours."

Marcus shook his head. He was beaten. Did he have any choice? To leave now meant certain death. To stay might mean death, but at least it gave him a chance.

"Certainly, Ekrem. I was hasty. I'll happily wait until after midnight tomorrow night." He leaned back against the wall, hands held out in resignation.

"That is a wise choice, Marcus. I'll be back tomorrow when midnight approaches."

As he left once again, Marcus got the distinct feeling that Ekrem was enjoying this situation far too much. If roles were reversed, he was sure he could have found a safe place that was less obnoxious than this one. But he couldn't choose, so he would have to maintain his composure for more than twenty-four hours.

He decided to while away the time thinking about his life and his plan to rid the city of the hated and feared cult.

What a grand plan! Paulus's head and the end of the cult, all in one spectacular night. I'll be the hero then. Magnus will honor me, and then . . .

But his mind played tricks on him and wouldn't go where he directed it.

Octavia flitted across his mind. He sat up straight. Why was he thinking about her?

She was one of the most useless females I've ever encountered.

He remembered the day he'd bargained with her father. He could tell he'd had him fooled, but the mother . . . well, that was a different story.

I think she saw through my words.

He chuckled, hugging his arms around himself.

But she was helpless. Her husband was greedy and wouldn't give up the money, even for his daughter. What fun it was breaking her. After the first night, there was no fight left in her. I wonder where she went.

In a momentary pang he remembered that she had told him she was bearing his child. He couldn't imagine what it would be like to be a father.

Maybe I've missed something important, was his wistful thought.

Octavia sat up in bed, trembling from a frightening dream. In it Marcus had found her and threatened both her and her baby.

He must never find us. Never, never, never.

She wept into her blanket.

Chapter Thirty-Five

Ekrem arrived right on time. Marcus heard his wheezy breathing before he saw him. He was standing, waiting for him, when Ekrem appeared among the tombs.

"The time has come." Ekrem slightly bowed his head toward Marcus. "There must be no talking once we leave this room. My life would be in as much danger as yours if we are caught. You'll find someone waiting to take you out of the city. Go wherever you're going. Just make sure the plan you have in place works. I'll watch for your return, which will only happen if you have been successful."

His hooded eyes gave away nothing, but Marcus caught the threat.

Ekrem led him back through the tombs, along the passageway with the torches, and up the packed earthen stairs. At the top, Marcus deeply breathed in the fresh air. Ekrem beckoned him to a doorway at the back of the temple. The torches were unlit, making the way difficult. As the door opened, Ekrem pushed Marcus ahead of him and quickly closed the door behind him.

Marcus looked around. No one occupied the darkness. Had Ekrem tricked him?

He moved away from the temple wall, determined to go on his own under cover of darkness. Where, he didn't know, but he'd not wait here for morning's light.

A slight whinny caught his ear.

"Over here," a ghostly voice said.

Marcus neared the sound and was relieved to see the outline of an old cart.

"There are tarps in the back," the unrecognizable voice said. "Make sure you're completely covered. No sounds at all."

He lost no time crawling onto the cart and covering himself. Once he was in, the cart began its creaky journey out of the alley.

Marcus tried to follow the turns in his mind, but it was impossible. He drifted off to sleep on the hard surface until presently the cart slowed.

A deep husky voice penetrated his sleep. "Pull in here, Luda . . . Watch that horse . . . slow and steady . . . There, there, that's good."

Another strange voice, this one jovial: "Almost morning, friend. Is everything ready to load?"

"Ready."

Marcus almost cried out as bulky objects were unceremoniously dropped on top of him. What could be in them to make them so heavy?

"Careful with these ones; they're eggs," the husky voice said. "Set them down gently."

More were added. He was aware of an earthy smell and decided the containers must hold vegetables as well as eggs. He didn't dare move or make a sound. His only hope of escape was silence and stillness.

"All loaded. Have a good day at market."

"Thanks. We should be to the gates about sunup, and then it's an hour to market. Things should still be fresh."

"I don't know how you fellows do it. Up in the middle of the night and then at market all day. Too much for me, but I'm happy you take my produce."

"See you next week. We'll be headed for a different market. The smaller towns are glad to welcome us."

The cart moved off again, this time more slowly since it was weighted down.

Sleeping was impossible with produce pressing down on him. Once the cart moved away from the voices, Marcus shifted his position to one of dubious comfort. It was a small price to pay for freedom.

He hoped his stay outside the city would be short. Once Izak finished his task, he could return in triumph. Until then, he could only wait.

"What is it, Octavia?" Juliana entered her room. She had heard her stirring. It was early morning before sunrise, although the sky was lightening.

"Just some pain in my back." Octavia stirred in her bed.

"How far along are you?"

"I must be nearly seven months." Octavia sat up in bed and rubbed her back.

Juliana sat on the edge of her bed. "Lie down and I'll rub it for you."

"Thank you. This means so much to me." Octavia rolled over to her stomach, arms stretched over her head.

"I'm surprised to hear you're so far along. I thought you were much earlier." Juliana rubbed rhythmically up and down her back.

"My mother was like this. Hardly anyone even knew she was having a baby until near the end." She sighed as the massage continued.

"How long has the pain been in your back?"

"Maybe an hour. Why do you ask?" She rolled her head around and looked at Juliana.

"I don't want to frighten you, but you may be in early labor." Her hand paused on her back as Octavia stiffened. She jumped up and stared at Juliana. Fear played across her features.

"I can't be, can I? Not yet." She put her hand over her mouth, her eyes wide.

"We'll hope not. But as soon as morning breaks, I'm sending Decimus for a friend who is a doctor. We'll get his opinion. Right now I'm giving you some powders I have that will help you relax." Juliana stood and covered her with the blanket.

"I don't deserve you, Juliana. You've been like a mother to me."

"Nonsense. I'm only doing what any good person would do." Juliana shook her head.

Octavia smiled as she lay watching her.

The doctor looked grave when he came out of Octavia's room. He was a kindly man, a believer who helped the converts any way he could. His white hair was pulled back off his face, and a matching beard flowed over his chest. Bushy brows were still dark, making an interesting contrast to his pleasant face.

"I do think she's in labor," he told a worried Juliana and Decimus. "You need to be prepared for a tiny baby before the day is out."

At Juliana's startled look, he assured her he would remain until the baby was born. Decimus prepared to go to their stall while Juliana would stay at the house.

"I'll be praying for Octavia and for you all day," Decimus said before he left. "It will be very special to have a baby in the house. You won't mind, will you, that it's not ours?" he asked Juliana tenderly.

"Oh, Decimus. I think that's the nicest thing you've ever said to me, so caring and loving. No, I don't think I'll mind. Octavia is like a daughter, and we'll both enjoy her baby."

She didn't voice what she was thinking.

If the baby lives.

Day turned into night, which then turned back into day, and still the baby didn't arrive. Juliana was alarmed as she watched Octavia, who moaned steadily and tossed and turned in a daze. The doctor slept when he could. Juliana had prepared a cot for him in a little room down the hall from Octavia. It was used for storage but satisfied the doctor.

By evening of the second day, the doctor asked to speak to Juliana and Decimus together. They gathered by the fire in the main room of the house. The doctor looked at them carefully before he spoke.

"Decimus, Juliana, things are not looking good. We may lose both mother and baby. I will try my best to save them both, but I wanted you to be prepared for whatever may happen. Octavia is weakening by the hour. I've just left her room. She's asking for you, Juliana. I'll stay here with Decimus while you sit with her for a while."

Juliana sat stunned once the doctor finished speaking. She gathered herself together.

"Of course, I'll go sit with her. I'll call you if I need you, doctor." She left the room and entered the bedroom. Octavia was very pale, lying still with her eyes closed. She seemed to be in a haze of pain. Juliana approached the bed and rested her hand on her forehead. It was clammy to the touch.

Octavia opened her eyes and focused on Juliana. A weak smile crossed her face. "Please, take my baby," she whispered so low Juliana could hardly make out the words.

"What do you mean, Octavia?" She bent down to catch the words.

She reached out and grabbed Juliana's hand. "I'm going to die and—"

"No." Juliana shook her head.

Octavia squeezed her hand. "Yes, I know it is so. I've talked to your God, and He's told me, and it's all right."

"Oh, don't say such a thing," Juliana cried, wiping the tears from her eyes.

"Please listen to me. I don't have much time left. I need you to promise me that you will keep my baby." She struggled as another contraction gripped her, then lay back on the pillow, spent.

Juliana began to see the truth in her statements. "I promise, Octavia. I don't want you to go, but if you do, I'll bring up your baby as though it were my own."

Octavia closed her eyes, a peaceful look on her face. She opened them quickly and gasped, "The baby's coming!"

Juliana raced to the door and called for the doctor. He came running into the room.

"It's time," he said. "Gather all those things I told you we'd need."

As the moon rose peacefully in the night sky, a tiny spark of life entered the world, passing his mother as she left it. A raspy cry broke the silence of the night as Gabriel filled his lungs with air for the very first time. The doctor handed him to Juliana, who gazed at him in wonder. So very small, but perfect in every detail.

Now their task would be to protect him from his father. A daunting task from a man who held so much power in his hands.

Chapter Thirty-Six

A slender beam of light burrowed deep between the containers, its tenuous appearance alerting Marcus to the arrival of morning. It faintly played across his face until he opened one eye. He was rewarded with a shower of tiny dust particles escaping from directly above him. He blinked rapidly and moved his head.

Voices raised in anger rose on all sides. They must be approaching the gates. The cart came to a halt with the load rocking dangerously.

Don't move, Marcus, he told himself. *Don't even breathe if you don't have to.*

This was a critical moment. The area would be swarming with guards, who watched the arrivals and departures as the gates opened. To be discovered now would mean death.

His right leg began to ache. He gritted his teeth and tried to ignore the pain.

"You, over there!" a guard called out. "Pull over to the side."

The cart began to move. Above him the load swayed as the cart eased through the gathering crowd. Travelers darted out of the path of the horse, filling the air with shouts and curses.

"Out of the way!" another guard yelled at the crowd.

Marcus froze in place. Would this be the end? More dust particles filtered over his face, invading his nostrils, probing his ears, creeping down inside his tunic.

I can't breathe, he thought.

A shiver of panic slid over his body.

No, don't panic. Keep calm. Your only chance is stillness and silence.

"Off your cart, farmer," a guard commanded with a snicker. "What's loaded in your cart? Something you stole from the market?"

"No, my lord. No stolen goods. I have vegetables for market in the small towns." The driver's voice quavered.

Don't give us away. Marcus willed his mind to reach the farmer with the message.

"Let's have a look," a deeper voice said.

Their military sandals clicked on the pavement as they approached.

"Take that first basket off," came the abrupt command.

The cart tipped slightly as the basket was lifted off the load.

"Take everything out," the same brutal voice said.

"Please, sir, the vegetables will be ruined if they're handled too much."

"I'll decide what's too much." A shout was flung into the air. "How's this?"

Someone close to the wagon whispered, "He put his sword through the vegetables. I can't believe how cruel the guards are."

A voice with a thick accent close by: "Shh. Don't let the guards hear you say that, or the sword could be through your heart."

The voices faded, and Marcus heard no more of their conversation.

"Another basket, you fool!" the guard shouted.

The cart swayed again. Still Marcus managed to maintain his pose.

Shouts rose in the distance.

"Over here! Guards, we need you quickly. Someone has been killed."

Again the sandals clicked as the guards worked their way to the crisis. The baskets landed back on the cart, and almost immediately the cart was in motion. He had earlier heard the gates open, and now they moved through amid the press of people and were soon safely on the other side. The farmer did not slow his pace for several leagues.

At last the cart came to a halt. With a final jolt it stopped. Marcus almost stopped breathing.

Are we safe? Or have the guards come after us? he thought.

By this time, sweat beaded his forehead since the heat of the day had begun to invade the cart.

The weight was lifted off him, and the tarp was pulled back, revealing the worried face of the farmer.

"No words, please. We're in a wooded area a distance off the main road. No one saw us enter, and I need to be on my way. I hope you find whatever you're looking for." The farmer gestured for Marcus to leave the cart.

Gingerly Marcus edged his stiff body from the cart. He turned to thank the farmer, but he was already in the cart and directing the horse back to the hard-packed path. Horse and cart lumbered away, and Marcus was left wondering where he was and what his next step should be.

He sat down under the nearest tree and from beneath his cloak pulled the pack Ekrem had given him. He found a goatskin of lukewarm water and a small loaf of bread. It tasted like a feast to him. He drank half the water, ate half the loaf, and saved the rest for the remainder of the day. He placed both back in the pack and secured it under his cloak.

The day was proving to be especially hot. In the distance, puffs of dust rose where horses and carts traveled the main road. He made a careful search of the surrounding area, assuring himself he was alone and sufficiently hidden from view. Once he felt secure, he settled under the tree again, this time to sleep.

He awoke as the sun hovered above the horizon and shadows deepened among the trees. He stretched and stood, watching the setting sun. After a brief meal, he began walking back toward Pergamum along a narrow path running parallel to the road. His jaw jutted out, and the determination in his heart matched his strides as he walked with a purpose.

Once I meet with Izak and the plans are finalized, I'll be on my way. The cave I discovered years ago has proved useful more than once. I should only have to stay there a few days. Then success!

When the gates of the city emerged through the edge of the trees, he stopped. The sun was now down, and the gates had been closed for the night. As he stood there, concealed, the outline of four figures emerged from the base of the wall. They moved toward the path where he waited.

"On time I see." Marcus jerked his head in their direction.

"Of course, did you expect any less?" Izak tossed his head and glared at Marcus.

"Well, are the plans in place?" Marcus asked.

"You'll get your money's worth," Izak said in a cool tone.

"When will you have executed my orders?" Marcus jabbed his finger in his chest.

"When the time is right—not before, not after." Izak snorted and backed away from Marcus.

"I don't like your tone of voice. Something feels wrong here." Marcus felt like he was losing control of the conversation.

As yet, the other three hadn't spoken.

"Everything is going as we discussed," Izak said. "Have no fear, my friend. You'll be satisfied with the results." He included the other three in his glance.

"I certainly hope so," Marcus said. "You will reap the consequences if things go awry." He shook his fist in his face.

Izak gave a coarse laugh. Marcus could just make out his eyes from the glow of the torches along the wall. The two glared at each other, while the other three moved silently. An oppressive darkness gathered behind his eyes as the first knife pierced his skin.

Chapter Thirty-Seven

Morning broke over Pergamum. Soft, pink clouds hovered on the horizon, welcoming the new day. The sun rose with dignity, thrusting its dazzling beams along the city's roadways. As the brilliant rays reached the temple of Zeus, a fledgling priest descended the steps to begin the morning preparations for the day's sacrifices.

He stopped and stared. With a gasp, he covered his mouth with his hands and fled back up the steps into the temple. Remembering his probationary vow of silence, he made haste to an inner room, where the senior priests would be breaking their fast. His body trembled as he pushed aside the curtain.

Ekrem saw him enter and speak to his mentor. The look of horror on the novitiate's face and the startled expression of the mentor made him rise from his position and approach them.

He invited the two with a gesture. "Why don't you come out in the hall with me?"

The mentor nodded in agreement, and Ekrem led the two from the room.

"Now, tell me, what is the problem that is so concerning both of you?" he asked them quietly.

The mentor indicated the novice should answer. The novice swallowed once or twice and ran his hand over his forehead before he looked into Ekrem's eyes.

"There's a body on the steps below the altar." He drew his shoulders together in a tight knot.

"A body? What kind of a body? What do you mean?" Ekrem blinked and pursed his lips.

"A man, master, a dead man. I could see blood and his face." A shudder shook his body. I don't want to talk about his face." The young boy wrung his hands and shook his head.

Ekrem turned to the priest. "Take the boy to his sleeping quarters and see if you can calm him. I'll look after things from this end." He flicked his hand at them.

As the priest led the novice away, Ekrem walked out onto the steps and approached the body. Finding a body on the steps was not uncommon; Ekrem had seen many of them in his day. They were nasty and difficult to get rid of, but all part of the job. Why people wanted to drop their dead before the altar, he couldn't understand.

He bent over the battered form, studying the features. He jumped back, alarmed, when he recognized the dead man.

"What's this?" His hand grasped his chest as he jumped, almost knocking off his turban.

He ran back into the interior of the temple and ordered the guards to follow him. When he appeared on the steps again, a crowd had gathered at the base of the steps, staring at the body. Whispers spread through the crowd.

"It's the captain of the guard. It's Marcus!"

Ekrem shook his head. There was no way he could keep this quiet now, no way he could deny this was indeed Marcus.

"Guards, carry the body into the temple," he said. He put his hand over his trembling chin, threw back his shoulders, and climbed the stairs with his back straight, chin up.

The guards were true to their training. They showed no emotion as they lifted the body of their chief and began the ascent into the temple.

Ekrem paced the quadrangle behind the priests' living quarters. One turn around the walkway, another turn, still another—and still he could come to no explanation for what had happened.

Did the thieves he was dealing with kill him? Was he overtaken by the guards at the gates? Did robbers on the road attack him? What happened?

He took another turn around the perimeter, arms clutched tightly behind his back, head bowed.

If it were robbers, no harm done. One less rogue in the world. But what if the ones he hired turned on him?

Step, step, robe swishing, shoulders slumped.

Am I *implicated?*

This was the big worry. His world could exist without Marcus, but he wasn't ready for it to exist without *him*.

How can I find out?

Question after question filtered through his brain, all unanswered.

Will the thugs still go through with the plan? I don't even know who they are.

At last he arrived at a measure of calmness.

There's really nothing I can do but continue the way things are and hope for the best. An extra sacrifice to Zeus wouldn't hurt either.

He made one final turn and reentered the temple. Once more he walked out onto the temple steps. The guards had done a good job. No evidence remained from earlier. Morning sacrifices were proceeding as usual. Smoke circled around the altar grate and spiraled into the clear sky. People lined up with their offerings for sacrifice, seemingly unconcerned about the earlier happenings.

But word spread through the city like a fire blazing out of control. Looks of dismay and alarm greeted the news. Cries of disbelief could be heard among whispered voices, expressing glee. The marketplace was abuzz with the story. The news eventually reached the stall of Decimus and Juliana.

Voices raised in excitement approached his stall.

"Decimus, have you heard the news?" cried a fellow vendor, coming up the pathway. He waved his arms in the air

Decimus looked up with interest. "No, what news?"

"Marcus is dead. Murdered. Knife right through his heart, they say." He accompanied his words with hand gestures of a knife stabbing his chest.

Decimus's mouth dropped open in shock. "Marcus is dead? It can't be true."

"Believe it, neighbor. It's true enough." The vendor clapped him on the back.

The group passed on to spread the news to the next stall. Decimus was left staring after them in bewilderment.

Juliana will be stunned with this news when I tell her tonight.

"It can't be true," he repeated to himself. *What will this mean for Paulus, for little Gabriel, for all of us? I need to get word to Paulus.* His hands trembled as he moved along the front of his stall.

"Friend," he called and waved his hand to the old man in the next stall, "would you do me the favor of keeping your eye on my stall? I've got an important errand to do."

"Certainly, friend. Anything for you. Sure know you've done enough for me over the years. Take your time. I'm not going anywhere." The man grinned a toothless grin, sitting on his stool.

Decimus pulled his hood over his head and set off in the direction of Paulus's house.

Paulus had just arrived at the front gate when Decimus hurried his steps and greeted him as he stepped down from his horse.

"Decimus, what's wrong? You look distressed." Paulus laid his hand on his shoulder and looked closely at him.

Decimus panted due to his haste in getting there and couldn't speak at first. "Paulus, I bring tragic news. I don' know how to tell you." His face flooded with heat from his hurried walk.

"Just say it, my friend. We'll discuss it once I know what this is all about." He kept his hand on his shoulder.

Decimus managed to get it out. "There's a rumor going around that a body was found on the steps of the temple this morning."

"Yes, yes, go on."

"The rumor is that the body is Marcus." Decimus let his head fall forward.

Paulus felt as though he'd been punched in the stomach. His head reeled for a minute before he could take in the thought. He gripped Decimus's shoulder tightly while he looked off into the distance. Finally he glanced at Decimus again.

"Where did you hear the rumor?" The words came out of clamped lips. His hand tightened on Decimus's shoulder until his knuckles turned white.

"At the market. Someone came to my stall and told me. I knew you needed to know right away, so a friend is watching the stall."

"We need to find out if this rumor is true. Let me think, Decimus." He wandered down the drive, trying to get his thoughts to focus on what steps he should take. He returned to where Decimus was patiently waiting.

"Decimus, I want you to go back to your stall. You may hear more news that will help us later. I'll go to the temple and see what I can find out."

The two men hurried away in different directions. Paulus pushed his horse hard until he neared the city center and the crowds on the street increased. He heard bits of conversation concerning the body as he passed people. He eased his way down the side street of the temple and left his horse in a public stable.

As he returned to the base of the altar, everything looked peaceful and normal. His thoughts turned to Antipas, who had been sacrificed on this altar, and now Marcus, who had supposedly been found dead at its base. The altar had dominated his family all through his life.

How can something so evil look so innocent? He shaded his eyes and stared up the steps. *The battle is not yet over*, he determined in his heart. *Zeus will not win.*

Reluctantly he made each foot step on a stair. He worked his way up to the doors that were closed since the time of sacrifice was over for the day. He approached the guards stationed on either side of the ornately carved double doors.

"I must speak with the chief priest," he said. "The matter is urgent." He kept his face neutral and spoke with confidence.

"You are Paulus, are you not?" One of the guards leaned toward him, causing his sword to clatter at his side.

"Yes, that is correct." He clenched his teeth as he waited.

The guard smiled a gruesome smile. "Then come with me. We have our orders concerning you." Each grabbed him by a shoulder and ushered him into the temple.

Chapter Thirty-Eight

The interior was dim and cool in contrast to the bright sunshine and intense heat of the day. Paulus needed a few minutes for his eyes to adjust to the muted shades. He distinguished several priests moving about, conducting their business, as well as visitors being led on a tour of the rooms.

The two guards did not pause and crossed the foyer with him in tow. They turned at the far side of the room and proceeded along an even gloomier hall. Part way along this passageway, they thrust him into a small side room, where a hooded priest waited.

"Thank you for bringing him to me," the priest said. "You can return to your duties." The priest sniffed once, then turned his gaze on Paulus. Two bright eyes peered at him from beneath the hood.

Paulus didn't recognize the husky tones of the priest. He waited and remained very still until the priest invited him to sit. He cautiously lowered himself into the only other chair in the room. The priest stood and closed the heavy, black curtain across the doorway, darkening the room.

"I suppose you must be wondering why you have been brought here." He sat again, resting his arms on the table.

Paulus spoke politely but courageously. "I presumed I was being arrested."

"Yes, I guess that is what you would think." The lips pressed together in a tight line. "Let me ask you a question before I begin. Why did you come to the temple?" A bony hand reached out from the depths of the robe, shaking a finger in his face.

"I heard a rumor that my brother has been murdered," Paulus said. "I came to find out if the story is true and, if it is, to ask if I may claim the body for burial." He looked directly at the priest. Honesty would be his best weapon. He sat still, awaiting the priest's next words.

"That is very noble of you." The priest coughed imperceptibly into the sleeve of his robe. "You realize you have put your life on the line?"

"Yes, I know that, but it seemed important that I find out the truth and that my brother be given a decent burial." Paulus clasped his hands together to stop them from shaking. He shifted in his seat, trying to find a comfortable position on the rough chair.

The priest sniffed softly several times while keeping his head lowered. Paulus couldn't see the man's face or distinguish anything familiar about him. He sat, watching him and hoping for a clue as to who he was and why he'd had the guards bring him here.

"You are more noble than your brother." The priest lifted his head and fastened bright eyes on Paulus. "You are aware, are you not, that he was plotting to kill you and to purge the city of your followers?"

"I have heard rumors to that effect, but I choose not to believe them." Paulus shook his head sadly. All his dreams for Marcus had shattered around him.

"Are you also aware that he was infiltrating your group?" The piercing eyes seemed to know everything.

"Again, I know some who believe that, but there is no proof that it is true." Paulus spoke with more confidence and lifted his chin in defiance of the words he was hearing.

The hood shook from side to side as the priest indicated his disagreement. Paulus wondered how much this priest knew.

"I am old and not well respected anymore in the temple," the priest said. "In fact, many would like me to just disappear and often treat me as though I had departed. That sometimes works in my favor as I can listen to things that are being said, and no one realizes that I am even there."

Paulus raised his eyes to study the bent head. The thin hands were clasped loosely in his lap, and the priest turned a ring round and round on his finger. Twisted knuckles and swollen veins lined the bony hands. The brown robe, worn in places, looked old and shabby.

He seemed to raise himself out of his reverie, fixing that gaze on Paulus again. "You are in danger. Marcus was not alone in this plot, and I have it on good authority that the plan will continue without him. His murder does not come as a surprise as he was not a well-liked man. His power had corrupted him. We will probably never know who was responsible for his death, but let's just say that many in power will be relieved that he has left this life. He was a dangerous man." He lapsed into silence, sinking down into his robe.

"I would like to see the body, and if it is Marcus, I ask for his body." Paulus leaned forward in the small space. He almost touched the priest.

"Do you want it, knowing that he would have killed you if someone had not killed him first?"

"He is my brother. Yes, I still want his body. I would like to be sure he has a decent burial."

"You amaze me. There must be something to this cult of yours, something that is lacking in Zeus or emperor worship, where it is every man for himself." He paused again. "I cannot give you what you want. I don't have the authority. But I do happen to know where they have taken the body. It may be that you can rescue it."

"You will never know how much this means to me," Paulus said, trying to keep the tears out of his voice.

"But first we have to get you out of the temple without being seen. There are those in this building who would like nothing better than to throw you in prison. If you will wait a moment, I may have a way out."

The frail man slowly rose from his seat, leaning on the wall with one hand. He steadied himself before he parted the curtains and shuffled out. Paulus was left alone. He knew it was not safe for him to be here, but he had no choice but to wait. He heard sounds of people talking outside the room and feet treading by. No one turned into the room.

"Father," he whispered, eyes closed, "this is a strange situation to be in. You know Your plans for Your church and for my life. If You still have work for me to do, then I ask that the priest be successful in getting me safely out of here. Thank You, Lord."

When he opened his eyes, the curtain was pushed to one side. Paulus held his breath, but it was only the same priest returning. He carried a bundle with him, which he laid on the chair before he closed the curtain.

"I have brought a priest's robe and sandals. Put them over what you have on and carry your own sandals under your tunic. I think I can get you safely out of the building. Please don the robe quickly, and we'll be on our way. The call has gone out for a meeting, which will mean fewer people for us to meet."

Paulus lost no time in wrapping the coarse fabric around himself and changing his sandals for the well-worn ones. When he pulled the hood over his head, he realized he looked very much like the old priest.

"Good, good. You'll pass," the priest said. He led the way from the room. They headed down the passageway away from the main entrance. Fortunately, they met no one, and Paulus soon arrived at a little-used side door.

The priest leaned close to him and murmured, "Go outside the eastern gate tonight, and you will see where your brother has been placed."

"Do you mean where they dispose of sacrifices and other unwanted things?" Paulus asked. He held his breath to calm his heart, which had begun to beat rapidly.

"That's the place." He gave Paulus a little shove out the door and closed it behind him.

Paulus and Mattias crouched behind a large boulder as the gates shut behind them. Darkness would soon be over the land, where men committed their evil deeds. The deed they were about to commit tonight was one of mercy and, yes, one of love. For Paulus did love Marcus and grieved deeply for him—grieved for the possibilities that had been opening up for them, for the years lost.

Paulus was no longer sure if Marcus had surrendered to Christ, but he had been hearing the message, and it must have had some effect on his life. Now that opportunity was gone.

"Are you ready?" Mattias breathed in his ear. "We need to get this done so we can get back into the city."

One of the newest converts was a guard who stood near a small gate a league to the left of them. If they could get there before he went off duty, he would open the small door set in the larger gate, allowing latecomers access when the other gates were closed. Paulus appreciated what his friend was doing for him since he could be in trouble if his entry was reported.

The two men eased out from behind the boulder and walked stealthily over the rough ground. Once they reached the refuse heap, they mounted the side and began their search for Marcus. The indignity of his resting place appalled Paulus.

"Over here," Mattias whispered. "I've found him, I think."

"This place reeks of death." Paulus joined Mattias and paused to look down on the frozen face of his brother, Marcus. Feelings of guilt, loss, and overwhelming grief flooded his mind. He was unable to stem the flood of tears.

This was his brother.

Mattias rested his arm across Paulus's shoulders. "Let all the grief out, Paulus. This is indeed a sad end."

"He had so much potential for good, but he chose evil. It's hard to come to terms with his death when such a short time ago I had big dreams and tremendous hope for him."

"Paulus, we need to move his body. Time is fleeting." Mattias put gentle pressure on his shoulder.

"Yes, I know." He knelt beside Marcus, leaning over the broken body. "Brother, I'm so sorry. Sorry for the life you had to live. Sorry for all the things we never got to do together." He reached out and laid his hand on Marcus's head. "Goodbye, my brother. I can only hope that at the end you turned to the One we talked about and that I'll see you again."

He rose. "I'm ready, Mattias."

Together they wrapped the body in the blanket they had brought and lifted him carefully in their arms. It was a solemn procession that arrived at the small gate and entered the city. They bore the body to Paulus's home, where they washed and clothed it in clean linen. When they had completed the ritual, Paulina and Eunice joined them.

When she saw him, Paulina wept sorrowfully. "My son, my son," she cried over and over.

Eunice held onto Paulus and gazed at this dead brother-in-law she had never been able to get to know.

A few of the leaders joined the family as they performed a simple farewell to him and buried him quietly the next day.

Marcus was dead, Paulus thought. He was no longer a threat to the fledgling church. But was the old priest right? Was the threat still real?

Chapter Thirty-Nine

The garden was redolent with the fragrance of blossoms as Paulus and Eunice walked arm in arm along its smooth paths. The sun made a spectacle of colors across the lower edge of the horizon. The last rays slanted along the path in front of them, designing a pattern of light and dark swatches. It was a restful place after the events of the day.

Eunice snuggled closer to her husband, who returned the pressure on her arm. He lifted his arm and encircled her waist, drawing her ever closer to his side. They slowed their pace as they came to their favorite spot, the bench overlooking the stream. Without comment, they sat together, watching the water flow in its perpetual motion. Two ducks paddled along in front of them, adding to the enchantment of the scene.

"Paulus, it was a hard, sad day." Eunice lifted her face to his. She smoothed the furrows on his brow and let her fingers linger on his face. "I've never experienced anything to compare to it. It was very sad when Antipas died, but it was also glorious. This was empty and hollow."

Paulus drew her closer, while they watched the ducks disappear around a bend.

"I felt so awful for you mother," she said. "The loss of a child is felt so deeply in a mother's heart, even though he is grown. This was especially hard as he was estranged from her." The tears hung on her eyelids.

"I'll need to visit Father tomorrow. He needs to know that his son is dead." Paulus stirred on the bench, putting his head in his hands.

"Do you think he'll understand?" She rubbed the tight muscles in his shoulders, resting her head on his arm.

"No, it's likely he won't know what I'm talking about, but I need to go nevertheless."

"What does this mean for the church now? Is the threat over?"

"I'm afraid not. I haven't had a chance to tell you about my visit to the temple." He encircled her again with his arm.

Eunice listened closely. She put her head on Paulus's shoulder, and he told her about the message from the priest. When he neared the end of his story, the garden had become darker as night descended on them. A slight breeze came off the stream, chilling the air.

"I want to be completely open with you, Eunice. You need to know what we're facing. I plan to meet with David and Emin tomorrow after I see Father. We'll need to make plans. I want to talk to Decimus as well. He may have heard something from his contact at the barracks."

"I know we're in danger, but I've spent hours in prayer this week and know the Lord is in control of this situation. I want to face this with you, whatever comes." She looked into his eyes.

"You are such a loyal wife; I don't know what I would do without you." He kissed her forehead and embraced her.

"Let's hope you never have to find out," Eunice said with a little smile.

The doctor's house looked foreboding when Paulus approached. He had never felt comfortable here and dreaded the interview with his father today. He knew his father had no use for him, and the news he brought would only increase the distance between them.

That is, if he even knows what I'm saying.

He knocked on the front door, which the doctor's assistant quickly opened.

"Good day to you." Paulus greeted her with a small bow. "Is it possible to see my father today?"

"Yes, I'm sure it is. Let me check with the doctor." She ushered Paulus into the building, which smelled like medicine and stale cooking. Paulus sat on a low couch while he awaited word from the doctor. The assistant returned with the message that he could visit but not for long. His father had apparently not had a good night.

He followed her down a dark, narrow hallway until they reached the room where his father was housed. He hadn't been here in some time, and his father's appearance shocked him. Tangled gray hair had been allowed to grow long and dirty. His beard was stained with food from many meals. Spittle dripped from the corner of his twisted mouth. Wild eyes looked at his son.

"Hello, Father," Paulus began, only to be interrupted by a low growl coming from his father's mouth.

"Out, out," came the cry from his lips.

Paulus tried to speak again.

This time wild laughter rolled from his father. "He thinks . . . he thinks . . . I'm nothing, nothing, nothing!" he shouted hysterically.

"Father, I need to talk—"

"Not your father, not, not . . ." Now the sounds were guttural. He waved his arms wildly about his head and tried to rise from his bed. It was then that Paulus noticed he was tied to the frame. When the cords held him back, he became more agitated.

"Away, go away, eeeeeehhhhh!" he shrieked.

The doctor entered the room and rushed to his patient's side. "You'd better leave," he said to Paulus.

Paulus's last glance at his father was one he would never forget. Hate seemed to pour from Julian's eyes and lips as he screamed at his son. Paulus left the house as quickly as he could.

A plan formed in his mind. He would give it more thought, but right now he needed to talk to David and Emin.

A servant met Paulus at the door of David's house and led him to the main room, where the men awaited him. The talk was subdued among those gathered.

"Brother, we're saddened by your loss," David said. "I know you longed to have a closer relationship with Marcus and see him grow in the faith."

As Paulus joined the group, he saw compassion in David's eyes.

"Come, sit with us." David extended his arm to Paulus, indicating a vacant seat.

"It's been very difficult." Paulus swallowed a lump in his throat. "It was sad when we lost Antipas, but we knew where he was going. This is devastating. It's a personal loss on so many levels—the time I had hoped to spend with Marcus, lost forever. We'll need God's strength to carry on from here. And that, my friends, is the good news; we have His strength. He's promised to stay with us always, and that means in dark times as well as light." He put his hand over his heart and looked at each present.

Emin leaned forward toward Paulus. "What can you tell us about how you found him?"

Paulus tapped his chin until he gained control of his emotions, then related all the details of his visit to the temple: the aged priest, the rumors—all of it.

Mattias nodded several times as Paulus related their experience in finding Marcus and bringing his body home.

"I'm glad you were able to find him and give him a decent burial." David's face reflected his grief in the lines across his forehead and between his eyes. He drew his lips together tightly. "God's hand was visible through that whole ordeal. It's the threats that cause me distress now. How accurate do you think these rumors are?"

"I'm afraid they're only too true." Paulus looked around the group, saw the concern in their eyes. "I think we need to be very cautious with our families. We don't want to cause them unnecessary fear, but we need to be wise. I've instructed my wife and my mother that they are either to always have a servant with them or wait until I can take them wherever they need to go."

Paulus surveyed the group before him. They were all solid members of the church, brave men who were totally committed to Christ and in spreading the word about Him. He knew he could count on them to continue the work with him. He made eye contact with each one of them, appreciating the special gifts each brought to the gathering. He stood and faced them.

"I'm going to be very careful with my family, but I plan to continue the work of the Lord here in Pergamum as if I had not heard the rumors. They may be Satan's way of distracting us from our message. I won't allow him to do that." He slapped his fist in his other hand, pressing his lips together with determination.

"Hear, hear!" Mattias jumped to his feet. "I'm with you, brother. If we can't stand up for Christ, we're not worthy to be called His sons." He moved up beside Paulus and clasped his hand in agreement.

David was the next to stand with them. "I'm with you too."

Emin quickly followed, as did several others until all were standing together. They broke into a psalm of praise for their God.

> I will praise you, O Lord, with all my heart;
> I will tell of all your wonders.
> I will be glad and rejoice in you;
> I will sing praise to your name,
> O most high. (Ps. 8:1–2)

They gathered in a circle and prayer rose from their lips. Prayer for their families, for protection, and for the courage to openly carry on the work.

Their support encouraged Paulus although his heart was heavy with the burden of the loss of Marcus. He walked home in the late afternoon, conscious of great danger from now-unknown sources. His mind filled with visions of his father from earlier in the day. The immediate future was uncertain. The old priest had warned him, and he realized the danger was very real.

Marcus, what secrets did you take to your grave?

That was the unanswered question.

Chapter Forty

Izak sat huddled underneath his flimsy shelter. The day was hot and afforded only a little shade. Insects buzzed annoyingly around his head. He swatted at them with increasing irritation. Food had been scarce to find today. The hotter the day, the more difficult the begging. The wealthy either stayed at home or were anxious to reach their destinations, so they had little time for beggars.

"It's a hard life," he grumbled to himself. Then he laughed uproariously. "I think I have everyone believing I'm a helpless cripple. If they only knew. Ha, ha! There would be surprised faces if they could see me after dark. That's when I really shine, when the real me comes to the surface. But it serves my purposes."

He leaned back against a box, which contained all his earthly goods, and dozed. Uneven snores could soon be heard coming from his direction. Children playing close by paused to listen and laugh. They didn't come close, and soon their play consumed their interest again.

As Izak slept, the brazen sun continued its journey, the air cooling as its rays lowered in the sky. By and by Izak gave one final snort, sat up quickly, and looked around suspiciously. Seeing no one in sight, he relaxed again.

"Soon, soon." He smiled to himself.

When darkness crept over the land, he stirred and prepared a simple meal for himself. When that was consumed, he took his place outside the shelter, watching the gate in one direction and the road to the gate in the other.

He watched the colorful guards as they prepared to close the gates. At one time he had hoped and dreamed he would be a guard posted on the gates. He loved the bright-blue tunics and the soft, dark cloaks, all completed with the sturdy military sandals. The guards had once stood high in his estimation.

But all that had changed. It was incredible how one seemingly insignificant incident could change the course of a life.

The brutality of the guards on the night his father was beaten to death for a crime he hadn't committed would forever stand out in his mind as the turning point. Then there were the long days and nights when his mother couldn't find enough food to feed him and his siblings, not to mention the dampness of sleeping under the bridge because the guards had taken over their modest home as payment for his father's crimes. It had all left a bitterness deep inside that only revenge could assuage.

He hated the guards, the governor, this new cult—anything that represented power and authority.

I'm my own power source, my own authority, he shouted inside his head. He dared not make the boasts openly. He knew he was being watched. Had been ever since that night.

But I'm more clever than they realize. To them I'm a worthless outcast from society, but they'll soon see what I really am. Marcus underestimated me, to his sorrow. Ha ha ha. The look in his eye was enough for me.

His thoughts continued along these mutinous lines while he continued to watch his surroundings placidly. His face gave away nothing.

While observers who always loitered around the gates watched the pageantry surrounding the gate, Izak watched the other direction. Out of the darkness several shapes materialized. He stepped from his shelter and moved away from the gates until he was behind the clustering shelters of the homeless.

The newcomers, led by Jamus, would follow his lead. He shortly reached an open field and picked his way across the rocky surface. A wooded area lay directly ahead, and he directed his steps toward it. Under the cover of trees he found the hard-packed earthen path. As he stepped on it, he was aware of others entering the grove behind him. No words were spoken as they proceeded to their destination.

At length the outline of a rough shack emerged. Hunters used it during the season, but it was deserted now. Though the door would be locked, getting inside would prove easy. He approached the battered door and pushed on it, surprised to feel it open at his touch. He eased through the opening and ignited a small torch he had carried under his cloak. A quick survey of the one-room structure convinced him they were alone.

He beckoned the others to enter and closed the door behind them. The torch was extinguished as they found places to squat on the rough floor.

Izak sat against the door where he could face all of them. He cleared his throat, covering his mouth with his hand. "Your identity is not important. We will use no names tonight." He spoke in a whisper. "You are here because the person who invited you knows you and has deemed you will be efficient for our purpose and, for whatever your reasons, will remain silent."

He cocked his head, listening for any outside noises. Determining there were none, he leaned forward.

Jamus held out his hand to interrupt him. "I assure you," he said, "each man here has been carefully chosen. You can count on each of us, provided the compensation is adequate." He dropped the words into the center of the circle.

Izak snorted. "I promise that each of you will be well paid for your trouble. Half tonight and half when the 'festivities' are over."

Murmurs of acceptance filled the shack.

"We have many plans to make tonight," Izak said. "Since we last met with your leaders, there have been a few changes in the plan. Since the death reported in the city, the plot has been enlarged and will take the city by surprise. Each of you will have an important part. There is no such thing as a small part. Each little section is needed for the whole to be successful."

Izak spent several minutes outlining his scheme. When he broached certain topics, some of the men gasped.

"Am I detecting cowardice from some of you?" he asked. "If this is too revolting for some of you, leave now, by all means."

He waited while restlessness rippled through the group, but no one spoke.

He snarled out the words. "Then I'm going to assume that all of you are with me and there'll be no more indications of trepidation. This is not for the fainthearted."

Once again, silence met him.

"We need to follow our plan exactly," he said. "Once we've decided on a time, we need to gather materials and decide how many teams we need, who will work together, places to meet when we have executed our plan, and alternate choices if something goes awry."

Heads bent together as the plot details unfolded. If anyone was still shocked, he kept it to himself. Ideas were presented, discussed, and accepted or discarded. Izak was well pleased with their progress. These men were with him. Each man had his own agenda for wanting success; that diversity made for a greater chance of attaining their goal.

When at last they slipped through the door, there was no turning back. The wheels of destruction had been set in motion, and no earthly force could stop them now.

Chapter Forty-One

Juliana sat by the open window of their small home. It had been a lonely dwelling for so many wasted years before they found Christ and their lives were transformed. Their humble living space had become a temple of worship and a place where love was utmost for the first time in many years. Juliana thought she couldn't want or ask for anything more. She was content.

Then Octavia had entered her life and now left them with little Gabriel. She gazed fondly at his sleeping form in her arms. So tiny, so perfect. His dark, curly hair clung to his darling, little head; he had unbelievably tiny lips, and his little eyes were closed. She watched his chest flutter up and down in baby-size breaths.

How can such a little body exude such life and such hope? She lovingly snuggled him closer.

"Lord, I still don't know why You took all my little babies, but I know You had a reason, and I accept that," she prayed. "I'm just so thankful that You have unexpectedly and lovingly placed this gentle baby in my care. I promise I will love him and care for him all the days of my life. Thank You for the joy of knowing his mother. Lord, I pray for him as he grows and will someday learn of his beginnings. Father, don't let this news taint his life. Amen."

The baby stirred in her arms as footsteps approached. A soft rap on the door indicated the doctor's arrival. He had been coming each day since Gabriel had been born to check on him and to make sure Juliana could care for him.

"I think this will be my last visit, Juliana," he said. "He is thriving, and you seem to be doing fine with him." The doctor looked up after checking the baby.

"Oh yes, thank you, doctor. I have never felt so fulfilled. I want nothing more in life than to raise him along with Decimus, who is quite foolish about him." She actually giggled like a young girl.

The doctor smiled to himself.

Juliana and Decimus sat together over their evening meal, discussing the events of their day. The city was always full of rumors, and now was no exception.

"The talk today was all about Magnus," Decimus said. "He's furious over Marcus's death, so they say. He had apparently given him a mission to do, and now that won't be possible. He seems very volatile." He dug his fork into the meal of lamb and vegetables Juliana had prepared. He stuffed it in his mouth and chewed vigorously.

"Oh, I remember the times he'd come through the market with his cohorts," she said. "We all hoped he wouldn't notice us. Each new governor seems to be worse than the last." She sipped from her cup. "What do you suppose this mission was that Marcus was to do?"

Decimus punctuated the air with his fork. "No one really knows for sure, but someone whispered in my ear that it had something to do with his brother. That would make sense as Magnus has no use for us Christians."

"It's frightening times we live in. I miss the market, but I wouldn't trade these days with Gabriel for anything. Is that young girl we hired to help of any use?" She set her cup down and wiped her mouth with her napkin.

"She's learning well. I think we can keep things together until you can bring Gabriel. How long do you think it will be before you can bring him with you?" Decimus glanced to where Gabriel was sleeping peacefully.

"He had such a good report from the doctor today that I may try him for a few hours next week. I'll see how it goes." She too looked at the sleeping baby.

"What a special gift from God he is." Decimus smiled. "We're a whole family now. You know, Juliana, I've been thinking."

"Oh dear. That often means trouble when you start that." She smiled at him fondly.

"Actually, this time it's serious. I think we need to take Gabriel to Paulus and tell him the whole story."

Fear gripped Juliana's heart. With wide eyes she stared at her husband.

He ignored her stare. "After all, Paulus is his next of kin. He needs to know about him and decide on his future."

"I know, Decimus, but I can't part with him. He's *my* baby now. I promised his mother." Tears threatened to release from her eyes.

"But Juliana, it's the right thing to do. We'll ask Paulus if he'll let us raise him." He rested his chin in one hand and contemplated his wife's face.

"I know you're right. I'm just afraid." She used the napkin to dab at her eyes.

That night, when the meal was over, Juliana wrapped Gabriel in his new blanket, the one she had made for him. Together with Decimus, she walked to Paulus's house. She determined to be brave and trust Paulus to make the right decision for Gabriel. She wanted the baby, wanted him badly, but she also wanted what was best for him.

Paulus was home and greeted them graciously when they appeared at his door. They asked to speak with him privately, so he ushered them into his private study and seated them comfortably. He looked at them with his eyes raised.

"Am I correct that this baby is the reason you wish to speak to me? Is this a relative?" Paulus asked. He looked from them to the baby in Juliana's arms.

Decimus glanced at Juliana, who bowed her head over the baby. He took a deep breath and faced Paulus. "You're right. We have come about the baby. It's quite a story, and you're part of it."

"Part of it?" Paulus's eyebrows shot up. "How could I be part of it?" He tipped his head and looked at Decimus.

Decimus related the tale, beginning with Juliana's encounter with Octavia at the market. Many expressions played over Paulus's face as the story unfolded: interest, disgust, shock, horror, and finally compassion.

"So we've come to you," Decimus said. "You're his next of kin, so you must make the decision about his future. Please know that nothing would give us greater pleasure than to be able to raise him. But even more than that, we want what's best for him, don't we Juliana?" He turned to her with his question.

Until now she had neither spoken nor looked up. She now lifted tear-filled eyes to Paulus. "Yes," came her faint sound, "I only want the best . . ." She was unable to complete the sentence.

"May I hold him, Juliana?" Paulus stretched out his arms to her.

She held Gabriel out to him, grief edging her heart. Paulus lifted the baby from her arms. He pulled back the blanket from his face and stared at the little one. He swallowed once or twice before he spoke.

Not taking his eyes off the baby, he said, "He looks like Marcus. I can see the noble brow and the dark eyebrows. There is no question in my mind that the baby is his. I need to think."

He stood up and handed the baby back to Juliana. "Will you wait here for a few minutes? I'll be back quickly."

Decimus was prompt to answer him. "Of course we'll wait."

Paulus left the room quickly. In the silence that replaced his presence, all Decimus could hear were sniffles coming from Juliana. He didn't look at her, afraid he might cry too. They sat without speaking, Juliana hugging Gabriel to her and Decimus staring at the wall.

When the door opened again, Paulus entered, followed by Eunice and Paulina. Both ladies looked serious and startled. Paulina wept softly.

"I've told both my mother and wife what you have told me," Paulus said. "They were unanimous that they wanted to see the baby. I hope you don't mind."

"No, not at all." Decimus jumped up to greet the ladies. Juliana said nothing, just held out the baby to Paulina.

Paulina took him in her arms, then sat on the couch where Paulus led her. She, too, folded back the blanket and gazed at the tiny face. Her tears joined Juliana's on his blanket.

"He's so beautiful." She sighed. "It's like holding a little piece of Marcus." She stroked his soft cheek and ran her fingers through his dark hair. Kisses were planted on his face, his ear, and his head.

"Decimus, Juliana, I've made my decision about him," Paulus said. "If you will agree that we will always be his family and can treat him as such, the three of us agree that we would like you to be his parents."

Juliana sprang to her feet and stared at Paulus. "Are you sure?" Her eyes darted back and forth between Paulus and the women.

"I'm very sure," Paulus said. "I can't imagine anyone who would be better suited. It was his mother's wish that you care for him, and we want to uphold her wishes as well. There is just one thing." Paulus paused for the briefest of moments.

Decimus watched him alertly.

"We would like to begin the process of adoption," Paulus said. "We would like to see you as his parents in the eyes of the law."

"We could never afford to do that." Juliana shook her head slowly.

"No, but *I* can," Paulus said. "And remember, you just agreed that we would always be his family. So, as his uncle, I will start the process." He smiled and nodded at her.

"This is more joy that I can hold." Juliana wept openly now. "We can never thank you enough." She fell at Paulus's feet.

He lifted her up. "Oh yes, you can thank me. By bringing him up in the ways of the Lord, by allowing us to see him on a regular basis, and by letting us help financially."

"I can do that," she laughed joyously, first embracing Paulus and then the women.

"You will never know what you have done for my mother and me today," Paulus said. "This has greatly lessened our grief over Marcus. This baby will help us come to grips with our loss over and over again." He placed his hand on Decimus's shoulder.

Eunice now held the baby. "You realize what this will mean to our children? He is their cousin. They will have no others as my brothers are too far away, if indeed they have any. This baby will be precious to all of us."

She handed the little one back to Juliana. The baby had managed to sleep the whole time.

Decimus and Juliana started back to their home, spirits high and hearts overflowing with happiness.

A dark shadow slipped along the side of the house and out of sight of the departing guests.

Chapter Forty-Two

Decimus and Juliana could hardly contain their joy at the thought of adoption. Like all citizens of Pergamum, they were familiar with the idea of adoption since many wealthy families used this method to provide sons for furthering their business plans. But adoption was rare among poor people like them.

"I can't believe this is really happening." Juliana beamed at Decimus. They sat before their fire long after returning from Paulus's home. Gabriel snuggled sleepily in Juliana's arms after he finished his feeding. She smoothed back the little curls from his forehead and enjoyed the feel of his soft skin.

Decimus choked up when he smiled at her in return. "We would have happily raised him, but this fulfills all our dreams," he said in a strangled voice.

Juliana looked at him lovingly. In all the days they had been together, she had never seen him weep. He had been deeply touched when they lost all their babies, but he had always been the strong one for her.

"We have to choose his name," she said. "I want to keep the name Gabriel as that is the name given to him by his mother. I always want to keep her memory alive. What do you think?"

Decimus appeared lost in thought for a moment. He rubbed his rough hands over his face. "I've been giving it some thought. I would really like to have some form of Marcus in it. I know he would never have acknowledged him, but Marcus is gone, and I think it would give great pleasure to Paulina and Paulus."

"Oh, Decimus, that's a lovely idea. I've heard of Marcellus or Marquis. Are there any other forms that you know of?" She cuddled little Gabriel closer in her arms.

"The only other one I can think of is Marcos, but I think I like your ideas better." His eyes focused on the sleeping form of the baby.

"Which one should we choose?" She looked to her husband expectantly.

"How about Marcellus? That has all of Marcus in it plus a couple more letters. Besides it has a certain noble ring to it."

"And one more thing, your name must be in there too." She looked lovingly at Decimus.

Again, tears threatened to release from his eyes. "He'll be my son, won't he? I never thought that would happen. What a lot of joy has entered our lives since we turned them over to Christ. We still have troubles, but oh the joy."

"You're so right, Decimus. But back to the name."

He closed his eyes while shaking his head. His head lifted, and his eyes opened to beam at her. "Then how about Gabriellus Marcellus Decio?"

"That's quite a name for such a little one. But I like it. We'll still call him Gabriel, won't we?" She ran her finger down the side of his face.

"Of course. That'll be our family name for him. But his full name will be a name that can go far in life." He leaned forward and laid his hand on the little head.

"Let's not tell anyone what his full name will be until the adoption ceremony," she said.

"I agree. It will be a surprise for Paulus." They smiled at each other.

Paulus made his plans for the adoption. He could hardly believe Marcus had a son. This little life was all that was left of him now. Maybe God would give him a second chance with Marcus's son. He had not been able to reach the father, but the son was there for his molding and training. He knew Decimus and Juliana would bring him up in the ways of the Lord.

He made his plans before retiring for the night and early the next day departed from home to set the adoption process in motion. His first stop was the office of Senator Quintus. He would know who to contact and would be able to assist Paulus.

He waited in the foyer of the senate building until Quintus was available to talk. A young clerk approached him with a deference he found amusing.

"My Lord Paulus, Senator Quintus would like to see you now. Please follow me." The clerk bowed low in a sweeping motion, then indicated the direction of his office.

Paulus rose and followed the clerk down a marble corridor lined with carvings embedded in the marble. He had seen this artwork before, but with the sun striking them this morning, they looked startling in their beauty. They entered a large, comfortable room with rich carpets adorning the marble floor and lounging chairs and couches scattered about the space.

Quintus sat upright at a desk in one corner. When he saw Paulus enter, he rose.

"My friend," Quintus said. "It's been many a long day since I have seen you. Welcome to my humble office." He rose and met Paulus in the middle of the room. The two exchanged greetings, and Quintus led them to a corner grouping of low couches.

"Let's sit here where we can be comfortable while we talk." He nodded to the clerk to leave them, then turned his attention to Paulus.

"It must be something serious to bring you to me so early in the day." Quintus gave him a questioning look.

"It's serious in one way but joyous in another." Paulus settled a cushion behind his back and sat for a moment before continuing. He needed to say this right.

"What I'm about to tell you must be held in strict confidence," he said. "It may well be known in time, but for the present, it must remain secret." He looked at his friend for agreement.

"Paulus, we've known each other for a long time, since we were children. Have you ever known me to betray a confidence?" He cocked an eyebrow at him.

Paulus raised his hands in agreement. "Never. That's why I've come to you."

"Then proceed." Quintus settled back on his low couch, eyes and ears alert for the story.

"You know my brother Marcus is dead." Paulus's voice trembled as he spoke the words.

"Yes, I think everyone in Pergamum knows by now. A sordid affair, if you'll pardon me for saying that." He shook his head.

"You're right. It *is* sordid but also very sad. We began as three brothers, and now I am the only one left." He lowered his eyes and struggled to gain control of his emotions.

"Please accept my condolences." Quintus reached out and touched his arm.

Paulus nodded his thanks. "I'm sure you also know that Marcus had a succession of women."

"Yes, that is also well known." Quintus shook his head sadly.

"What you probably don't know is that Marcus has a son." He watched for a reaction.

Quintus blinked at Paulus. He looked at him seriously before he answered. "It would be very surprising if he didn't have more than one."

"That is quite possible, but this one is known to me. I held him in my arms last night."

Now Quintus sat up straight. His lips parted, and he raised both hands, palms up. “How did that ever happen? From knowing you all these years, I would say you wouldn’t be a part of all that Marcus indulged in or even move in the same circles. How ever did you find this child?” His face registered his surprise.

“I’d like to tell you the story . . .”

The telling provoked many shakes of the head from Quintus as well as frowns and looks of incredibility. When Paulus finished, he sat back and waited for Quintus to speak.

“And now you want this poor, old couple to raise the child? Is that sensible?” Alarm sounded in Quintus’s voice in response to the story he had just heard.

“Yes, that is exactly what I would like to do.” Paulus leaned forward, fixing his eyes on Quintus. He held his gaze for a heartbeat.

“I think Marcus would be shocked.” Quintus broke eye contact and looked at the wall over Paulus’s head.

“But remember, Marcus had put aside the mother when he knew she was carrying his child. He would never have acknowledged him. This way the baby has a chance at being legitimate and a son under our laws. This is a much better prospect for him. Besides, I’ll be a big part of his life as he grows.” He found Quintus’s eyes again and scanned them. Quintus adjusted his robe and returned the look.

“I see your point. Paulus, after the way Marcus treated you and your family, why are you doing this?” His brows drew together in a frown.

“There are many reasons, Quintus. As you already know, I am a follower of Christ now, and His teachings include showing love wherever we can.”

“Yes, I’ve heard of these strange teachings. Magnus wants all of the Christians wiped out of our city. Marcus was in on that too, from what I can determine. Are you not placing yourself in danger by doing this, even by coming here today?” He swung his hand in a circle and leaned toward Paulus.

“My life is in the hands of my God every day. I no longer fear what man can do to me. I’ll not hide away; I’ll live my life openly. Whatever comes, comes. I’m willing to take the risk.”

“I can’t say I agree with your choice of god, but I have to admire your approach to danger.” He placed a finger on his chin. “This will have to come before the senate for their approval. We can hardly tell them the whole truth. How shall we handle this?”

They discussed how best to present the adoption petition without bringing in Marcus’s name. When they were both satisfied, Quintus said, “I’ll do what I can to make sure this adoption takes place. You know there is a cost to this?”

"Yes, I've come prepared with the payment." He reached into his bag and withdrew several valuable coins. He placed them before Quintus. "If it takes more than this, I'll bring you whatever you need."

"Thanks, Paulus. I would think that'll be enough to grease the palms of the greedy lawmakers." He laughed a hollow laugh.

"Quintus, you'll never know how much I appreciate this. Many of the senators would have shied away from doing anything for me or even for Marcus. I appreciate your willingness to still do business with me."

"I just hope I've done the right thing. I'm not a brave man, but loyalty still means something to me. I'll send word to you when we're ready for the next step."

Paulus left Quintus's office well pleased with his dealings of the morning.

I think we've covered everything. What could possibly go wrong?

Chapter Forty-Three

Ekrem fumed to himself. He marched around the temple library, wanting to kick the walls. His face warmed as he stormed around in circles.

"What now, what now?" He ground his teeth and muttered under his breath. He didn't dare speak any louder since priests were in the hall outside the room.

"These peons of the emperor who call themselves governor make me ill. Justus Anthony was bad enough, but Magnus is so filled with himself, there's hardly room for him in his palace."

He raised his foot, then changed his mind. He pounded a fist into his other hand instead. His diatribe continued. His arms flung around, and his robe swung as he went. At last, he stopped long enough to take a breath and decide what he would do.

"A summons," he cried, almost losing his temper again. "Of course I'll go. He made it clear this was not an invitation but a command." He tugged his beard until he felt the pain, then took a deep breath. He smoothed his clothes, which were now in disarray, and moved through the deep curtain covering the entryway. He walked with dignity through the groups of priests going about their daily duties.

The bright sunshine was a shock to his eyes, so he pulled the fringe of his turban lower on his forehead to provide some shade. The walk to the governor's palace was short, but each step was agony for Ekrem today.

He presented himself to the guard at the door, indicating he was expected. The guard led him into a waiting room and entered the great room. When he returned, he marched past Ekrem without a word. Ekrem had no choice but to sit where he was and hope someone would soon let him in.

At first it was interesting watching people come and go from the interview room, but soon Ekrem became agitated again.

Why have I not been announced?

His eyes darted back and forth as he watched the guards and the steady stream of people.

A group of inappropriately dressed girls trouped into the room, giggling and fixing each other's hair as they went by. Ekrem was disgusted. He lifted his eyes to avoid the sight but stole quick glances as they went by. Laughter and coarse singing drifted through the doors as they opened and closed.

He rose from his seat and strutted to the door. It was partly open so he could see a section of the room. Young maidens scurried about with cloths and baskets of utensils, setting long tables for what appeared to be an approaching feast. He couldn't see Magnus, but he could hear his vulgar laugh and the tittering of the girls.

What a revolting sight.

Clucking his tongue, he shook his head and charged back to his seat, dropping into it.

Should I stay or should I go?

He debated with himself, fingers tapping out a rhythm on one cheek.

To go would bring swift and severe retribution on my head, but I'm not sure if I care.

Before he could decide, the door opened fully, and an inner guard, ostentatiously garbed, appeared in the doorway. "Ekrem, the governor wishes to see you at this time. Please enter."

Ekrem jumped up and followed him into the vast room. The guard led him past the decorated tables to a far corner, where Magnus lounged with his ladies.

"Leave me now, girls." The governor dismissed them with the wave of his hand. They skittered away, taking a large basket of fruit and pastries with them. Their departure was noisy, and Magnus didn't speak until they were out of hearing.

He stared stonily at Ekrem, a frown forming on his formerly smooth brow. After straightening himself in his chair, he raised a hand and pointed. "You." The word was filled with scorn.

Ekrem seethed but refused to be intimidated or show his anger. He waited.

"What happened to your friend Marcus? The one who was going to solve all our problems? How did you manage to make such a mess of that?" The finger never stopped pointing at Ekrem's face.

Ekrem bowed low, sweeping the floor with his turban. "My lord, I have no knowledge of that which you speak."

"No knowledge?" the incensed governor roared. "Do you think I don't know what goes on in this backwards city? I know everything—every conversation you've ever had, every whisper uttered in a back room, every traveler on a back road. Everything." His voice rose with each word until he shouted, gesturing wildly with his hands. He stood now, spewing out the words.

Ekrem stood his ground, never wavering. "You are mistaken, my lord, if you think I had anything to do with Marcus's death." He said this in a steady, monotone voice.

The calmness of his words seemed to have a slightly soothing effect on Magnus, who sat down on his seat. He dropped his hands to his side, and his face lost some of its dark hue. He took a deep breath and exhaled slowly. He began again in a subdued voice.

"Our problem still remains. The cult is as strong as ever, and his brother walks the streets in safety. We need a resolution to this situation. What do you suggest?" Magnus sat back with arms folded over his silk robe.

"All is not yet lost. There is a plan . . ."

Magnus watched the floor as Ekrem talked, never moving a muscle. He shook his head from time to time. When Ekrem finished, Magnus looked up at him, lips clamped tightly together.

He rubbed one ear, pulling on the lobe as he observed Ekrem. "Perhaps you are more clever than I at first determined." His smile was tight. "If your plan works, you shall be rewarded." A flick of the wrist told Ekrem he was dismissed.

Ekrem bowed his way out of the chamber.

Magnus relaxed against the cushions.

Fool. Your plans may work, but you have no idea what my plans are, and they will work.

His laugh echoed across the empty room.

After returning from his meeting with Quintus, Paulus sought his mother. He found her in the solarium, stitching on a piece of fabric. She gazed at her son with a welcoming smile. Paulus was so pleased to see her looking happy again. Holding little Gabriel last night had changed her whole outlook.

He paused just inside the door, inhaling the fragrance of the blossoming flowers. "Mother, may I speak with you for a minute?"

"My son, nothing gives me greater pleasure. Come, sit beside me." She folded her work neatly and laid it on a white table beside her.

He sat and took her hand in his. "What I have to say may not be welcome, but I am convinced that it needs to be said."

She searched his eyes while squeezing his hand. "I fear the serious tones in your voice. Have I done something to make you unhappy?" Her eyebrows lifted in question.

"No, Mother. I can't imagine you doing anything but bringing great joy to me and to any others who are fortunate enough to come under your blessing." He rubbed his thumb over the back of her hand.

"Then what is it, my son? Please tell me quickly." Her eyes widened and her chin came up.

Paulus swallowed hard. "I went to see my father after Marcus died. I felt he should be told the truth."

His mother's hand tensed under his. He gently rubbed her hand as he continued to talk. "I know this is hard for you, but you need to hear this."

"Keep going, Paulus. I trust you to tell me what I need to know." She smiled sadly at him.

"The place where he is being kept is a depressing place. Not only that, but he is not receiving good care. His hair is unkempt and dirty, as are his clothes. They've tied him to the frame of the bed. He . . . he didn't want to see me. I had to leave without being able to tell him about Marcus."

Paulus paused as the scene played itself again in his mind. He squeezed his mother's hand before going on. "When I left the house, a plan entered my mind. I really think it was from God."

"Go on, Paulus. I'm listening." Her voice betrayed her calm words.

"I'd like to bring him home."

The words seemed to hang in the air just above them.

Paulus wasn't even sure if he had uttered them. His mother sat perfectly still. The only sound in the room was from the birds just outside the window, sitting in bushes and celebrating the day.

Paulina stood up and walked over to the window. Paulus watched for her reaction. She didn't speak.

"Mother, I would never do anything to hurt you. If this is too hard for you, I'll never mention it again." He sat with slumped shoulders, his head resting in his arms.

She turned from the window. "How would we look after him?"

He was shocked that she had moved so quickly into the practicalities. "We would hire a nurse to look after him, two nurses. I was thinking about the set of rooms on the other side of the house from where our sleeping and living quarters are, the ones that open onto the side garden. They're bright and airy and away from the busyness of the house."

She nodded, apparently deep in thought.

"You wouldn't even have to see him," he said. "He would be given his meals there as well. But he would be in our home and well looked after. I feel it's the least I can do for him. He wants nothing to do with me, and I can cope with that if I know he's well cared for." He shook his head as he looked at her.

"I think it might work." Paulina smiled at him this time. "You have no idea how proud of you I am. Most sons who have been treated the way you have been would leave him to rot where he is."

He went to the window to stand beside her. The two watched the birds in silence. Finally he turned and embraced her.

"Thank you, Mother. I'll talk to Eunice and approach the doctor."

Eunice quickly agreed with his plans.

"I'm so proud of you. You have such compassion." She stood before him, cupping his chin in her hand. "This won't be easy for any of us, but it's the right thing to do." She placed a gentle kiss on his cheek.

He hugged her to him. "That's how I feel about it, too. Will you sit with Mother for a while? I want to approach the doctor without delay."

Once again he found himself in front of the desolate building that housed his father. The same female assistant opened the door. She looked surprised to see him again but said nothing.

"I'd like to meet with the doctor if he is in at present," Paulus said politely, tilting his head slightly in her direction.

"I'll see if he can see you." She did not invite him in, and he was left standing outside the house. Even the street was depressing. Low, run-down dwellings lined both sides of the street. A few dirty, ragged children played in front of a house. A dog slunk between two of the buildings. Paulus decided he was probably seeking food.

The door opened again, and the doctor appeared. “Is there something I can do for you?” The doctor stood stiffly before him, no expression on his face.

“I would like to talk with you. It’s urgent.” Paulus again inclined his head.

“I’m really quite busy right now.” His hand was on the door; he began to close it.

“I won’t take up much of your time, but it is imperative I speak with you today.” Paulus stepped toward the doctor.

“Then follow me.” The curt command was followed by a swift turn of his sandal. He preceded Paulus into the house and led him through the dingy hall to a back room. Once inside he swung around on his heel and faced Paulus. No seat was offered. “What do you want to speak about?”

“It’s about my father—”

“Your father is well looked after” came the abrupt reply. “Have you any idea how difficult he is?”

“Yes, I’m certain he’s very difficult. I’m not here to make complaints—”

“Then what is it you want?” His demeanor was fierce, with his lips pulled into a straight line, eyebrows drawn together, and his words almost a snarl.

“I want to remove him from here to my own home.” Paulus folded his arms across his chest and lifted his chin. He would not be cowed by this man.

The doctor stared at him. He laughed a short, sharp bark. “And just how do you think you could handle him?”

“That is *my* concern. I want him ready to be moved by tomorrow noon.” When the doctor gave no reply, Paulus turned to leave the room. The voice behind him gave a low growl. He took one last look.

The doctor’s eyes were hooded in a squint, his teeth bared. “You’ll never get him. I’ll never let you have him.”

Paulus threw his words back into the room. “Tomorrow at noon.”

“Never! Never! Never!”

The shouted words followed him down the hall and out the door.

Chapter Forty-Four

As Paulus left the building, he knew he couldn't wait until tomorrow. Something else was at play here, and he had his suspicions.

Marcus must have paid the doctor well. There must be some way that he is still getting money; otherwise why would he not want to release Father?

He brooded as he walked, head down, hands behind his back.

Maybe Marcus convinced him to keep father on medications so he wouldn't be trouble to Marcus's career. It's a mysterious affair.

He walked swiftly to David's house. He needed wisdom.

David leaned his head toward Paulus as Paulus spoke. When he paused, David closed his eyes and bowed his head. He nodded and looked at Paulus.

"I think you're probably right in your guesses," he said. He bent forward and placed his hand on his arm. "I think we need to move right away on getting your father out of there. If you wait until tomorrow, it may be too late. He could move your father almost anywhere, and we might never find him."

"That's my thinking." Paulus's lips pressed together in a straight line. He sighed deeply, rubbing his hand across his forehead.

"Just one question before we make our plans." He tightened his grip on Paulus's arm. "Are you sure you really want to bring him to your house? He isn't an easy man, and with his condition, it could make life difficult for you and your family."

Paulus nodded and clenched his hands into fists. "I appreciate your concern, and I have thought about that, but I really feel God is prompting me to bring him home. My family knows the risks involved and is willing to take them."

David released his arm and punched the air with his fist. "Then let's find Mattias and a few of the others, and we'll get him out of there."

"Before we do that, do you know of any women in our midst who might be willing to care for him in my home? I've thought of Maria."

"Maria is a great choice," David said. "She is skilled dealing with sickness, and she is lonely. I know she would appreciate the chance to work for you. What about Livia?"

"That's a good idea. Can we stop by their homes on the way to get Mattias?" Paulus's face relaxed. It was good to have David with him.

"I've got a better idea. Why don't I ask Miriam to do that for us, and they can meet us there. That way we won't lose any more time."

"Excellent." Both men jumped to their feet.

David talked with his wife, who immediately saw the great need and was agreeable to approaching the women.

Paulus and David set out to talk to Mattias and others, and soon had a group of six men with them. Once again, Paulus stood in front of the doctor's house. Their first knock was not answered. Mattias gave a mighty rap on the door, and the frightened-looking assistant answered.

"What do you want?" Fear played across her face. Her eyes shifted back and forth just below their gaze.

Paulus stepped up to the door. "We've come to take my father to my home." He stood quietly before her, but his voice was firm.

She tried to shut the door, but Mattias was too quick for her. He wedged his strong arm against the door. She jumped back out of his way.

"Really, you must go," she said. "I have orders not to admit anyone this morning." Tears hung in her eyes, and a tremble flitted across her chin.

But it was too late; the six men were already heading down the hall to the doctor's office. The door was closed, so Paulus knocked.

Nothing.

He pushed on the door, and it swung open. The office was empty. He turned quickly and led the way to his father's room. This door, too, was closed but not locked.

A pitiful sight met their eyes. Julian was strapped to the narrow bed, eyes closed, chest rising and falling as he breathed heavily. His physical appearance was no better than it had been yesterday, and the smell in the room was caustic. As the men entered, they covered their noses.

Mattias quickly untied the tethers on him, and two of the men picked him up and carried him out of the room. Paulus made a quick search but could find no personal belongings. When he returned to the front entrance, the assistant was gone.

Back on the street, David opened the blanket he had been carrying, and they gently placed Julian on it. A farmer passing by with his wagon stopped to look, and David paid him to carry Julian to Paulus's house. Paulus sat in the wagon with his father, while the others walked.

As they bumped along, he looked at his father carefully. Due to the lines on his face, he was nearly unrecognizable as the man who had raised him. Instead of anger, Paulus felt intense pity for him.

Julian never once opened his eyes during the journey across the city. Paulus knew he must have been heavily sedated.

As they proceeded through the streets, the wagon's progress was slow, so the others had no trouble keeping up. People stared at them from all sides. A few recognized one or more of the men and shouted questions at them, but no one answered.

When they arrived at their destination, they carefully lifted their burden from the wagon and carried it into the house. The servants had prepared the room for their reception, and Miriam had managed to get Livia and Maria there before them. Eunice met them at the door and led the way to the rooms. Paulus gently laid his father between the cool sheets and covered him.

"Maria, please let him sleep off whatever the doctor has given him," he said. "Then your job and Livia's will be to see to his comfort. I will send clean night clothing to you, and servants will be available to bring hot water and whatever you need."

He kept his face a rigid mask to hide his feelings from those around. He swallowed once, then took a deep breath. "Leonius has agreed to work with you and carry whatever you need to you. Your rooms are just off this one and should be ready for both of you. I'll speak with you later with more details. Right now I'm sending one of the servants for our doctor. I want him to check my father over carefully."

Paulus's gaze shifted between the two women, assessing their understanding of his instructions. Once he felt they were ready to take over the care of his father, he nodded to them and left the room.

Back in the main room of the house, Paulus thanked the men for their help and support. "I could never have gotten him out of there without your help. The hardest part is probably still to come." He embraced each one.

"Brother, I think we should pray with you before we go." Emin put his hand on his shoulder. "This may be a very difficult road for you."

"Yes, I appreciate your prayers." Paulus bowed his head as each man stood beside him and placed a hand on him.

When they finished praying, the men left to return to their own work. David was the last to leave.

"Please be careful, Paulus, and send for me anytime you need me." He rested his arm around Paulus's shoulders.

"I will, David. Thank you, Miriam, as well." Miriam and Eunice had entered the room after the others had gone. David and Miriam left, leaving Paulus and Eunice alone.

"Well, it's done," he said. "Now we'll see what will happen." Before his wife he let the mask slip and allowed his face to twist in pain and grief. "Thank you, my dear wife, for everything you've done to make this possible."

She wrapped her arms around her husband. "I'm happy to do anything that will bring you happiness. I truly hope this move will eventually bring all of us happiness."

Later that night, Paulus stole quietly into his father's room. Maria sat beside his bed. She looked up and laid aside the needlework she had been holding.

"Good evening, Paulus." She struggled to stand from the low chair, but he motioned for her to remain seated.

He took his eyes off her and moved close to the bed. With hands behind his back and head bowed, he stared at the form lying there. His mind jumped from the present to his childhood, when his father had been strong and handsome. He had once greatly admired him, even loved him. Paulus remembered that he had always been distant from the children in those early days, but never cruel.

Maria coughed softly behind him, shattering the images and forcing him back to the present. "He looks much cleaner than when we brought him here," he said. He glanced back at Maria, then studied his father's face again. "You've done wonders with him."

"He was in bad shape when he woke up. Didn't know where he was and screamed a whole lot of abuse. Leonius helped Livia and I hold him down until he relaxed." Maria reached out and smoothed the blanket covering him.

"I'm so glad you're here. We would never have been able to handle him." He knew his voice was quavering and swallowed a few times to still the shaking.

Maria smiled up at him, adjusting the scarf covering her graying hair. "I'm happy to be here. He may not be easy, but I was so lonely, it's good to be among people again." Maria's tone was wistful.

Paulus turned from the bed and stood beside Maria. He focused his full attention on her so as not to dwell on his father's face. "Did he make any sense when he talked?"

"None whatsoever. We couldn't make out anything at all except some words we wouldn't repeat." She sat up straighter and folded her arms.

Paulus went closer to the bed and gazed down on his father again. His father's eyes opened slowly, and he looked right into the eyes of his son.

"Get out!" his father cried. "Out! I never want to see you again. Out . . ." He tried to sit up in bed, eyes wild, arms thrashing. He displaced all the bedding around him.

Paulus turned and left the room.

Chapter Forty-Five

The screams could be heard through most of the house. Servants came running to see what had happened. The children had awakened and were both crying for their mother. Marina tried to comfort and assure both of them that all was fine, but she, too, turned her head in the direction of the diabolical sounds.

Eunice met Paulus in the hall outside their rooms. She hugged him closely and felt his shaking body.

"What have I done, Eunice? Bringing him here felt so right earlier." He wrapped his arms around her and leaned his cheek against hers.

She caressed his head while speaking softly to him. "It will still be right, Paulus. You must give him time. He's been under heavy sedatives and is dealing with demons we know nothing about."

"I know you're right. I must be patient. And even if he never accepts me, he's still in a better place than he was. I'll know he's well cared for." He leaned back to look into her eyes and mustered a smile for her.

A servant approached to tell them the doctor had arrived. He bowed his head to Paulus. "Would you like to speak with him before he sees the patient?"

"Yes. Tell him I'll meet him in the library." Paulus straightened and grabbed Eunice's hand.

"I'll come with you, Paulus, if I may." Her eyes pleaded for him to allow her.

"Yes, please. I'd like you by my side." Together they hurried to the library. He gripped her hand tightly.

After they spoke with the doctor, he promised to return to the library when he had finished his examination. They waited without speaking. Wild sounds rang out again from the room, then stopped abruptly. They looked at each other in surprise. Paulus started for the door, but Eunice put her hand on his arm.

"No, Paulus. We said we'd wait here." He relaxed the muscles of his face as he returned to her side.

When the doctor returned, he explained to them that he had to sedate Julian again. "I've given him a small dose of medication. It isn't powerful, but it will help him to sleep comfortably."

The doctor's piercing eyes now focused on Paulus. "The nurses have been given instructions on how to administer more if needed. I think it will take several days before we can really assess his state. It may be he'll never recover, but we'll wait and see. I'll come back later tomorrow unless you need me sooner."

After glancing from one to the other, he took his leave.

Quiet once more settled over the house. The moon shone through Paulus and Eunice's bedroom window, waking Eunice in the early hours of the morning. She slipped from her bed without waking Paulus, wrapped a warm robe around herself, and silently stole from the room.

The windows facing the garden provided a scattering of light in the hallway, the moon casting muted patterns on the tiled floor. She softly made her way toward the section of the house where Julian was housed. Listening at the door and hearing no sound, she pushed the door open and slipped into the room. Maria still sat by the bed, but her head was bent in slumber. As Eunice approached her, she stirred.

Eunice leaned over her and spoke in low tones. "Everything seems peaceful at present."

"Yes, he's been asleep for quite some time." Maria rubbed her eyes and straightened in her chair.

"Why don't you go and lie down? I'd like to sit with him for a while." Eunice patted her shoulder.

"Oh, Eunice, you don't have to do that." Maria reached for her hand and squeezed it.

"I know, but I want to. Go now and let me sit in your place."

The night was very still as she watched her father-in-law, whom she had never met before. She was amazed to see the look of both Paulus and Antipas in his face. This man had borne two wonderful sons; but the third son, unfortunately, had never found his way. Was there hope yet for the father?

She prayed earnestly for him as she sat by his bed. Time went by as she prayed and thought about her husband, her children, and the danger that threatened their lives. Her eyes were closed in prayer when a rustle came from the bed. She rose and bent over him.

"How are you feeling?" she asked gently. She didn't dare touch him.

"Who are you?" he asked in a hoarse voice.

"My name is Eunice, and I've been sitting with you." She folded her hands in front of her.

"I've never seen you before. Should I know you?" He lay still. Only his eyes and lips moved.

How much should I tell him? she wondered. "I live here in this house."

"Is this where I live?" His eyebrows rose in question.

"Yes." She wanted to keep her answers as simple as possible.

"Will I see you often?"

His lips were dry and cracked. *They must make speech difficult*, she thought. She leaned forward to catch each word. "As often as you wish."

"I think I would like that to be very often." He closed his eyes and fell back into slumber. He didn't wake again while Eunice was there.

This started a nightly pattern. Eunice came to his room either late in the evening before retiring or during the night. Each time she was there, he expressed how much he wanted to see her. No one else had been able to break through whatever was binding him.

Maria and Livia watched over him and cared for his needs, but he spoke to neither of them. Only when Paulus tried to approach did the screaming begin again.

Late one night, he was awake when Eunice arrived. She let Livia go and sat by the bed.

He turned his head toward her. "Would you sit closer to me, please?" His voice was low, but his eyes begged her.

She pulled her chair against the side of the bed and smiled at him, waiting for him to continue.

"Tell me about yourself. Who are you?" he asked again.

"I am Eunice—you remember." She smiled again, nodding at him.

"Yes, yes, I know your name. But who *are* you? You aren't one of the servants—I can tell that." After speaking, he lay there panting.

She waited until his breathing became quieter. "You're right; I'm not one of the servants." She sent a quick prayer heavenward for the right words to say. "I'm actually married to your son."

A frown gathered on his forehead. He appeared to be turning her words over in his mind. He turned his dull eyes on her again. "Which son?"

"Paulus is my husband."

"Paulus."

"Yes."

Lines deepened in his forehead. He turned his head toward her. "I haven't been very nice to him, have I?" The words were barely a whisper.

She chose her words carefully. "No, you really haven't been."

His head moved slightly from side to side. "Is this your house?"

"Actually, the house belongs to Paulus."

"Then why am *I* here?" His eyes widened, and his jaw slackened.

"Paulus brought you here because he was upset by the way you were being treated where you were."

His bony hands plucked at the blanket, gathering it in little bunches. "He did that for me?"

"Yes."

Sleep overcame him, and Eunice soon left the room to report the conversation to Paulus.

"He said all that?" Paulus asked, his tone incredulous.

"Yes, I've tried to tell you the exact words he said." She ran her hand down the side of his face.

Paulus shook his head, then laughed. "Why should I be surprised? You completely won my heart, and you charm everyone you meet."

Eunice blushed but couldn't stop the smile that curved her lips. "You embarrass me, my husband. It was you who won *my* heart."

Paulus let a few days go by before attempting to see his father again. Eunice's encounter encouraged him, but still he wondered what would happen when he saw him. The reports coming from the nurses were mixed. He ate his food with gusto and was beginning to fill out again, but they had made no headway with his mind. He either refused to talk to them or screamed obscenities to the point that they wished he hadn't spoken.

Therefore, Paulus approached the room with trepidation. He knocked softly and waited for Maria to appear. She opened the door slowly, a sleepy look hovering around her eyes.

"Maria, I would like to try to see my father again. What is his mood today?" He slipped into the room as Maria held the door open for him. The room was dark compared to the lighted hallway, and his eyes needed time to adjust. He peered at her, watching her lips as she responded.

"He's been quiet, master. He hasn't spoken, but we've had none of those awful outbursts. I think it might be safe to see him. He's sleeping at the moment." She backed away from Paulus, rubbing her palms on her robe.

Why did she always seem nervous when he was around? He smiled to ease her discomfort. "Then I'll sit by his bed until he awakens. You take a break. I think the cook has just taken fresh bread from the oven. Why don't you go see if she'll spare you a piece?"

She bowed, wiping her hands again. "Thank you, my lord. I'd be pleased to do that." She padded noiselessly from the room.

Paulus sat on the same chair that had held Maria and where Eunice had sat the night she spoke with his father. As he scanned his father's face, he was pleased to see how much better he looked. His face had filled out, and his color was much improved. He was clean and tidy, a vast improvement.

Even if he never regains his mind, he's still much better off here than at the other house, Paulus thought. Memories of childhood with Antipas and Marcus filled his mind. His parents had seemed to have everything in the eyes of those who knew them.

But look at our family now.

He rested his head on his folded hands and continued staring at the man before him.

Antipas gone, Marcus gone, father incapacitated. Antipas, at least, is in a better place, and mother and I have the hope of joining him. But what does my father have? Nothing. Nothing.

While he contemplated the past, his father must have awoken. As Julian tried to lift himself in the bed, Paulus jumped up to help him.

Curses rolled from his lips. With his returning strength, he threw his pillows and bedding at Paulus. "Out! Out! Help! He'll kill me."

Paulus tried to restrain him, but Julian seemed to possess a fierce strength. He managed to stand and twisted away from Paulus. He grabbed items from the low table beside the bed. They soon followed the pillows. Fortunately, Leonius was passing outside the room and came running in. The two men were still no match for Julian.

Paulus had never heard such foul language pour out of his father as Julian continued his rampage around the room. He yanked curtains from the windows and ripped down wall hangings. The room was in chaos, and still Paulus and Leonius were unable to restrain him.

At last, Julian fell to the floor, spent. Broken pottery lying beneath him cut his skin; blood seeped from several scratches. Livia must have heard the commotion; she looked in and went to find assistance. Now other servants and the women arrived. Eunice bent over Julian's still form and pressed her hand to his forehead.

"Paulus, why don't you and Leonius go and get cleaned up," she said. "Maria, Livia, and I will look after Julian's needs." She gave Paulus a gentle shove in the direction of the door.

He left the room, crushed by the display and lacking hope of any improvement. Julian was lost to him.

Chapter Forty-Six

"Jesus is the Son of God. He came to save you . . ." David preached from the steps of the altar. Paulus stood beside him while some of the other men were dispersed throughout the crowd. Tensions were high in Pergamum. Rumors darted through the city with a rapidity that defied speed. None were favorable to the Christ followers.

Paulus fixed his gaze on the temple guards, who hovered on the fringes of the crowd. An undulating mass of people swarmed the steps and the street below the altar. Children played at their parents' feet, while the usual detachment of dogs sniffed around the edges, seeking discarded food.

The day was unbearably hot under the noonday sun, but still the people came.

What an opportunity to present Christ, Paulus thought. *The people are hungry for the Word of the Lord.*

A disturbance at the left side of the crowd caught his attention. Paulus couldn't see what was happening, but the temple guards forced their horses through the press of bodies. Shouts sounded from that general area.

David's amazing. How can he keep preaching with all the distractions?

Paulus tried to see what was happening. He stretched his neck and craned it to see around the crowd.

The guards milled around but seemed disinclined to intervene. A man was being lifted onto waiting shoulders.

Someone in the crowd began to chant.

"Miracle. We want a miracle!" Others took up the cry, adding their voices to the confusion.

"Make way."

Four men worked their way through the crowd toward the altar, one carrying the man on his shoulders while the others supported him. Fists jabbed heavenward as the great multitude took up the chant.

"We want a miracle. Want a miracle. A miracle. A miracle."

David stopped speaking and watched as the group drew near the steps. The noise was deafening as more and more joined the chant, "Miracle! Miracle! Miracle!" Heads bobbed, arms pierced the sky, shoulders jostled, colors of turbans and robes blended and faded, voices rose higher in pitch, and over all the tableau of the bearers continued. They dropped their burden at David's feet. A stillness fell over the crowd as they watched the drama reach this climax.

Paulus watched David out of the corner of his eye. This was unexpected. No one had performed a miracle since Antipas had been sacrificed.

One man separated himself from the others and mounted the steps. "People of Pergamum," he shouted, both arms raised to the heavens. "If this god is real, it's time we saw what he can do." With disdain in his voice and bearing, he turned to David. "If this god has any power, heal this man or accept the consequences." Closed fists reaching for the sky accompanied his shouting.

Paulus wondered what David would do. He didn't want to interfere. The challenge was issued to David. He would wait and see what would happen. He moved to stand side by side with him in a show of support.

David closed his eyes, bringing instant condemnation on his head.

"The man is afraid." The man issuing the challenge pointed at David as he jeered. His eyes swept the mass of people before him. "He can't do it. Bring the guards in closer."

David opened his eyes and looked directly into the face of the brash man. He then let his gaze wander over the restless crowd. He drew himself up and thrust his shoulders back.

"Men of Pergamum, know that the God we speak of has great power," David said. "He is able to lift the fallen, heal the diseased, raise the dead." At that point the crowd roared in protest. David waited until they had settled down before speaking again.

"He can do all these things and more than you can ever imagine," he said. "But He never does them for show. His power is not for entertainment, nor at the whim of man. This man"—he pointed to the figure lying at his feet—"this man will not be healed today."

Great bursts of hissing and jeering greeted his words.

"The other reason this man will not be healed today is because he is not sick. You have been tricked."

The roar of the crowd was deafening. Several men pushed toward the front while they thrust women and children out of their way. Curses poured from opened mouths. Clenched fists towered over heads. The guards rushed to the altar, jumped from their horses, and ran at top speed up the steps to where David stood waiting for them. They grabbed him and bound him without resistance. Paulus expected to be taken as well, but just as quickly as they came, they departed, dragging David down the stone steps and onto a waiting horse. The guards swiftly mounted their horses and rode off through the multitude.

Paulus was stunned.

So the rumors are true. The priests are looking for a way to arrest our leaders. I'm sure this whole setup was a plot. Once the people turned against us, the time was right. It's a miracle I'm still here.

In front of him, the man who was reportedly sick simply stood up and walked away from all the fuss. His friends left with him. The crowd, recognizing that the action was over, began to disperse. Only Paulus was left standing alone—utterly alone.

Chapter Forty-Seven

"The atmosphere in Pergamum is heating up," Decimus said.

"I heard about the crowd wanting a miracle. What will happen now?" Juliana arranged a platter of fruit at the front of their stall.

"Well, the crowds were certainly disappointed. I think public opinion is turning against us."

"Why, did something else happen?" Juliana asked.

"It might be my imagination, but some of the vendors turned their heads the other way when I walked through the market this morning."

"Oh oh, here comes an old one looking for gossip. I'm going to the wagon to get more wares." Juliana headed behind the stall.

Decimus turned to see the man approach him. The gnarled market seller leaned on the side of Decimus's stall. "Did you know that cult is out to ruin the city?"

"What cult is that?" Decimus asked.

"Those crazy followers of that new god. They're going to ruin us."

"How could they do that?" Decimus kept on working, rearranging the merchandise and not looking at the talker.

The seller lowered his voice so no one else could hear. Moving closer to Decimus, he lifted his hand to shelter his lips. "I hear they plan to destroy the great altar."

Decimus almost dropped the wooden spoon he was holding. "How could they do that?"

"Well, they have strength from an unknown god, you know. He'll tear it down. They only have to ask him." He wiped his face with the end of his turban.

Decimus looked up at that and studied his acquaintance. "Where did you hear such nonsense?" He wanted to hear more but not scare the seller away.

"Oh, everybody knows that," was the disdainful reply. "They've already destroyed a military building outside the city." He gestured broadly with his wrinkled hands.

"I think you're listening to gossip, my friend." Decimus smiled at his neighbor, but the smile didn't reach his eyes.

"No, no. These are the facts." The seller spit in the dirt and wiped his face again. "Now that I come to think about it, aren't you one of them?" He narrowed his eyes at Decimus.

"Yes, of course, I'm one of them, as you say. And I tell you, this is all nonsense. You need to stop listening to them and come with me to one of our gatherings and listen to the truth." Decimus reached out and clapped the man on the shoulder.

"No, I won't be coming. I fear for you." The man laughed scornfully and backed away from the stall.

"You've known me for years," Decimus said. "Have you ever known me to be involved in something destructive?" He shuffled along with the man and gripped his shoulder tighter.

The man straightened and backed farther away from him. He shook his robe and adjusted his turban, lips curled over yellowed teeth. "I'll have nothing more to do with you. I don't know you at all. For your own sake—and I tell you this as a former acquaintance—you need to get out of that cult and hide yourself away until this blows over. You're probably in danger. And I'm leaving before someone thinks I know you." He moved away from the stall as quickly as his bent form and twisted legs would allow.

Decimus later reported the conversation to Paulus.

"There's a different feel in the market, master. Men are not as open to our message." Decimus shook his head. His turban tilted, and he grabbed it with both hands to straighten it.

"But that doesn't change our message, does it?" Paulus asked.

"Oh, you can count on me, Paulus. Juliana and I are fully committed. But it will be dangerous until this is settled. It feels as though the city were waiting for something." He placed his hands over his chest and nodded.

"I think you're right, Decimus. There is a feeling in the air of something coming." Paulus crossed his arms and paced the length of the room.

"What have you heard about David's arrest?" Decimus followed behind him.

Paulus completed the length of the room, and the two men returned to their low seats. He slowly shook his head. "Nothing. It's as though he's been swallowed up by the city. I've just come from Miriam's. She's holding up very well. She and

David talked about this possibility many times before his arrest. She feels this may be the end but is trusting the Lord for the strength for each day."

"These are dangerous times for the converts." Decimus sat in silence, his face clouded in thought. Paulus could see he was aging.

Decimus finally glanced up at Paulus again before rising. "I need to get back to the stall." He pulled his robe more tightly around him and adjusted the belt.

"Will I see you tonight at the meeting?" Paulus stood and walked with him to the door.

"We wouldn't miss it for anything." His face transformed into a wide smile. Waving his good-bye, he began his trek back to the marketplace.

After Decimus was gone, Paulus pondered the rumors.

Lord, times are getting tough for the church here in Pergamum. May Your will be done. Pour out Your strength on our people, Lord. Give them the courage to carry on in the face of this opposition. Give me wisdom as I meet with many of the converts tonight. Let me be like Paul and be able to say, "I rejoice."

An angry wind tumbled down the main street of Pergamum, swirling debris in wide arcs as it shifted from side to side along the street. Pedestrians held cloaks tightly around them, and ties from turbans were wrapped over noses. The wind had no respect for friend or foe, poking into openings, probing empty spaces, and violating privacy. The rain hadn't started yet, but the gusts hinted that it wouldn't be far behind.

Out in this tempest, converts from all over the city emerged from their homes. A less-important gathering would have convinced many to remain at home. Decimus and Juliana left the warmth of their hearth and entered the fray. Juliana had bundled Gabriel so closely that Decimus was concerned that she would smother him. Juliana just laughed at him.

Paulus and Eunice chose to walk and bent their heads into the wind. "I hope this isn't a sign that things are getting worse for us," Eunice said to Paulus.

"I agree."

The roar of the wind prevented further conversation, so they continued without speaking.

A large warehouse was their destination. No house was large enough to accommodate the crowd they expected. Paulus wanted to speak directly to as many Christ followers as possible. A recent convert owned the facility. Offering the use of the facility to Paulus was a brave thing to do since the business segment of Pergamum was rapidly becoming anti-Christian.

"I wanted a large area. It's always better to hear things firsthand," he had said to Eunice. "Information passed on loses some of its accuracy."

The building loomed in the darkness ahead, with its sinister façade and drab stone siding. Hampered by the intrusive wind, two small torches bravely tried to light the way.

Inside, the vast room was filling up with men and women, many of whom shivered from the contest with the wind on their way. The atmosphere was somber since all had heard of David's arrest and the many rumors running rampant in the city.

Paulus worked his way through the crowd, listening to a brother here, gripping a shoulder for encouragement there, and generally helping to make people feel comfortable. The owner had assembled a makeshift platform from a few bales of packing materials. To this dais, Paulus now moved. He mounted the platform and faced the group. A hush fell.

"People of Pergamum." He tried to make eye contact with those closest to the front. "I've asked you to come tonight as I need to talk to you about a number of things. I know you are concerned about David. Most of you know how he was taken. I'm sad to say that we have been unable to find out anything about him since. We don't know where he's being held and if there are any charges against him. Keep praying for him. Pray that God will use him where he is and give him the strength to face whatever comes. Pray for his wife and family."

He paused to take a drink from a cup that had been handed to him. Very little noise came from such a large gathering. A cough here and there, the rustle of a robe, the scrape of a sandal—that was all. The people stood, watching and listening.

"Many of you have heard the rumors that are circulating in our city," he continued. "We are in graver danger than we have been for quite some time. I believe that things are coming to a head. I can't tell you what is to come, but you need to be prepared. I believe hard times are near; our day of persecution has come."

A woman cried out only to be quickly silenced by the man at her side.

"But brothers and sisters, don't let fear and discouragement fill your hearts. The God we serve is greater than the wicked ones who seek to destroy us." He gazed out over their heads, lifting his arms high in the air. "God will be victorious.

Will some of us suffer? Yes, we will. But we suffer for Christ who suffered for us. He will be by our sides through the suffering."

He lowered his arms and pointed at the crowd. "Each of you must choose how you will react to the persecution. Once again, we will move some of you to safer places if that is what you desire. I already know that many plan to continue their everyday lives as usual. It's a personal decision. Don't make it without prayer."

The same woman cried out again. This time she was led out of the gathering. Other faces bore masks of fear, but shoulders were thrust back and chins lifted.

"Eunice and I have decided to stay where we are. You will need your leader close by if a crisis comes. I will still be visible in public places. Be careful where you walk, who you talk to, what you say. It may all be held against you." He once again lifted the cup to his lips.

"We will continue to meet in our small groups, but we will not again meet as a large group until the persecution is past." He lifted his arms in benediction over the large crowd. "Go in peace, my children, and remember, God loves you more than you can imagine. May His peace steal over you. May His presence be felt in you. May you walk in His ways as you leave this night."

As people quietly left, a lone figure separated itself from the larger group and slipped into a narrow alley. It was very dark, and he stumbled a few times but managed to exit into a back laneway and leave the center of the city. His cloak, a dull, nondescript gray, blended in well with the night.

He soon disappeared into the darkness. He had achieved his purpose.

Chapter Forty-Eight

Once Decimus had Juliana and Gabriel safely back home, he ventured out again into the night. Rain now slanted down, agitated by the wind. A wet gust slapped him in the face as he stepped from his door. He bent low and hurried away from the house.

Military Row was deserted at this late hour. That and the storm kept most indoors. Drenching blasts from the wind and teeming rain had long since extinguished many of the torches along the barracks and outbuildings.

Decimus felt his way along the side of the building. When his hand no longer found a place to rest, he knew he had arrived at the alleyway leading to his friend's workshop. He turned into the rutted lane, carefully placing each foot on the slick mud.

As he expected, up ahead he could see a light coming from the window of the shop. Aulus was inside. When he knocked on the door, it opened quickly. Aulus put his finger to his lips and hauled Decimus inside. Decimus straightened and shook out his robe. Then he removed his turban to let the water drain from the folds.

"My friend, I'm sorry to disturb you on a night like this." He looked toward Aulus as the silence stretched out.

"What is the matter, my friend?" Aulus continued to stare at him. "You mustn't stay here," he whispered. "Someone might see you."

"I'm not afraid." Decimus stood straighter. "I—"

"It's not you I'm worried about," Aulus said. "I worry about me. I don't want to be seen talking to you. Someone might think I belong to the cult. My life would be worth nothing if that were to happen." He paused, took a deep breath, and raked his fingers through his hair.

"My friend—"

"You must never call me 'friend' again. I'm no longer such a person." Aulus talked faster and faster until he panted out the words. "Please go before I raise an alarm and have you arrested for treason."

"I'm sorry to hear this, Aulus. I merely wanted some information. Won't you reconsider?"

Decimus took a step toward him, but Aulus swept by. He opened the door to the rainy outside and pointed. "Leave. Leave now. You are no longer a person I know or wish to know."

"I will pray for you, friend," Decimus told him. Then he went out into the blast from the wind. The door slammed shut behind him, and the interior light went out.

Decimus was left with no means of seeing the way ahead of him. Slowly he crept along the lane until he reached the street again.

What a disappointment, Lord. I had so hoped that Aulus would soon be one of us. Open his eyes to Your truth.

He faced the rain and pulled the hood of his cloak over his turban. He pulled it down over his face as far as it would go as he battled the elements on the way home.

Paulus and Eunice arrived home thoroughly soaked. Hot water, soft towels, and clean, dry clothes soon remedied their situation. Leonius had met them at the door and instantly promised them a hot drink. They now sat together in Paulus's office. Paulina sat with them.

"Mother, I'm glad you didn't try to come with us tonight. The weather is terrible. I haven't seen such wind and rain in a long time." Paulus's body shivered from the cold and wet he had just experienced. "It almost has a sinister feeling to it, tonight of all nights. Meeting in a warehouse with the wind howling around outside and the rain beating against the side of the building made the atmosphere inside somber indeed." Paulus folded his hands and rested his chin on them.

"How did the people take your message?" Paulina leaned forward on her lounge, her lovely face turned toward her son.

"On the whole, there was a positive response. Some want to hide away until the persecution settles down, but most plan to stay right where they are and continue their day-by-day routines. I was very proud of them." Paulus smiled at the memory. "They're being very brave for Christ."

Maria appeared at the door. She tipped her head toward Paulus. "Master, your father is asking for you."

"Then I'll come right away." He quickly rose, following her from the room.

Eunice and Paulina glanced at each other with puzzled expressions.

"I think we should pray," Eunice said to her mother-in-law.

"I agree."

As Paulus walked toward his father's room, the prayers of his wife and mother surrounded him.

Maria entered first. Paulus followed slowly, searching the room with his eyes until he saw Julian sitting up in bed, looking better than he had for some time.

Maria tiptoed up to his side. "Paulus is here now. Do you want to see him?"

"Yes, yes, bring him in." Julian's voice trembled, but he waved his hand at her.

Paulus advanced into the room and took the chair beside the bed his father indicated. His father seemed deep in thought, so Paulus hesitated to disturb him. Slowly Julian's head turned, and he rested his eyes on his son.

"I hardly know you anymore." The bright eyes roved his son's face.

Paulus acknowledged his remark with his head slightly bowed. "It has been a long time since we've really talked."

"Where is Marcus? I need to talk to him. I thought you might know where he is." The lined hand scratched the bedclothes.

Paulus stared at his father in stunned silence. How should he answer him? He turned ideas over in his mind, discarding them as quickly as they came. He studied his father's face, trying to decide if he was in his right mind at this moment or if this was part of the madness.

"Father," he began. Julian flinched when he said the word.

Paulus shifted his weight on the chair. He wanted to look away but forced himself to look his father in the eye. "Marcus has met with some trouble."

"Trouble? He's all right, isn't he?" More scratching with his fingers.

"Well, no. Not really." Paulus coughed lightly into his hand.

"What do you mean—not really?" His father's face started to tremble. He stared at Paulus.

"Marcus is dead." The words sounded flat to Paulus, but he didn't know how else to break the news to him. He watched the transformation on his father's face.

A deep flush rushed up his neck until it covered his face. Deep furrows dented his forehead while his eyes closed tightly. A slight tremble intensified until his body began to shake, continuing until his entire frame was engulfed.

"Who are you?" he whispered hoarsely. His voice had taken a deeper tone. The bony fingers now gripped the blanket so tightly the knuckles turned white.

As he watched the change in his father, Paulus was dismayed. For a moment he had begun to believe in hope for his father's recovery. Now he wasn't so sure.

Spittle spewed from his stiff lips, and his head thrashed from side to side.

As he raved, the words were garbled and almost unrecognizable. "Get out! Get out. Leave me alone."

On his feet now, Paulus slowly backed away from the bed. He didn't want to cause any more stress for his father. He called softly to Maria, who was instantly at his side, followed by Livia.

"We'll take over from here," Maria said. "He's often like this." She shooed him away with one hand. "You go, and I'll bring you word once he's under control."

Paulus sadly watched from the doorway as the two women ministered to his father. They soothed his forehead with a damp cloth and spoke calmly to him. Once they had stilled him, they mixed the powder the doctor had left and administered it to him. His body began to relax as they eased him down on his pillows. Paulus slipped away and returned to his wife and mother.

"Paulus, what's wrong?" Paulina asked.

"Is your father upset again?" Eunice hurried to his side and embraced her husband.

"I'm afraid the news isn't good. I had hoped that bringing him here would help him regain his senses, but I seem to have been mistaken. The madness has him in its grip." He rested his head against her hair, struggling not to let his emotions show.

"I'll try to see him again tomorrow," Eunice said. "If we surround him with love, we may yet see some improvement."

"Oh Eunice, I'm so sorry you have to be involved in all of this," Paulina said. "I know I'm not the person to see him. It would be too painful and too filled with unhappy memories for me. But he is still my husband and father to my sons, so I'm glad that he's getting good care. Thank you both." She put her hands over her face and wept.

Eunice was instantly by her side. She wrapped her arms around her mother-in-law and gently rocked back and forth.

"You never have to see him, Paulina," she said. "I have no memories of him, happy or otherwise, so I can approach him as someone who needs the love of Christ in his life. Don't be sorry, Mother; I see it as a ministry for me. I can't go out and help people like I used to, so this is one way I can serve my Lord right in my own home." She smoothed the hair back from her mother-in-law's face.

Maria knocked softly at the door. All three looked at her expectantly.

"He's sleeping peacefully now, master," Maria said. "I don't think we'll be disturbed by him again tonight. It usually takes several hours for the medication to wear off."

"Thank you, Maria. I appreciate all you do for my father," Paulus said with warmth.

Long into the night hours, Paulus lay awake. So many things were happening on so many levels.

Lord, I just need to lay all of these things at Your feet. I've been trying to carry it alone. There's joy mixed with sadness as we look at little Gabriel . . . grief whenever I think of Marcus or my father. There's fear for David's life. Wherever he is, Lord, let him feel Your peace tonight. Pergamum needs You, Lord, but they've rejected You. Lord, help me to be wise and bold for You. Whatever comes, I want to stand true to You.

At last he fell into an uneasy sleep, dreams of trouble filling his mind. The face of Marcus kept flashing across the dreams, a cruel smile twisting his face.

Chapter Forty-Nine

"Paulus, you must come at once." A breathless Decimus caught up to him just as he was leaving the house for the city. When he reached Paulus, he grabbed his sleeve.

Paulus gripped his arm. "Decimus, slow down. You can hardly breathe. What's wrong?"

Gasps burst from Decimus as he tried to regain his breath. He was perspiring freely, and sweat soaked the top of his robe and ran through his beard. His turban was tilted to one side of his very red face. He tried to speak but continued taking deep breaths. A look of horror had taken possession of his face.

"Are you all right, friend?" Paulus encircled his shoulder with his arm to help support him. "Here, sit down by the side of the lane for a moment."

"No time," Decimus was finally able to say. "You have to come with me." His face was streaked with dirt from the dusty road.

"Then let's take it slowly, and you can tell me what's wrong as we walk." He kept his arm around him as they moved away from the house.

He forced the words through his teeth. "It's David."

Paulus stopped and faced him. Words tumbled out of him in his excitement. "What about David? Have they released him? Where is he?"

Decimus shook his head and took another gasp of air. "It's not good. A body was found in the alley behind the temple. Some of the merchants in the marketplace told me this morning. They heard it's David."

Paulus gripped his shoulder and stared at Decimus through eyes widened with disbelief. "Are they sure?"

"No, not sure. I came for you right away." They started walking again, faster this time.

Paulus was perspiring now, and sweat ran down his forehead, smarting his eyes. "You did the right thing. We'll go there and see what we can find out. Is the body still there?"

"I don't know." Decimus moaned.

As the two moved toward the marketplace, the city streets were busy with carts clattering over the pavement, horses clopping rhythmically, and farmers shouting to each other. A crowd had gathered in front of the temple to watch the priests prepare the altar for the morning sacrifices. They were abuzz with the day's news.

Decimus and Paulus skirted the back of the throng, who jostled and shoved each other in their attempt to get closer to the front. The two squeezed through the last of the crush and stepped into the open area to the side. They hurried along the side of the temple and entered the laneway behind.

Now that they were away from the bright sun, the light was muted here. They carefully stepped over pieces of broken pottery and other debris. As the stench of rotting refuse assaulted their nostrils, Decimus put a hand over his nose. They turned over discarded waste as they thoroughly searched for a body.

"There's nothing here." Paulus straightened and wiped the back of his hand over his forehead. He put his hands on his hips as he scanned the alley.

Decimus stood as well. He was filthy by now but seemed unaware of it. "You're right. We've left nothing undisturbed. If his body was here, we would have found it."

"It was either a false rumor, or they've taken the body elsewhere," Paulus said, still giving the area a sweeping glance. "Let's go back around by the altar. We might overhear something that would help in our search."

Decimus wiped his hands on his cloak and followed Paulus back the way they had come. The crowds had increased, but they were able to slip into a gap along one side. The priests were carrying a wrapped bundle down the steps from the temple to the altar.

"It's one of the cult leaders." A shout went up from the crowd.

Paulus froze in place. The awful reality hit him. It did look like it could be a body. Surely not.

"Sacrifice the cult leader," a voice said.

Decimus leaned toward him and grabbed his wrist. "Did you hear that?"

"Yes, but I'm not going to believe it just yet," he whispered back.

"Burn the infidel," another voice shouted.

More and more cries filled the air as the crowd surged forward. Temple guards moved among them on horseback, challenging anyone getting out of control. The priests had now reached the altar with their burden and stopped on the step above. Ekrem, the high priest, moved in front and faced the people.

"People of Pergamum," he said. The crowd gradually stilled when they noticed Ekrem's attempt to get their attention.

The altar had been lit earlier and now blazed beside the priest, making a macabre picture. A shadow of foreboding hung over the now-silent crowd.

"Men of Pergamum," the priest began again, "this is a day of triumph for our great city, a day of victory for our exalted god Zeus."

Wild cheering broke out in the crowd. The swelling mass of people renewed their pressing and shoving in one giant surge forward. An old woman near Paulus was thrust aside, lost her balance, and disappeared in the mass of bodies. Paulus pushed his way toward her, reaching out a hand to help her up. She smiled a toothless grin in thanks. Her arm upraised, she continued shouting with the rest.

The priest once again called for quiet. "Men of Pergamum," he again cried out over the clamor of voices.

Silence was longer coming this time, but eventually he had their attention again. "I have here"—he gestured toward the wrapped object the priests held—"the body of a traitor."

"Burn him, burn him" could be heard above the din. "Throw him on the altar."

"Zeus will be avenged this day." The priest raised his arms high as he shouted. "You are witnesses to this act of justice. No one can defy Zeus and live!"

"Down with the cult. Kill the traitors . . ."

"Burn him, burn him . . ."

The crowd was in a frenzy, wanting blood, wanting revenge. The priest stood stiff and still, eyes roving over the mass of people. A slow, evil smile spread across his face as he watched the tumult before him.

Paulus leaned in close to whisper to Decimus. "I would say he's enjoying this."

Decimus kept staring at the altar and the priests while he answered Paulus. "That's what I was thinking. Do we stay or go?"

"I think we'd better stay. We need to see this through to the end." It was hard to talk over the noise. Paulus bent closer to Decimus again. "I'm wondering what's in that package. It could be a body, but we have no proof, only the priest's word." He nodded in the direction of the priest.

"I hadn't thought of that. You're right; we need to stay." Decimus nodded and took a quick glance at Paulus.

The two continued to watch the strange scene before them. The priest continued to stand, watching the people. He seemed to be looking for someone but not finding him. Paulus was aware of a disturbance behind him. As he turned to look, an imperial chariot approached.

"Magnus," he whispered to himself. His eyebrows drew together in a frown.

The priest cast his gaze in that direction, then turned to the people once more. When the roar began to abate, he seemed to come to life. He raised his arms high over his head, made a complete circle on the steps, then let his voice ring out over the crowd. "Zeus will be avenged!"

"On the altar with the infidel." The shout came from somewhere back in the crowd.

Amid the agitated cheers from the crowd, the priests threw their burden on the flames. Sparks rose high in the sky, snapping and hissing as they went. People danced around each other, clapping and singing. It was a bizarre sight, one Paulus would not soon forget.

He glanced over his shoulder in time to see the imperial chariot race off away from the melee. The guards moved in closer, separating some of the crowd into smaller groups. Amid the fracas, the priests disappeared into the temple, leaving the altar to burn out on its own. Paulus kept his eye on the flames, noticing that they died down quickly after the priests retreated.

Something is not right.

He pursed his lips as he pondered what he had seen.

He nudged Decimus and nodded to indicate they should leave. The two men turned away from the altar, slipping through the still-maddened crowd until they were clear. They talked as they walked, discussing the scene over and over again.

"We're missing something," Paulus said. He had taken a cloth from under his cloak and wiped his face vigorously.

"What are you thinking?" Decimus turned to him, stretching out his hands, his lips drawn together in a tight line.

"It just seems to me that a body would burn longer and with a more intense flame. It's also out of character for the priests not to show the body. If they have a traitor to sacrifice, they exploit the opportunity to the fullest; but today, nothing. Why?" He clasped his hands behind his back and bowed his head in thought.

Decimus gasped as if realizing what Paulus was indicating. "Are you saying you don't think that was David?"

"That's what I'm saying. Someone wants everyone to believe it was, but the evidence points in the other direction." They kept walking, both now with bent heads.

"I see your point. Then if that wasn't David, who was it, and where is David?" Decimus's eyes widened as he looked at Paulus.

"I don't know where David is, but I'm quite certain that bundle didn't contain a body at all."

"Why would the priests do that? Why the big show?" Decimus asked with a shrug.

"That's what I'd like to know. Was this a message for us?"

Chapter Fifty

The swish of a priest's ornamental robe could be seen and heard as Ekrem hurried down the long hallway to Magnus's receiving room. An angry scowl furrowed his face. His shoulders showed a tenseness not usually seen in him. As he approached the guards at the door, he slowed his pace and replaced the scowl with a halfhearted smile.

"I believe Magnus is expecting me," he said to the guard in a commanding voice.

"We have orders to usher you right in," was the brusque reply.

The guards stood at attention, spun on well-oiled sandals, and ceremoniously threw back the entry doors.

"You may enter, Lord Ekrem," one said, a hint of sarcasm edging his voice.

Ekrem barged into the presence of Magnus, who was all business today. There was no sign of the usual ladies hanging around his chair. He was alone except for a stiff-looking servant.

"You are dismissed, Manium." Magnus nodded toward the servant, who gathered his robe about him and left without a backward glance.

Meanwhile Ekrem stood before Magnus, not speaking.

Magnus was arrayed in a bright robe of yellow silk with an intricate pattern of vines and urns delicately worked over the fabric. Gold arm bracelets covered his upper arms as well as one ankle. His feet were shod with sandals dyed a royal purple.

A garish attire, Ekrem thought. He showed nothing on his face.

"I'm sure you are aware of the reason for my summons." Magnus sat straight in his chair and spoke the words through clenched teeth.

"My Lord, I'm afraid I do not." Ekrem politely bowed. He kept his lips clamped firmly together while making eye contact with Magnus.

"You have not heard the rumors circling the city with feverish haste?" He flicked his hand toward Ekrem, curling his lip.

Ekrem shook his head. He looked straight at Magnus, defiantly staring him in the eye.

A red flush stole over Magnus's face. He drew his brows together, breathing heavily through his nose. He slowly and deliberately rose from his chair, drew himself up to his full height, and spat in Ekrem's face.

Ekrem did not flinch.

"I will not be made a fool of!" Magnus shouted. He gave Ekrem a hard shove out of his way and proceeded to storm around the room, muttering to himself as he went. When he returned to where a still-silent Ekrem stood, he thrust his face in front of Ekrem's face until they were almost nose to nose.

"You will give an account of yourself." Each word was deliberately pronounced and flung in his face. "Where is the infidel David?" he shouted.

"My lord and master, that is obvious." Ekrem again bowed his head. "You yourself watched him burn on the altar. The remains will be buried before the sun sets outside the northern gates." He indicated the direction with one hand.

"That's not the word I've received from my spies. And I do have spies. You are watched, my less-than-loyal subject." He threw himself down on his chair and looked intently at Ekrem. "What do you say now?"

"I say your spies have brought you lies instead of truth." His kept his back straight, shoulders back, chin elevated.

"And I say *you* are lying." Magnus jutted out his chin and leaned forward in his chair.

"But, my lord, you were a witness. I saw you myself." Ekrem held out his hands, palms up.

"I saw a wrapped parcel burn on the altar. But I did not, nor did anyone else, see what the parcel contained." His forehead was drawn down in a frown, his eyebrows almost touching.

"But what else would it contain?" Again the lift of the palms.

Once again Magnus rose from his chair. He drew his restless hands into fists and released them a number of times before he spoke. He drew a deep breath.

"You tell me." He jabbed his finger at Ekrem. "You tell me what it contained." He was once again in Ekrem's face.

Ekrem remained straight. "And I tell you again, it was David."

"Then I need proof. You have until the sun sets to bring me proof. Go." He pointed to the door and called for the guards. Ekrem was abruptly escorted from the room, down the long hallway, and out the front door. The guards closed the doors behind him, leaving him alone on the street.

He glanced once at the building behind him before he escaped through the crowds and fled back to the safety of the temple.

"He's onto something. I don't know how much he knows or if he's just bluffing. We'll need to move with care."

"How did you manage to bungle that? I thought it was incredibly simple, you fool."

"How dare you call me a fool? I could have you whipped for that."

"But you won't. You need me." The smirk on Izak's face deepened. Arms folded over his chest, he watched his partner under lowered eyelids.

Ekrem fell silent. The darkness surrounded him inside and out.

I'm in too deep, he thought. *I'll need to be clever to play this right. I should never have agreed to work with him, but when he approached me, it seemed right.*

He forced himself to speak calmly. "What do we do now? Casting blame won't help the situation. So far, it's only gossip about the identity of the sacrifice. Surely you have cronies who can change that." He hissed the words in Izak's face.

"Leave that part to me," Izak said. "You just find more money. Anything is possible with enough coin." He rubbed his hands together and grinned.

"I'll get more. But that's all. You do your job, and you'll be well rewarded." Ekrem turned from Izak and moved away with dignity. He looked over his shoulder as he went, flinging back the words. "Just make sure that you've got everything ready when I send the signal."

Izak spat on the ground and wiped his lips on his sleeve.

"And just where is David?" he shouted after the retreating figure.

He could hear moaning clearly now. Weakly he lifted his head and scanned his surroundings. By the little light seeping in from somewhere, he could see damp, dark walls—possibly a cave, he thought. Chains held his wrists and ankles tightly, causing excruciating pain. His body was twisted at a grotesque angle.

As consciousness returned, he realized the moaning had come from his own lips, cracked and swollen as they were. His nostrils encountered the musky odor of his surroundings, and a shudder coursed through his body. He moaned again.

"Quiet in there!" The authoritative voice jarred him. "Quiet or you'll feel the sharp side of my whip."

He settled down again on the coarse, hard surface, his face pressing into the hard-packed earth.

I need to think, he told himself. But then darkness fell over his eyes, and he slipped away.

Chapter Fifty-One

"There is a young man at the entrance who wishes to speak to you." Leonius bowed to Paulus, who sat with the family, enjoying his evening meal. He quickly followed Leonius to greet the visitor.

"Yes, what is it you wish?" Paulus asked.

The young boy standing before him appeared to be out of breath. "This is for you." The boy thrust a small scroll into his hands, then jumped down from the entrance and took off running down the street.

"That's strange." Paulus stepped outside and watched him disappear. He shook his head. "Why is he in such a hurry?" He closed the door and entered his office rather than returning to the family. The scroll bore an official seal, which he pondered. Then he recognized the seal of Quintus. He quickly slit the wax and unrolled the scroll.

"To Paulus from Quintus." The words were formed precisely and looked stark on the scroll. "It is with regret that I inform you that I am not able to produce the papers you requested. The situation in the city has changed, and I am no longer able to do business with you. I wish to distance myself from you and your associates."

Paulus looked up from his reading and stared at the wall opposite him, deep in thought. He turned back to the scroll. "Please do not approach my business in the future or attempt to have any communication with me. I wash my hands of any agreement between us."

Paulus stood, contemplating the words in front of him. "Why?"

He glanced at the scroll again and noticed small letters in the lower corner. He peered at the writing, his eyes widening. "Be careful. You are in danger."

Paulus rolled up the scroll and placed in with his other documents.

This will be a blow to Decimus and Juliana.

He stood thoughtfully, rubbing his hand over his face.

They were anticipating this adoption. But that can't be changed now. There is no going back. Quintus will see me no more.

He sat down on a low seat beneath the open window. Outside all looked peaceful; within his mind all was turmoil. As he sat pondering the problem, an idea surfaced.

"We'll do it." He slapped his hands and walked with purpose back to his family.

Heat. Overpowering, overwhelming, suffocating, draining heat. Pergamum was steeped in it. A listless breeze poked at the litter in the gutters, then decided on another plan and left it where it was. Market vendors wiped sweat from brows below hot turbans. Little children played in the dust without energy. Even the mangy dogs were silent in the sun.

As afternoon wore to a close without any lessening in the temperature, Decimus closed the stall early to relieve Juliana. She had stayed at home today, not wanting to subject Gabriel to the sultry conditions. He walked through the streets, feeling the sweat gathering on his face and neck. He thought about the message Paulus had conveyed to them regarding the adoption.

I'm so sorry, Paulus had said. *I had wanted this almost as much as you. But we'll plan something special just the same.*

And that's tonight. Decimus smiled to himself as he thought about it. *I wonder what he's planned.*

He entered their home to find a weary Juliana.

"I'm so tired and hot. My clothes are just clinging to me." She wiped her forehead with the back of her hand. "I'm so happy to see you. Are you still willing to watch Gabriel while I rest before this evening?"

Decimus reached out for Gabriel, and she gratefully handed him over. She sank into her bed and was asleep almost instantly. When she awoke, the three were soon on their way through the airless streets. Gabriel fussed in Decimus's arms as he tried to breathe in the stifling heat.

Leonius led them to the garden, where they found some shade for protection from the burning sun, which still had not set. The shade was pleasant under the trees, and the baby stopped fussing almost immediately. Paulus and Eunice welcomed their guests graciously. Eunice lifted Gabriel from his arms, allowing Decimus to greet Paulus properly.

"You both always make us feel welcome," Decimus said to Paulus and included Eunice with a nod. "It's an honor for us to come."

Eunice smiled mischievously. "Just wait until you see what's happening tonight." She hugged Gabriel closely, and her eyes danced.

"Here, make yourselves comfortable on these benches by the arbor." Paulus pointed out where he wished them to sit. Decimus led Juliana to the offered seat and sat beside her once she was comfortable.

"What a beautiful spot this is." Juliana gazed around the garden, which was in full bloom. The scent of hidden flowers surrounded her on the bench. "It must be a little like the garden God created. Wouldn't it have been wonderful to see that?" Juliana's face reflected her joy as she watched Eunice with Gabriel.

Leonius appeared with several people behind him. Paulus walked toward them, welcoming each warmly.

"Come greet our guests of honor." Paulus led the newcomers to the bench, where Juliana and Decimus sat. They looked up as the group approached. Both Decimus and Juliana had bemused looks on their faces.

"Dear friends." Paulus addressed Decimus and Juliana but included all the others with a sweep of his hand. "All of us were troubled that we could not have an adoption ceremony. But that is a legal ceremony and doesn't include our God." He paused to look toward the sky. "We talked about it and decided we needed a ceremony that would honor our Savior. My mother and I, as Gabriel's only blood relatives, have drawn up a document appointing you as Gabriel's legal guardian for as long as you live. Then as church leaders, we want to dedicate this baby to God and commit you and Gabriel into his care."

Juliana wept openly but with a loving smile on her face. As he gazed at Paulus, Decimus needed to clear his throat a few times.

"Come, friends, stand with me and the other church leaders." Paulus stretched out his arms toward them. He offered his hand to Juliana, who took it willingly and rose to stand before him with Decimus by her side. Eunice passed the baby over to her and stood on her other side. Emin joined the group, and the others found places to stand or sit to watch the ceremony. Paulina joined Paulus with tears in her eyes.

"Brothers and sisters, tonight we come before God as a gathering of his people, people who love Him and who have been brought together by His grace." Paulus folded his hands together and looked at each of them individually. "We want to honor Him and do what is pleasing to Him. Times are uncertain, but God is unchangeable."

Several people joined in. "Yes, yes."

"He sees what is happening in our lives and in our city, and He wants to draw closer to us. We stand in His presence in awe of Him and the marvelous things He does for us." He turned to look at Gabriel, snuggled in Juliana's arms. "Consider this baby before us. His very life is a miracle. Not only is his life a miracle, but his having come into our hands is an even greater miracle, all brought about by our loving God."

Paulus paused for a moment with head bowed. He took a deep breath, raised his head, and continued.

"My mother and I are pleased to recognize that God placed him in the loving hands of a couple He has called to Himself, Decimus and Juliana. We all know and love them and marvel that God would bring together a couple who so longed for a child, and a child so in need of loving parents. God is good."

Several voices were raised, repeating, "God is good."

Juliana hugged Gabriel closer, and tears flowed freely down her cheeks. She kissed the top of his curly dark head and hugged him closely.

"My mother and I now present you with this document," Paulus said. "It is not legal in the eyes of the law, but binding under God's law and witnessed by all of us present."

Paulina moved forward and placed the scroll, tied tightly with bright fabric, in the hands of Decimus. She embraced him and kissed him on each cheek. She then embraced Juliana and, before stepping back, placed a kiss on Gabriel's forehead.

"My grandson, you have this day received a great gift," she said, "the gift of a loving mother and father." She placed her hand on his head. "May you grow up to be a strong man of God, a man who honors his parents and a man who lives to please God and serve others."

She stepped back beside Paulus. There were many eyes wet with unshed tears as they watched this woman of God, who had seen so much tragedy in her life, exhibit a love so warm it could have come only from a heart in tune with her Savior.

Paulus looked at Juliana. "May I hold Gabriel please?"

Juliana held the little bundle out to him. He took Gabriel carefully in his hands, gazing at his little face.

He looks so much like Marcus, he thought. *Would his little life have softened Marcus*? It was a question they would never have the answer to.

He brushed his fingers over the dark hair, which curled around the baby's scalp. Holding him closer to him, he looked up. "Decimus, will you stand beside me?"

Decimus stepped from beside Juliana, whom Eunice had encircled in her arms, and stood tall and proud beside Paulus.

"Would you tell all of us the names you have chosen for Gabriel?" Paulus's voice sounded shaky.

Decimus lifted his eyes to heaven. In a strong voice he said, "Gabriellus Marcellus Decio." His lips curved upward, and his eyes disappeared into his smile.

Cheers and clapping erupted from the guests. Juliana smiled as tears slid down over her cheekbones and dripped off her chin. Paulina pulled both Eunice and Juliana into a tight embrace. Paulus clapped Decimus on the back and waited for the cheers to quiet.

"What a strong name you have given Gabriel," Paulus said. "Our family will always be grateful that you included Marcus's name," he whispered while the noise level dropped.

Paulus now lifted the small bundle high in his arms. He closed his eyes and turned his face toward the sky. "Father in Heaven, we lift up our newest member before You. Please bless Gabriellus Marcellus Decio. May Your face shine upon him. May he early know You and serve You all the days of his life. May his parents be blessed by his presence in their lives. Protect and keep him from all harm. In Jesus's name we ask this. Amen."

While he prayed, all the people lifted their arms in prayer. Many murmured their own requests and blessings for the tiny babe. Hands lowered after they finished until all were silent. A shrill cry from Gabriel broke the stillness, and one by one they began to laugh and talk. Paulus handed Gabriel back to Juliana, who took him inside to change and feed him.

Servants arrived with platters laden with honey-stuffed dates, fresh bread, olives glistening with oil, and grapes. The guests found seats scattered throughout the garden, and a sweet time of fellowship with each other followed.

As the festivities came to a close, Emin moved in beside Paulus. "I wish it could be like this always," Emin said as he laid his hand on Paulus's shoulder.

"Yes, I too wish that. But I sense more trouble coming. There may not be many more gatherings like this one. The city is restless and filled with conflicting falsehoods, none of which are favorable to us." Paulus drew his brows together and shook his head sadly.

Chapter Fifty-Two

Large open scrolls were fastened to the walls of the temple for all to see. The city was abuzz with the invitation to all citizens to gather below the altar, when the noonday sun was at its height. Word had spread quickly that something of great magnitude would take place.

Emin was strolling through the business section of the city when he heard yelling. He listened in without giving any indication that he was doing so.

"Are you coming to the temple at noon?" one voice asked.

"What's going on?" the second voice said.

"There are signs everywhere asking everyone to come. Something big's happening for sure."

The voices faded, and Emin walked on. He moved toward the temple to see the signs for himself. He read each word carefully, then hurried away to warn the Christ-followers.

"Paulus, I think we need to stay away. This may be a plot to get us all in one place," Emin said. He crossed his arms and sighed deeply.

Paulus gestured with his hands as he responded to Emin. "On the contrary, I think at least some of us need to be there. We need to keep a finger on the pulse of the temple. There may be an announcement we need to hear. I, for one, plan to be there."

"Then I'll go too. I won't see you go alone." He sighed again, making eye contact with Paulus.

As noon fast approached, the two turned their steps in that direction. When they arrived, the street was filling with crowds of citizens. A hum of voices greeted them. Cheers broke out here and there. Excitement filled the air, a festive feeling in the crowd. The talk was all about what great thing they were going to see.

A stir on the temple steps drew all eyes toward the opened door at the top of the stairs. The murmuring ceased as onlookers crowded together, craning necks for a better view. The weather was still hot in Pergamum, and the crush of bodies made everyone uncomfortable.

As Paulus watched between two bobbing turbans in front of him, Ekrem appeared. Once again he was elaborately dressed. This time his robe was white with dark-blue trim. The harsh sunlight reflected off his white robe, which seemed to shimmer in the glare. He stepped onto the top stair, shoulders back and arms high in the air.

The crowd held its collective breath as four priests followed him, carrying a man between them. Ekrem slowly descended the steps until he was opposite the altar. The priests took their places beside him, easing their burden down. The man they had been carrying was clad in a dark-brown robe with a thick veil over his head and shoulders. His face could not be seen.

Many in the crowd shouted questions to the priests, but they gave no answers. Tension filled the air as bodies surged forward in one mass. The heat from the sun warmed Paulus's face.

"People are going to start fainting if something doesn't soon happen," he whispered to Emin. "It's beyond hot here."

"Men of Pergamum," Ekrem shouted over the crowd. He extended his arm out to embrace the people. "Several days ago I watched as you asked for a miracle from the evil cult so prevalent in our city."

Several voices chanted, and arms waved throughout the crowd.

"That day you were not given your miracle," Ekrem said.

"No miracle. No miracle." The words erupted from many voices, the sound hovering over their heads.

"And do you know why you didn't get one?" Ekrem now stretched both hands out to them

"No, no!" The shouts rang out in a deafening roar.

"I'll tell you why." He paused to swivel his body from side to side, taking in the people on all sides. "It's because their so-called god has no power. He can't do miracles." His hands, now clenched in fists, pierced the air over his head.

"Yes, yes, yes. No power, no power." Many voices joined in with shouts of confirmation.

Ekrem waited until the crowd was quiet again.

"Zeus is the one who is all-powerful." Ekrem almost shrieked in his excitement.

"Zeus, Zeus, Zeus, Zeus," The crowd roared. Bodies swayed back and forth as they took up the chant. Paulus wondered if he and Emin would be crushed in the mass of people. Just then Ekrem held up his hand for silence.

"Do you still want a miracle?" Even from where Paulus stood, he could see the priest's reddening face.

"Yes, yes, yes, yes . . ." Arms waved, and turbans bobbed as their shouts pierced the blistering air.

"Then here is your miracle." He whipped the veil from the head of the shrouded man beside the priests. There before them stood David—bound and gagged but unmistakably David.

A gasp rippled through the crowd.

Ekrem faced them again. "Zeus has raised David from the dead!" He gave a great victory shout. "Hail Zeus, hail Zeus, hail Zeus . . ." The crowd took up the chant.

Ekrem paced along the steps in his excitement. "David has renounced the cult, has renounced this Jesus, has turned his eyes to the truth that Zeus is all-powerful. You watched him die. You are witnesses to his death and his resurrection."

"Hail Zeus, hail Zeus . . ." Their shouts reverberated through the street and up the temple steps.

"Destroy the cult that says otherwise. Destroy the people who try to tell you that Zeus is not all-powerful. Destroy the infidels in our midst. Destroy, destroy, destroy . . ."

The scene that followed would forever be etched in Paulus's mind. The crowd swarmed up the steps and surrounded David and the priests. David fell in their midst. The priests scrambled to grab him, but the crowd was too powerful. Many willing hands seized David and thrust him high. The crowd descended the stairs with him and passed him from person to person over the heads of the crowd.

As he watched this spectacle, Paulus was sick at heart, powerless to help. He could only stand and pray.

At last the crowd tired of their game and turned him back toward the steps. Two powerful men grabbed his arms and hurled him in the air. He landed at the feet of the startled priests, while Ekrem continued shouting, "Victory! Victory!"

The four priests gathered him from the steps and disappeared into the temple. Ekrem gave one last cry of victory, then swung his robe as he pivoted on his sandals, and followed the priests. The crowd continued to mill around the steps, but soon began to disperse when nothing further happened.

Paulus and Emin slipped down a side street, shaken by what they had seen.

Emin turned to Paulus, his face twisted as though in pain. "What will happen to David now?"

"This can only mean more persecution for the church," Paulus said, putting his hand on Emin's shoulder. "Brother, I sense a darkness imbued with evil descending on the church of Pergamum."

Chapter Fifty-Three

Behind the curtain of the temple, a different scene played itself out. The priests unceremoniously dropped David in a heap on the floor of a small windowless cell. Ekrem entered the room behind them.

"Ha, your usefulness has reached its end," Ekrem said. "Unless, that is, you really do want to recant your belief in this false god." He placed a well-aimed kick into David's side.

A low moan was the only reply. Blood oozed from the side of his mouth, where the rough cloth had dug into the corners of his lips. His hair was matted with sweat and dirt. Only his eyes remained clear.

Ekrem turned away from their gaze. He nodded to the priests. "Blindfold him and lock him up for now. I'll give you further instructions later." With a final sneer, he left the room.

Once the blindfold was in place, the four priests looked at each other, then hoisted him to once again carry their burden. They eased him through the door, scraping his side in the process.

"Watch where you're going," one of them said with a growl. "You almost caught me on the side of the wall." He grunted as he pulled himself after the others.

"Watch your own self," the burly priest said. "It's bad enough that we have to do this, but we have to listen to your whining and complaining, too."

"Both of you, focus on what we're doing and stop the talk." This came from Tacitus, the oldest of the group. "You're going to draw attention to what we're doing, and Ekrem won't be happy with that. Keep your mouths shut and walk." The effect was silence for the remainder of their passage through the halls and into the old section of the temple.

"In the narrow room at the end," Tacitus said. He exerted his leadership again, and the rest followed his directions. The young one pushed open the low door with one arm and backed into the space. They squeezed David's body through and threw it on the hard-packed dirt. The four left him there, barring and bolting the door as they left.

He lay still for several minutes. His heart pounded as he tried to process what had just taken place. His eyes were blindfolded, mouth gagged, and his hands and feet bound. He had no way of discerning his surroundings, but his brain was fully awake.

Lord, don't let the others believe that I've turned my back on You, David prayed. *Let them know that I would never do that. I feel my death is near, and that's acceptable to me. I will soon see Your face. Please protect and comfort my family . . .*

A soft shuffle outside the door alerted him. Someone was at the door. He paused his prayer to listen. Wood scraped against wood as the bar was lifted. David sensed the door opening and lay still, awaiting his fate. Gentle hands touched the material at the back of his head, and soon the blindfold was off. Next his hands and feet were freed and the gag removed. As he looked around to thank his rescuer, he saw only the back of a robe. Then the door shut again.

Thank You, Jesus.

Gingerly he sat up. The room was dark and damp, with a musty smell prevalent around him. He reached out in all directions, surprised by how small it seemed. The ceiling was low and rough, as were the walls. It was more like a cave than a room, but at least he could move, thanks to his visitor.

He was tired and spent. The last few days had been arduous; the several men who guarded the cave where he had been kept had ill-treated and interrogated him. His body slumped against the wall, and he fell into an uneasy slumber.

"Where are the bindings that were on him when last I saw him?" A strident sound filled the room.

David came rudely awake and looked toward the voice.

"Bind him quickly," the voice said.

The discarded bindings were soon back in place, and he was held fast again. Someone pulled him to a sitting position and dragged him out the door.

"I will want to know who was responsible for this, but later." Ekrem snapped his fingers in the faces of his companions. "Now we need to get him out of here."

David was aware of being moved through the now-silent passages of the temple. His body felt each twist and turn as he was jostled between his captors. No further words were spoken. A breeze ruffled the cloth over his face, and he knew they had gained the outdoors. In his mind he pictured the turn and movement along the side of the building.

"Stop." The whisper was like the crack of a whip. "Tacitus, move up ahead and make sure the way is clear."

David felt someone letting go and someone else taking his place at his side. Footsteps receded in the distance. His captors kept their silence until once again they began moving him with grunts and sighs. The heat was oppressive, and the smell of sweaty bodies soon penetrated the bindings and invaded his nostrils. When at last they stopped, their panting and heavy breathing filled the air.

"We've reached our destination," someone said.

Lanterns flickered and flared around the front entrance of Magnus's dwelling as Ekrem neared the door. The guards became alert and flung open the doors through which Ekrem led his procession and continued up the stairs.

Interior guards stopped them outside the audience room, but Ekrem approached and engaged them in a heated discussion. One of the guards turned abruptly and entered the room. When he returned, he indicated that Ekrem was to enter.

The five priests crowded into the room with their charge. Magnus stood, waiting for them. They advanced to within a short distance of him. Ekrem put his hand up, indicating they should stop. The room was thick with tension as he waited for Magnus to speak.

Magnus's arms were folded over his chest, and a deep frown creased his brow. "I'm going to assume you have a valid explanation for your intrusion." The haughty words fell from his lips, which puckered in a frown.

"Yes, my lord, I do. I've brought you the prisoner." Ekrem bowed stiffly and pointed at the captive. He hoped the tremble in his hand could not be seen.

"The one that was dead?" Magnus curled his lip into a magnificent sneer.

"Yes." Ekrem ground out the word between clenched teeth.

"What kind of a fool do you think I am?" Magnus took a step toward Ekrem, raised his fist, and pointed it at him. "You may fool some of the people, but you certainly don't fool me. Speaking of fools, there seems to be one in my presence."

“Yes, my lord, whatever you say.” Ekrem tilted his head forward.

I’m not going to let him see how nervous I am. All the rumors are true; he is cruel.

Magnus may have detected sarcasm in his voice, or the lateness of the hour may have made him crazed. Whatever it was, something in him seemed to snap. He rushed to the door, ordered the guards in, and with the turn of his head gave the command to kill.

The guards needed no further prompting. They fell on the unsuspecting priests and David with their swords slashing. The priests had no defense against the power of Rome and were soon reduced to piles of corpses steeped in blood. David lay dying beside them.

Ekrem had tried to defend himself but to no avail. Magnus shouted hysterically throughout the massacre.

At last all lay still before the guards.

“Clean up the mess and dispose of the bodies” was Magnus’s curt command. He turned his back and left the room.

Chapter Fifty-Four

Dawn in Pergamum. The sun poised on the horizon as if reluctant to rise and illuminate the desecration. The breeze held its breath from the streets. Trees hung their branches low in protest of the spectacle before them.

Blood on the altar steps. Blood spilled from bodies heaped in grotesque shapes just below that altar. Costly fabric stained with its flow. Faces white in contrast to the blood.

Wailing in the streets. Early risers viewed the terrible scene in disbelief. Women threw their scarves over their faces in an apparent attempt to erase the picture forever etched on their mind's eye.

Shocked faces on young priests. They stood in small groups several steps above the carnage. No one seemed to know what to do. No one seemed eager to be the one to approach the bodies.

Angry voices rose to the sky. Men in dark robes and turbans tore their clothes in protest of the destruction before them. They railed at any god they thought might listen.

Blame was assigned. Whispers began to circulate through the crowd.

"The cult. They're responsible."

Shrieking voices now took up the theme.

"Wipe them out."

"Rid our city of this plague."

Still the bodies lay where the guards had dumped them in the early hours of the morning. The guards left no indication of responsibility and had returned to their master.

Word of the slaughter reached Paulus. He collected Emin, and together they approached the crowd. The sight was terrifying. The crowd had now worked itself into a frenzy.

Emin bent his head to whisper in Paulus's ear, gripping one of his arms. "Paulus, it's not safe for us to be here."

"Yes, I know. But we must identify David so we can take the tragic news to his family." Bile rose in his throat, and an ache stabbed deep in his heart. "Let's move to the other side. There appears to be a break in the crowd close to the steps." Paulus gave Emin a nudge in the direction of the break. The two men moved untouched through the crowd, which had no thought for anything except hysteria. The bodies were visible from their new vantage point. Their identities were easily discernible. David's face was strangely peaceful and untouched by the blood from his wounds.

Paulus groaned. "I'm satisfied it's him. We need to go quickly." He shook Emin's shoulder, turning him away from the spectacle.

The setting at David's house contrasted to the frenzy they had just left behind. Miriam received them solemnly and graciously.

"I can see by your faces you bring unwanted tidings." She stepped aside to let them enter. She appeared calm except for a tremble in her voice.

"I'm afraid you're right," Paulus said with reluctance.

"Then come sit in the garden with me. Bad news is always easier to bear surrounded by God's creation." She turned and headed toward the garden entrance. They followed her through the house and to the garden, where she led them to a low bench beside the fountain.

"Please tell me your news. I think I'm prepared for what it is. God has been especially near me this morning." She sat on the bench, her hands folded in her lap. Dark eyes searched their faces.

Paulus broke down as he related the information he knew. Miriam's eyes were moist, but no tears fell as yet.

She removed a small, dainty square of fabric from her robe and twisted it in her hands. "I came to the conclusion a while ago that he was not coming back. I came to terms with that as much as that is possible humanly speaking." Her restless hands continued to twist the cloth. "It doesn't lessen the shock or the finality of the death of a loved one, but God has promised me that He will give me the strength to carry on."

The tears that had hung immobile now spilled over and down her cheeks. Paulus and Emin moved to her side and wrapped her in an embrace. The tears were soon spent, and she lifted her tear-streaked face to them.

"I need to gently break the news to the children," she said. "Thank you for bringing me the news and so sympathetically dealing with me. We'll have many plans to make in the coming days." She paused to wipe her eyes. "Do you think there's any chance to claim his body?"

Emin spoke softly, taking her hand in his. "I think it's highly unlikely. I think just knowing what happened to him is the best we'll be able to manage."

"I agree," Paulus said. "The crowd is in such a frenzy and it sounds like people are blaming the Christians, so any attempt on our part to retrieve him would meet with instant death. No, we have to be thankful for at least knowing."

"And I *am* thankful. You men risked your lives just doing that."

"We'll leave you alone to talk to your children. I'll send Eunice to you within the hour."

"That is the best thing that you could do for me. She will be such a help to me. Thank you," she said once again as she ushered them from the house.

A small gathering of believers sat silently in Miriam's home to pay tribute to David's life. Meeting for the larger group was unsafe, so she had given the invitation only to intimate friends. The mood was somber as Paulus spoke of their dear brother. His voice broke once or twice, but he bravely carried on. Miriam face was immobile as she sat clutching her children close to her side. Eunice sat on her other side with an arm around her friend.

"And now, dear friends," Paulus said, "it is time for you to leave the city for the present. The situation is volatile." He moved his head and scanned each face before him. He swallowed twice and took a deep breath. "We'll get word to you when it's safe to return. We all discussed our plans several months ago when the trouble was just beginning. Now it is full blown, and it would be wise to flee." The people moved restlessly and looked at each other. Some shook their heads, while other wept softly.

"A few of us will stay to keep abreast of happenings and to await the Lord's leading," Paulus said. "Do not linger, my friends, but go as quickly as possible."

Many embraces and tears followed this pronouncement. Promises were made to keep in touch; offers of transportation and help in many other ways were extended and accepted. The gathering slowly broke up, eventually leaving Miriam with Paulus and Eunice.

"Where will you go, Paulus?" Miriam asked. She pulled her robe closely around her. Tears hung around the edges of her eyes.

"We're staying here," he said calmly. He reached for Eunice's hand. She smiled at him and then at Miriam.

"Would you allow me to stay with you?" Miriam asked. She leaned forward and held Eunice's arm but never took her eyes off Paulus.

Paulus and Eunice exchanged glances before Paulus answered the question. He gazed out into the garden, deep in thought, considering options. He walked to the open door without seeing the beauty before him. At last he turned and faced the two women.

"Do you understand the consequences of your request?" he asked her quietly.

"I think I do, Paulus. I know we're in danger, but David was taken from me, so I know the worst. Safety is not my concern; friendship with your family and closeness with Christ is now my desire. God can protect me if He chooses. If He sees fit to take me, I'll be with Him and with David all the sooner. Please consider what I've asked." One tear slipped from the corner of her eye, but she let her lips curve in a small smile.

Paulus smiled back at her. He stepped in beside Eunice, placing his arm around her. A meaningful look passed between them again before Paulus faced Miriam and answered.

"We'd be honored to have you stay with us. We, too, feel this is in God's hands. We'll face it together with God's help. I'll take both of you to our home. Then I must return to the city to see what is transpiring today."

Miriam dismissed the servants, suggesting they return to their homes and seek safety wherever they could. She quickly gathered what she would need for herself and the children, and they were on their way.

Paulus left them sorting out rooms where they would be comfortable. He smiled to himself as he thought about how empty his house had been before Antipas was martyred. It had been lonely; safe, but oh so alone. Now it was almost full to capacity with his mother and father, the extra servants needed for his growing household, Eunice and the children, and now Miriam and her family. God had chosen to gather them all under one roof for purposes known only to Him.

Crowds still milled about the central point of the city. The bodies had been removed earlier, and the blood had been washed off the steps. The doors of the temple were open, allowing a glimpse of the priests moving around inside. Paulus kept his head down, trying not to attract attention to himself.

He slipped through the streets to visit the marketplace. Here everything looked the same as it had when he and his brothers had come here as children. Then everything had been happy and light in the carefree days of youth.

So much has happened since then, he thought. *But I wouldn't trade what I have found in Christ for one single day of youth.*

Both Decimus and Juliana were at the stall today. He glanced around before nearing their stall.

"Greetings, friends," he said as he approached.

Juliana looked up quickly. "Paulus," she said with evident pleasure in her voice. "We didn't expect to see you here today."

He leaned in close to them as he spoke. "I've been trying to find out what the feel is in the city. I thought you might have heard more here in the market."

"We have heard much." Decimus kept his head lowered and his voice low. "We're in the process of packing up what we can and closing for now." He glanced around without moving his head.

"What have you heard?" Paulus felt a frown crease his face.

"Apparently Magnus is incensed and threatening anyone and everyone. The guards were out in full force this morning, and several arrests were made. He's promised to clean out the city of the infidels, as he calls us." Decimus shook his head. His lips turned down and lines crowded between his eyebrows.

"Where are you headed?" Paulus laid a hand on his arm.

"We've made arrangements to go to Juliana's sister in the country until this settles down." Decimus looked Paulus in the eye before asking, "What about you?"

He gripped Decimus's arm more tightly. "We've decided to stay."

At his words Juliana gasped and put her hands over her heart. "But it's not safe, Paulus."

"I realize that, but I need to be here." He smiled a little smile that did not reach his eyes. "I must go before someone recognizes me and I put you in even more danger. You are leaving today, I trust?" He squinted and searched their faces.

"We'll be on our way within the hour. We've brought everything with us so we don't need to cross the city again." Decimus wrung his hands together.

"Then may God watch over your departure, and may we meet again soon." Paulus embraced them in parting and disappeared into the market crowd.

Chapter Fifty-Five

Life settled into a routine in Paulus's home. He continued to enter the city each day to learn what he could. Many of the converts had been able to escape successfully, but others had been arrested, and deaths continued to be reported, including one of Emin's grown sons. The city was in a frenzy, with riots in the streets almost daily. Paulus wondered how long he would be able to move freely through the city.

With Decimus gone, Paulus had no contact in the city. Businesses were closed, and market stalls were empty since the exodus of the Christians.

One day Paulus became aware of a procession winding its way down the main thoroughfare toward the temple. Several guards marched in front, helmets gleaming in the morning sun. Swords were polished to a punishing shine and carried aloft. The tramp of boots could be distinctly heard as they neared their destination, short uniforms swaying to the rhythm of their feet.

The guards were followed by the imperial carriage, decked out with drapes of red and purple fabric pulled back at the sides and tied in place. Four black horses pulled the carriage, which contained Magnus. Citizens had fallen in behind the procession, shouting their praises to Magnus.

At the foot of the steps, the soldiers stopped with a sharp tramp of both feet. Their leader mounted the first step and gave instructions for them to part to allow the passage of Magnus. The carriage drew close and paused in front of the soldiers. Magnus alighted from where he had been sitting.

With back straight and chin elevated, he mounted the steps with a fanfare of trumpets played by musicians who had silently appeared through the open doors of the temple. To Paulus, the display was reminiscent of Rome.

At the top of the steps, Magnus turned with dignity and faced the gathering crowd. The ones following him had been joined by others who had heard about the arrival.

Magnus lifted his arms high over his head, feet apart, and face lifted upward. Slowly he dropped his arms and faced the crowd, speaking with authority.

"I am your high priest. There will no longer be a distinction between the worship of the emperor and the worship of Zeus."

The crowd was strangely silent. This news didn't appear to be what they had been expecting. The guards on horseback drew their swords and sat alertly on their mounts. Whispers began to spread through the mass of people.

"This is an order from Rome!" he cried. "There will be no debate. I am your high priest. I am in control." The words reverberated across the crowd. Faces showed signs of disbelief, and soldiers raised their swords in readiness.

"From now on, there will be sacrifices each morning, noon, and evening. You will gather here to honor your emperor. I am his representative." He paused and scanned the crowd. The priests had ventured onto the top step. They seemed uneasy, unsure of what part they played in all this.

"Bow down and worship!" The command exploded in the air, causing instant reaction. Many people turned to leave, but the soldiers were there instantly, swords brandished, horses high stepping. The masses began dropping to their knees wherever they were. Fearful cries split the air from those who refused and were cut down by the vigilant guards.

Paulus faced a quick decision. He had to get out of here—and fast. He turned from the altar, bent over at waist level, and burrowed his way through the now-mesmerized crowd. He was able to propel himself around the side of the temple without the guards spotting him. Once out of sight, he walked briskly out of the area and headed for home.

As he hurried away, the noise and confusion was audible for many steps. Now came cries of, "Worship Magnus . . . Hail Magnus . . ."

At the next crossroads a solitary man on horseback accosted him. Paulus would have dashed by, but the horseman drew up in his path. The horse rose up on its two back legs and whinnied in protest. The man, obviously skilled in horsemanship, soon had the animal under control.

Paulus had nowhere to turn. He wisely stopped and waited for the man to speak.

"You are Paulus." The statement drifted down to him from the stranger's rigid lips.

Before offering an answer, Paulus studied his challenger. He was attired in a dark cloak that covered most of his body, including his head. Flashing eyes, visible beneath the hood, peered over a hooked nose. Thick lips curled in a grimace.

"Are you satisfied with what you see?" The stranger pulled back on the reigns of the restless horse.

"Do I know you?" Paulus finally asked, staring directly into his eyes.

"That doesn't matter," the stranger said. "What matters is that I know you."

"How do you know me?" Paulus shifted his position, hoping to find a means of circumventing the horse and continuing his way home.

"Don't bother looking for an escape route. You'll be let go when I'm through with you."

"What is it you want?" Paulus asked in a quiet voice. Fear rose inside his chest, but he determined not to let the stranger see it. He clenched his hands under his robe. Too bad he didn't have his sword or knife with him.

"I don't like your tone of voice," the stranger said. He slipped from the back of his horse. When he landed on both feet in front of Paulus, a short, sharp blade gleamed in his hand.

"Stand back if you know what's good for you," the angry voice said. The stranger took a fighting stance and faced Paulus. A thrust of the knife—a twirl of it in the air—quickly followed.

Paulus lifted his hands in acquiescence and backed up a few steps.

"I have a message for you if you're ready to listen," the stranger said. "If not, you'll receive a message from my knife."

"Speak. I'm listening." Paulus slightly bowed his head.

"Your brother Marcus was known to me," the man said.

Paulus jerked his head up at the name of Marcus. He took a step toward the stranger. His reward was the slash of the knife across the back of his hand. Blood trickled from the cut.

"Stand back!" was the harsh command.

Paulus's knees felt weak, but he hastily complied.

"Marcus had plans for you, but now he's dead."

Paulus waited, watching his opponent. What was his game? He shifted his feet slightly to be ready for whatever would come next. Every muscle in his body tensed. He breathed deeply, noticing a slight breeze that freshened the air.

Funny the things you notice when your whole world seems to be stopped, waiting in expectation, he thought.

Without warning, the invader lunged at him, thrusting his knife toward the folds of his robe around his chest. Paulus jumped to the side, barely avoiding the blade and infuriating the stranger. As he lunged again, Paulus managed to swing around the horse, where he had left it. The movement startled the horse, which once again reared on its hind legs in terror.

Paulus grabbed the reins and managed to get the horse back on the ground. The interloper tried to circle the horse, but the still-panicked horse rewarded him with a swift kick.

"You stupid brute!" the stranger shrieked at his horse. He held his leg and, as if trying to keep his balance, hopped around on one foot, screaming in pain.

Paulus saw his chance and ran.

"I'll get you yet!" the stranger cried. "You haven't seen the last of me. Marcus will have his revenge."

Paulus didn't pause to ask what he meant. He ran until he could no longer breathe. With great gasps, he threw himself down on the grass at the side of the road. There was no sign of the stranger.

Chapter Fifty-Six

Paulus lay still for several minutes. He wasn't sure which event had upset him most—the encounter with the stranger or the scene at the altar.

No, it has to be the performance at the altar, he thought. *The stranger was a threat to me personally, but the episode on the steps will have wide sweeping consequences. There's no doubt it was a show, but I don't quite see why.*

He continued to ponder what he had witnessed.

Since he saw no sign of his attacker, he gathered his cloak around him and resumed his course toward home.

Behind him Izak watched from a hidden vantage point.

"He's a worthy opponent." He shook his head with a grin on his face. "Too bad he has to die, but a job is a job."

He turned and headed back into the city.

The tableau was winding down as Magnus majestically ascended the stairs. The priests, who had been hovering just outside the door, quickly stepped out of his way. Inside, Cato, now the most senior of the priests, stepped forward to meet him.

"Welcome to the temple, Governor Magnus." Cato simpered and bowed low before him.

"'High priest.' I prefer to be called 'high priest.'" Magnus's voice resounded through the massive room. "On your knees, priest." Magnus pointed to the floor with an outstretched arm.

Cato stood still. "I welcome you as governor and give you all the honor that is due your office, but I cannot and will not recognize you as high priest. Zeus would not be pleased." He spoke these words with bravado, shoulders back, eyes fixed on Magnus.

The two men stared at each other. Magnus was much the larger of the two, but the other had a distinctive strength visible to all. Magnus closed his eyes, and the furrows deepened between his brows. He folded his arms across his chest. No one in the room moved while watching this battle of minds.

Cato never let his gaze wander from Magnus's face. He had a reputation among the other priests for being stubborn. A palpable tension filled the room as the two men stood close. Outside, the cheers and ruckus continued, but in here, the silence was deafening.

Magnus opened his eyes, and a slow smile spread across his face.

"Priest"—the word rolled smoothly off his tongue—"I'm sure we can come to an agreement. Let's find a quiet room where we can talk."

"As you wish, governor." Cato led the way down a side hall. The two entered a small room, and Cato adjusted the curtain back in place over the entrance once they were inside.

When they emerged later, neither spoke a word to those waiting in the hallway. A small smile of what appeared to be satisfaction spread over both faces. Magnus left the temple by a side door, while the priests stared after him. When they turned back to seek information from Cato, he looked sternly at each of them.

"Back to work. We have much to do. It is past the time for the morning sacrifices." He swept away from them, and neither then nor later did he reveal what had transpired in the tiny room.

Paulus arrived home, somewhat out of breath and disturbed in his soul. Eunice met him at the front entrance.

"What's wrong, Paulus? You look like you've had a troubling morning." She searched his face with concerned eyes.

"Let's go to the garden where we can talk privately. But first I want to see the children. I just need their hugs right now." He pulled Eunice to him and embraced her tightly.

Simon and Helena were playing happily in their room, while Marina watched over them.

"Father, come see what we've built." Simon greeted him enthusiastically, pulling on Paulus's hand to lead him to their creation. Helena jumped up and down with her arms in front of him. He reached down with his other arm and scooped her up. She covered his face with kisses. He hugged her to him while following Simon.

He knelt down beside the tower Simon had built out of pieces of wood Leonius had sanded for him.

"It's amazing, Simon," Paulus said, encouraging him. "Did you and Helena do it all by yourselves?"

"Yes, yes!" Simon shouted, smiling.

Paulus played with the two for several minutes, allowing Marina a short break. When she returned to the room, he gently disengaged himself from their grasps. He hugged and kissed them before leaving the room.

"You really are their father." Eunice spoke quietly as they passed through the house to the back entrance leading to the garden.

"I feel that way, too," Paulus said with some sadness in his voice. "It's such a privilege to have them to love and raise. I have often longed for a child of our own, but God seems to have other ideas. I am so thankful He has entrusted them to my care."

"Everything in God's timing, Paulus. I, too, would love to have another child, but we'll just have to be patient and wait to see what God has in store for us."

The two sauntered, arm in arm, to their favorite place at the back of the garden. The sun shone on their special bench beneath the trees along the bank of the river. They sat, feeling the warmth of the sun on their faces.

"It's so peaceful here," Eunice said when Paulus remained silent.

"If only that peace could be felt in Pergamum," he said with sadness in his voice as he looked out over the gentle flow of the water.

"What happened today?"

Paulus told her every detail of his morning, from the arrival of Magnus to his escape from the attacker.

"I'm sorry to have such dismal news," he said, "but you need to know exactly what is going on. There will be no secrets between us. We're both in danger, and we've counted the cost, so to know is to be prepared or at least as prepared as possible in these unstable times."

"I'm so sorry you had to go through that, Paulus." She put her head on his shoulder and sighed. "But you're right, I need to know as much as you do, and I appreciate your candidness with me. Many husbands wouldn't share that news with their wives."

"But I'm not just any husband, now am I?" He smiled in a teasing way. "Just sitting with you helps me to put everything in perspective."

"What will you do?"

"I'm not sure. I'll want to talk to Emin because he needs to know what he faces as well. Most of the others have left the city, but Emin, like us, refuses to go."

Eunice spoke softly. "Well, nothing has changed here, at least for now. We'll just enjoy the peace we have for the present and leave the future to God."

"You're an amazing woman." He kissed the top of her head.

"In honesty, I have to admit that inside I'm terrified." She looked up into his face.

"I guess I have to admit that even though I'm trusting the Lord, I quake on the inside as well. I don't know how I'll stand up under whatever persecution comes our way. I think I could bear something happening to me, but I don't know how I could handle anything happening to you."

The two continued to sit and absorb the light. The gathering darkness was all around them. Evil stalked the city streets. Satan was engaged in full battle for his throne, and many gleefully joined forces with him.

Chapter Fifty-Seven

Magnus brooded in his chair. The news from Rome wasn't good. Word of the riots had somehow made its way to the emperor, who was incensed and threatened to arrive in Pergamum to deal with the situation in his own way.

I can't let that happen, he thought, tapping his foot repeatedly on the marble floor. Today his girls surrounded him, waving their fans over his head, trying to drop bites of fresh figs sweetened with honey into his mouth, smiling bright smiles. He was tired of them. He was tired of the priests. He was tired of the Christ cult. He was tired of Pergamum. Truth be told, he was tired of himself.

He jumped up from his chair, scattering the figs and fans as well as the girls in every direction. Flinging his arms in disgust, he brushed them all away from him. His white toga had been stained from the honey, which only added to his displeasure. He snarled savagely at one of the girls who tried to draw near.

His voice rose in volume. "Get out! All of you. Can't a person have any peace?"

The girls didn't need to be told twice. They left everything where it was and fled the room, arm and ankle bracelets tinkling as they hurried away. Magnus watched the last of the colorful costumes, which showed more of the girls than was acceptable in the culture, leave the room.

Think, Magnus, think, he thought. Around the room he paced over and over, trying to work out a plan. "If I only knew what Marcus had intended . . . it would be easier to make decisions. Who would know?"

He rushed to the door, flinging it back roughly.

"Guards!" he shouted. They came to attention at the sound of his voice.

"You." He pointed at the taller of the two. "Inside." He pointed back into the room.

Once they were behind closed doors, he asked for a report from their surveillance.

"Master, you asked me to follow the market stall owner, Decimus," one of the guards said. "I followed your orders through wind and rain—"

"Stop the drama. You were well paid for your trouble. Just tell me what you were able to discover."

"He walked daily to his market stall."

"Are all the inhabitants of this city as dull as you?" Magnus cried. "I know he went to his stall daily. I want to know what you discovered that he *didn't* do daily, you fool."

The guard wiped his hand over his face and swallowed once, then dropped his hand to his side. A muscle in his cheek twitched. He shifted his feet before raising his eyes to Magnus.

"My lord," he said again, "I followed him day and night. The only unusual visit he made was to the small shed behind the barracks. He's been there twice. I checked the next day and discovered that the occupant of the shed is one named Aulus."

Magnus spoke curtly. "Bring him to me."

"Yes, my lord." The tall guard gave a stiff military bow, then marched from the presence of Magnus.

Magnus had calmed considerably since the abrupt departure of the guard. He folded his arms across his chest and observed Aulus without speaking. It was a sight worth watching as the man seemed to come apart before his eyes.

His face wore a startled look, mouth open but no sound escaping, eyes wide with fear written on his face. His shoulders slumped in such a way as to appear that his legs could no longer hold him. A tremble could be observed in his arms and legs, and he clutched his robe over his heart as though in pain.

Magnus snapped out the words in a staccato bark. "State your name."

Aulus worked his lips, but nothing came out.

With a snap of his fingers in Aulus's face, the command hit the air. "Now."

At the sound of his voice, all pretense of standing left Aulus, and he slumped to the floor.

"Guard. Water. Quickly." Magnus looked down at Aulus with disgust.

The guard grabbed a large pitcher from the nearest table.

"Here, pour the water over his head. That should revive him."

The cold water was effective. Aulus sat up, sputtering and trying to wipe the water from his face. It apparently did nothing to ease his fears, but only increased them. His eyes were wider than ever as he cowered on the floor. Saliva ran from his lips along with the water.

"Rise to your feet" came the brusque order. "I've had enough of your theatrics. Stand before me with the respect I demand."

Aulus rose to his feet, his whole body shaking—whether from fear or the cold water couldn't be determined. He seemed to be trying to gather himself together as he lifted his shoulders and his chin and looked at Magnus. He held his gaze for only a few seconds, then collapsed again.

"Carry him out and throw him in the dungeon. That will bring some sense to him." Magnus stepped away from the shaking form on the floor, turning his back on the scene.

Once more Aulus appeared to be struggling with his inner self. He managed to get on his knees.

"No, my lord, not the dungeon. I'll tell you anything you wish to know. Just don't imprison me." Aulus clasped his hands together and lifted them to the governor. His face was twisted and tight.

Magnus turned and stared sharply at him. "Can I be assured that I'll witness no more histrionics?" Another snap of his fingers at Aulus.

"Yes, yes. I'm under control now. You have my word." White showed around his knuckles as he continued clenching his hands together.

"We'll see how good your word is then."

Magnus sat down on his chair and observed Aulus. What he saw satisfied him, and he slowly nodded. He leaned forward with his hand on his jaw.

"I want to ask you some questions," Magnus said.

"Anything, my lord," Aulus replied with a slight bow.

"You have a friend I desire information about." Magnus tilted his head to one side.

"I have many friends, my lord." Aulus lifted his chin, a hint of pride in his voice.

"Perhaps you should have fewer friends and make sure they are all loyal to the emperor." Magnus thrust out his chin and pursed his lips.

"I'm sure all my friends are loyal citizens of Pergamum, my master." The shaking had started again. He lowered his hands to his lap but remained on his knees.

Magnus leaned forward and barked the words. "And I'm certain they're not."

Aulus jumped back from the force of Magnus's words, that look of fear fleetingly crossing his face again. "You must be mistaken—"

"I do not make mistakes!" Magnus shook a fist at Aulus.

Aulus backed up even farther. "Yes, my lord."

"You have, I believe, a friend named Decimus." Magnus lifted his face and gazed at the ceiling.

Silence. Aulus's eyes darted back and forth as if looking for an escape.

"What have you to say to this?" Magnus let a slow smile crease the edges of his face. He lowered his gaze to Aulus and never took his eyes off him, while Aulus looked everywhere but at Magnus.

"Answer or the dungeon will come with great haste." He pounded the arm of his chair.

Aulus pulled his shoulders up and sputtered out the words. "He's no friend of mine."

Magnus spoke in a low, dangerous voice. "Are you saying you don't know him?" His eyes bored into Aulus. Aulus seemed to be mesmerized, his eyes fixed on Magnus.

Aulus's voice came out in a high-pitched whine. "I've met him, but I don't consider him a friend."

"That remains to be seen," Magnus said in a thoughtful voice. He rubbed his jaw and nodded.

"Are you loyal to the emperor?" The question came sharply.

Aulus stammered out the words while shifting uneasily on his knees. "Yes, my lord, oh yes."

"Are you ready to prove your allegiance?"

"I'll do anything you ask, governor." By now Aulus looked as though he might topple over again. Magnus watched him through eyes almost shut.

Magnus barked the order directly in his face. "Then find Decimus and bring him to me."

Aulus paled and backed up, raising his arms as if in defense. "But, my lord," he managed to get out, "I really don't know where he is. He must be in hiding somewhere. I haven't seen him lately."

Magnus rose from his seat, tall above Aulus, and stared down at him with scorn. He folded his arms over his chest and hissed through his teeth. The grimace on his face deepened as he observed the nervous response in Aulus, who had backed up even farther.

The words came out smooth as a silken robe. "Then find him. For one as clever as you, that should not be a problem." Still the words were soft and sweet. The atmosphere in the room was charged with tension.

Magnus slowly moved toward Aulus, who once again cowered. When he was directly in front of him, he lowered his head and looked right into Aulus's eyes. "If you know what's good for you." Still softly sweet.

"Take him away!" he cried with an intensity that shook Aulus. The guard stepped forward, grabbed him, and dragged him from the room. He was deposited on the front steps, and the door was resoundingly shut.

Chapter Fifty-Eight

While Aulus lay on the steps, stunned, Paulus was having difficulties of his own. His father had taken a weak spell during the night and now lay unconscious in his bed. Livia had alerted Paulus to the attack as soon as it happened, and Paulus had been at his father's side since. Eunice entered the room quietly. She had been coming back and forth for several hours, bringing food and drink for Paulus and the two women.

"Has there been any change?" she whispered to her husband. She put her hand on his shoulder.

He looked up at her and smiled. It never failed to amaze him how she handled so many things at once and still maintained a calmness of spirit. He took her hand in his and pulled her down beside him on the chair.

"No, no change," he said, watching his father. "Have I told you lately how much you mean to me?" He rubbed her hand and leaned his head against hers.

Her lips curved in a smile he knew so well. "No, not for the last hour or so."

"Then I have really been remiss." He planted a kiss on her nose.

"Why don't you take a little break? The children have been asking for you this morning." She wrapped her arms around him. "You could take them for a walk in the garden and stretch your legs. You must be stiff from sitting for so long."

"You're right. I could use a walk, but I hate to leave him in case he regains consciousness." He scanned his father's face, tilting his head to one side. "I guess I keep hoping he'll accept me again. But I'll go for a few minutes. I'll call Maria."

"No need. I'd like to sit with him while you're gone." The curve of her lips deepened as she looked into his eyes.

"Are you sure, Eunice?" He raised his eyebrows in question.

"Absolutely. Now go."

He stood and stretched his muscles, then bent down and kissed her once more. "I love you, you know," he said with a grin.

"I know." She smiled in return.

As he left the room, Eunice adjusted the blankets around Julian, then settled comfortably into the chair to begin her watch. Her gaze roamed around the room they had prepared for Julian, hoping it would stimulate his brain and bring him back to them. So far, it had made little difference.

A sound from the bed drew her attention to him.

"Water," he said weakly. He tried to sit up, but the effort was too much for him, and he slipped back down on his pillows.

Eunice quickly poured water from a pitcher on the bedside table and held his head up to help him drink. He sipped slowly, then pushed the cup away. Eunice placed the water back on the table and eased him down again. He looked around, seeming to take in his surroundings for the first time.

"Your name?" It was only a whisper, but she heard him.

She leaned over his bed so he could see her without turning his head. She spoke distinctly though softly. "Eunice."

"Yes, I remember." He was silent for a few minutes, but his glance moved around the room. Eunice followed his gaze as he stared at the paintings on the wall at the foot of the bed. She remembered how Paulus had chosen them so carefully since they were some of his father's favorites.

"Where . . . ?" He couldn't seem to complete the sentence.

She leaned close to his face again. "Where are you? Is that what you would like to know?"

"Yes . . . yes."

"You are in Paulus's house, your son." Eunice brushed back his hair from his forehead, feeling for fever as she did so.

"My son . . . not Marcus?"

"No, Paulus, not Marcus."

"Paulus." Saliva slid from the corner of his mouth. Eunice reached for a small towel on the night table and gently wiped it away. He was silent for a few minutes.

"Will he . . . ?"

Eunice leaned over him again; hearing him was very difficult since his voice was so weak.

"Will he what, Julian?" she prompted.

"Forgive . . ."

"Are you asking if Paulus will forgive you?"

"Yes."

He was perspiring. She wet the small towel in cool water and wiped his face before trying to answer him. As the cool water dampened his face, he sighed.

"Do you want him to forgive you?"

"Oh yes," he answered without hesitation. Tears trickled down the wrinkled cheeks. Eunice used the cloth again and wiped them away.

"If you really want forgiveness, I know Paulus will forgive you."

The ghost of a smile touched his lips. He closed his eyes and leaned back into the pillows. Eunice heard Paulus returning and slipped from the bedside to meet him at the door. In a soothing whisper, she related her conversation with Julian. Paulus looked bemused as he glanced at the bed.

"I can hardly believe it," he managed to whisper.

"I'm going to leave you alone, so when he wakes again, he can talk to you in private. This is just between you and him." She reached up and touched his face.

She left the room, and Paulus slid into the chair she had just vacated.

Can it really be true? he thought. *I've prayed for this so long.*

He sat quietly and studied his father's face. A deep longing to know this man, to have a meaningful father-son relationship with him, overcame him. He became aware of eyes staring at him.

He leaned forward and placed his hand on his father's shrunken one.

"Paulus?"

"Yes, Father, it's Paulus."

Julian squeezed his hand lightly before continuing. "Forgive . . ."

"Are you asking me to forgive you?"

"Yes . . . please . . ."

Paulus knelt down beside his father. "I've already forgiven you, a long time ago." Tears stung his eyes.

When he looked up, Julian wept openly. He opened his arms to receive his son—the son he had abandoned, the son he had hated, the son he had hoped to kill.

Paulus embraced his father, and all the longings of many years came rushing to the surface. He was finally accepted!

"Please, help me sit up," Julian said weakly.

Paulus tenderly lifted his shoulders and placed pillows behind them. Once Julian was settled, Paulus pulled the chair closer to the bed and sat, still holding his father's hand.

"We have much . . . to catch up . . ."

"Nothing would please me more."

They talked for a long time, with breaks when Julian needed to rest. Paulus was able to answer many questions but told him only as much as he could handle in his weakened state. Later would be soon enough to hear about all the troubles in Pergamum.

At last Julian fell into a peaceful sleep after a promise from Paulus that he would spend time with him each day. Paulus left the room with thankfulness in his heart, but also a heaviness because of all he would need to share with him in the days ahead.

But it was a start. It was enough.

Chapter Fifty-Nine

Paulus was sitting in his office and praying for his family, the Christians in hiding, the city of Pergamum, and the triumph of good over the evil so prevalent. Maria's knock on the door startled him.

"Yes, Maria?" He raised his eyebrows and looked at her.

She bowed her head and spoke politely. "Your father would like to speak with you."

"I'll be right there." He gave her a big grin. He felt like a child again now that he had his earthly father back.

He was soon seated beside his father, who had chosen to remain in his chair.

"Son, I have so many questions, I don't know where to start." His face was a mask of confusion; lines ran deep between his eyes and across his forehead. He opened his hands in a gesture that spoke consternation to Paulus.

"Just take your time, Father. Ask me any questions you would like." He patted his father's knee and offered a smile of encouragement.

"I would like to see your mother, but I'm reluctant to ask. She must hate me for the way I treated her for years." He hung his head and leaned back in his chair with a deep sigh. His ran his hands over his face.

He sat up straighter and looked Paulus directly in the eye. Leaning toward him, he asked hopefully, "Do you think she might visit me . . . in time?"

"I can't speak for her, but I will certainly express your wish to her." He nodded at his father.

He lowered his head, his voice a little more than a whisper. "Do you know where she is?"

"Yes, she's actually living right here with us."

His head snapped up, and his eyebrows rose in his forehead furrows. "In this house?" he asked, incredulity in his voice. "In this house?"

"Yes, Father. Once you went to the doctor's house, I convinced her to come live with Eunice and me." Paulus tried to keep his voice and face from showing emotions. Inside he yearned for a possible reunion between his parents.

Julian appeared to think this over before speaking again. He peered at his son through watery eyes. "Why are you so different?"

"In what way, Father?" Paulus's heart beat faster. His father was asking all the right questions.

"Ever since you left Marcus and me to join with . . ." He stopped before finishing his sentence. He looked at Paulus imploringly.

"Do you mean joining Antipas?" Paulus thought his father would be able to hear his heart thumping in his chest. He observed his father closely.

A silence passed while Julian kept his head bent. "Yes, I guess that's what I mean."

Paulus wanted to shout for joy. His father was actually asking about Antipas. This was the first time since they were children and he had banished Antipas. Paulus drew in a quick breath. "It's because I have Christ in my life that I've changed. Turning from evil and embracing the truth of Christ makes a difference in a man's life."

"It's too late for me, I know that." Julian sighed and folded his hands in his lap.

Paulus leaned toward his father, taking one of his hands in his. "Father, that's where you're wrong. It's never too late. Christ is waiting for you to acknowledge Him. He wants to come into your life and bring you joy."

"Joy?" Julian shook his head from side to side. "I can't remember the last time I ever felt joy."

"Father, I've been praying for you for a long time, and God is answering those prayers."

His eyes lifted to Paulus's face. "You prayed for me? Why? All I ever did was curse you." Tears slid from his eyes.

"I prayed for healing of your mind and body, and that's happening, even when the doctors had given up hope. I've also been praying that you would open your heart to Christ and accept Him as your Savior."

"I think I need to lie down now." When he started to rise from his chair, Paulus was instantly at his side. "My mind can't absorb anymore right now. But, Son . . ."

"Yes, Father?" Paulus helped Julian back in bed.

After he was settled, Julian said, "Would you keep praying for me?" The voice was small, almost humble, as he looked into his son's eyes with longing.

"You can be sure of that. Just keep thinking about what I said, and we'll talk later."

Aulus slumped on the steps where he had been dumped, his head swimming with confusion and disorientation. He pulled himself up on his knees and gazed around. No one paid any attention to him. Seeing strange sights in front of the governor's house wasn't unusual.

He breathed deeply several times, then made an effort to stand. He had just regained his feet when the door opened again and the same guard came out.

"Oh, *you're* still here, are you?" He leered at Aulus. "Come now, we'll never find Decimus that way." The guard descended the steps and stood beside Aulus. "Let's go. You lead the way."

Aulus stared at him, confusion clouding his brain. His clothes were in disarray with a tear down the side of his robe, where the guard had pulled him through the hallway. He opened his mouth, but no sound emerged. His mouth stayed open until the guard snapped it shut with his hand.

"Get moving. We're wasting time."

Still without a sound, Aulus walked away from the governor's house. His feet seemed to move of their own volition, and he frowned deeply as he walked. The guard followed on his heels. When they turned into the market street, Aulus brightened, and the frown left his face. When he paused in front of Decimus's stall, the guard moved in beside him.

"This is Decimus's stall, is it not?" the guard asked, shaking his sword at his side.

"Yes, I believe it is." Aulus stared at the empty space.

The guard moved toward the flimsy structure and began to demolish it. Other vendors looked the other way, probably fearing the same destruction might happen to them. When he had finished, he moved to the neighboring stalls, asking questions about Decimus.

He received the same answer everywhere.

"Decimus is gone. We haven't seen him in several days. We heard that he went into the country."

When the guard continued to hear the same story, he prodded Aulus with his knife. "Keep moving. He's not here."

For the next hour they circled the city until the guard stopped him. "Where is Decimus?'

"I really don't know. I promise you, I would tell you if I did. He's no friend of mine and not worth being imprisoned for. Please, just let me go home." He wrung his hands together.

"Go. But I'll be watching you. If you so much as look the wrong way, you'll see the inside of the dungeon before you know what's happened."

Later that night, Aulus had a visitor. The morning light revealed Aulus's body in the alleyway to his shop.

Chapter Sixty

Paulus stuck his head in the doorway of their bedroom, where Eunice was folding clothes. She looked up with a welcoming smile.

"Eunice, I feel I must see my father again before I retire for the night."

"Certainly, Paulus. I'll say good night to the children while you see Julian."

He waved at her and left the room.

Scent from a small candle burning in the room caressed Paulus's nostrils, but it wasn't strong enough to erase the acrid smell of medication in the air. Julian was awake and watched him enter.

Paulus told Livia to take a break; he would sit with his father for a while. Once she left the room, Paulus smiled at Julian as he sat by the bed. The smile was returned.

He reached out and held his father's hand. "You're looking much better tonight, Father." He scanned his father's eyes as he squeezed his hands.

Julian cleared his throat. "I've been thinking all evening."

"About what?" Paulus leaned forward so as not to miss a word.

"About what you said I needed to do." He tapped his free hand on the bed-covers and clenched his lips tightly. He looked up at his son. "Do you really believe it's not too late for me?"

"I know it's not. Christ is waiting for you. He wants you to confess your sins and enter into His salvation." Paulus stood and adjusted the pillows behind his father's back. He needed time to get his emotions under control.

"If you're sure it's not too late, I think I'm ready," Julian said, tears running down his cheeks.

Paulus swallowed hard, not wanting to weep when it was time for joy. He knelt beside the bed and took both his father's hands in his.

"What do I need to do?" Julian asked in a shaky voice.

The moment was almost too much for Paulus, but he sent up a quick prayer for help. "We'll talk to our heavenly Father. You need to confess your sins to him and ask him to come into your heart and save you."

Julian lifted up his voice to his heavenly Father. “I’m so sorry,” he managed to say. “For everything. Please, if You’ll have me, I would be so grateful.”

The room seemed to radiate with love and joy as father and son embraced. Paulus could no longer contain his tears, but they were tears of joy.

At last Julian fell back on his pillow. His face relaxed, and the lines on his forehead were gone. “Do you think it’s too late to send for Paulina? I really want to see her.”

“I’ll be right back,” Paulus said. He tiptoed out of the room, softly closing the door behind him.

Paulina hesitatingly slipped into the room a few minutes later. Her heart beat rapidly, and she clasped her hands to hide her agitation. Julian struggled to sit up when she entered. Paulina slid into the chair beside the bed, silent and waiting.

“Thank you for coming, Paulina. It couldn’t have been easy for you.” He lowered his eyes and picked at the blanket.

She was unable to speak, and she twisted her hands together in her lap.

“Did Paulus tell you what I’ve just done?” He rested his gaze on her face.

“Yes,” she whispered.

“I’ve asked God to forgive me, and He has. Now I need to ask you if you’ll forgive me.” His voice was low and faltering.

One word came again: “Yes.”

“Oh Paulina, thank you.” He spoke her name reverently. He tentatively reached out to touch her hand. She didn’t pull her hand away but entwined her fingers in his.

He looked deeply into her eyes. “How much I’ve missed with you. How much I’ve caused you to miss. I’m so sorry.”

She timidly moved to sit on the edge of his bed.

“I believe that God can work miracles,” she said, “and so I believe that you are changed.”

“I am. I’ve never felt anything like this. I . . . I . . . love you.”

With that she fell into his arms, and all the tears over their lost years mingled together as they clung to each other. She sat up and brushed the hair back from his forehead.

“I’m going now,” she said, “but I’ll be back tomorrow and every tomorrow we have left together. We can’t make up the lost years, but we can claim the days, one at a time.” She leaned over and kissed him softly on the forehead.

Chapter Sixty-One

Darkness descended over the land. A darkness so deep that all the host of Satan rejoiced in it. Clouds rushed to cover any light from moon or stars, obscuring the night sky. It was a night for evil. A night for evil deeds. A night for revenge. A night for victory over light.

The darkness reigned.

A fever of activity sprang up under the bridge by the north gate. Torches sent out their uncertain light, held by hands ready for evil deeds. The fitful light danced in grotesque shapes on the walls under the bridge. Shouting filled the air, together with tension, arising from the anticipation of the night.

Thieves rubbed shoulders with beggars; the misfits of Pergamum gathered in this one place. Wariness gleamed from hooded eyes as they took each other's measure. Smoke stung the hooded eyes, bringing unusual tears to eyes that had forgotten trust and decency. The conspirators of evil deeds gathered together. They jostled each other as more and more gathered in the confined space and spilled out into the vacant areas on either side. A sense of waiting and expectation filled the air.

"Watch where yer goin'!" a crusty character cried.

One push and the fight was on. Others joined in with swinging arms and butting heads. One rebel was shoved to the ground, unable to get up as the fight continued over him. Shouts mingled with cries of distress as others tried to intervene.

Izak came upon the scene. "Stop," he cried. "Stop now!" He grabbed robes and arms, and separated bodies. "This is a night to work together, not fight with each other." His thick eyebrows drew together in anger.

He pushed his way to the center of the waiting group. One of his followers shouted for him to mount a large rock close by. Hands quickly helped him up, and he faced the crowd, which had now swelled to over a hundred.

"Gather around. This is your night." He raised a fist high over his head. "Tonight you are partners in darkness, rebels with a grudge that wants—no, demands—to be avenged." He turned to glare at the waiting crowd. "Whatever your reasons, tonight the dark side will be victorious." By this time he was shouting as cries from the mob ebbed and swelled around him.

"What we do," he said, "we do because we have seen the glint on the edges of the coins that will pour into our pockets once the events of the night are fulfilled."

The crowd became more and more agitated and excited. Shouts rang out. Raised fists punched the night air and mingled together in one mass. As they cried out, Izak continued to raise their fervor.

"The cult must be silenced forever. You have been given that assignment. You have been chosen to fulfill this duty."

The noise became deafening. Izak stood back and watched them with eyes keen and sharp. He let them rant and cheer, stomping their feet on the damp ground. At last he stepped forward and faced the mob again.

"Quiet now while I give you your instructions."

Gradually the furor stilled. Tension filled the atmosphere.

"I have appointed ten leaders who will each be responsible for one strike tonight. You will be under one commander and will receive your orders from him. I will lead one group with a chosen few. When this night is over, ours will be the victory! The victory! Victory!"

The mass of aberrant humanity took up the call of victory. It echoed along the banks of the river, across the fields, around the gates, and into the night sky. When Izak judged the rabble was at fever pitch, he spoke again and brought order.

"Into your groups. Find a leader and join for instructions for your mission. I will meet here with my troop. When each leader is satisfied that you know your assignment, I will lead us into the city to begin our night of destruction."

A figure squeezed through the gate just before it clanged shut.

"You almost missed it. Another moment and you would have been out until sunrise," an angry guard said to him.

"Yes, thank you. I am very late, but I do appreciate entrance to the city."

The young man wandered along the path beside the river. The living conditions of the poor and homeless, the blind and lame, always appalled him. All the misfits of Pergamum, all the ones unacceptable to Pergamum society, seemingly collected near this gate for shelter, what food they could find, and miserable company. Whenever he came this way, he tried to relieve some of the suffering.

This night was no exception. As he picked his way through the wet grass and debris that littered the landscape, he directed his steps to the hut of an elderly woman. As he approached, he could see she still sat on her mat before the opening to her hovel. He pondered her situation, and pity filled him when he thought about the events that had brought her to this place.

After an accident left her with a crippled foot, she was no longer of any value to her family. She had eventually found her way to this refuse of humanity.

This night he brought her a few coins with which to purchase the little food she consumed during the day. She waved a withered hand his direction, then pointed toward the bridge. He stopped and followed the direction of her hand. What he saw caused him to hurry to her side.

"What's going on?" he asked.

She scraped out the words with a voice worn out by many years of overuse. "Do you think they tell me anything?"

"Now, now, don't be too hard on yourself. What have you seen this evening?" He shifted his cloak on his shoulder and leaned toward her to catch every word.

"They've been gathering there all afternoon and now into the evening. Listen to how noisy they are. A woman can't get any peace here at all."

"They're certainly very loud, whatever it's all about. I think I'll just take a look before I move on. Here, I've brought you a little something." He handed her a small linen purse.

She reached out with her bony misshapen hand and snatched the purse from him. Quickly she opened it and began counting the coins, chanting to herself as she did so.

Having convinced himself that she was as well as could be and that he could do nothing else for her tonight, he said farewell to her and directed his steps toward the bridge.

He slowed his pace a good piece back from the mob and circled around to cross the river at a shallow spot a stone's throw from the crowd. Once he reached the other side, he concealed himself among the small tarps and makeshift shelters of the wandering people. He proceeded to the place where the opposite side of the bridge met the shore, noiselessly slipped down the muddy bank, and slid under the bridge in the darkness to watch.

By now the crowd had swelled, and the noise increased with loud voices raised in anger. When the leader mounted a rock and began to speak, his eyes snapped open. He listened to each word and grew more and more alarmed.

When the mob broke into sections for their instructions, he could no longer make out the individual voices. He searched the faces for recognition but couldn't distinguish features, not from this distance. When he felt it was safe, he wrapped his robe tightly around him, pulling the hood over a portion of his face. He lifted the edge of the hem to avoid the muddy dampness underfoot and clawed his way up the bank, hastening away.

Although the night was dark and cloudy, no rain had fallen. He reached his home as speedily as possible and burst through the door to the side entrance. The cook looked up, eyes wide.

"Where's master?" he asked her, urgency filling his voice.

"In with the children. And if you know what's good for you, you won't disturb him." She shook her fist at him and noticed the mud on the floor from his sandals. "And take off those sandals. Where have you been?"

Leonius ignored her and sped through the house to locate Paulus. He had been on an errand for Paulus and knew the cook was wrong. Paulus wouldn't be angry, especially after he heard the news he had to tell.

"Paulus, my lord," he said when he reached the children's room.

"Leonius, whatever is the matter?" Paulus jumped up and met him outside the door. "Here, sit on this couch." He led him to a low bench along the hallway. "Get your breath, then tell me what's wrong."

As Leonius recounted his encounter with the mob, the story tumbled out of him.

"I'm sure there'll be some type of attack tonight." Leonius's eyes widened as he looked directly at Paulus. "What can we do, master? I'm afraid. They'll kill us all as we sleep." He started to shake.

Paulus put his hand on his shoulder and shook him gently. "Leonius, you must be calm. We need to make plans and be prepared. You won't be of much help to me if you don't get control of yourself."

The soothing tones of Paulus's voice had an immediate effect on him. Leonius straightened his shoulders and closed his eyes. When he opened them again, he seemed to have found inner peace. He wiped his face on the edge of his robe, then stood beside Paulus.

"Can I really help you?" Leonius asked.

"I will count on your help."

"Then I'm ready." The sound of pride rang in his statement. "What would you have me do?"

"There are very few Christ-followers still in the city, but there are some. If I give you names and addresses, can you find them and bring them back here with you? I think we need to be in one place tonight."

His voice was firm. "I'm ready, my master. I'll do whatever you need done."

"Good. Then let's prepare."

Once Paulus had given him the names, Leonius once more went out into the night. This time he held his head up and walked with purpose in his step.

I'll bring every one of them back here safely, he promised himself.

While Leonius gathered the Christians together, Paulus went to talk with Eunice and Paulina. He found them sitting together on the low couches in their main living area. Paulina had pillows piled at her back and looked comfortable and serene. They had both noticed a difference in her since the night she reconciled with Julian. Eunice, wrapped in a blanket, was chatting with Paulina.

When Paulus entered the room, they both looked up. Eunice threw off the blanket and went to his side, putting her arm around him.

"What's wrong, Paulus? And don't try to tell me there's nothing wrong. I can see it in your face."

"I agree," Paulina said as she rose to her feet. "You can't pretend around mothers and wives."

"Please sit down, both of you. Yes, there is something wrong, and we need to pray for direction and guidance."

He proceeded to tell them the story Leonius had brought home.

"We've known for some time that things were coming to a head," he said. "We just didn't know when, where, or how. We've been given a gift in now knowing when."

Paulina pressed hands to her mouth. Panic stared from her eyes. Eunice was very still, obviously deep in thought. She now looked at Paulus, taking his hand in hers.

"I feel it's all right," Eunice said. "Yes, wicked things will happen tonight, but we're like those old Jewish patriarchs we've heard about. They were always in danger, but God was right there with them. He's here with us, too."

"Well said, Eunice." Paulus squeezed her hand. "Mother, are you feeling better about this?"

She moved her hands from her face and rubbed the back of her neck. Her lips turned up in a small, brave smile. "Yes, thank you, Paulus. You and Eunice are such great examples for me. I'm still afraid, but if you are with me, I can cope."

As they finished speaking, the sound of voices drifted from the front of the house. A few of the converts had arrived. They were quickly ushered into the house and joined Paulus and the women.

"Leonius told us to come quickly," one man told Paulus.

"Yes, we need to be together tonight," Paulus said. "Come in everyone." He beckoned to the small group that stood in the room's entrance, looking around uncertainly. "Please be welcome in our home. There is enough space for all of you. Make yourselves comfortable. As soon as the others arrive, we'll make our plans."

Leonius soon arrived with the rest he had been able to find. Few talked as they found places with the others. The atmosphere was fraught with tension as they settled themselves and their frightened children around them. Most of the children had been asleep when they were carried from their beds.

One mother and baby cried together softly. The mother hugged him to her and whispered soft sounds in his ear. Gradually he calmed and drifted off to sleep again.

"Friends, we know not what this night will bring," Paulus said. "It seems certain that evil is afoot and that in some way we will all be touched by the events of the night. The forces of Satan are powerful, the followers of Zeus are zealous, and the priests are crafty and without trust. The forces of evil are lined against us tonight. God may not spare our physical lives. We do not know. We only know that He will be with us through whatever comes our way. And if some of us pass on to eternity, He'll be there to greet us on the other side."

He paused to allow them to take in his words. Restlessness was evident in each shuffle of sandals, each clearing of throats, each shrug of shoulders, each clutching of a child. No one could predict what wicked deeds were about to be unleashed on them.

"We'll prepare to the best of our ability," he said. "A team of men will be on guard duty through the night hours. The women and children will be housed in the center core of the house away from doors and windows. One of us will be posted beside the door at all times." He watched their eyes, trying to gauge their level of fear. "Try to get your children to sleep and get some sleep yourselves. Tonight may be dangerous and unpredictable, but tomorrow we will need to deal with the aftermath of the deeds of tonight."

Servants appeared and led people to their assigned places. Once the women and children were settled, the men drew names for guard duty. Those not chosen for first watch found places to rest until their time for duty had come. Paulus was content with all that was in place. It might not protect them from anything, but they would feel they had done all they could.

He left the men either resting or taking up their places of duty and made his way down a silent hallway to his father's room. How different it was to come now that his father was a believer who was hungry to know as much as he could about the Lord. He slipped into the room to spend some time with him before he would need to be on duty.

"Father, are you still awake?" he whispered since his father's eyes were closed.

"Yes," Julian whispered and opened his pale eyes.

"I wanted to tell you what is happening tonight." Over the last several days, he had told his father all that was happening in Pergamum. Now that Julian's eyes had been opened to Christ, he mourned over his part in what was taking place.

"I'm responsible for much of this," he had tearfully said to Paulus.

"God has forgiven you for every sin in your life," Paulus had said. "You can rest in His promises that it is gone. You could not stop the progression of evil rampant in this city."

He listened now as Paulus told him of the mob congregating near the bridge, of the threats to the Christ-followers, and of the precautions he had taken.

"Well done, Son." Julian reached out a veined hand and touched his arm. "I am so proud of you. Whatever happens tonight, know that I am ready to meet God face-to-face."

The two men embraced, and Paulus sensed a feeling of finality to their farewell. He returned to the men on duty and circled the house to assess the needs for the night. All was going according to plan. Paulus knew he would not sleep but would keep his vigil, whether on duty or while watching over the house. He had insisted that the children move in with Eunice for the night.

He now entered their bedroom. Eunice still sat up and watched the children sleep. She smiled at him as he neared the bed.

"They look like little angels when they're asleep, don't they?" she said in low tones.

"They certainly do, and from where I'm standing, I see an angel watching over them." He smiled and gave Eunice a kiss.

"You won't be coming to bed tonight, will you?" she asked with certainty in her voice.

“No, I want to keep an eye on things. You try to sleep. I’ll check in on you every hour or so. Good night, my love.”

“Paulus, if we should not make it through the night, I want you to know that our time together has been amazing. I couldn’t have asked for a better husband. Your love and care and concern have been more than I deserve. You are a very special person.” Tears hovered on her eyelashes as she spoke her declaration of love to her husband.

He leaned over to give her one last hug. “Oh, my love, words are inadequate to express my love and gratitude to you. Always know that you are the best thing that ever happened to me.” He ran his fingers through her hair and looked lovingly at her. Foreheads touching, they said their good nights.

As Paulus traversed the hallways back to the central location where the men spent the night, dark thoughts swirled in his mind. Would he and Eunice still be alive when day broke? Would the church of Pergamum still exist? With a sinking heart, he entered the room that had become the center of his universe for this night.

Chapter Sixty-Two

"Kill the infidels."

"Long live Zeus."

"Down with the cult."

"Let's cut their lying tongues out of their treasonous bodies."

"Kill them all. Don't leave one standing or breathing."

The scene was madness. The oppressive darkness made a backdrop of blackness for the torches thrust high in the air. Eyes gleamed in the flickering light, and shouts went up to join the darkness overhead. The glint of unsheathed knives added to the exhilaration of the night. From the torches, smoke circled the scene, adding the pungent smell of burning wood to the already-volatile setting.

Izak watched the spectacle play out before him. With arms folded across the front of his robe, feet apart, and shoulders back, he looked with disdain on the sight.

What fools, he thought. *But I need them to fulfill the night's undertaking.*

He would work alone if he could and leave the rabble behind him, but the plan was too big.

I hate to admit it—he groaned to himself—*but I need them. But after tonight, I'll be the victor, the hero. There won't be anything I can't have.*

When he determined that the mob had reached a highly agitated state and was ready to storm the city, he motioned for the leaders to come close. As they approached, he hated them in his heart. Maybe some of them would need to be eliminated after tonight. He had chosen them because of what he knew about them. They disgusted him.

He clipped out the order through clenched teeth. "Get the horde in order. We're ready to march."

It was an ungainly sight. The masses swelled to more than two legions, all drunk on the thought of dispensing destruction on the innocent. They moved slowly at first, then with increasing speed as they swarmed into the city streets. Voices lifted in uproar, and torches trembled dangerously in uplifted arms. It was a scene from hell as Satan and his demons pushed their way into the heart of humanity.

A cry split the night; a torch found its mark in the dwelling of a poor man. He stumbled into the street, eyes round with fright, and clutched his robe around bony shoulders.

"Spare my house!" he shouted to the mob. "I've done ye no harm."

His words only incensed them further. A long, thin knife sank into his back. The spilling of blood along with the burning inferno incited the mob to more violence. House after house in this poor district was torched and left to burn to the ground. Most of the houses were empty, a fact that further agitated the mass of evil.

When they entered the street where Decimus lived, Izak spotted his house. He'd been waiting to personally pull the inmates from their beds and murder them in the street. He stormed through the door, bursting through each room, only to find them empty. His anger knew no limit, and he began to demolish the house with his bare hands. Others joined him in his destruction. When the torch finally ignited the remains, they no longer resembled a home.

The clamor and commotion in the streets brought others out of their homes to see what was happening. Upon hearing that the Christ cult was being destroyed once and for all this night, many joined the mob, adding their voices to the din.

In street after street the houses of the Christ-followers were destroyed. The smoke rose up into the blackness, obscuring the clouds and choking the destroyers. Eyes stung from the assault of smoke, but still they toiled on.

As Izak left one dwelling, a young boy observed the mob from the side of his house. As they marched on, they trampled him with the stomp of many feet. No one stopped to help him as his life's blood was spilled before his home. Dark was the night, but darker were the deeds of evil as they spread their venom through the city streets.

Izak separated himself and his group from the mob as they neared the center of the city. He had no doubt in his mind that the mass of demons wouldn't stop until every designated home was torched and every Christ-follower still in the city was rooted out and killed.

It was time for the main event.

Chapter Sixty-Three

Darkness deepened as the hour approached midnight. A thin fog hovered above the ground, winding its tendrils in and around rocks and bushes. The backdrop to the night was eerie.

At midnight, Paulus slipped from the house to take up his position on guard duty. All was quiet within and without. He exchanged a soft greeting with the guard he replaced and began his slow circuit of the house and property. He detected nothing amiss.

He passed other guards, who patrolled their assigned spots. Nothing was astir in any area. As he concluded his second round and reached the pathway to the garden, a spark of light caught his eye. He stopped, barely breathing, and stared into the distance. When the flicker failed to appear again, he wondered if it had been his imagination. He carefully moved to the front.

A servant approached him with a request that he reenter the house; some of the guests were anxious and wanted him to pray with them. He spoke with two of the guards, promising to send a replacement before he went in.

Outside, the night remained calm.

"This way." With this command, Izak pulled his band away from the mob. The fires continued to burn behind them, and flames lit up the night sky. The crackling of the blazes rose clearly over the howling of the mob. It was a night scene fueled by the demons Satan had sent to avenge Zeus.

The small band ran through the city toward the ever-alert household of Paulus. That Paulus was aware that they were coming, Izak was certain. The fires had to be visible from great distances. He would need finesse to take this house, but he had a plan, a daring plan. Because of its boldness, he felt it had a chance to work.

He stopped his group a league from the house for a hurried consultation. When he laid out his plan, everyone laughed together at the audacity of his scheme.

"Brilliant," one clever thief said, slapping him on the back. "It's so daring, it just might work."

"Is everyone certain of their part?" Izak asked. In the darkness he could see only outlines of the men. Glints from their eyes reflected the flames from the city.

Assured that they were with him, he continued. "Then it's silence from here on."

The band of evil cunning fell into place behind him. The pace was slower now. Nothing must give away their approach. Within sight of the house, he signaled them to stop. He watched intently, surveying the guards and the outline of the house.

It must be perfect, he thought. *No room for error.*

With a touch on the shoulder and a brisk motion of the hand, he directed each group to their location. They melted into the darkness toward their goal. The ones remaining with him made no movement, though he was aware of their presence. Once he was sure everyone was in place, he lit his torch; this was the signal for the others to light their torches and move. He gave a loud rallying cry and set off toward the front entrance at a run.

Because of the noise, the guards were immediately on the alert. The ones guarding the sides of the house came running to the front to investigate the disturbance, leaving the sides open. Izak propelled himself forward, brandishing his torch. He continued to yell, now accompanied by the others in his band.

Before the guards could react, Izak and his group of five hurled their torches onto the building's roof. In the initial seconds of the attack, the front door opened, and two of the torches found their mark inside the building. Once they had discharged their torches, Izak and his followers engaged the guards in hand-to-hand combat. Knives gleamed in the glare of the quickening fire behind them. The guards, now alert and fighting for their lives, spilled their blood as knives found flesh willing to accept them.

Groups repeated the attack on both sides of the house and the rear entrance. By now the fire had a tenacious hold. People emerged from doorways, coughing and clutching throats as the smoke filled nostrils, throats, and lungs. Cries and tears joined the yells of the attackers and the roar and crackle of the fire.

Paulus was everywhere. He herded people from the house and ran through the rooms, urging people to hurry and carrying those who were unable to move fast enough. He made sure Eunice and the children were out, then moved on to the wing where his father was housed.

Here the scene was different. As he hurried toward his father's rooms, a wall of flame met him. He took a deep breath and charged the flames, but the power of the inferno threw him back. As he recovered and prepared to make another attempt, a large burning beam broke away from the roof, effectively blocking off the entrance.

With a cry of frustration, he turned back and headed for the nearest doorway. He ran out the back entrance and into the garden. The battle raged here as well. Timbers had fallen and littered the ground as guards and attackers engaged in combat. Paulus glanced at them and hurried past on his way to the outside of his father's rooms.

But it was of no avail. The blaze consumed that section of the house. There was no way in or out. With devastation in his heart he realized he couldn't rescue his father. He fell to the ground and wept. Leonius found him there minutes later.

"Paulus, are you all right?" Leonius cried with alarm.

Paulus stood up and put his hand on Leonius's shoulder. "Thank you, my friend. But no, I'm not all right. My father is . . ." He gestured toward the wing, now completely engulfed in flames, and shook his head in helplessness.

"Come, Paulus. We need you around at the front. There's nothing more you can do here." Leonius put a hand on his shoulder and turned him to face the front.

The fighting was over in this area. Izak lay dying at the feet of the guards; the other attackers had slipped away once their leader was mortally wounded.

Paulus approached the fallen villain and knelt beside him. Angry thoughts raced through his mind until he looked into Izak's eyes and saw fear. Compassion filled his own eyes, and he reached out to touch Izak's shoulder when a snarl erupted from the fallen man.

"Don't touch me, you foul scum!" He gasped and swallowed while blood ran from his mouth. "I die knowing I've won." His eyes closed and he was gone.

Paulus stood and looked down on his foe, feeling helpless.

"Paulus, come, we need you."

Like a man in a dream, Paulus followed Leonius. By the time he reached their destination, he had recovered his composure and once more became the leader all knew him to be.

Paulus brought everyone to the front, where he and the guards moved all the families away from the blazing inferno. The entire house was now engulfed in flames, which leapt into the night sky. Entering the structure again was impossible. Nothing could be saved from the raging fire.

As all gathered a distance from the house, Paulus counted heads to determine who had escaped the flames. All were present except Julian and the two nurses who had so faithfully ministered to his needs. The believers stood and watched the house burn with disbelief in their eyes. Mothers clutched their children tightly, knowing they had almost lost them. Husbands hovered over their families.

When Paulus knew there was nothing else he could do, he drew Eunice and Paulina into a tight embrace. Both women held one of the children, and the five of them wept for their loss. When the tears were spent, they drew apart.

"Mother, would you sit with the children while I see what I can do to help?" Eunice asked Paulina. She laid her hand on her arm and leaned her face in close to Paulina.

"Yes. They'll bring comfort to me. You go. You'll be needed in the hours ahead." Paulina gathered the children to her while tears streaked her face. She buried her face in their hair and silently sobbed.

Hand in hand, Paulus and Eunice moved among the guards first and then the families. Leonius brought water from the well to wash wounds. Paulus gave Eunice his cloak to tear into bindings for wounds. Following her example, other women left their families and assisted in helping the wounded against the backdrop of fiendish flames writhing in their macabre dance.

By first light the fire had done its worst. Its relentless work of the night before had leveled the proud house of Paulus. Smoke continued to rise from the ruins with a ghastly stench that assaulted the nostrils.

The early morning light touched the heads of the survivors. Those awake were shocked at the sight. Families lay in each other's arms, some still in a fitful, uneasy sleep. Fire residue coated their faces and clothing. As they began to awaken, they rose in a group and turned toward the house which had so recently sheltered them. As one they moved closer and stood, observing the ruin with shocked faces.

People from the city began to arrive. They had seen the flames in the night and had come to help. They brought welcome food as well as hot drinks. Many of the ones who had so recently lifted their voices with the mob were now ashamed and threw themselves into helping their former neighbors and fellow workers.

A group of men approached Paulus.

"What can we do to help?" one of them asked. They exchanged the usual bows and embraced Paulus.

Paulus stood back and spread out his hands, indicating the group of Christians around him. "Our biggest need is going to be shelter. Do you have any tarps we can borrow? We could hang them under the trees."

"Done," said the man who had asked the question. He clapped his hands together. "We'll be back with everything you need to erect them." They turned and headed toward the city.

Others brought news that a violent mob had burned several homes in the city the night before. Paulus guessed these were homes of other Christ-followers. Once the tarps were in place and the groups had been fed, Paulus approached some of the converts, asking who would go into the city with him to assess the damage from the fires there.

"We need to see for ourselves what damage has been done and then get word to those in hiding," he told the group. His robe was dirty from ashes, and his cloak had been shredded for bandages, but still he put others first and showed his concern.

"Won't it be dangerous to enter the city?" one of the men asked. He rose from the ground where he had been sitting; dirt streaked his face.

"Yes, I suppose it will be, but I feel we owe it to the others to be able to give them a full report on what has happened to their homes." Paulus wiped his hands over his face. He was weary, but he refused to stop until everything possible had been done to assess the situation.

Three men agreed to go with him, while the others would look after the women and children.

The devastation was total. As they followed the streets of the city, home after home lay in ruins. Sadly, many pagan homes had been destroyed as well. Small groups of people stared forlornly at the ruins. Women buried their faces in their cloaks and wept, their wails stinging the air. Little children played in the streets, untouched by the horror of the night.

Paulus and the others turned away sadly. They could do nothing to relieve the pain and loss. Two of his men agreed to journey into the country and report the loss to the Christ-followers who had earlier left the city and were in hiding. Paulus and his companion returned through the city to join the believers at Paulus's destroyed home.

Magnus was caught off guard when an emissary from Rome was announced and stormed into his audience room. Magnus stood and watched the Roman stride across the space between them. He recognized his former enemy, Octavian.

"Sit, Magnus." Octavian pointed at Magnus. "What I have to say will be easier to digest sitting down."

"I'll do as I please," Magnus said with a sneer and squared his shoulders. "It'll be a sorry day when I take orders from you." His chin jutted out, and his lips locked in a grimace.

"Then you can count this as a sorry day, Magnus. For taking orders from me is exactly what you will do." Octavian flicked his hand in Magnus's face and drew his heavy brows together in a frown.

Magnus took a deep breath and breathed noisily through his nose, exhaling loudly. One step forward was all he managed before Octavian turned toward the door.

"Soldiers, enter." Octavian snapped his fingers sharply.

The guards on duty for Magnus stormed into the room, while a contingent from Rome followed on their heels. Magnus watched as alarm fought for control of his face.

"Seize the prisoner!" Octavian stood aside, and the guards approached Magnus in brisk military fashion.

Magnus lifted his hands. "There's no need for force here. What is it you want, Octavian? I'm sure we can work it out." His stomach muscles clenched, and his knees began to tremble.

His words were useless. Roman soldiers surrounded him, pinned his arms to his sides, and wove a chain around his body. He protested loudly but to no avail.

"You are under arrest." Octavian faced him, feet apart, hands on hips.

"But why? What have I done to warrant arrest?"

"You are under arrest for failing to keep the peace in Pergamum." Octavian turned his back and walked away.

"B-but it's not my fault these cultists have invaded the territory," Magnus stammered. He gripped his tunic with his bound hands, while sweat pooled in the lines of his face and neck.

Octavian spun around and faced him again. "But it is your fault that you were unable to control the mob. The city is in disarray. The emperor is not pleased."

Octavian folded his arms across his chest and glared at Magnus. His lip curled up in a scornful gesture.

The rest of Magnus's body began to shake. Octavian watched him, a look of triumph glinting in his eyes.

Magnus protested as the guards unceremoniously dragged him from the room, down the long hall, and into the morning sunshine. Those who had apparently seen the Roman soldiers enter the building crowded around. They hung back and watched through hooded eyes, making no eye contact with Magnus or the Roman soldiers.

Magnus hung his head in embarrassment as the guards threw him into the waiting chariot. Black, shiny horses stomped impatiently as others joined him. Octavian gave the command, and the chariot hurled off down the street and away from the city.

Chapter Sixty-Four

On a hillside beyond the city gates, four figures toiled up the grassy slope. Behind them, the plain, stretching out in flat monotony, was filled with silent people, who milled around its base and watched the climbers. They stood in small groups or singly, watching and waiting.

The climbers meanwhile continued their journey up the steep ascent. The air was chill, and dawn had not yet broken, though it gave signs of its imminent arrival. Pink, feathery lines were visible on the distant horizon behind them. Bird calls pierced the silence of the new day.

The couple and their two children, though aware of the stirrings of the day, remained focused on reaching the summit. A level ridge hugged the headland above them. The boy held the mother's hand, while the father carried his little girl.

Eunice smiled at Paulus as their family edged up the mount. He returned her smile and hugged Helena closer to him. The events of the last few days had taken their toll on this little family, but their peaceful steps showed evidence of inner battles fought and won.

The ridge at last gained, they paused to take deep breaths and rest weary legs. Together they looked westward toward the city. It lay before them, just touched by the early morning light. The gates were still closed as if awaiting the first touch of the sun above the horizon. Trumpeters were visible on top of the wall, ready to announce the morning and the opening of the gates to begin another business day in the city.

Smoke still rose from the fires of the past two days. The destruction was invisible from this distance, but the harsh fumes from the fires still hovered in the morning air.

Paulus lowered Helena to stand beside him and reached out for Eunice. She moved into his embrace, hugging Simon to her side.

They turned together and beckoned for the others to join them on the ridge. Those who were able to make the climb soon joined them at the top. The others continued their wait on the lower portions of the hillside. A psalm broke from the lips of one of the newcomers, and soon the hill resounded with praises to God the Lord. As the sun rose behind them, illumining the scene before them, the Christ-followers lifted arms high over their heads in praise and worship.

The church in Pergamum would grow again; its members had emerged from the fires of persecution and were stronger than ever. Houses would be rebuilt, home churches reestablished, preaching on the temple steps resumed, and relationships rebuilt with ordinary citizens. Christ's church would grow and take root in the hostile soil.

Satan's victory was a hollow sham. Christ alone was the Victor.

As the first rays of the rising sun touched the backs of these pilgrims, a great cheer arose from the very depths of their hearts.

"Holy, holy, holy is the Lord God Almighty. Holy, holy, holy is the Lord God Almighty. Holy, holy, holy is the Lord God Almighty."

The cry rose to the heavens, where Christ watched over His people, who were strong, triumphant, victorious.

Acknowledgments

Many people come together to produce a book like *Pergamum: Satan's Throne*. In *Meditation XVII*, John Donne wrote, "No man is an island, entire of itself; every man is a piece of the continent, a part of the main." And so it is for an author.

Thank you to the many who came alongside me as I wrote and published *Pergamum: Satan's Throne*. My husband deserves my biggest thank-you as he reads every word I write, suffers through uncreative dinners when I am in the midst of writing or editing, and encourages me at every step along the way. Friends and family members have encouraged and supported me, always asking with anticipation for the next book. Adam Blumer, my editor, deserves credit for the attention to detail he brought to the manuscript and for his words of encouragement.

The Pergamum Prayer Team faithfully prays for each step in the process. I am so appreciative of their willingness to bring all matters before our Heavenly Father.

The team at Deep River Books made the entire process so easy. They answer questions, offer suggestions and professional advice, and give warm encouragement. Thank You.

And to you, my dear readers: Without you, there would be no purpose in producing books. You have made my heart sing with your praises of *Antipas: Martyr* and your continued requests for more. Your enthusiasm for my stories has given me the desire to keep writing. I trust you will enjoy *Pergamum: Satan's Throne* as much as you did *Antipas: Martyr.*

Sharon Dow